KEEPING AMANDA

RESCUE ANGELS
BOOK 2

SUSAN STOKER

This book is a work of fiction. Names, characters, places, and incidents are products of the author's imagination or used fictitiously. Any resemblance to actual events or locales or persons living or dead is entirely coincidental.
Copyright © 2025 by Susan Stoker
No part of this work may be used, stored, reproduced or transmitted without written permission from the publisher except for brief quotations for review purposes as permitted by law.
This book is licensed for your personal enjoyment only. This book may not be re-sold or given away to other people. If you would like to share this book with another person, please purchase an additional copy for each recipient. If you're reading this book and did not purchase it, or it was not purchased for your use only, please purchase your own copy.
Thank you for respecting the hard work of this author.
Edited by Kelli Collins
Cover Design by AURA Design Group
Manufactured in the United States

CHAPTER ONE

Amanda Rush was scared. Not just a little scared either. *Terrified.* According to her calculations, it had been two weeks, give or take a day, since she and twenty-three kids had been taken from their school in Guyana, put into a truck that had crossed into Venezuela, and then forced to walk day after day deeper into the Amazon rainforest.

She was exhausted, dirty, hungry, and petrified over what the men holding them hostage could possibly want. They hadn't spoken a lot, just prodded them along with their rifles when they slowed down too much. They hadn't explained where they were going or why they'd been taken in the first place.

Even though she wished she was anywhere other than where she was, Amanda wouldn't change what she'd done. If she hadn't stayed with the children, if she'd run in the opposite direction when the men stormed into the classroom, like the other adults had done, the children would be out here all alone.

And while she didn't think she was anything all that special, Amanda was proud that she'd stayed with them. Even though it probably meant she'd die as a result.

But she wasn't dead yet. And even though things were bad,

they could always get worse. So far, none of the rough-and-tumble soldiers guarding them had made any kind of move toward her. They hadn't beaten her or any of the kids. They'd kind of seemed like robots...quiet, blank...unmoved by the children's crying. Immune to Amanda's begging on their behalf for food, water, to be able to sit for a moment.

So on they walked.

Rain was falling, as it had been for basically two weeks straight. Not constant, but just when she thought she might have a chance to dry out, inevitably it would start raining again.

But today things had changed. They'd arrived at a sort of makeshift camp. There were quite a few ratty canvas tents in a small clearing in the trees. A large firepit sat to one side of the camp, smoking as the rain did its best to extinguish the flames. She didn't see anyone there when they arrived, but someone had to be close, since the fire was lit before their arrival.

The man who she assumed was in charge—since the other soldiers did whatever he ordered without hesitation—gestured to the tents. "Boys over there, five to a tent. Girls, there," he said, pointing to the other side of the camp. "All eight in the far tent."

Looking where he was pointing, Amanda realized it was going to be a tight fit to get all eight of the girls into the smallish tent he was pointing to, but she didn't protest. She actually preferred they all stay together. The girls ranged in ages from four to eleven, and the boys were anywhere from three to thirteen.

She gave Michael a small smile, trying to let him know that she was okay, that everything would be all right. The boy had stayed near her side for the last two weeks, doing what he could to protect her. It was both heartwarming and heartbreaking at the same time. Because she knew without a doubt if the soldiers wanted to harm her, there wasn't anything he'd be able to do to stop them.

"We want to stay with the girls," Michael told the leader.

He ignored him, turning his back on the group and heading toward a bigger tent near the edge of the trees.

"Hey! We want to stay with the girls," Michael said again, louder and more forcefully.

The man stopped, and Amanda's heart nearly quit beating in her chest. Something bad was going to happen, she knew that as well as she knew her name.

He turned around and stared at Michael for a long moment. Then he slowly walked toward him.

Michael's shoulders went back and he lifted his chin. His refusal to back down to this man was impressive...and not very smart.

Before Amanda could utter a word to tell the leader that Michael was tired and hungry, that he hadn't meant to be disrespectful, his arm swung. He backhanded the boy so hard, Michael went flying backward, landing in the mud several feet from where he'd been standing.

The leader nodded at one of the other soldiers, and the man leaned down, hauled Michael to his feet, and shoved him toward the trees.

Amanda could barely breathe.

"Please don't!" she begged. She had no idea what the soldier had in store for Michael, but it couldn't be good.

The leader turned his icy gaze on her, and for the first time since she'd been taken, Amanda felt as if he was seeing her. *Truly* seeing her. His gaze roamed up and down her body, but she couldn't tell what he was thinking.

She'd never seen herself as very attractive. She was...cute? At five feet tall, she'd been mistaken for a teenager more than once, even though she was almost thirty. Back in Virginia, at the school where she'd taught, she was shorter than many of her seventh-grade students. Her hair was a mix of light brown and blonde and she kept it short, simply because it was easier to take care of, something she was very glad for here in the rainforest. Her eyes blue, her weight average. Not too skinny and not overweight. In truth, she was average. Not height-wise, but in every other way.

But when the leader looked at Amanda, her skin crawled.

"You want to join him?" he asked in a low, smooth voice that lacked any real emotion. His khaki pants and shirt were sweat-stained and dirty, just like Amanda's and the kids' clothing. He had dark hair, a square jaw covered by a full beard. The rifle strapped around his chest was a vivid reminder of her current situation...that it was in her best interest not to piss this man off.

"No, sir," she said, as respectfully as she could. "Michael is just worried about the girls. He's always done his best to look after them."

"They are no longer his concern. He has a new job...to become a soldier."

Amanda's belly clenched. She'd been pretty sure that's why the kids were taken, but to hear this man say it so nonchalantly was still a shock.

"That's what you all will be!" he said a little louder, looking at the rest of the boys, who were huddled together. "You will learn everything you need to know here. You will be trained, and as long as you cooperate, you will earn the right to sleep in the tents and eat. If not..."

He didn't have to finish his sentence, it was obvious what would happen if they didn't. Michael's pained cries seemed very loud in the clearing.

He'd been taken deep into the trees, so Amanda couldn't see what was happening to him, but her heart broke with every sound he made.

"And you," the leader continued, looking at the girls, as if he couldn't hear the pathetic cries of a child echoing through the forest, "will be responsible for cooking and cleaning, at least for now. Husbands have already been chosen for you, and they will begin arriving to retrieve you in a few days. Your job is to serve your husbands and make babies who will further our cause."

If she thought she'd been horrified before, Amanda was even more so now. Bibi was only four. And Natasha, the oldest, was eleven. The thought of anyone hurting them made her physically sick.

"What about Mandy?" Sharon asked. She'd been extremely clingy throughout their trek through the rainforest, and while Amanda also wanted to know her fate, she wished the girl had kept her mouth shut at that moment.

The leader smiled then—an evil smile that made the hair on the back of Amanda's neck stand up.

"Ah yes, the brave teacher who refused to leave her students. We definitely have plans for her. But for now, she continues to do what she's been doing…keeping you all in line."

And with that, he turned and headed in the direction he'd been going when Michael interrupted him.

A shiver swept through Amanda from head to toe. She wasn't going to make it out of there. That much was obvious. She was being used to keep the children calm and compliant, but as soon as the girls were given to whomever came for them, and the boys were cowed from exhaustion or beatings, she was expendable.

And the looks of the faces of the men around her were suddenly a little too eager. As if they'd been wondering what the leader had in store for her, and now that he'd spoken, they assumed she'd be nothing more than a plaything to use as they saw fit until her death.

"Mandy?" Sharon whined.

Turning her thoughts away from her inevitable future, she straightened her spine and faced the girls. "Come on, let's go get settled in our tent," she told them. Looking at Joseph, the oldest boy, she added, "Joe, look after Richard, James, and Mark. Split them up amongst the rest of you." The three boys she'd singled out were the youngest, and would need looking after if they were going to survive.

Joseph nodded, and Amanda was glad to see the boys immediately split themselves up, each tent housing a mixture of older and younger kids.

Natasha, the oldest girl, picked up Bibi and carried her toward the tent they'd been assigned. The other girls followed suit, the older girls pairing up with the younger ones, holding their hands as they trudged toward their new home for however long they'd be there.

Amanda wanted to ask if they'd get some food. Some water. If they'd be able to wash their clothes. After two weeks of walking, they were all pretty ripe. But she also didn't want to bring any more attention to themselves than they already had. As much as she wanted to come up with a strategy to escape, to run into the jungle and get away from whatever this group of men had planned, she knew that wasn't exactly viable.

She had no idea where they were. Couldn't survive on her own in the jungle, forget about taking twenty-three boys and girls with her. And Amanda would no more leave the kids to fend for themselves than she'd kick a wounded puppy in the streets.

No, she was going to be here until she died. No matter how this played out.

She had zero confidence that a miracle would happen, that they'd either let them go or someone would come to their rescue. Life only worked like that in movies and novels. The reality was, the boys would be forced to fight for these rebels, and the girls...

She didn't want to think about their fate.

Refusing to cry, as that wouldn't solve anything, Amanda herded the girls to the tent.

One minute at a time. That's all she could do. That's all she had the mental bandwidth to deal with. Whatever would happen would happen, but when the time came for *her* fate, she vowed to fight to the bitter end. She wouldn't make it easy for them, no matter what their captors had in store for her.

* * *

Nash "Buck" Chaney clenched his fists under the table, trying to hold on to his patience. He and his copilot, Obi-Wan, were currently in Guyana, preparing for a rescue mission. Twenty-three children and one American teacher had been kidnapped from their school near the border of Venezuela and taken into the rainforest. They'd just been briefed by the director of the school about what had gone down that day just over two weeks ago, when the school was raided, and nothing they'd heard was making him very happy.

He and Obi-Wan might not be in the middle of a war zone, but knowing there were innocent children going through something horrific right this moment was making him more than a little anxious to get this mission started.

The location of the kidnapping victims was currently unknown, but the Guyanese government had an idea of where they might be, or at least of the direction they'd gone. There were several training camps in the depths of the rainforest they were keeping an eye on, since they were relatively close to the border. Tensions with their neighboring country had ramped up in the last few years, and no one wanted to be surprised by an invasion via the forest.

Hostilities were even higher very recently, because Venezuela announced the annexation of Guyana's western territories in something they called the Venezuelan Referendum. Guyana had strengthened their military partnership with the US in order to help protect their people and land from their larger neighbor.

But nevertheless, they *had* been surprised by the kidnapping. It happened so fast. The men had crossed the border without detection, driven straight to the school, loaded up the children and teacher and crossed back into Venezuela, all within ten minutes. There'd been one fatality—a teacher was shot—proving the men weren't afraid to use lethal force if threatened.

The reason Buck and Obi-Wan were there was because the vice president of the United States had a connection to the small country of Guyana, and he'd pressed the president to take action. To authorize the use of the Night Stalkers to see if they could rescue the children.

Officially, the involvement of the specialized Army unit was because of the American teacher taken with the kids. That was their "in," so to speak. Sending a message that kidnapping American citizens wouldn't be tolerated.

It was a tenuous excuse at best. Because Amanda Rush had no connections to the military or government. She had no intel that any foreign military would deem desirable. She was a volunteer, spending time in Guyana helping an organization educate a school full of orphans.

But the longer Buck sat at the table and listened to intel about the group who took the kids and their teacher, the more uneasy he became. This was no unorganized, ragtag group of men. They were terrorists, plain and simple. Reports of the things they'd done in the past made his blood boil. They were ruthless, and they didn't care if the soldiers they "recruited" were nineteen or nine.

Those children would be forced to do heinous things, whether they wanted to or not.

And worse was the way the group treated women. *Girls.* They were disposable. Second-class citizens. Only good for the children they could birth. It was a barbaric and old-school way of thinking, and it made Buck genuinely concerned for the well-being of Amanda Rush and the eight girls who'd been taken.

Buck's question was—why had this school been targeted at all? It wasn't as if it was full of rich children. It was a school for orphans. Children who had no family. No money. Buck supposed if the rebels simply wanted boots on the ground, it made sense. But there were even other schools closer to the border. So why *this* school? Why pass up two other significantly larger schools with a lot more children? There was even an all-boys academy with older kids, ages thirteen to eighteen, that the rebels had to have passed in order to get to the small orphanage.

It was possible they chose the smaller school because that meant potentially fewer adults to have to deal with...but would that really stand in their way if they'd hoped to grab a significant number of children?

In the grand scheme of things, Buck supposed it didn't really matter. All that mattered was getting to those kids and their teacher before they disappeared forever.

That's where he and Obi-Wan came in.

They were going to fly into the jungle, rescue the kids, and bring them all back to Guyana. To safety. They were taking half a dozen members of the Guyanese military with them, as that was all they could fit in the chopper once the kids were rescued. He and Obi-Wan had been reassured that the six men were more than capable of taking on the dozen or so militants who were hiding out in the jungle.

It seemed like a huge risk to Buck, but he had to believe the army knew the capabilities of both their special forces soldiers, and the men they were hunting. His main concern was the kids... and Amanda.

He didn't know what it was about the woman that intrigued him so much. She'd quit a job in Virginia—ironically in Norfolk, where he was currently stationed—to fly to South America and volunteer her time and expertise with the orphans at the small school. He didn't know many people who'd be willing to give up their lives to do such a thing. Yes, people joined the Peace Corps all the time, but many were younger, not already well established in a career. He supposed it wasn't unheard of, but Amanda's actions still impressed him.

And something that concerned Buck was the fact that Amanda was twenty-nine, single, no parents, no siblings...and apparently didn't have one person worried that she was missing. He didn't even know if anyone *knew* she'd been kidnapped.

His parents were currently living in Kansas, and while he didn't talk to them every day, he was still close with them. He reached out at least once or twice a month to touch base. His sister was married with two kids and living in Washington state, but if something happened to him, he knew she'd drop everything and come to Virginia to see if she could help.

Not only that, but he had his Night Stalker family, the fellow pilots he worked with on a daily basis. Who had his back in the air and on the ground. He'd die for them, and he knew they'd do the same for him.

The thought of Amanda not having a single person in the world who cared where she was or what was happening to her...it didn't sit well with him.

From everything he'd heard from her coworkers at the school here in Guyana, she was a hard worker, considerate, compassionate, and kind. It seemed all sorts of wrong that she was caught up in whatever was going on.

Buck only wished the rest of his team—Casper, Pyro, Chaos, and Edge—were with them to assist. Instead, they were in Mexico, helping with the aftermath of the latest hurricane. Their skills were needed to help rescue stranded victims, and to deliver food and water to those who were cut off by raging floodwaters. He and Obi-Wan had volunteered for the Guyana mission, and they'd meet up with their fellow Night Stalkers afterward in Mexico.

"Are we set on the plan?" Colonel Samuel Khan asked. He was in charge of the rescue mission, and would be monitoring how things were going from a small military base not too far from the Venezuelan border.

Joining them around the table were several other military officials, including the captain in charge of the special forces men tasked with taking care of any resistance from the rebels; the administrator of the school, Blair Gaffney; and her assistant, Desmond Williams.

Blair and Desmond had been tense throughout the meeting, and they'd brought with them a folder with names and pictures of all the children who'd been taken. Looking at them now made Buck's chest hurt all over again. They were all so young. So innocent. He hated that this had happened to them. Hated that they were probably scared out of their minds. He wasn't exactly glad that their teacher had also been taken, but he guessed without Amanda Rush, the kids would be even worse off.

"Buck? You good?" Obi-Wan asked.

Forcing his attention back to the present, Buck closed the folder. The faces of those kids were etched in his brain...but it was their teacher at the forefront of his mind. She looked eager and happy in the staff picture that had been included in the packet of information provided by Blair and Desmond.

"What's the contingency plan?" he asked. He'd already approved of the plan to fly over the jungle, use the helicopter's technology to find heat sources, make sure they were the right targets, then swoop in and spirit the hostages away in the middle of the night. But even the best plans didn't always work the way they were intended. The kids may have been split up, the chopper might have engine failure—doubtful, but it could happen—or a hundred other things could go wrong.

He wanted to know what the plan was if they weren't successful on the first go-round. Because once the rebels understood their location had been compromised, they'd scatter. Possibly taking children with them, or even killing them outright.

It was that thought that had Buck hesitating to call this meeting over so they could get started.

"This is a delicate situation," the colonel said.

"No shit," Obi-Wan said under his breath.

Buck did his best to keep his face expressionless as he stared at the man in charge.

"If this mission fails...I'm not sure we'll be able to launch another rescue attempt for some time," the colonel explained. "The rebels know that jungle better than we do, so they'll be able to hide in places that might be impossible to reach. And if they split the children up—"

"That can't happen!" Blair exclaimed, interrupting. "If they split up the kids, we'll never see them again."

"They might have already split them up," one of the special forces operatives said matter-of-factly. "It's been sixteen days since they were taken. They could be in Caracas by now, for all we know."

Buck didn't disagree, but he was really hoping that wasn't the case.

"I don't know why they took the girls," Blair said, wiping her eyes with a handkerchief. She was in her early seventies, if Buck had to guess, and looked way too fragile to be in charge of an orphanage in the tiny South American country. Originally from Texas, she'd apparently decided to do something different with her life after her husband passed away unexpectedly a decade ago. That something was move to Guyana and start a school for orphaned children.

Desmond was a Guyanese man born and raised, who'd been hired as a liaison between Blair and the other locals.

Over the years, the popularity of the school had grown, and the local people had learned to trust Blair. The school turned into a full-time orphanage, and now children were brought there by locals, the government, or they found their way to Blair themselves.

"If we don't get the children back, we're done here," she said tearfully.

Buck couldn't keep his lip from curling in disdain. She was worried about the reputation of her *school?* What about the kids? What about Amanda Rush? The safety of the children who *hadn't* been taken? It seemed to him there were other things the woman should be worried about.

Desmond patted her hand. "They'll find them, Blair. I know it."

"Those kids are innocent. They didn't deserve this," she said between sniffs.

"Yes, ma'am. We're going to do our best to bring them all back to you unharmed," the captain told her.

"As to a contingency plan," the colonel said, his tone hard, "there isn't one. You have to succeed in getting the kids out on your first pass. Otherwise..."

He let his sentence hang.

Buck knew what he didn't want to say in front of the civilians. It was likely the rebels would simply shoot any younger kids, because they'd be a liability. They might keep the oldest boys, but that was about it.

And Amanda Rush? She'd be as good as dead as well.

They had to use the element of surprise and rescue the hostages. If they didn't...

Buck knew there was as much point to finishing that thought as there was to the colonel finishing his directive. He was well aware of the responsibility that sat upon his and Obi-Wan's shoulders. The same one he had every time they loaded up a chopper full of Navy SEALs or Delta Force operatives before heading into any other hostile territory.

He was a Night Stalker. One of the best pilots in the world. It didn't matter if he was flying into a jungle or the mountains. He could handle the chopper and the terrain...but it was the unknown factors that would make the mission succeed or fail.

And Buck refused to fail. Not today. Not when the stakes were so high. Not when so many innocent lives depended on him and Obi-Wan, and the soldiers they would carry into the jungle. They had to not only find the missing kids and teacher, and get them back to Guyana, but mitigate any threats in the process.

There were a few other details that needed to be discussed, but after another twenty minutes, the meeting had disbanded and Buck and Obi-Wan were standing. They had two hours before they'd be heading into the jungle on their search-and-rescue mission.

Blair stopped them before they could leave. She put a hand on Buck's arm and said in a low, tearful voice, "There's a girl. Bibi. She's the youngest. Only four. She's like a daughter to me. I want all the kids back safely, but she's..." Tears spilled onto her cheeks as she struggled with her emotions.

The woman's white hair was messy, and any makeup she'd been wearing had long since worn off. She had bags under her eyes and it didn't look like she'd slept much recently. Buck felt bad for her...and a little guilty for his earlier thoughts. The woman's entire world had shifted, and it seemed she was barely hanging on.

"We'll bring her back. We'll bring them all back," he impulsively promised. It was a stupid pledge to make, as he had no idea if they'd even be able to find the missing children, but he couldn't stand there and *not* reassure the woman in some way.

"Thank you," she whispered, before Desmond put his arm around her shoulders and led her down the hall, in the opposite direction from where Buck and Obi-Wan would be headed.

"That was intense," Obi-Wan observed.

"Yeah."

"Civilian missions are hard. I think I prefer being a bus for SEALs."

Buck understood where his copilot was coming from. At

least when they were ferreting military personnel to and from hot zones, everyone knew what was expected of them. What they were getting into. That there were no guarantees anyone would survive the extremely dangerous missions they were sent on.

Kids were a completely different thing. They were precious. Innocent. Unpredictable.

As he and Obi-Wan headed to the nearby hangar to check over their chopper one more time and make sure everything was as it should be, Buck couldn't help but think about Amanda Rush yet again. Everyone's focus was on the kids, and rightly so. But that didn't keep him from wondering how she was coping. If she was even still alive.

If the rebels had decided to use her to assuage their baser needs.

He frowned at the unpleasant thought. No woman should have to experience that. Ever. It was the ultimate degradation.

Even if the teacher *had* managed to escape that fate, she still had to be extremely stressed. Being responsible for over twenty kids, who she probably thought of as her own children, in some ways. She was in an impossible situation, and Buck hated that for her.

He took a moment to hope and pray that they'd be successful. That the intel they'd received about the direction the rebels had gone, and where their suspected camp was located, was correct. If it wasn't...

It was very likely Amanda Rush and the children under her care would be lost forever.

Gritting his teeth, Buck was filled with determination. He'd do whatever it took to find them. He didn't know why this mission felt so much more personal than any other he'd been on...was it because it involved kids? Civilians? Orphans who already didn't have much in this world?

He wasn't sure. But if he and Obi-Wan found them, he was going to do everything in his power to get them out of the jungle safe and sound.

CHAPTER TWO

Amanda was exhausted. It wasn't easy being a mother to eight needy girls, while also trying to reassure and comfort the fifteen boys who were still being kept in different tents on the other side of the makeshift camp.

Not that she had much time for mothering of any kind. During the day, while the boys were being forced to run through crude obstacle courses and shoot at targets in the trees with weapons that were too large and powerful for them to manage, Amanda and the girls were cooking, cleaning, and washing their captors' clothing.

Everyone was tired and scared and cranky. Amanda made sure the younger girls were given the easier tasks, and that she herself did the bulk of the chores, but as a result, she was on the verge of collapse after just two days.

So far, no men had arrived for any of the girls, but the tension in the air remained thick. Especially for her. Because every time she turned around, she saw one of the rebels watching her. And she didn't like the looks in their eyes. She wasn't sure what they were waiting for, but she had a feeling her respite would soon be over.

The last couple of days since arriving at the camp had felt like an eternity. Her back hurt. Her feet hurt. Her heart hurt at seeing the pain and exhaustion of the children. She hadn't been at the school for long, but even in her short time there, she'd been able to make a difference in the children's lives. At least, she *thought* she had.

They'd seemed lighter. Had laughed more readily and more often. Had begun to openly show affection toward her, especially the younger kids. She made a point to hug everyone as much as she could and to compliment them on every little thing. The confidence they'd gained was remarkable, and it made Amanda feel as if she was finally making a difference in the world.

And now? They were back to being closed off. Emotionally and physically. They didn't meet her gaze and their little shoulders were slumped at all times. Amanda felt as if she'd failed, even though none of this was her doing.

She so wanted to steal the kids away in the middle of the night, but that would be impossible. First of all, she couldn't exactly sneak away with twenty-three kids, and she wasn't willing to leave even one behind. Second, going off into the jungle was stupid. She wouldn't survive a day. Some of the older kids, like Joseph, Michael, Andrew, and Natasha, probably knew more about jungle survival than she did, but she wasn't willing to risk everyone's lives on that.

Finally, there were too many rebels to even contemplate trying to fight back. And they were all armed. There were around a dozen men constantly watching and guarding them.

But today...something had happened. All morning, their guards were extra chatty. Amanda knew some Spanish and could pick out a few words here and there. Tomorrow, reinforcements were arriving. Supplies. "Husbands" for the girls.

Amanda was almost frantic with worry. She had no idea what to do, but she kept her mouth shut. There was no point in distressing her kids any more than they were already. Being taken away from their friends would be traumatic for everyone. And Amanda dreaded the sun rising on the next day more than she could express.

Her belly hurt so much from the stress, she hadn't been able to eat more than a few bites of the nasty stew she and the girls had made for dinner. During the meal, she'd caught Michael's eye across the hard-packed earth. He'd given her a small smile, which made her want to cry. He had a black eye and bruises all over his arms and legs. All the boys did. They were being treated harshly as they were "trained"...and yet, with that smile, Michael was still doing what he could to reassure her that he was okay.

He'd apparently been beaten almost to the point of unconsciousness when he'd been taken into the jungle that first day, but he hadn't let it break him. He'd also limped for a short while afterward, but either his leg wasn't injured so badly that it hurt for long...or he'd refused to give their captors the satisfaction of seeing his pain.

Amanda had never felt as helpless as she did at that moment. She'd wanted to go over and hug the boy—*all* her boys—letting them know she loved them. But she knew if she'd tried, the second she stood, one of the rebels would have been at her side, pointing his rifle, ordering her to sit back down.

Now, she was back in the girls' tent, with Sharon under one arm and Patricia under the other. Michelle held Bibi as she slept, and the other girls were side by side, sleeping as best they could on the hard ground. They hadn't been given any blankets—not that they needed them, as it was hot as hell, even at night. But even that small creature comfort would've made their situation seem a bit more humane.

Amanda couldn't sleep though. Too many thoughts were rolling around in her brain. About what the future held, for her *and* her kids.

And that lack of sleep was why she heard the faint sound of... something. It was an out-of-place noise, one she hadn't heard in the jungle before. It took her a moment of listening intently to understand what she thought she was hearing.

A helicopter!

Acting on instinct, she quickly and quietly woke the girls, telling them all to stay silent. Thankfully, they were more than willing to do as she asked, and they all sat in the dark, eyes wide, waiting, listening, praying that the helicopter was there for them.

As outlandish as the thought was, Amanda couldn't help but hope against hope that it was a rescue. But it could just as easily be more rebels joining the group that had kidnapped them.

Whoever it was, Amanda wanted to be ready. She had no idea what time it was, just that it was dark, with only the moon to light the area. There were no sounds of anyone else stirring, and she hoped that was because the men were all still asleep, too used to the various night sounds of the rainforest for their brains to make note that the helicopter was out of place.

Amanda thought about the boys. Had they heard it too? Or were they too exhausted from all the physical activity they'd been forced to do for the last couple of days? The need to run over to their tents to see if they were awake was hard to resist, but she stayed where she was, not willing to risk the wrath—or lust—of their captors if they caught her outside the girls' tent in the middle of the night.

So she waited. Holding her breath. Praying against all odds that the chopper was there for her and the kids.

One moment the sound seemed far off in the distance. The next, it was as if the helicopter was right over their heads. The walls of the tent were even blowing from the rotor wash.

Their captors heard it now too. Of course they did; it was right over top of them. Shouts came from outside the tent, and Amanda held her breath. Not excited shouts, as if they were greeting friends or fellow rebels—but shocked, angry sounds.

It was the sound of gunfire that had Amanda moving,

however. She wasn't going to be a sitting duck in this tent, waiting for a stray bullet to pierce the canvas. Or even for the rebels to decide killing their hostages was better than allowing them to be rescued. And one thing she refused to do was sit back and let someone else do all the work. If it meant getting out of here, getting all her kids out, she'd do whatever was necessary.

"Hurry, girls, this way!" she whispered urgently, gesturing toward the back side of the tent. She'd tested it out two days ago, realizing that the bottom wasn't secured to the ground. She lifted the canvas and lay down on the ground, peering out into the darkness. All she saw was trees. Whatever was happening was going on in the clearing on the other side of the tent.

She gestured for Natasha and Patricia to move forward. "Scoot out, but stay by the tent," she ordered.

Natasha nodded and took Patricia's hand. Next came Michelle and Jennifer. Then Karen and Sharon. Sandra reached for Bibi's hand, but the four-year-old refused to take it, instead holding her arms up for Amanda.

As much as it tore her heart out, Amanda shook her head. "Go with Sandra," she told Bibi as sternly as she could. "I'll be right behind you."

She loved that little girl. She was adorable, and sweet, and loving. She'd been orphaned very recently, after her parents were killed in a motorbike accident. She was lost and confused when she arrived at the school, but before the kidnapping, she'd slowly begun to open up, attaching herself to Amanda in particular.

Hating that the little girl was experiencing such trauma, that all the kids were, she was right on their heels, slithering out of the tent to join the rest of the girls. She hurried toward where Michelle was standing near the edge of the tent and peered around the corner.

Her eyes widened at what she saw. Men she didn't recognize —who seemed to be wearing uniforms of some kind, not the shorts and T-shirts most of the rebels wore—were hiding behind trees, shooting at their captors. She saw several rebels lying motionless in the dirt while the rest fought back almost desperately.

"Head in that direction!"

Amanda let out a screech and jerked at the sound of the accented voice behind her. Spinning around, she saw it was one of the newcomers. A man in a military uniform.

"There's a clearing about half a kilometer through the trees that way," he barked. "Take the kids and go!"

The girls didn't need to be told twice. Natasha and Michelle took charge and herded the rest of the group in the direction the man had pointed. Amanda didn't want to let them go alone, but she needed to make sure the boys were being rescued as well.

"The rest of the kids?" she asked the man.

"We'll get them."

She should've trusted him—but she couldn't leave that camp without seeing the boys. Without knowing they were coming too. She watched as the man ran toward the other tents. Spotting Michael and the other boys streaming out of them was a huge relief.

But when one of the rebels saw what was happening, he screamed in rage and made a beeline for little Richard and Leon.

Michael purposely dodged in front of him, and was knocked on his ass as the man ran smack-dab into him. They fell to the ground in a tangle of limbs. Thankfully, the soldier who'd spoken to Amanda was there. He and the rebel exchanged blows. Punching each other as hard as they could.

In the meantime, Michael was frantically yelling for his fellow orphans to run as fast as they could into the trees. Except they weren't orderly about it. They scattered like leaves in the wind, and Amanda was having a hard time counting heads, making sure everyone was escaping. With the darkness and the chaos of the fight occurring all around them, she had no idea if they even knew which way to go toward the chopper.

Panic hit hard and fast.

"Run! *Now*," a different soldier said, as he grabbed Amanda's upper arm and practically threw her in the direction the girls had gone. "We'll get all the kids!"

It was the best she was going to get at the moment, and Amanda knew it. She turned and ran into the trees after the girls. The second she left the clearing, any light there was from the moon disappeared. It was like running blind. Amanda had to slow down, resort to walk as quickly as she could with her arms in front of her, so she didn't smack into a tree.

Adrenaline was making her shaky, but she kept going. Freedom was close. So close she could smell it. Or maybe that was the scent of her own fear.

The sound of the helicopter got louder and louder, the only way she knew she was headed in the right direction. The second she broke out of the trees into another clearing, she could see once again, thanks to the moonlight that wasn't able to penetrate the canopy of the jungle. A huge helicopter was on the ground, its rotors turning, a man standing by the open door and helping kids into the huge cargo area.

Excitement surged through Amanda's veins. She took off toward the chopper, knowing as soon as she got inside, she'd finally be safe and this ordeal would be over.

But before she got more than a few steps closer, Michael appeared at her side as if by magic.

"Mandy! I can't find James!"

"What?" Amanda practically shouted to be heard over the sound of the chopper.

"James! He was with Patrick, but he got lost in the trees somewhere on the way here!"

"Shit," Amanda muttered. "What about everyone else?"

"I think they're all here. I tried to be last and count as

everyone ran by me. We headed for the sound of the helicopter because we saw the girls going this way. He was there by the tents, but by the time we got here, I didn't see him anymore!"

"All right. Don't panic. I'll find him!" Amanda shouted. "Get to the helicopter! We don't need two of you lost. Tell the soldiers that I'll be back with him. Okay?"

"Okay!" Michael said with a nod, then continued toward the chopper and his friends.

Thankful he'd been looking out for all the kids, especially the younger ones—James was only five, and he'd been struggling hard with the physical activities he was forced to do at the camp—Amanda gave one long look at the helicopter that represented her freedom, then turned and headed back into the trees.

* * *

"What the fuck is she doing?" Buck asked, more to himself than anyone else. He saw who could only be Amanda Rush running toward them, and the relief he'd felt was huge. She looked okay. Tired and dirty, but on two feet and moving without too much trouble.

Then she'd stopped to talk to one of the older boys—and turned around and headed back into the jungle.

"We need to get the hell out of here!" one of the special forces soldiers said in Buck's ear. They were all wearing radios so they could communicate. After they'd fast-roped out of the chopper, Buck and Obi-Wan had landed in the clearing to wait for the children to be extricated. He'd gotten out of the pilot seat to help the kids into the helicopter as soon as they'd appeared in the clearing.

When the girls started arriving, Buck and Obi-Wan had been relieved.

"Reinforcements incoming," another soldier said. "We've mitigated the immediate threat, but there are trucks approaching from the west. They'll be here in two minutes. There are over three dozen men, too many for us to keep at bay. We're coming in hot for the chopper. Get the kids in and get ready to take off!"

Every muscle in Buck's body tightened. Amanda. Where was she?

"How many kids we got?" Buck asked Obi-Wan through the radio.

"Twenty-two."

"Twenty-three with this last boy," Buck returned grimly.

A tall, slender boy with more bruises on his body than any kid should ever have was running toward the helicopter with wild eyes.

"Amanda!" he blurted, as soon as he was within earshot. "She went to look for James!"

"James?" Buck asked.

"Yeah! He's five. He got lost in the trees on the way here!"

"No, he didn't. There are fourteen boys and eight girls inside. You make a total of twenty-three. Everyone is accounted for." Unless their numbers had been wrong. Unless there were actually twenty-four kids taken.

The boy immediately frowned. Looked confused.

Buck didn't hesitate. He lifted him up and into the back of the chopper.

The kid stood at the entrance for a moment, his gaze scanning over the other children before he turned around, looking absolutely devastated. "I didn't see him! I thought he was lost!" he cried.

Buck turned back toward the trees and prayed he'd see Amanda running toward him once more. But the only people he saw were the special forces soldiers. They were running hard—as if being chased.

Fuck, fuck, fuck! This wasn't good. Why the hell did she have to go off by herself? Why couldn't she have double-checked to make sure all the kids were there before acting? Hell, she should've come straight to *him* for help, instead of running off into the jungle like a damn idiot.

Buck made a split-second decision.

He wasn't leaving her.

He was going to get his ass chewed for leaving his chopper. A Night Stalker never, *ever* left his chopper. Recently, Casper had done just that, leaving Laryn vulnerable and allowing her to be taken in Turkey. And now he was following suit.

But he could *not* leave Amanda Rush in this jungle. Not knowing there were dozens of rebels about to descend on the area. Knowing that she'd sacrificed her own safety for that of a five-year-old boy.

"Go," he told Obi-Wan, turning to meet his gaze. "I can't leave her, and you have to get these kids to safety."

"Buck, I don't think—"

"I'll find her and circle around and head east. If that's not possible, we'll head south. I'll get her across the border and meet you back in Guyana."

With that, Buck ripped off his headphones and threw them into the back of the chopper at the same time the soldiers returned. Without hesitation, he sprinted across the clearing, heading in the direction Amanda had disappeared. He had to get out of the clearing before the newcomers arrived. If they knew he was still on the ground, or that Amanda was, they'd be hunted like animals. It was possible they'd figure out she'd been left behind, anyway, but if he was lucky—*really* lucky—he and the teacher could sneak off in the darkness and chaos of the night.

He felt the wind from the rotors, heard the motor revving as Obi-Wan expertly lifted the chopper. Shouts sounded, and Buck slipped into the trees just before six men burst into the clearing a dozen yards away, rifles in hand. They stopped and lifted their weapons, all their attention on the sky as they aimed for the helicopter, which was ascending at a rapid rate and already beginning to fly out of range.

As gunshots rang out, Buck saw something out of the corner of his eye. Instinctively he turned, reaching out as someone ran by him. Knowing immediately this was Amanda, even as they went down to the ground hard.

He covered her mouth with his hand, cutting off anything she might say to give away their location to the now very pissed-off rebels.

Her eyes were huge in her face, and he could feel how fast she was breathing as he lay on top of her, trying desperately to communicate to her without words how important it was to stay absolutely silent and still.

She didn't fight him, simply stared back as her nostrils flared with each labored breath she took. Buck could feel her heart beating against his chest as the rebels continued to shoot at the helicopter, which was now way out of range.

A huge wave of relief swept over him. The kids were safe. The soldiers were safe. Obi-Wan was safe. They'd succeeded in rescuing the children. Even though he and Amanda were fucked, he was still glad the mission had succeeded as well as it had.

But he and Amanda couldn't stay here. They were way too close to the rebel camp. And those men in the clearing were beyond outraged. He didn't know who they were in relation to the rebels, but since they were connected to the kidnapping of twenty-three children, he figured it wasn't good regardless. They were either there for the girls, or to force the boys to kill or die for their cause.

They were the scum of the earth, and Buck wanted to avoid detection at all costs.

Especially since he had no gun. Hell, he had no supplies, period. No food, no water, no nothing. All he had was the KA-BAR knife he always carried in his flight suit and an old-school compass. His dad had given him the latter for his high school graduation, before he'd headed off to boot camp. And he'd carried it on every mission since becoming a Night Stalker. It might be his only saving grace. His and Amanda's.

Leaning down, he put his lips right near her ear. Speaking in a tone lower than a whisper, he said, "We need to put space between us and them."

She nodded, and Buck took a chance and removed his hand from her mouth. She immediately lifted her lips toward his own ear.

After turning his head so she could reach him better, and so she didn't have to speak any louder than necessary, he heard her tortured words. "There's a boy missing."

He shook his head. "No. They were all in the chopper."

She looked confused. And now she shook *her* head. "James. He's five."

"He was there. They were all there."

Buck saw the second the information sank in. The exact moment she realized that her desperate search for a missing boy had been in vain. Saw the despair in her eyes. The fact that she'd missed the chopper for nothing.

He wanted to soothe her. Tell her it would be okay. But things were far from okay at the moment. They were in deep shit, and only time would tell if they made it out of the area without being detected.

He should be pissed at her. Furious that she'd run off on her own. And he was. But he also understood making split-second decisions based on limited intel.

Hadn't he done the same thing less than a minute ago?

"Stay low. Stay quiet. And follow me," he ordered.

He waited for her to nod, then slowly slid off her body and motioned with his head to the west. They'd have to circle around the camp. Couldn't afford to get too close to it.

Well, *she* couldn't. Buck would infiltrate their base to see what he could scavenge.

KEEPING AMANDA

But first he needed to ensure Amanda's safety. Find a place to hunker down. Then he'd see what he could steal from the rebels and they'd head east, if possible.

Obi-Wan knew his plan. Buck would lead Amanda to the border one way or another. The jungle had never been one of his favorite places, but it was better than the desert. He hated sand, and would choose being wet over being cooked alive in the desert heat any day.

Ever so slowly, he began to army crawl, keeping his head down and checking on Amanda every few seconds. It would be slow going to get out of the area, but he wasn't willing to risk being captured. Because he knew without a doubt the rebels wouldn't give anyone a chance to mount a second rescue attempt.

Their *only* chance of making it out of there alive was staying under the radar. Making the rebels think everyone had left in that chopper.

CHAPTER THREE

Amanda felt sick. She hadn't hesitated to run back into the trees to look for little James...and there'd been no need. He was already in the helicopter. She didn't blame Michael for the mistake. There were a lot of little bodies, and it was dark, and they'd been awoken from a deep sleep to complete terror.

But as a result of her rash decision, she'd missed her chance to escape.

The chopper had left without her.

It hurt. A lot. But she didn't blame the pilot either. Was glad he'd chosen the children over her.

She had no idea who the man was who'd basically tackled her before she could run into that clearing, screaming for the helicopter to come back. He was American, she could tell that much by his lack of accent. And she couldn't believe he hadn't left with the rest of the rescue team.

Why did he stay? For *her*? That couldn't be right. Maybe he'd been off looking for James too, and was also left behind.

But no...he knew James was in the helicopter already.

She couldn't think straight. Her mind was spinning. Adrenaline was making her shaky. Making it hard to think rationally.

But for the moment, all she had to do was exactly as she was told...which was a good thing, because Amanda didn't think she could make any decisions right now. Not good ones at least.

Doing her best to copy the man, she crawled on her elbows and knees across the wet jungle floor. She refused to think about what kinds of critters she was disturbing as she slithered over their hiding places under leaves and dirt and mud. She felt a little shell-shocked. Happy that the children were safe and out of this stinkin' jungle, but terrified for herself.

She had no idea how long she and the man had been crawling away from the clearing where the helicopter had landed, but when the man stopped, Amanda had never been more relieved.

She dropped down onto her belly and tried to ignore her shaking muscles. Crawling while trying to stay as quiet and low as possible was hard work. Much harder than it looked.

Resting her forehead on the backs of her hands, Amanda closed her eyes. She was tired. Bone-deep tired. The adrenaline that had been fueling her flight had waned and now all she felt was exhaustion.

"We'll rest here for a bit," he told her.

At that, Amanda's head came up. The man had turned around to face her, and he was talking a little louder than the barely there whisper he'd used earlier, but not by much. "Shouldn't we get as far away from here as we can?" she asked, mimicking his low tone.

Her rescuer stared at her without speaking for a long moment.

"Probably. We *should* be putting as much space as possible between us and the assholes who kidnapped you and the kids, but the thing is..." He sighed, then continued. "We have no provisions. I hadn't planned on leaving my chopper, so I have nothing with me. No food, no water container, no way of lighting a fire. We need that stuff if we're going to get back to Guyana."

He wasn't wrong, but the thought of having to retrace the path she'd been forced to take to get where she was now was extremely disheartening. "The helicopter can't come back and pick us up?" she asked, knowing what the answer was, but needing to ask the question anyway.

"We surprised them once. We wouldn't be able to do it a second time. And I have no way to communicate with my partner and the rest of the rescue team. I can't tell them where we are. My friend and copilot could try to find us by using thermal radar, but that would also bring attention to the fact we're in the jungle, and pinpoint our location to the rebels. Bottom line is that we're most likely going to have to walk back to the border."

Amanda wanted to protest. To tell this man she couldn't do it. That she was too tired, too dirty, too hungry, too thirsty, too... weak. But the words wouldn't come. She was overwhelmed and scared. And she had a feeling if she opened her mouth, she'd lose the little composure she was currently hanging on to by the skin of her teeth.

Instead, she simply nodded.

But the man seemed to understand how close to the edge of control she was. He scooted closer so their heads were right next to each other. "You're doing great. Just keep hanging in there."

His words were gentle and encouraging...and they did nothing to make the tears Amanda was desperately holding back go away. She nodded again and swallowed hard. After about ten seconds, she thought she could talk without breaking down. "So what are we going to do about supplies?" she asked.

"You're going to stay here. I'm going to go recon the camp. See what I can steal. I'll grab what we need, since it's still dark, meet back up with you here, then we can go."

Amanda felt extremely uneasy about that plan. But he had a point about seeing what he could get now, while it was dark. The last thing she wanted to do was hang around for a whole day, waiting for nighttime to fall again.

As if he could sense her unhappiness with his plan, he went on. "We have no idea what they'll do come morning. They could all just up and leave, taking the things we need with them. I have to see what I can get now, while they're all still confused about what just happened and wondering how the kids were taken right from under their noses."

"Won't they be pissed though? Making them more dangerous?"

"Yeah," the man said, and Amanda appreciated that he wasn't trying to downplay the situation. "But I'll be careful."

Making a split-second decision that she had a feeling she'd regret, Amanda said, "I should go with you."

Her rescuer shook his head firmly. "No. You'll stay here where I know you're safe."

Amanda snorted.

"Shhhh," he reprimanded.

"Sorry," she whispered once more. "But I don't think there's any such thing as safe right now. I could get bitten by a suntiger tarantula, or some rebel trying to find a place to pee could stumble over my hiding spot. Besides, I've been in the camp. You haven't. I can tell you where everything is. Where you're most likely going to find stuff we can use." She didn't know why she was arguing to go back to the place where she'd been completely miserable and terrified, but she was even more scared of being left alone here in the middle of the jungle. What if something happened to him and he didn't come back? She'd certainly die out here.

His facial expression didn't change as he stared at her.

"I'm sorry I ran off," she said a little desperately. "It was irresponsible and stupid. I realize that. But when Michael said James was missing, I panicked. I couldn't leave any of the kids behind. I just *couldn't*. I should've checked myself. Counted heads before running off into the trees. You're here because of my asinine decision. I'm sorry. I'm *so* sorry."

"It was brave," the man said without hesitation. "Maybe impulsive, but extremely unselfish. That's pretty rare these days."

Amanda stared at him. "I'm still sorry," she told him.

"Me too. I wish you weren't in this situation. Wish things had gone a little smoother in the extraction. But they are what they are, and we have to deal with the hand we've been given. I could use some intel about the camp, and if you're willing to tell me what you can, that should be enough for me to be able to get in and out without detection."

"It would be easier if I could point things out in person," she argued. Again, she didn't want to go back to camp, to the men who were planning on doing horrible things to not only her, but the kids as well, but the fear of being left alone was stronger than her fear of sneaking back to the edge of her makeshift prison.

"I'm Nash. Nash Chaney. My flight name is Buck."

Amanda blinked. She hadn't expected introductions in the middle of this intense conversation. They were both lying on the jungle floor, covered in dirt, and it felt like the oddest time to be exchanging names. But she went with it. "Amanda Rush. People call me Mandy."

"It's good to meet you in person. For the record, so you don't find out later and get upset…I know a lot about you already, from reading the file we were given when we came down for the rescue."

"There's a file on me?"

"Yes."

Amanda wasn't sure how to feel about that. But ultimately, she decided she didn't care. If the people sent to rescue her needed to know every minute detail about her life in order to do so, what did it matter? She had nothing to hide. "Okay."

"Just okay?"

She shrugged as best she could from her position on the ground. "The kids are safe, that's all that matters. Not whatever's written about me in some random file. I haven't done anything illegal or that I'm ashamed of in my life. It's like surveillance cameras. I don't mind them because I'm not doing anything wrong. If they want to film me driving, walking through a parking lot, down the street, or through the aisles of a store, I don't care. If I was doing nefarious stuff, maybe I'd give a damn. But I'm not, so I don't."

Nash chuckled softly. "Nefarious stuff?"

"Yeah. Shoplifting, speeding, running innocent people off the roads...that kind of thing."

"Right."

"So...about coming with you to camp...I promise not to do anything else on impulse. I'll do everything you say, as soon as you say it. I'm not stupid, I don't want to get caught. I just want to help. I put us in this situation, and I want to help get us out of it."

"You didn't put us here. The assholes who kidnapped you and those kids did."

"Yeah, but I was the one who ran *away* from the helicopter instead of *toward* it," Amanda argued.

"All right. But I'm going to hold you to your promise to do everything I say. Even if you don't understand why. I've had training, Mandy. I can handle things if they go wrong. But I *can't* handle you falling back into their hands. Got it?"

"Got it," she agreed immediately. "I think the other guys who arrived were here to take the girls away. As wives. Or slaves." She shuddered. "Thank you for risking your life to come get them."

"And you. We came for you too," Nash said.

Mandy shook her head. "The kids are what are important. Not me."

"Don't sell yourself short. You're the reason we were sent on this mission. Because an American was kidnapped. If you weren't with those kids..." He let the explanation trail off.

Amanda was glad she was the excuse her government needed to rescue the children.

"All right. It'll be light before we know it. If we're going to do this, we need to get going," Nash said.

Amanda nodded. Her stomach immediately rolled, thinking about what was to come. But he was right, they needed supplies if they were going to walk back to Guyana. And the best place to get them was at the camp she'd just escaped.

Nash cocked his head, as if that would help him hear if anyone was close. All Amanda heard was crickets and birds. And the sound of water dripping from the leaves overhead after a break in the constant rain.

"Follow me," Nash ordered, slowly getting to his feet.

Relieved they weren't going to have to crawl all the way back to camp, Amanda got to her feet—and almost faceplanted right back down to the ground. Would've done just that if Nash hadn't grabbed her arm, keeping her upright.

He frowned. "Maybe this isn't a good idea."

"It's fine. Great. I just stood up too fast," Amanda rushed to reassure him. She'd stay on her feet or die trying. Anything was better than being left behind. She just had to ignore her body's need for sleep. Or food. Or water. Piece of cake.

The skeptical look Nash gave her wasn't unexpected. Amanda did her best to smile in return.

To her surprise, after he let go of her arm, he reached for her hand. Holding it in a firm grasp as he began to head toward the camp. It was obvious he was holding her hand to try to prevent her from falling, but the warmth and comfort the small action provided was everything at the moment.

She'd been solely responsible for the twenty-three kids for so long, and the stress of that responsibility was immense. Simply having another adult to help make decisions felt amazing. As did knowing the children were safe. In part because of Nash.

She made a mental vow not to do anything that would cause her to be a burden on him. Well...any more than she already was. She was so out of her element here, and she had no choice but to rely on him for just about everything. But she could do her best not to be the stereotypical "city girl" dropped in the jungle. She could suck it up and get through whatever she had to if it meant getting back to Guyana and safety.

Life had certainly thrown her a curveball in the last two weeks, and it didn't look like her unexpected adventure was over yet. All she could do was hang on for the ride and hope that no one got hurt because of her. That was literally her worst nightmare.

Pushing the dark thoughts from her head, Amanda trudged behind Nash, concentrating on where she put her feet so she didn't sound like a huge elephant making its way through the trees. Stealth was their friend. The fact that the rebels didn't know they weren't on the chopper was a huge advantage. And she'd do whatever it took not to blow that.

CHAPTER FOUR

Buck could admit that he'd been annoyed with Mandy. Annoyed that she'd done something so stupid like running away from the helicopter, forcing him to chase her down and thus miss their ride out of there.

But the feeling didn't last long. Because honestly...hadn't he done the same thing?

He had no gun, no supplies, had left the safety of his chopper and rashly raced into the jungle after her. How could he stay annoyed with Mandy when he'd been just as reckless himself? Besides, she'd thought she was rescuing a child. If there was ever a good reason for her behavior, it was that.

So no, he was no longer annoyed. In fact, the longer he was around her, the more impressed he became. She was obviously scared, but not hysterical. He could work with that. And he'd known she was compassionate from reading her file. The fact that she hadn't been able to resist going to look for the allegedly missing boy wasn't out of character for her. It just sucked that she'd been going on bad intel.

And Buck wasn't one to rehash mistakes over and over. It did no good. All he could do was pivot and come up with a new plan.

He and Mandy would either cross back into Guyana on their own—if nothing went wrong on their hike east—or Obi-Wan would browbeat the colonel and his special forces to fly over the jungle to find them.

One way or another, Buck would get him and Mandy out of the jungle alive. But the first step was to get supplies. And the only place he'd be able to do that was back at the camp where Mandy and the kids had been held captive. Bringing her along wasn't ideal, but it would make getting the hell out of the area faster, which was a good thing.

Looking up at the sky as they quietly made their way through the jungle, Buck frowned. He didn't have a lot of time left before it got light. And he and Mandy needed to be far from the camp before that happened. He could hear the men at camp now, which was both a relief and an added stressor to an already tense situation.

A few more yards and he stopped and crouched down behind a large tree, pulling Mandy with him. Buck had no idea why he hadn't dropped her hand by now. He'd grabbed it to make sure she didn't fall on her face and give away their location, but once they'd been on their way, and she was steady on her feet, he could've let go of her.

Truthfully, he wanted to comfort her in some way. She'd had a hell of a couple weeks and things weren't about to get any easier. They had a long way to go, and she was obviously struggling. Though he was impressed with her attempt to keep her chin up and pretend she wasn't at the end of her rope already. Holding her hand was a small way to help her continue to stay strong. To maybe give her some of his strength.

"What's wrong?" she whispered anxiously when they'd stopped.

She was crouched next to him, staring at him with wide eyes. Her short hair was greasy and sticking up in every direction. She had dirt on her face, under her nails, and her clothes were covered in dirt and mud as well, after they'd crawled away from the clearing.

And yet...there was something about her that was immensely beautiful to Buck. Physical beauty he could take or leave, but inner strength and kindness were two things he'd always been a sucker for. And Amanda Rush had both in spades.

"Nothing," he told her. "I just need you to tell me, quickly, everything you can about the layout of the camp."

Without hesitation, she did just that. Telling him about the four tents the boys had used, where the makeshift obstacle course was located, the tent the girls had slept in—and most importantly, where the one the kidnappers used as a kitchen was located, in relation to the others, as well as how it was set up.

She did such a good job describing everything, Buck had a clear vision in his head of the entire camp. He asked a few more questions—mostly about the supplies in the kitchen tent and about weapons—but before too long, he was ready to head out.

"I need you to stay here," he told her, expecting her to protest once again. So he was pleased when she simply nodded.

"Is there anything I can do to help you from here?"

"Stay quiet. Do not under any circumstances, no matter what you hear, show yourself to the rebels. Understand?"

"I don't want you to get hurt," she said, a deep furrow in her brows.

"I don't want that either. But if I am, if they discover me, you rushing in to help isn't going to do anything but give them someone else to fuck with. Understand?"

Still frowning, she nodded. "Can we steal a truck?" she asked.

Buck had thought about that, but decided stealth was a better option. Yes, the truck could get them to the border faster, but the rebels would follow, and the last thing he wanted was to get into a car chase in the middle of the freaking jungle. The rebels knew this area like the back of their hands. He'd be more likely to drive them into a ditch or river. He was better off stealing what he needed and sneaking out of the area with Mandy. At least then, they stood a chance of the rebels not even knowing they were out here. Hopefully.

"Not a good idea," he told her. "They'd know immediately we were here."

She nodded. "Right. Okay. I'll hunker down right here by this tree. Wait for you. But I can do my fair share of carrying whatever it is you get."

Impressed all over again, Buck nodded. He wasn't going to make her carry a damn thing. She'd have a hard enough time just walking to the border as it was. He hoped to find a duffel bag or something to put supplies in while he was at camp.

Though now, for some reason, Buck was reluctant to leave her. He needed to get going. It would be light way too damn soon, but the thought of leaving Mandy behind was making him hesitate.

"I'll be back," he forced himself to say.

"I'm counting on it," she said calmly. "Because if you aren't, I'll be walking in circles in this damn jungle until I can't take another step, then I'll just lie down and die. And I'm not being dramatic. I have no sense of direction and don't know the first thing about survival stuff. Sorry."

"Don't apologize. I don't know a damn thing about teaching. We all have our strengths and weaknesses."

She gave him a small smile.

Buck forced himself to give her a nod, then he turned and headed for the camp. Every step felt like a mistake, but he had to do this. Had to find provisions.

By the time he got to the outskirts of the camp, he'd calmed somewhat. Became focused on the mission at hand. The rebels had set up lights in the clearing, which actually worked in his favor. They could see what they were doing, but everything outside the circle of light would be darker. Their vision would be slightly impaired...hopefully enough to let him do what he needed to do and get the hell out without being detected.

The camp was set up exactly as Mandy had described. He could see the obstacle course the boys had been forced to run over and over. The tents where they'd slept, and the kitchen tent was right where she said it would be. On the far side of the camp was the large firepit. It looked like most of the men were currently sitting around the fire, bitching about the rescue and the fact that the girls, in particular, had slipped through their fingers.

It was disgusting, but Buck forced himself to forget about vengeance and concentrate on what he was there to do.

Just when he was about to head toward the kitchen tent, something caught his eye.

It was a dog.

At least, that's what he *thought* it was. The animal was lying on the periphery of the group of men. Every time one of them brought a hand up to their mouth, the dog's gaze followed the movement. He, or she, was super skinny, from what Buck could tell from his vantage point, its fur matted and covered in dried mud. The thing looked pathetic…and it hurt Buck's heart to see it. He had no idea if it had arrived with the men or if it was a stray, but the latter seemed unlikely since they were so far from any kind of civilization.

As he slipped around the camp to where the kitchen tent was located, Buck did his best to keep his temper in check. His job was such that he couldn't really have a pet, but he had a soft spot for animals. Why anyone would ever have an animal if they couldn't care for it, he didn't know. Why would the rebels keep a dog around if they weren't going to feed it, at least?

Doing his best to put the dog out of his mind, for his own sanity if nothing else, he concentrated on the job at hand. From talking to Mandy, he knew there wouldn't be anything useful inside the tents where the kids and Mandy were kept, because their captors hadn't given them blankets or spare clothes. Most of what they needed was inside the tent where all the females were forced to make food.

Getting down on his belly, Buck slowly lifted the edge of the canvas tent, listening and looking for anyone who might be inside. Relief filled him when he saw it was empty. That didn't mean someone couldn't enter at any second. He needed to be fast. It would be easier to cut the canvas than wiggle under, but a damaged tent would instantly indicate someone had been there. And he needed every second of time it would take the kidnappers to realize they'd been raided. The longer that took, the farther he and Mandy could get before they began hunting them down.

With luck, they'd never miss the things he pilfered.

But that hope died as soon as he was inside the tent. Mandy had warned him that she and the girls hadn't had a lot to work with, as far as cooking items went, and she hadn't lied. There was one large stockpot, which wouldn't be practical to take, and two smaller pans. There were a couple of spoons and a pair of tongs. One fork, and two dull kitchen knives. Anything he took would definitely be missed before too long.

However, he *did* spot a backpack lying in the corner. It had seen better days, the seams were coming apart, but it was better than nothing.

Working quickly, Buck packed one small pan, the fork and a knife. He padded them with the random dirty cloths lying around the tent so nothing would rattle as he walked.

Even though there wasn't much in the way of cooking items, Buck was extremely pleased with the amount of food. Mostly canned goods, which wasn't ideal, but once empty, the cans could be used to hold water and as cook vessels. That was why he didn't bother taking both pans. The cans would do in a pinch.

Better yet were the several matchbooks scattered haphazardly on the ground.

But the best item he found was the packet of purification tablets. They made water taste funky, but would kill any bacteria that could otherwise make them extremely sick.

Voices outside alerted Buck to the fact that his scavenging mission was quickly coming to an end. He needed to be gone by the time whoever was coming his way entered the tent. He shoved the backpack under the canvas at the back, then quickly lay down and crawled out himself.

He made it out just in time. Freezing in place, not wanting to make any noise whatsoever, Buck held his breath as two men entered the tent.

They were speaking Spanish, of course, and complaining about having to make breakfast for everyone. Thankfully, it didn't seem as if they noticed anything missing; they obviously hadn't spent much time in the kitchen tent, so they didn't know what supplies were normally available.

Moving slowly, Buck eased the pack onto his back and carefully moved away from the tent. There were more items he would've liked to have taken, but he'd have to be satisfied with the things he'd managed to grab.

Moving as stealthily as he could, Buck crept back through the trees to where he'd left Mandy. For a moment, he panicked when she wasn't crouched behind the large tree. Then a soft sound had him spinning around, and every muscle in his body sagged when he saw her. She'd moved away from the tree a little and was lying on her side in a ball, snoring lightly.

The fact that she'd felt safe enough to fall asleep wasn't lost on him. Or maybe it was just sheer exhaustion. Whatever it was, he felt horrible that he had to wake her, but they needed to get as far away from the rebel camp as possible before they could truly rest.

He put a hand on her shoulder and gently shook her.

She woke instantly, eyes wide with panic as she lurched away from him.

Feeling sick that he had to grab her to keep her from making any noise, Buck was on top of her with a hand over her mouth before she could let out even the smallest squeak.

"Sorry!" he apologized immediately. "I'm so sorry. Are you okay? Awake now?"

When she nodded, he quickly dropped his hand. "Did I hurt you?"

"No. Sorry. I didn't mean to fall asleep. Did you find the things we need?"

Buck nodded. "Got us some good stuff. But we need to go. Now."

She was on her feet almost before he'd finished speaking. Obviously more than ready to leave a place that was a source of some horrible memories.

"I'll lead. Stay right on my ass. Hold on to the backpack if you need to. Step where I step. Try not to make any noise. Understand?" He was being extra brusque, but the hair on the back of his neck was standing up. It was too light outside now, even under the canopy. They needed to be gone.

"Yes." Her reply was short and to the point.

Taking her at her word, Buck turned and headed north. They'd go that way, then circle back around to the east. Taking the long way around the camp, but he'd rather be safe than sorry.

Just when he thought they'd done it, that they'd gotten away without anyone knowing someone had been left behind by the chopper, a shout rose from the direction of the camp.

"Someone's been here. There's food missing!"

"*Fuck*. We need to run," Buck said. "Can you do that?"

"Yes!"

He didn't hesitate, just took off at a jog. They were still way too close to camp. And from the yelling he heard, Buck could tell the rebels were both pissed *and* excited.

The thought of them getting their hands on Mandy was enough to spur him to run faster. He could hear her breathing hard behind him, but she didn't complain, simply did her best to keep up.

At least the rebels had no idea who or how many people they were looking for, or what direction they'd gone. They probably thought they were looking for a kid or two—which again would work in their favor.

Still, the more distance they could put between them, the better off they'd be. Buck had no doubt the rebels wouldn't give up easily, but eventually when they didn't find anyone, he hoped they'd second-guess themselves...think perhaps the kids had stolen food before they'd been rescued, and just give up the search.

How long they ran, Buck had no idea. But it wasn't until it occurred to him that he didn't hear Mandy's breathing that he looked behind him.

His heart literally stopped beating when he didn't see her anywhere.

"Shit," he whispered, spinning around to backtrack.

He didn't have to go far. When he found her, he knew immediately they weren't going to be able to go much farther. Her face was bright red from exertion and tears were streaming down her face.

"I'm sorry!" she whispered. "I'm coming. I'll do better."

"Shhhh. *I'm* sorry," Buck told her, as he wrapped an arm around her waist, taking some of her weight. "I've got you."

"I can keep going. I just needed a second to breathe," she told him. "And I didn't want to call out to let you know in case someone could hear me."

She was being smart, but Buck still felt bad that he'd been so focused on escape that he hadn't even noticed she'd fallen behind. He vowed to do better. To *be* better. He wasn't in this with one of his Night Stalker pilots or a special forces operative. Mandy was a civilian. One who'd been through hell and was nearing the end of her rope. He wouldn't let her down again.

"Come on, I'm pretty sure we lost them. We need to find a place to hole up anyway. Rest. Eat something."

"Are you sure? What if they find us?"

"They won't." Buck didn't know that for certain, but at the moment, he'd say whatever he needed to in order to reassure Mandy.

Keeping his arm around her waist, Buck headed back in the direction they'd been going before Mandy fell behind. As they walked, he looked for a place they could hole up for the day. It was more dangerous to travel at night, but the cover of darkness would also help hide them in case the rebels were out searching.

What Buck *really* wanted to do was circle back around and kill each and every one of the bastards. It was a bloodthirsty thought, but he could feel Mandy trembling against him. They'd put her and the children through hell, and they deserved to suffer. But his only concern right now was the woman at his side. Making sure she survived. Getting her to safety.

Being this up close and personal to someone he rescued was a new thing for Buck. As a helicopter pilot, his role was usually only to transport people from one place to another. Anyone who'd been a prisoner of any kind was usually accompanied by a team of special forces. He and his fellow pilots rarely even spoke to whoever they transported. He felt out of his element right now. Unsure what to say to reassure Mandy. He wasn't good at this. He was good at flying, not soothing traumatized victims.

"How are you holding up?" he asked, immediately wincing at the stupid question.

"I'm okay," she surprised him by saying.

"I don't want you to tell me what you think I want to hear," Buck replied. "If you feel like shit, tell me that. If you're scared, I want to know. The only way we're going to make it through this is if we're honest with each other."

He was used to being on missions with his Night Stalker brethren. They had no problem telling shit like it was. They were probably a bit *too* honest at times. But one weakness could actually get the entire team killed if it wasn't dealt with or brought to light. They were stronger together than they were individually, and right now, he needed Mandy to be his teammate. A team of two.

"How are *you* holding up?" she asked, turning the question around on him.

"I'm pissed. Not at you," he said quickly, "but at the situation. At the men who thought it was okay to kidnap children and force them to become soldiers for their cause. I'm irritated they realized so quickly that things were missing from the kitchen tent. I'm worried about you. It's obvious you haven't been eating enough, and the last thing I want is for you to faint from lack of sustenance. I'm hot and uncomfortable in this flight suit. And I'm stressed because we need to find a place to hide so you can get some food and rest."

Her eyes had widened when he first began to speak, and by the time he was done, she was staring at him with an expression he couldn't read.

"Too honest?" he asked, as he looked down at her. Buck wasn't a very tall man, only five foot eight, but Mandy was still tiny compared to him. She only came up to his shoulder, and with his arm around her waist, he could feel how skinny she was. He was worried about her physical *and* mental state.

"It actually makes me feel better that you're dealing with all that," she told him. "You seem so...I'm not sure how to explain it."

"Try," Buck urged.

"Competent? Larger than life? You came swooping down and scooped us all up...well, you would've if I hadn't been an idiot by running off."

"You weren't an idiot," Buck said.

She shrugged. "I'm scared," Mandy whispered. "And hungry. And thirsty. And I've got chafing in places I've never chafed before. Clothes that never dry *suck*. And I'm worried about the kids. How they're doing. They have to be terrified. They don't have anyone to hold them tight and tell them they're okay, that things are going to be all right."

"The staff at the school won't do that?" Buck asked. "Blair and Desmond?"

"They will. But..."

Buck waited for her to finish her thought. When she didn't, he encouraged her to continue. "But?"

"Blair is a good director. But she's a little old school. A little stricter than I think some of the kids need. She loves the little ones—Bibi has become one of her favorites, she dotes on her. But Natasha and Michelle seem to irritate her. As do Joseph, Michael, and Andrew. The older the kids get, the more stand-offish she can be.

"Desmond's great, but he has his own family, so he isn't always around when the kids might need something. There are part-time volunteers who take turns staying with the kids at night, and the staff that works in the kitchens and stuff, but they're not as...invested? That's not really the word I'm looking for but my brain isn't firing on all cylinders right now. The kids need hugs and reassurance that they're safe, and I'm just not sure they'll get that. Especially not the older kids."

"You love them," Buck said.

"Of course I do," Mandy said without hesitation. "If I could adopt them all, I would. But I can't. So the best I can do is show them unconditional love and try to make them see that just because they don't have parents, that doesn't make them any less worthy than anyone else."

Buck was impressed. Yes, some people would think she was naïve and tell her that she couldn't change the world. But he admired her empathy. How much love she had in her heart for a bunch of kids society might deem not important because of their circumstances.

He opened his mouth to reply, but was distracted by exactly what he'd been searching for as they walked. He stopped and looked around the area, wanting to triple check that they were alone. Buck hadn't heard anyone following them, but since he and Mandy had been talking, he might've missed something.

When he heard and saw nothing out of the ordinary, he glanced at Mandy. "Stay here a second. Okay?"

She nodded without hesitation, and Buck was glad she didn't question him. He'd answer any questions she had, but he needed her to be able to follow orders because it literally could be a matter of life or death for them both.

He left her standing next to a group of trees and headed for the boulders that caught his eye. The huge rocks were actually unusual in the rainforest, but he wasn't going to walk away simply because they were out of place. They both needed somewhere dry to spend the day, and if he was lucky, the formation might offer just that.

First, he needed to make sure there weren't any animals that had already taken up residence.

Pulling out his KA-BAR knife, Buck slowly approached the boulders. It didn't take him long to see there was indeed a small space between two of them that would provide a perfect place to get out of the weather. There was moss, leaves, and other greenery covering the formation, and he was surprised he'd even spotted the boulders in the first place. At first glance, they looked like just another small hill in the jungle. Another overgrown pile of roots and earth.

Luck was on his side for sure, because on the other side of the formation, he discovered that over time, water had formed a natural vertical trough in one of the rocks. Fresh water would be easy to secure by putting one of the cans under the trough, catching rainwater as it was channeled through the depression in the rock.

Hurrying back to where he'd left Mandy, Buck found her

standing unnaturally still, as if she was afraid to move even one muscle.

"It's okay," he said gently. "Come on, I found a place you can rest during the day."

He took her hand in his, and once more it felt more natural than he ever would've thought. He led her to the rocks and pointed to the small cave-like space. "After we eat, you can crawl in there and sleep for as long as you're able."

"What about you?"

"What about me...what?" Buck asked.

"Where are you going to sleep?"

He frowned. "Out here."

"No. Not acceptable."

"What? Why?"

"I'm not going to take the only shelter if that means you're out here in the rain. And don't tell me it's not going to rain. It *always* rains. Every damn day."

"Mandy—" he started, but she lifted her hand, palm out toward him.

"No. Not happening."

Buck couldn't help but chuckle. "Did you just hand-palm me?"

"Yes. Because you were about to say something stupid."

This entire conversation was ridiculous, but Buck found himself smiling anyway. "You're at the end of your rope. You need the rest," he cajoled.

"So do you. More than me, actually. Because without you, I'm as good as dead out here, and we both know it. You're the one carrying the pack of supplies. You have the compass. You know what you're doing. I'm just along for the ride. I can handle being hungry, tired, thirsty, whatever. All I have to do is put one foot in front of the other. *You* need to stay sharp. Keep us going in the right direction. Stay strong so you can continue to carry the backpack. I'm extra baggage here, Nash—you're the important one."

"No," he said firmly. "Not true. If I'm constantly worried about how you're doing, I won't be able to fully concentrate on other things. And if you fall over with exhaustion, neither of us is getting out of this damn jungle, because I'm not leaving you. So you need to get it out of your head that you're expendable here. That you're not as important as me. A team is only as strong as its weakest member. And I don't intend for either of us to be weak."

Mandy's lips were stubbornly pressed together, and Buck was surprised to find how much he enjoyed sparring with her. If this could be counted as sparring. And she was fucking adorable when she was being all bossy.

She was a complete mess—dirty, sweaty...she even had a bug bite in the middle of her forehead—and Buck couldn't help thinking if he was *this* drawn to her when she wasn't at her best, what would it be like when she was rested, not stressed out, and all cleaned up?

She looked at him, then at the hole between the rocks, then back at him. "You aren't huge. I mean, it might be different if you were like, six-six or something. But I think we can both fit."

Buck frowned harder. "No."

"Why not?"

For the life of him, Buck couldn't think of a single reason why they shouldn't get comfy in that tiny little space together. In fact, the idea appealed to him. He tried to tell himself it was simply because he'd be able to keep watch over her easier if he was holding her. Could monitor her breathing and heart rate. Make sure she was resting comfortably. And if someone did happen upon them, he could communicate with her more easily, tell her what to do, since they'd be right next to each other.

"Right," she continued, when he came up with no good reason to avoid sharing the space. "We'll eat, then get some sleep. And when it gets dark, we can start off again. I do have one question for you though."

"What's that?" Buck asked.

"How do you feel about creepy-crawlies?"

"What?"

"Creepy-crawlies," she said matter-of-factly. "Bugs. Spiders. Snakes. Because lying on the ground under those rocks and leaves is gonna mean bugs crawling on us. That happened in the tent back at the camp where we were held. And I figure if it happened inside a tent, then it'll definitely happen out here in nature."

"I'm good with it. As long as nothing bites us, we'll be fine."

She nodded. "Yeah. That's what I told the girls. Okay, what's for breakfast? Or lunch, or whatever it is we're having?"

This woman. The longer he was around her, the more impressive she seemed. She took things in stride. If he'd been with almost anyone else, he figured they'd be freaking out. About being dirty. About the bugs. About sleeping on the ground. But not Amanda Rush. She was one of a kind, and that wasn't even taking into account the fact that she'd quit her job to help teach orphans in a country most people probably couldn't even find on a map.

Buck vowed right then and there to do whatever it took to make sure she got back home without a single hair on her head being harmed. It was the least he could do after all she'd been through. He'd pull any strings needed to make it happen.

And it wasn't lost on him that "home" was the same city where *he* lived. It was a huge coincidence...but then again, he didn't believe in coincidences.

"I'm not one hundred percent sure of what I grabbed. Have a seat and we'll check it out," he told her a little gruffly, not wanting to admit that he was having all sorts of feelings he'd never experienced before...and was confused as hell about every single one of them.

CHAPTER FIVE

Amanda wanted nothing more than to crawl inside that hole in the rocks and sleep for days. But she refused to be the stereotypical city girl...out of her element in the jungle and all whiny about it. Besides, everything she'd told Nash had been the truth. She needed him. Wasn't getting out of this without him. He had to stay strong, because she certainly was not. She was a huge manacle around his ankle, and he had to drag her along every step of the way.

Without her there, he'd be halfway to Guyana by now, she had no doubt. So she'd do whatever it took, sacrifice what she had to, in order for him to stay strong.

It wasn't that she was unselfish—she wanted to grab one of the cans he was taking out of the backpack he'd stolen and stuff all the food in her mouth as fast as she could—it was more that she was being practical.

She felt a little disconnected as she watched him pull out the cans he'd pilfered. Thank goodness they all had pull tabs and they didn't need a can opener. Wouldn't that have just sucked to have all this food and no way of getting into it?

But then again, he had that big-ass knife. He could probably get into a weak little can without any problem with that thing.

"What are you smiling about?" Nash asked as he glanced up.

"Nothing really."

"No, come on. Tell me," he urged.

Amanda wasn't sure she'd ever met a man who actually *liked* to talk as much as Nash seemed to. Who encouraged a woman to tell him what she was thinking all the time. Granted, circumstances right now were very different than normal. He was probably completely different when he was at home with his friends.

Now that they were in full daylight, she took the time to study him more closely. His eyes were unusual—a blueish-green color. And judging by his gaze, he looked as if he had the ability to read her deepest, darkest secrets. His nose was a little crooked, as if it had been broken at some point. He had dark hair, short on the sides, longer on the top, with a bit of scruff on his face. And even though he was wearing one of those flight suit things, which zipped from his crotch to his neck, she could tell he was muscular.

Of course, right now that flight suit was covered in dirt and mud from crawling on the ground. He had streaks of dirt on his face and his hands were just as dirty. Amanda had a feeling she probably looked ten times grubbier than he did.

"Are you always like this?" she blurted.

"Like what?" he asked, with a cute tilt of his head.

No. No, no, no. She couldn't start thinking of him as cute. He was her rescuer. That was it. Once they got back to Guyana, she'd have a few more months to go in her agreement with the school, then she'd head home and figure out what to do with the rest of her life.

"Chatty," she said succinctly.

Nash chuckled. "Yup. Drives my friends crazy. It drives my copilot, Obi-Wan, *especially* crazy."

"Obi-Wan?"

"Yeah. He's a huge *Star Wars* fan. Obviously."

"I assume he wanted to fly a starfighter growing up."

"Bingo," Nash said with a smile.

"Why are you called Buck?"

To Amanda's surprise, she thought she saw his cheeks flush. Was he embarrassed about his nickname?

"It's not very interesting," he said. "Do you want green beans or pinto beans?" he asked, holding up two cans.

"I want to know why your nickname is Buck," she replied with a grin.

Nash sighed. "Fine. I made a bet with one of my battle buddies when I was in basic training that I could get all of us an extra ten minutes of sleep one morning."

"Let me guess—for a buck?"

Nash grinned, and it made him seem so much more...approachable...than the serious soldier he'd been so far. "Yup."

"Did you win?"

"Of course I did. I snuck into the CQ desk while the drill sergeant on duty was in there—sound asleep—and changed the alarm on his phone. Not by much, just the ten minutes, but it was enough to win me the bet...and to get my nickname. The DS never did figure out why all the privates were suddenly calling me Buck, but eventually he and all the other drill sergeants started calling me that too. It stuck."

"What's CQ stand for?"

"Charge of quarters. The drill sergeants weren't supposed to sleep while on overnight duty, but I knew that this guy's wife had just had twins. And when he went home from work, he wasn't getting much sleep because of the babies."

Amanda smiled. The story was silly, but sitting here in the middle of the rainforest, trying to stay ahead of the rebels who would certainly want to kill them both if they found them, it was a nice dose of normalcy.

"Now, do you want green or pinto beans?"

"Green. Please."

Amanda tried to make the can of beans last, but it was impossible. As soon as the first bite hit her taste buds, she was shoveling them into her mouth so fast it was ridiculous. She finished way too quickly, and her belly felt almost bloated, even with the tiny amount of food she'd eaten. Being so full also made her extremely tired all of a sudden. So tired she could barely keep her eyes open.

"Go ahead and climb in there," Nash said gently, as he took the now empty can out of her hand.

Amanda realized she'd been sitting there staring into space almost catatonically for who knew how long. "You're coming too, right?" she asked suspiciously.

Nash chuckled. "Yes, ma'am. As soon as I secure the pack so no critters can get inside or take off with it. If you can lie on your side, that'll make it easier for me to get in there with you."

She nodded, then crawled on her hands and knees and backed herself into the small space between the rocks.

Amanda watched as Nash secured the backpack, putting rocks on top of it, probably to not only keep animals from getting into it, but also as camouflage as well. He'd already put the lids inside a pocket on the outside of the bag, not wanting to litter, but also in case they could use them for something later and to avoid leaving any trace that they'd been there, in case the rebels were looking for them. Finally, he took the empty cans and placed them around the backside of the rocks.

Then he was there. Squeezing into the small space. Making her wonder if they'd fit together after all.

They did. Barely.

Nash was curled up behind her, spooning her, with one arm around her waist and the other under her head, providing her with a pillow of sorts.

"Is this okay?" he asked in a whisper. "If not, I can sleep right outside near the pack."

"It's fine," Amanda told him quickly, surprising herself with how *fine* it really was. She wasn't a cuddler. Never had been. She tended to run hot and didn't like anyone touching her while she slept. But right now? Even though it was hot and moist as fuck outside, her clothes were sticking to her sweating body, and she felt as grimy and disgusting as she'd ever felt in her life...having Nash at her back, holding her, made her feel safe. And not quite so alone. She could finally let down her guard for the first time in over two weeks. Let someone else take responsibility for the time being.

"Thank you for coming for us," she said in a barely audible voice. "For not leaving me even after I did something extremely stupid."

"You're welcome."

The two words were simple but heartfelt, and exactly what Amanda needed to hear.

She fell asleep feeling positive for the first time in ages. She was still in deep shit. Had a long way to go before she'd be truly safe. But with Nash at her back, literally, she felt as if it just might be possible.

* * *

Amanda wasn't sure what woke her up. Or even what time it was. But several hours must've passed, because it wasn't nearly as bright outside as it had been when she'd fallen asleep. It looked like that time right before the sun went below the horizon. Kind of greenish and hazy.

She felt sweaty and claustrophobic. Then she remembered why. The heavy arm around her waist was a reminder of where she was and who she was with. The light snoring in her ear was also a good clue. She smiled as she listened to Nash's deep breaths, glad he was able to get some sleep, as she'd done.

But then another noise made her smile die. Tilting her head

back, not wanting to wake Nash up unless it was an emergency, she froze.

About two feet away from their heads was a fox. It was lying on the ground, ignoring the rain that was falling. It had its head on its paws and was staring at them with unblinking eyes. It was matted and dirty, and it seemed to have some sort of injury on its head. She could see what she thought was blood near its ear.

But it wasn't moving. Wasn't growling. Wasn't acting aggressive in the least. It was simply lying there, staring at her and Nash.

The angle Amanda had wasn't great. Not with being on her side as she was and smooshed up against a rock.

"Nash," she whispered, not wanting to agitate the fox if she could help it. If it decided to attack them right now, they'd be fucked. They couldn't exactly fight back in the tight space.

Amazingly, her soft whisper immediately woke Nash. His arm tightened—and then she felt every muscle in his body tense against her back.

"There's a fox," she told him, not wanting him to think the rebels were there or anything.

She felt him lift his head to see what she was talking about—and to her surprise, he whispered, "Hey, boy. What are you doing here?"

Amanda frowned in confusion.

Thankfully, Nash kept talking.

"It's not a fox. It's a dog. I saw it when I went to get supplies at the camp. I don't know if he belongs to one of the rebels or what. But he didn't look like he was in great shape then, and even less now."

"How did it find us? Do you think it tracked us? Are the rebels on our heels?" Amanda asked, not able to keep the panic from her voice.

In response, Nash wiggled his way out from between the

rocks. To her surprise, even though she immediately felt cooler, Amanda also felt...adrift.

The dog had quickly scurried backward when Nash moved, out of reach. But it didn't run off. Amanda scooted out of the shelter of the rocks, arching her back to stretch her achy muscles. She was getting used to sleeping on the hard ground, but that didn't mean she liked it.

"What's it doing? Do we need to get out of here?" she asked.

"I don't know, but I think we're okay. From what I saw, no one paid any attention to the little guy. I highly doubt they trained it to track people. Hey, boy, you hungry? You look hungry," Nash crooned.

Amanda swore her lady parts twitched in her pants. Listening to this skilled pilot talk baby talk to the pathetic-looking dog was sweet.

Nash glanced at her. "When we stop again, I'm going to set up some traps, see if we can't get some fresh meat. But I'd be more comfortable setting a fire to cook meat once we put more distance between us and that camp."

The thought of fresh meat made Amanda's mouth water with anticipation. She wasn't a huge meat eater, but right now, her body was craving fat and protein. She nodded in agreement.

"For now, it's going to be a breakfast of canned...whatever. And water."

Nash went around the rocks, making the dog back up a little more at his movements, and came back holding two cans full of rainwater.

It was a little silly to get so excited about something as boring as water, especially when it was falling steadily from the sky, but seeing him holding those cans as if they were delicate glasses made Amanda feel more human than when she'd had to slurp water out of her hands back at the rebel camp.

Looking inside her can, she saw the water looked clear and fresh, unlike the stuff that had been collected by the rebels. They'd had a system for catching water, but it was always full of dirt and leaves. And they didn't allow her or the children to use the cans as cups.

Today's breakfast was olives for her and more beans for Nash. They were saving the canned chicken and spam for a time when their bodies really needed the nutrients.

The dog didn't move from where it had lain down when they began to eat. But its eyes followed every movement their hands made.

Amanda couldn't stand it any longer. She leaned forward and held out an olive. "You want some, boy?"

The dog licked its chops but didn't make any kind of move to take the food from her.

"He was probably abused by the rebels," Nash said softly.

"Yeah," Amanda agreed. "You want to try?"

"Sure." But the second Nash knelt next to her and held out his hand, the dog sat up and backed away. "Shoot, it's more scared of me than you. Probably because I'm a guy. You keep trying." With that, Nash backed up toward the rocks where they'd spent the night.

"It's okay, he won't hurt you," Amanda said softly to the dog. To her relief, it lay back down again instead of running off into the trees. "I know you want this olive. It doesn't taste that great, but when you're hungry it doesn't really matter, does it? Watch, I'll eat, then it'll be your turn. Ummmm, yummy. Here…now you take one."

The dog wanted the food. That was clear as day. But it was too scared to come any closer. So Amanda took a chance and gently lobbed an olive in his direction.

It had barely bounced a foot in front of his face when he moved. Snatching it up and backing up again all in one motion.

"There you go," Amanda said with a small laugh. "Good, right? Here, I'll eat one, then it's your turn again." She ate another olive, then lobbed another at the dog. Once again, he gobbled it up as if he hadn't eaten in weeks.

Then to her amazement, the dog scooted forward on its belly, closer to her.

"That's right. Come on. I'm not going to hurt you. We can share the rest of this can. Because honestly? Olives taste horrible. But not to you, huh?" She kept up the one-sided conversation, all the time aware that Nash was behind her, watching and listening.

Amanda was a sucker for kids and animals. Especially strays. She supposed she might be considered a stray by some people. She had no family and was kind of wandering aimlessly, trying to figure out what to do with her life. The kids at the school and orphanage were also like strays. Doing their best to survive in this big ol' unfair world.

"Here, if you don't like the olives, take my beans. Let the dog have the rest of your breakfast."

Amanda turned her head to see Nash holding out his half-eaten can of beans. "You should eat that," she told him. "You need the calories."

"I'll be fine. We'll eat better tonight, once I can hunt. If you don't like the olives, you shouldn't eat them, and we can't let them go to waste. The dog can have them, and you can have the beans. I'm full anyway."

He was full of shit, but Amanda felt like crying over both his kindness and his lie about being full. She seriously doubted he wasn't at least a little hungry. She reached out and took the can from him, her fingers brushing against Nash's in the process. Their gazes met, and time seemed to freeze for a moment. Something intense passed between them, but it was over as soon as it began.

"Look," Nash whispered, nodding toward something over her shoulder.

Turning her head, Amanda barely stopped a surprised gasp

from leaving her mouth. The dog had crept forward again while she was talking to Nash, and was now lying right in front of her. Within touching distance.

"Hey, boy. You like those olives, huh? Well, Nash was kind enough to say you could finish them." Amanda slowly picked up the can of olives and poured a few on the ground in front of the dog. He ate them just as quickly as he had the others, then looked up at her with a hopeful expression on his face.

She chuckled. "All right, give me a second." She alternated between eating the beans Nash had so unselfishly offered, and tossing the dog an olive. She didn't think she should give him the entire rest of the can at once, for fear it would upset his tummy.

All too soon, both the beans and the olives were gone.

The dog looked at her with hopeful eyes, and she felt horrible that she had nothing else to give him. "I'm sorry, but that's all there is. We ate everything."

To her total shock, the dog wiggled closer and began to lick the juice off her fingers. It would've been sweet if it wasn't so sad. If the dog wasn't so desperate for calories he was willing to lick the smallest bit of leftover juice from her hand.

Making a split-second decision, Amanda poured some of the water Nash had caught the night before into the olive can, twirling it to mix the water with the remaining olive juice. Then she tilted the can so the dog's tongue could reach the liquid. "How about some olive-flavored water?" she asked.

Before she finished her sentence, the dog stood and stuck his muzzle into the can, eagerly lapping at the water.

Turning, Amanda smiled at Nash. "He's drinking," she whispered ecstatically.

"I see that," Nash responded with a small grin.

"Good boy," she told the dog.

After he'd finished the water, he sat back on his haunches and stared at her.

"Well, that's *really* all we can offer," she told him sadly. "And we need to be on our way. Good luck, boy. Stay safe out there."

As if he could understand, the dog bobbed his head, then turned and ran off into the trees.

Amanda stared after him for a long moment before taking a deep breath. "Right. I need to pee, then I guess it's time for our nature hike to start, huh?"

She'd stood as she was talking, and when she turned, saw that Nash was also standing. And staring at her with a look she couldn't interpret.

"What?" she asked, running a hand over her head a little self-consciously. She knew she was a mess. Thankfully, she had short hair so it wasn't as much of a bird's nest as it might've been. But she was still grubby and stinky, and soaking wet—again—from sitting in the light rain.

"You're not what I expected," Nash said after a moment. "And before you ask, I'm not sure *what* I expected. Maybe more along the lines of someone scared. Weaker. More out of your element."

Amanda couldn't help it. She laughed. "I'm terrified, actually. And I'm as out of my element as I can be. But I've learned that if I fake it, I can usually convince those around me, mostly my students—and even myself—that I know what I'm doing."

"Well, you're doing a good job of it. I like your positive attitude. And most people wouldn't give some of their precious food to a stray dog if they were in your situation."

Amanda shrugged. "He needed it more than I did. A few olives isn't going to make much of a difference to me, but it could mean the world to that dog. Give him just enough energy to get back to wherever he belongs. To outrun something bigger and stronger that wants to eat him. I don't know. I just believe in good deeds coming back tenfold. Besides, did you see his eyes? How in the world could I resist?"

"Why do you think I gave you my beans?" Nash asked, smiling. "And I swear if that dog could talk and asked me to open all the cans and let him eat them all, I would've agreed without hesitation."

Amanda grinned. She liked this man. True, she hadn't known him long and it was possible he was very different when he wasn't in a crisis situation. But she couldn't deny she was attracted to the man he was right now.

Though, this wasn't the time or place to have *any* kind of feelings toward Nash. He was doing a job—a job he wouldn't even have to be doing if it wasn't for her rash decision to go look for James instead of making sure he was really missing.

She couldn't change the past. She'd learned that over the years. All she could do was keep going forward. One step at a time...even if each step was extremely painful and lonely.

Taking a deep breath, she watched as Nash shrugged on the backpack with their meager supplies. Then she reached out and grabbed hold of a strap before they once again started their trek through the jungle.

CHAPTER SIX

"Why'd you come to Guyana?" Buck asked Mandy a couple of hours later. The rain really started coming down not too long after they'd set out, and his clothes were soaked, as were Mandy's. They weren't moving too fast, since the undergrowth in the jungle was thick, and he wasn't about to attempt using any of the trails or the occasional road they came across. Not only that, but it was now fully dark. The flashlight he'd taken from the rebel camp didn't do much to penetrate the blackness. Which was good, as he didn't want to be a beacon for anyone who might be looking for them, but it made getting anywhere quickly difficult.

He'd already made the decision that they were going to need to transition to walking during the daytime after tonight. They should be far enough away from the camp that it would be safe. It was too dangerous to continue walking in the dark. He preferred nighttime himself; it was what he was used to, since most of the Night Stalker missions were done under the cover of darkness. But it was one thing to operate at night from behind the controls of his MH-60, with night-vision, radar, and all the other fancy technology to help him see in the dark.

It was another thing altogether to be trudging through the jungle with a civilian who'd already been a captive for over two weeks, with a stolen flashlight whose batteries could go dead at any moment. Not to mention there were critters that came out at night that could kill either of them with one bite faster than a terrorist with an RPG.

Mandy hadn't complained. Not once. And he appreciated that, but it also worried him. She hadn't said much in the last hour at all, and he was concerned that she was once again hiding how she was feeling from him. He suspected this woman would pass out from exhaustion before making one peep of complaint.

She was hanging on to one of the straps of the backpack to make sure she didn't get separated from him. A few times, when he'd stopped abruptly, she'd run right into him, apologizing profusely afterward even though it definitely wasn't her fault.

Buck wanted nothing more than to stop, but a sixth sense told him that they weren't far enough away yet. That they needed to keep walking, just in case. He didn't feel as if there were any rebels in the immediate vicinity, so they didn't need to stay silent, just vigilant.

And that was why he'd asked Mandy the question about why she'd come to Guyana. He was curious about her, and he had a feeling a lot of Americans wouldn't have the slightest idea where the country was in the first place.

"Mandy?" he asked, when she didn't respond. Glancing over his shoulder, he saw she was walking with her eyes closed. It wasn't as if she could see much with her eyes open anyway, but the trust she was giving him was almost overwhelming. Buck was going to try even harder not to let her down.

"Are you asleep?" he asked with a small chuckle.

"Shhhh," she said with a smile, not opening her eyes. "I'm pretending I'm on the beach, taking a pleasurable stroll that will end at my hotel room, where I'll get into a huge Jacuzzi tub after eating the enormous meal I ordered from room service."

Now Buck found himself smiling. "With a huge cup of coffee."

"And a piece of peanut butter chocolate pie."

"Buttered garlic bread."

"A medium-rare steak."

Buck's smile widened. As much as talking about food was making his stomach hurt, it was also kind of fun. "So... Guyana?" he asked, still wanting to hear the answer to his question.

She sighed, and when he looked again, he saw her eyes were now open.

"After work one day—a very tough day, during which I'd been spit on, got my ass chewed by a parent for something I had nothing to do with, and was reprimanded by my principal—I was at home, doom scrolling on social media, when a video caught my attention. At first I rolled my eyes, because it reminded me of those ads for the humane society that showed all these animals in deplorable conditions—you know the ones...where puppies are shivering in the snow while the narrator talks about how for just thirty-two cents a day, you too can help save an abused and neglected animal? Anyway, the longer I watched, the more intrigued I got.

"I clicked on the website and saw more pictures. Not of sad-looking children sitting in the dirt looking pathetic...but happy children, running around and smiling. They weren't playing with electronics, weren't dressed in expensive clothing...most weren't even wearing shoes. But they seemed content. Unlike my students, who just seemed annoyed most days because they had to put their phones away in class.

"I researched as much as I could, then contacted Blair. She seemed excited that I was interested in joining them. She explained that their little school-slash-orphanage wasn't sponsored by the government, so they only got by with private donations. She further explained that if I came down, I'd be a volunteer, so she warned me that I needed to make sure I could afford it."

"I didn't think teachers made a ton of money," Buck said, not wanting to be rude, but genuinely curious.

"They don't," Mandy said. "But my parents were killed in a car accident when I was seventeen. A drunk driver hit them going seventy miles an hour on the interstate. There was a lawsuit, and an online fundraiser for their only child...me. I used some of the money for college but saved the rest, and it had just been collecting interest ever since. I had enough to quit my job back in Norfolk and do something new and exciting. It wasn't going to be my new forever, I just desperately needed a change."

"This is a change, all right," Buck said dryly.

Mandy chuckled from behind him. "Yeah. The thing is, being down here, interacting with these kids...it gave me my love of teaching back. They're all so eager to learn, they soak up every scrap of info you give them, and they have so much love in their hearts. There's nothing better than being greeted at the door with a huge hug and a 'good morning, Miss Mandy!' If nothing else, it made me realize that when I go home, I want to update my teaching certificate so I can get a job with younger kids. There's nothing wrong with middle school, but I think my passion is teaching kids of a younger age."

"That's great," Buck said.

"Yeah. Your turn. Tell me about you. About your copilot, the one who loves *Star Wars*. How exactly did you end up flying a helicopter to South America to rescue a bunch of kids?"

"Apparently the vice president has ties to Guyana. He worked down here after college with the Peace Corps. When word got to the White House about the kidnapping of a bunch of orphans, he pushed for something to be done. And me and Obi-Wan were that something. We volunteered, while the rest of our team went to Mexico to help with recovery after the hurricane."

"There was a hurricane?" Mandy asked. "Jeez, I love being

down here, but I feel so out of the loop. The break from social media has been great, I don't miss it, per se, but I do feel as if I'm not as informed as I should be. How many other pilots do you work with?"

"There're six of us. Casper and Pyro usually fly together, as do Chaos and Edge."

"I've always wanted a badass nickname like that," Mandy said with a sigh.

"Trust me, they're usually not as cool as they might sound. You already know how I got mine."

"I know, but it still sounds impressive, and that's what counts, right? I mean, if a dog's name is Fluffy, that gives a very different impression than if its name is Killer, even if it wouldn't hurt a flea."

Buck chuckled. "True. So, what would you pick? As a nickname?"

"I don't know. Viper? Shadow? Storm?"

"Rebel," Buck blurted, not sure where it came from, but as soon as the word left his lips, he realized how well it fit. "You defy expectations, fight back against the odds, and you do what you want, even when it goes against what society thinks is normal or proper."

When he looked back at Mandy, he saw she was smiling.

"Rebel. I like it. Tell me more about your friends."

"Casper is our team leader. He has a twin who's a Navy SEAL. He and our mechanic, Laryn, recently realized they were perfect for each other."

"Oh, that's cool."

"It is. Because Laryn's awesome. Not only is she the best helicopter mechanic in the country, she's now tied to our unit because of Casper. So she's not going anywhere."

"You know how awful that sounds, right?" Mandy asked with a chuckle.

"Yup. But seriously, the woman has skills. And because

Casper has recently destroyed two helicopters, she's been kept very busy."

Mandy inhaled sharply. "Two?"

Time went by quickly as Buck explained the circumstances behind his team leader's two chopper incidents. He then went on to tell her all about his other teammates.

When he got to Obi-Wan, he did his best to explain his relationship with the man he trusted with his life on a daily basis. "When you're in the cockpit, in the middle of an op, it's pitch-dark outside, you only have the instruments in front of you to know where to fly and what's going on, so it's vital that you trust the person sitting next to you. Obi-Wan, he's...he's like my brother. We clicked the first time we met, when we were assigned to our new unit. There's no one I trust more."

"Is he going to be pissed that you're here now? That you didn't leave with him?" Mandy asked quietly.

Buck hesitated, but ultimately decided to be honest. She'd been through hell and deserved that much. "Here's the thing—we aren't supposed to leave our chopper. Under *any* circumstances. Casper did that on the mission I was telling you about before, and he'll kick his own ass for it for the rest of his life, because it allowed Laryn to be taken."

"But he saved those SEALs. Right?"

Buck nodded. "Yeah. He did. Which is why he did it. It's not in our DNA to literally sit by and let someone on our watch get hurt or die. You asked if Obi-Wan would be upset that I came after you, and the answer is no. He'd probably be *more* pissed if I'd gotten back in that chopper and left you out here alone. I had no doubts about his ability to fly the kids and those special forces soldiers back across the border. Further, I know that even now, he's doing everything in his power to try to come back for us."

"But it's not that easy," Mandy surmised.

"It's not that easy," Buck confirmed. "But Obi-Wan won't be

pissed that I came after you. That I can guarantee. My boss? He might be a different story."

Mandy tugged on his backpack, making him stop walking and turn to look at her.

"What? Are you okay?"

"You're going to get in trouble for what I did?" she whispered, sounding aghast.

"No."

"But you said—"

"I can handle the colonel. I made a split-second decision, one I don't regret for a second. As a Night Stalker pilot, I have to make life-or-death choices on the turn of a dime. Pretty much on every mission. Every moment I'm in the air. I constantly have the lives of the men and women I transport in my hands. One moment of second-guessing myself, or my copilot, could mean everyone dies. I made the decision to come after you, and I stand by it because it was the right thing to do. Besides, I don't think the colonel will say much because ultimately, the only reason we were able to come and get the kids was because of you."

"I'm still having a hard time believing that," Mandy said. "I mean, I'm nobody. Definitely not important enough for a rescue."

"Wrong. You're an American. You were the reason the mission was approved. Why the vice president was able to sign off on the paperwork needed to get Obi-Wan and myself down here. *You* were the objective, Rebel. How would it look if we came back without you?" Buck interjected humor into that last bit, hoping to make her smile, at least a little.

It worked. Kind of.

She gave him a small grin, but the worry returned to her expression right afterward. "Thank you, Nash. Seriously."

"You're welcome." He wasn't going to dismiss her need to express her gratitude. She was feeling overwhelmed, that much was obvious. "I'm thinking it's time for us to stop," he said, changing the subject.

"But it's still dark," she replied, sounding confused. "I thought we needed to walk in the dark to try to stay hidden."

"We did. At least when we were close to the camp. But I think we're far enough away that it's okay for us to rest now and walk in the daylight tomorrow. We'll have to be vigilant, on watch for anyone else out here, but we can make better time when it's light out. I'm thinking we stop, get some sleep, then head out around lunchtime, after I make us that huge steak and peanut butter pie you were talking about earlier."

"And some coffee for you," she said, with a teasing glint in her eye.

"That too. Come on, let's see if we can find another hidey hole like we did last time. Although I'm guessing we won't be quite as lucky."

And just like that, memories swept over Buck. How well he'd slept with this woman in his arms. It made no sense. He'd been on plenty of dangerous missions before, even some that had gone sideways like this one, when he'd had to flee from the enemy with civilians in tow. But he'd never felt as protective about any of the others as he did Mandy. And he wasn't sure why.

It made him a little uncomfortable. But recently, he'd felt as if he'd been in a rut. Seeing how happy Casper was with Laryn was forcing him to rethink certain aspects of his life—namely, the fact that he was almost forty and didn't want to spend the rest of it alone.

Did that mean he'd marry the first woman to strike his fancy? No. But he was more open to the possibility that a new relationship could become a long-term thing. Something he'd never truly contemplated in the past. Heck, he hadn't even *been* in a relationship in years.

Was he happy he was getting this time with Mandy, to get to

know her? No. Because the circumstances sucked. He'd much prefer to have met her back in Virginia, taken her out for coffee, lunch, a movie. *Anything*. But it was what it was. He'd learned a long time ago to take life as it came. Buck had no idea what would happen in the coming days. One of them could get sick or hurt. They might be found by the rebels. Or nothing would happen, and they'd arrive back in Guyana tired, dirty, and ready for those foods they'd fantasized about.

Worrying about it wouldn't make their current situation any better. All they could do was take things one day at a time.

Not sure he was any less confused about his feelings toward the woman at his back, Buck started walking again, keeping his eyes peeled for a place to hole up for the rest of the night. They had some hard walking over the next few days, and they needed to get some much-needed sleep, where and when they could get it.

* * *

Amanda was confused.

She could admit that, but only to herself.

This situation sucked, and she couldn't help but constantly berate herself for being here. It was her fault, after all. If she'd taken precious seconds to check for herself whether James was really lost or not, she'd be back at the school with the rest of the kids and Nash wouldn't've had to put himself in danger because of her.

But at the same time, even though she was completely out of her element and hungry, tired, and grubby...she wasn't having a terrible time. And that was *completely* messed up.

Having Nash with her made all the difference in the world. Without him, she'd be in big trouble. But he *was* here. And she trusted him completely to do what was best for the both of them. Walking through the night had gone a long way toward solidifying that trust. She couldn't see anything, and had to hold on to his backpack and know that he wouldn't walk them into a raging river or straight into the hands of the rebels.

Nash was so different from other men she'd known. More rugged. Rough around the edges. But also funny and protective. She liked him. A lot. And that concerned her. Because she wasn't sure if it was because of her situation, the fact she was relying on him, that was skewing her feelings. She didn't want to think that was the case, but she wasn't completely sure.

If they were back home, Nash taking charge the way he had out here would probably annoy her to no end. But it was what she needed right now. She needed his expertise.

Like last night, for example. He'd told her to sit against a tree and relax while he checked out the potential spot he'd found for their rest. The Amanda from Virginia would've protested, insisted she could help. But the Amanda she was out here was perfectly willing and grateful to sit and wait for him to come back.

It wasn't a crevice in rocks this time, but a space between two huge tree trunks, their canopies thick and dense overhead. Once again perfect for one person, but tight for two. And again, Amanda insisted he stay with her. For her own sanity. She'd never get any sleep if she couldn't be sure she wasn't alone.

She had no idea what time it was when she woke, but the sun was peeking through the trees around them. For once, it wasn't raining, and for that she was *more* than grateful. She had no illusions that her clothes would actually dry out, considering how humid it was, but not to be rained on felt like a gift.

Nash was once more plastered to her back, and again, she didn't hate it. The man was turning her into a cuddler. She felt him stir, and smiled a little when he murmured, "Morning," before climbing out of the small space they were smushed into.

But it was when he said, "Holy shit," that Amanda woke completely. One second she was floating in that in-between state before you had to get out of bed, and the next, her adrenaline was flowing and she was sitting up ready to do...something. Run, fight...she wasn't sure what.

Looking around frantically to see what had Nash sounding so surprised, she blinked when she saw the same dog they'd shared their food with the day before, sitting not too far away. Staring at them with the same beseeching look he'd had yesterday.

His hair was still matted, he still looked pretty pathetic, but Amanda could've sworn she saw recognition in the dog's expression.

"What is he doing here?"

"I guess he followed us?" Nash said with a shrug.

"In the dark? Through the jungle?" she said skeptically.

"There've been many instances of stray dogs latching onto groups of people in the wilderness. I remember reading a book about a dog here in South America—I *think* it was South America—who followed a group of men and women doing some sort of extreme foot race. And then there's *The Call of the Wild*, *Old Yeller*, *White Fang*...and tons of other fiction books I can't remember right now, that're about loyal dogs."

"Wait, I've read that book. The first one you were talking about. Arthur was the dog, right?"

"No clue, but if you say it is, then it is."

"This dog kind of looks like the one in that true story. You think it's a terrier of some sort?"

Nash tilted his head as he studied the stray just as intently as it was watching them. "Maybe. But it's bigger than a terrier. I'd guess at proper weight, he should be around forty or forty-five pounds. Right now, he looks more like twenty-five. Long legs, scruffy hair, short ears...there's no telling what his pedigree is. He could be part wolf or lynx, for all we know."

"Just like there's no telling what color he really is under all that dirt," Amanda said with a snort. "He's as dirty as me. He needs a name..." she mused.

"Not sure that's a good idea," Nash warned. "To name him. It's likely we won't see him again after this morning. When we get too far away from wherever it is he came from."

"You said yourself that you thought the rebels brought him with them. And they were mean to him. Why would he want to go back there? And he's probably just as lost as us. Not that we're lost, but you know what I mean. I think we should call him Rain. Because we found him, or he found us, in the rainforest."

"Seems appropriate."

Amanda was relieved Nash didn't say anything else about the dog disappearing or about not giving him a name. She was already enamored with the pathetic-looking creature. She was well aware that no good could come from her getting emotionally attached to the dog, but everything right now was out of the norm for her. Might as well go with it.

"Hey, Rain. How'd you find us? You aren't leading anyone else to our location, are you?" Amanda crooned.

Of course, the dog didn't respond, simply tilted his head as he listened to Amanda speak.

"I'm going to see if the trap I set last night caught anything," Nash told her. "Will you be all right here by yourself while I'm gone?"

"I won't be by myself," Amanda told him. "I have Rain."

"Right. Well, if something happens, just scream. I'll be back in a heartbeat. Okay?"

"Thanks. I will."

After Nash left, Amanda didn't feel as stressed as she might've otherwise because she truly didn't feel as if she was alone. It was silly, it wasn't as if the dog could actually do anything if a rebel leaped out of the trees and ambushed her. But simply having someone to talk to, to interact with, to concentrate on instead of thinking about her itchy skin, her empty belly, and the confusing thoughts running around her head about the man who'd risked his own life to stay behind with her, kept her calm.

The entire time Nash was gone, Amanda kept up a running commentary with Rain. Not about anything in particular, but the way the dog kept his gaze locked on her, his head tilting now and then as if he were truly listening, made it feel as if he could honestly understand.

When Nash returned, Rain let her know someone was near right before he reappeared. The dog turned his head and looked in the direction he was coming from, before Amanda even heard his footsteps.

Rain didn't seem alarmed or concerned with his reappearance, and Amanda hoped that was a good omen. That the dog was getting used to Nash. She hadn't missed how wary he was around Nash the previous day. She hated to think about why that was. Because he'd likely been abused by men in the not-so-distant past.

"Success!" Nash said with a smile as he held up a porcupine.

Amanda was torn. She hated to see any animal killed, but just thinking about the meat they'd soon be eating was enough to make her stomach growl. Loudly.

So loudly, Rain's ears perked forward.

Nash chuckled. "It won't take me too long to get it ready to cook. You want to see if you can find any sticks that aren't soaking wet?"

It was Amanda's turn to laugh. "Seriously? *Everything's* wet. Including me."

As soon as the words left her mouth, she wanted to take them back. They sounded way too suggestive. But any hopes of Nash letting her unintended inuendo slide were dashed when his smile grew and one of his eyebrows went up.

"Sorry, that came out wrong," she said, feeling her cheeks heat.

Thankfully, he didn't prolong her embarrassment. "Look

under leaves. And under other branches that might be on the ground. Anything buried under other stuff won't be quite as damp." Then he looked over at Rain and said, "Watch her, boy."

As if the dog could understand exactly what Nash said, he got off his belly and stood, looking like he was patiently waiting for Amanda to go looking for wood so he could do just as Nash asked—keep watch over her.

"Don't go far," Nash warned.

He didn't have to tell her that. Amanda wasn't going to go out of sight of the man who'd become her lifeline. She was well aware it probably wasn't healthy for her to get so attached to someone who'd be leaving as soon as they arrived back in Guyana. But she couldn't help it. He was not only kind, and obviously competent in the jungle...he was easy on the eyes.

She felt like the worst kind of hypocrite for thinking that way, though it was difficult not to. Seeing the man with his flight suit plastered to his body because of the constant rain wasn't exactly a hardship. But she would've been just as grateful and relieved she wasn't alone in this...adventure—could she call it an adventure, when it wasn't something she'd chosen to do?—if the man who'd stayed with her had been a hundred pounds overweight and as out of his element as she was.

Turning her attention to the task at hand, she set out to look for branches and sticks that would be dry enough to build a small fire.

She made several trips back and forth from the trees around them to where Nash was skinning and gutting the animal. By the time he was ready, she'd managed to find a decent amount of sticks for a fire.

The look of approval on his face warmed Amanda from the inside out. He quickly got a fire going with the matches he'd pilfered from the kitchen tent—which was impressive, since everything was so damp—and heated the small pan they'd also stolen from the rebels.

The smell of the meat cooking was almost torture. Amanda could literally feel herself salivating. The porcupine looked huge when she'd first seen it, but based on the amount of meat in the pan, she realized it was only going to provide a few decent mouthfuls for each of them.

Even Rain was completely focused on the fire, or more specifically, what was cooking over it. He kept licking his lips, and he drooled as he patiently waited for the meat to finish.

"Eat slowly," Nash warned, as he moved the pan off the fire. "Not only is the meat hot, you don't want to upset your stomach. It would not be good if you threw it up."

Amanda nodded, but didn't take her gaze from the meat. Minutes later, it had stopped sizzling and cooled enough that Nash deemed it safe, and she was more than ready to try it. They didn't have any kind of spices or salt—but when the meat hit her taste buds, it was one of the best things she'd ever eaten in her life.

Being hungry changed everything. How she looked at food, portions, the world at large…and it made any pickiness she might've had disappear forever.

As she ate, she was aware of the dog's attention. His gaze was locked on her fingers as she licked them after each bite, and on her mouth as she chewed. After a moment, guilt hit Amanda hard. Rain was probably just as hungry as she was, maybe even more so.

As much as she wanted to shove the rest of the meat into her mouth, she tore off a small piece and held it out toward the dog.

"Mandy," Nash warned, but she ignored him. What she was doing wasn't smart. But she could no more ignore the dog's starving state than she could ignore one of the kids back at the school when they needed a hug after a bad day.

Rain trembled with the desire to take the meat, but fear held him back. He wouldn't take the two steps necessary for him to get close enough to accept the food from her fingers.

Amanda could've tossed the meat to him, but she didn't want it to land in the dirt. Which was silly, as Rain definitely wouldn't have cared...but she simply couldn't do it. So she grabbed a nearby rock and put the meat on that, then slid it as close to Rain as she could get.

The second she leaned back, the dog moved, snatching up the meat and swallowing it without chewing.

Amanda giggled. "Did you even taste that, boy? Come on, you have to eat slower, enjoy it."

She appreciated that Nash didn't say anything as she continued to share her meal with Rain. After each small bite, she tore off a smaller piece to give to the dog.

After a moment, Nash said, "You've got a tender heart."

Amanda shrugged. "He needs it as much as I do."

"He's probably catching rodents or something. He's most likely getting more calories than you are."

But Amanda didn't care. It felt good to be able to provide for another creature. She certainly wasn't very able to provide for herself, was relying on Nash for her basic needs. She liked being able to do the same thing for the dog. "One more piece, then it's all gone," she warned, as she held out the last small piece of meat. She'd eaten her last bite, and as much as she wanted to eat the bite in her hand, she couldn't deny the little dog the luxury.

As she leaned over to place the meat on the rock, Rain stepped forward. He took the food from her fingers so delicately, it was almost as if someone had trained him to do that exact thing.

Amanda turned toward Nash. "Did you see that? He took it straight from my hand!"

"I saw, Rebel." Then he nodded toward the dog.

Turning her head, Amanda saw Rain was standing almost right next to her.

Moving slowly, she brought her hand up toward his chest. She knew better than to try to pat the top of his head. Her fingers stroked the matted fur of his front left leg. "Hey, boy. Was that good? You starting to trust me a little more?"

She could feel him trembling, but he was allowing her touch. Wasn't trying to bite her and wasn't running off. For a moment, she felt him lean into her hand, then, as if thinking better of what he was doing, he stepped backward once more, out of her reach.

"Here. I figured the three of us could share a can of olives," Nash said, holding a can he'd already opened out toward her.

The three of us. Even though he disapproved of her sharing her meal with Rain, he wasn't berating her, telling her how stupid she was to waste what little they had. Instead, he was making it clear that he was aware she would continue to share her food with the stray.

Strangely enough, Amanda was happier in that moment than she'd been in a very long time. Which was crazy. She was lost in the middle of the jungle, with a group of pissed-off rebels who may or may not be hunting for them that very moment. She was absolutely filthy, thirsty, in pain from walking so much and sleeping on the ground...and yet the simple joys of having a full belly and of earning a little bit of the stray dog's trust was enough to make her truly feel content.

Not to mention, the man she was stranded with. He made her feel as if she could let down her guard. Not worry so much about the next minute, hour, day. Whatever happened, they'd figure it out together.

He would get them back to Guyana, of that she had no doubt.

"Thank you," she said softly. "For not yelling at me for feeding him. For being so patient with me and for knowing what to do when I have absolutely no idea."

"You're welcome. Go ahead and eat those while I douse the fire and see if I can remove any signs we were here. At least as much as possible."

Amanda wanted to help, but she also didn't want to be in the way. So she did as he asked and sat where she was, eating an olive and then throwing one toward Rain—laughing when he caught it in midair—before holding up one of the small treats for Nash.

He shocked the hell out of her when he leaned down and took the olive from her fingers with his mouth.

He smiled and held up his hands, which were covered in soot and dirt from trying to put out the embers of the fire.

The feel of his lips against her fingers was shockingly intimate. And Amanda felt it between her legs. It was surprising, and so inappropriate for the situation it almost felt wrong.

Almost.

It wasn't as if she was seriously contemplating having sex with the man.

At least...not when they were on the run in the jungle. Not before she'd been able to scrub the last couple of weeks' worth of grime off her body. She'd read books where the hero and heroine in the story had wild monkey sex in some jungle stream while on the run, but it always seemed a little gross to her. She couldn't understand how the characters could even *think* about sexy times when they were in that situation.

But all of a sudden, she got it. She still didn't *actually* want to have sex right now, but the spark she felt as he ate olives from her fingers was certainly eye-opening.

By the time the can of olives was empty, Nash had gotten the fire out and they were ready to start walking again. For some reason, Amanda was reluctant to leave this little oasis in the jungle. It wasn't anything special, just another few meters in the vast wilderness, but she felt as if her world had tilted on its axis in this place.

The progress with Rain, the sudden and unexpected sexual feelings she had toward Nash, and of course, another memory of sleeping in the cradle of his arms. Amanda was confused, and a little angry that all of this was happening *now*. Thousands of miles from her home back in the States, with a man *any* kind of relationship with would likely be impossible, and while on the run from the people who'd kidnapped her. It wasn't fair.

But then again, life wasn't fair. You simply had to deal with whatever was thrown your way as best you could.

Taking a sigh, Amanda tried to shove her deepening feelings toward Nash out of her head. He was doing a job. She needed to concentrate on not falling on her face from exhaustion. On what was going to happen once she arrived back at the school. At how happy she'd be to see all the children again.

They started walking, and this time Amanda didn't need to be so close to Nash, since she could see where she was putting her feet. There was no need to hang on to his pack in the daylight.

Ignoring the pang of disappointment, Amanda looked behind her as they headed out of the area where they'd slept.

The day before, Rain had run off after eating. But today? He was there, following along as if it was the most normal thing in the world.

She couldn't help but smile as she walked. Life wasn't perfect, it was damn hard at times. But the dog's presence reminded her that there was beauty in the world. She simply had to be alert enough to see it.

CHAPTER SEVEN

Five days later, Buck was pleased with the progress they were making. Mandy was holding up much better than he'd expected. She didn't say much as they walked, but that was fine because it allowed him to stay alert for any signs they were being followed or that the rebels had managed to drive their trucks ahead of them.

It didn't take a rocket scientist to know that anyone who'd escaped them would be trying to get across the border. But Buck still wasn't sure whether or not the kidnappers knew anyone had missed the rescue helicopter. It was possible *no one* was looking for them. That they'd assumed some of the kids had stolen food from the kitchen. Mandy had told him that she and the girls were left in the tent unaccompanied when they prepared meals.

That would be the best-case scenario, and the one that Buck was leaning toward. He hadn't seen or heard signs of anyone in the jungle except for him and Mandy...and Rain, of course.

The little dog was tough. He kept up with them as they walked for miles every day. He'd disappear every once in a while, and Buck could see how worried Mandy was about him each time, but he always showed up again, his tongue out, loping along as if he was on a grand adventure. Buck wished the little guy could talk, he was sure he'd have a hell of a story to tell.

They were running low on cans of food by now, but he'd been able to catch some kind of fresh game almost every night. They'd had squirrel, another porcupine, and amazingly, even a pacarana. Buck hadn't even thought they were in this part of the rainforest, but he'd obviously been wrong.

A pacarana looked like a guinea pig, with black fur flecked with white dots running along its sides. The one he'd caught was smaller than usual, probably why he'd been able to catch it in his snare. They were usually around thirty pounds, but this one had been about half that. It provided some much-needed meat for all three of them.

And yes, Buck was now considering Rain a part of their traveling party. The dog was still wary of him, but at least he no longer flinched away every time Buck stood up or shifted.

So even though they were doing okay with food—and water, since it rained all the time, and he set up a catchment system with all their empty cans every night—the more immediate issue was hygiene.

Buck felt disgusting in his flight suit. He would've taken it off long before now, but all he had on underneath was a pair of underwear and a thin tank top. He'd unzipped it so he could get some air while he walked, but the wet and humid environment were doing damage to his feet in his boots. He had sores in places he shouldn't have sores and chafing all over his body from the suit. He'd lost weight since they'd been walking, and the material was extremely uncomfortable against his skin now.

And he knew without a doubt Mandy was feeling the same way. She was wearing sneakers, and when she took them off the other night, he could see her feet were in the same bad condition as his. Her clothes were torn and caked with dirt and sweat, and at night when they lay down to sleep, she'd lower herself gingerly, trying not to flinch. She had to have bruises all over her body from sleeping on the hard ground.

Something had to give. Buck wasn't sure how much farther they had to go. He'd estimated how far they'd walked every day, and knew how far it was to the border, but since they weren't going in a straight line, it could be another week until they reached Guyana. Mandy said she and the kids had walked for two weeks to get to the rebel camp, but they'd been moving very slowly. It was tough to walk fast with twenty-three children.

It was ironic that even though they were surrounded by water—falling from the sky every day, puddles they walked across and through, and even the occasional pond—there wasn't anything appropriate to clean with, other than the fast wipe-downs they did each morning with the rainwater he'd collected overnight. Whatever they didn't need for drinking.

So that was why, when Buck heard what he thought was running water, and more than just a trickle, he didn't believe his ears at first. But he couldn't fight the huge smile when all of a sudden he was face-to-face with a good-size stream with fast-moving water. Even more amazing, off to the side and not far from where he was standing, a small pool had formed thanks to a large tree that had fallen across the stream, diverting the water.

"Holy cow, how are we going to get around that?" Mandy asked, as she came up beside him to stare with wide eyes at the obstruction in their path.

She didn't understand how fortunate they were right that moment.

"We aren't going to go around it. We're going *through* it," Buck told her, still grinning. "It's not a Jacuzzi, but it's the best I can do at the moment." He remembered that she'd said a few days ago she wished she was on the beach, in a hotel with a Jacuzzi.

Her eyes widened as it hit her what all this running water meant. "Is it safe?"

"Safer than the stagnant pools we've come across before now," Buck said. "Come on," he cajoled, holding out his hand.

He smiled when Mandy put her hand in his, and he led them toward the pool.

He shrugged off the backpack, leaned down to take off his boots and socks, took his KA-BAR and compass out of his pockets, then walked into the pool of water with his flight suit on.

"Nash!" Mandy said with a laugh.

"What?" he asked, turning around and smiling at her. "My clothes need washing almost more than I do. I mean...I could get totally naked if you'd prefer. Don't think I've missed the way you've ogled my ass, woman." He was teasing her, but the blush on her cheeks told him he might've been closer to the mark than he thought. Which was fine, considering he'd done his share of checking out *her* ass over the last few days.

"Get in here, Mandy. The water isn't too cold and it feels divine!" Buck lay on his back and stared up at what little blue sky he could see between the canopy of leaves. For once it wasn't raining, and with every step they took away from the rebel camp without seeing or hearing any sign of anyone being after them, the more confident he was that the men didn't know they hadn't gotten onto the helicopter.

Mandy copied his actions and leaned down to take off her shoes—except she left her socks on—and entered the water with him.

"Oh my God, this feels *amazing*!" she moaned.

And the sound went straight to Buck's cock. It was a good thing he was still wearing his flight suit and was under the water, because the last thing he wanted to do after all their time together was make her wary. And seeing his erection might make her think she wasn't safe with him after all.

She ducked below the water and stayed under long enough for Buck to get a little worried. Just when he was about to go over and haul her back up, she stood and shook her head, spraying water in every direction.

The smile on her face transformed her. Until that moment, Buck had never seen Mandy carefree. But watching her now was like watching a butterfly emerging from its cocoon. She lifted her arms out to her sides and tilted her head back with her eyes closed.

She was a fucking goddess—and Buck wanted nothing more than to worship her the way she deserved to be worshiped. The water made her T-shirt and shorts cling to her body in a way he hadn't noticed before now. Yes, she'd been wet from the rain, but there was something inherently different between then and now. And he couldn't take his eyes off her.

After a moment, she lowered her head and arms, and when their gazes met, Buck could've sworn something arced between them.

He desperately needed to focus on something other than how beautiful this woman looked. Squatting down, he scooped up some sand from the bottom of the pond. "Look. You can use sand as a scrub. Not as good as soap but it should help, at least a little."

Of course, he realized he was covered from his wrists to ankles in cloth. He needed to peel off at least the top of his flight suit so he could clean his skin. Without thought, he reached for the zipper and yanked it down, shrugging the material off his shoulders and letting it float in the water around him. His tank top was disgusting, and he quickly pulled it up and over his head, sighing in relief at the feel of the water on his bare skin, of being able to essentially "air out" his upper body.

He crouched in the water once more and ran the sand over his arms, then his chest and underarms, reveling in the rough abrasion of the grains against his skin. He'd acted out of pure instinct, simply wanting to get clean and enjoying the impromptu bath, but when Mandy made a noise, he looked up—and froze.

She was staring at him with wide eyes, and it didn't look as if she'd moved an inch.

"Mandy? Are you all right?" he asked.

When she didn't respond, Buck got nervous. He moved toward her, the water lapping at his hips, his flight suit trailing behind him. It wasn't until he was a foot in front of her that he understood the look on her face.

Desire.

Seeing it ramped up his earlier feelings tenfold. And now that he was so close to her, he could see what he'd missed before. Her pupils were dilated, her nipples hard under her shirt and bra. She shifted where she stood but couldn't take her gaze from his chest.

"Mandy?" he said softly, needing this woman more in that moment than he'd ever needed anything in his life. He admired her. Respected her. Was in awe of her. She'd soldiered on through some very tough times recently, and had done so with a positive attitude. She hadn't complained, hadn't made him even once regret his decision to go after her while Obi-Wan took the children to safety.

She licked her lips as her gaze slowly lifted from his chest. The want in her blue eyes matched what he felt in his soul. Buck took another step, bringing him within inches of her. She was a tiny thing, making Buck feel more masculine, like more of a man at that moment than he'd ever felt. She made him want to slay all her dragons, protect her from anything and anyone who dared hurt her, claim her as his own.

This wasn't the time or place, and she was extremely vulnerable. He didn't want her to do anything out of a sense of obligation or gratitude. But he could no more ignore the feelings coursing through his body than he could turn his back on an animal or child in need.

"I want to kiss you," he whispered. "But I want you to want that too. Not agree out of some sense of obligation or payback or because you think you have no choice."

He wasn't sure what he expected her to say or do. Maybe nod. Maybe blush and drop her gaze. Maybe tell him that this wasn't a good idea, which it certainly was not.

But what he *didn't* expect was for her to close the remaining distance between them, reach up and pull him toward her with a hand on the back of his neck, and plant her lips on his.

* * *

What was she doing? Amanda had no idea. All she knew was that she needed this man more than she needed to breathe. When he'd turned and smiled at her from the middle of the pool, she'd followed him without question. If he said it was safe to bathe in, it was safe to bathe in. And she'd already been struggling to think of him as nothing more than an escort back to safety in Guyana, but when he'd unzipped his flight suit as if he were a performer at a strip club working the crowd, all she could do was stare.

If that wasn't bad enough, he'd peeled off his tank top, exposing his sculpted chest and abs. She felt like a voyeur, watching something she had no right to witness. But he seemed oblivious as he scrubbed his body with the sand on the bottom of the pool. Then he'd stood up and his body was on display once more.

The flight suit floating in the water drew her gaze—right to his hips. He was hard, his erection straining against the tight underwear he wore. The water was clear enough to not leave much to her imagination. Nash might not be the tallest man in the world, but he'd gotten more than his fair share in the reproductive department, that was for sure.

All Amanda could do was stand there and stare at him and

try to control the lust coursing through her body. Hadn't she just been thinking about how gross sex in the jungle would be? But now that was all she could think about. Walking over to him and pulling his underwear down and touching and tasting his beautiful cock.

He might have said something to her, but her ears were ringing so loud, she didn't hear what it was. Then he was standing in front of her. She looked up to meet his gaze and inhaled silently at what she saw. The desire she had for *him* reflected back in his eyes.

"I want to kiss you," he whispered. "But I want you to want that too. Not agree out of some sense of obligation or payback or because you think you have no choice."

Without realizing she'd moved, Amanda was touching him, pulling his head down and latching her lips onto his.

She didn't want to give him a chance to change his mind. To come to his senses. She was boring Amanda Rush. Men didn't look at her with lust the way Nash was. It felt as if she didn't kiss him right then, she'd lose her chance forever. And she knew without a doubt she'd feel the loss for the rest of her life.

But to her amazement, Nash didn't seem interested in a quick kiss. He immediately took control, wrapping an arm around her waist and yanking her against his body. The water sloshed around them, but Amanda barely noticed. All she could do was feel. Nash's lips and tongue against hers was something out of a fairy tale. She immediately broke out into goose bumps as he tilted his head to more deeply explore her mouth.

She wasn't thinking about where they were, or any danger they might be in, or how long it had been since she'd been able to brush her teeth. All she could think about was how all-consuming it felt to kiss him. All her worries disappeared, and she couldn't think about anything other than how good this man was making her feel.

It was Nash who finally lifted his lips from hers, making Amanda whimper pathetically.

"Shhhhh, I know," he soothed. He pressed her head to his shoulder and held her tightly.

Being in his arms felt like coming home. It was an odd feeling, one she'd never experienced before. Amanda had the thought that maybe it was because of the situation she was in, but she dismissed that idea immediately. Nash Chaney was everything she'd always wanted in a partner. Calm, even-tempered, competent, smart, kind, and funny.

And now she could add good kisser with a hot body to that list.

A whine caught her attention, and she felt more than heard Nash chuckle. Since she was plastered to his naked chest, she felt the vibrations move through him and into her. It was almost as intimate as the kiss they'd just shared. Almost.

"Looks like Rain isn't happy and is probably wondering what the hell we're doing," Nash said.

Turning her head, Amanda saw the dog who had inexplicably attached himself to them, following them for the last few days, sitting on the shore next to their shoes and the backpack, staring at them with a concerned look in his eyes.

"We're all right, boy," Nash told him.

And just like that, the spell she seemed to be under was broken. All of a sudden, Amanda felt self-conscious. Yes, he'd made the first move by asking if he could kiss her, but she'd been all over him. Practically jumped him.

Proving he was a perceptive man, Nash leaned back a little and stared down at her. "Well, that was a surprise, huh?"

She gave him a small smile and nodded.

"Do you regret it?"

That was an easy question to answer. "No."

"Good. Neither do I. This is horrible timing, and probably the last thing we should be thinking about, but I can't help it.

You live in Norfolk, right? I mean, when you aren't here in South America."

"Um, yeah."

"I'd like the chance to get to know you when you get home. I'm stationed there myself. It feels like kismet or serendipity or something. I'd like to see if this chemistry we have is still as explosive and intense when we aren't escaping through the jungle. When we aren't maybe or maybe not on the run from assholes who want to do horrible things to you. I want to take you out to dinner. Maybe a movie. Go for walks. Introduce you to the rest of my team. To Laryn, Casper's fiancée. Would that be something you'd be interested in?"

Interested in? Amanda wanted to jump up and down in giddy glee.

But the practical side of her kicked in. "I have about three more months on my agreement here."

"I highly doubt time is going to dull this ache I feel for you. The desire to get to know you better."

That was something her dream man would say for sure.

"Unless you don't feel the same. I mean, you could have any man you want, so why settle for a pilot whose work schedule is unpredictable at best. I can't guarantee I'd be able to be with you every time you needed me. I have to go where the Army, and sometimes Navy, sends me."

Amanda hated the uncertainty in his voice. She put a hand on his chest and looked up at him, hoping he could see the honesty in her eyes and hear it in her tone. "I've been alone for quite a long while now. I don't mind that you have to travel for your job. That doesn't matter to me, as long as you're safe."

"I have a feeling if things work out the way I'd like them to, my days of doing impulsive things like running away from my chopper during an op instead of keeping my ass inside are over."

That made goose bumps break out over her arms once more.

She realized she never answered his original question. "I'd like that," she said simply. "To see you when I get back to Virginia."

"Awesome!" Nash exclaimed with a smile. "Now, I'm going to go back over there," he said, nodding toward the other side of the pool. "And take off this flight suit, scrub it as best I can, take off my underwear and do the same thing. I'm sure you want to do the same with your clothes. I give you my word I won't look until you're dressed again."

Amanda added honorable to this man's list of attributes. "Thank you."

He lifted a hand and brushed the backs of his fingers against her cheek. "No need to thank me. If you knew the thoughts I had, you'd probably be running in the opposite direction."

"Oh, I know what thoughts you have. I'm pretty sure they're the same ones *I* had when you did your little strip tease earlier."

He chuckled. "Honestly, all I was thinking about was getting that nasty tank top off. Speaking of which…where did it go? Shit, did it get sucked off downstream?"

Amanda wanted to make a joke to go along with his "sucked off" comment, but decided this wasn't the time or place. "I think that's it, over there," she said, pointing toward the bank, not too far from where they were standing.

"Whew. All right, let's get this bath thing done. Our clothes aren't going to be dry, but maybe since it's not raining for once, they'll only be damp by the time the sun goes down."

"How much farther do we have to go, do you think?" Amanda couldn't help but ask. She'd refrained from asking that very question many times over the last few days, simply because she didn't want to be a pest and didn't want to sound like a little kid on a road trip asking that annoying question over and over. *Are we there yet?*

"You want honest, or do you want me to make something up?" he asked with a small tilt of his head. Nash hadn't let go of her, and it felt...good, comforting, being in the circle of his arms as they talked.

"Honest. Always."

"I don't know. You said it took you and the kids about two weeks to get to the camp?"

"That's what I think, yes."

"I have a feeling we're moving only a little faster than you did with the children. Simply because we aren't using any convenient roads or trails, but trudging through the jungle. We're also weaving a bit, zigzagging to try to throw off anyone who might be tracking us."

"So, you think we still have at least a week of walking to go. Maybe more," Amanda deduced, feeling her shoulders slump.

"We've got this," Nash said quietly. "We're doing all right."

"We're almost out of the food you took," she felt obligated to point out.

"But I'm also catching fresh meat almost every night with my snares. Thanks to the empty cans, we've been able to catch plenty of water as well. We might be a little hungry by the time we cross the border, but we'll get there one way or another."

He was right. Amanda knew he was, but the thought of walking for another week was daunting. She was exhausted. "Okay," she said softly.

"Hey, look at me, Mandy."

Sighing, she did as he asked, tilting her head up to meet his eyes.

"You're doing amazing. We've got this. All it takes is one foot in front of the other. Baby steps."

"Baby steps will just prolong this," she said firmly. "I'd prefer to take giant Nash-size steps, thank you very much."

He smiled. "That's my girl."

His words were a little condescending, but she took them in the manner he'd intended. As encouragement. Besides, being called *his* anything made her heart do silly flip-flops in her chest.

"If we're going to have a chance to dry out at all, we need to finish bathing and get out of the water," she said as sternly as she could. Though honestly, she didn't want to leave this pool, for fear it would all turn out to be a dream. Or Nash would come to his senses. "Besides, Rain is going to have a coronary if we don't get back to shore soon."

The dog was whining more often now, and pacing back and forth as he watched them from the safety of the shore.

Nash nodded, then leaned down and kissed her briefly. He licked his lips after he pulled back, and Amanda almost melted at the tender look in his eyes.

He backed away from her and wagged a finger. "No peeking, woman."

She giggled, having a feeling he wouldn't care in the least if she did. He seemed like a man who was secure in his masculinity and wouldn't give two little shits if someone spied on him while he was bathing.

But fair was fair, and since he'd promised not to look at her while she was getting clean, she wouldn't disrespect him by not doing the same.

It didn't take long for her to scrub her body with the sand at the bottom of the pool, and then do the same to her clothes. They weren't exactly clean, but mentally it felt as if she'd somehow shed several pounds of dirt by the time she'd redressed.

"What about you, Rain? You want to get clean? Come 'ere, boy. Let me give you a bath, get some of that icky dried mud and blood off your fur."

But the dog wanted nothing to do with the water. He backed away when Amanda tried to coax him into the shallow edge of the pond. She could only laugh. She wasn't going to force the dog into doing anything for fear he'd go off and leave. She'd gotten very used to having the dog around. He didn't walk with them all the time, but several times over the course of each day he'd pop back up, as if checking to make sure they were still there, before heading into the underbrush of the jungle once more.

Something occurred to her then. "Nash? How are we going to get Rain across the stream? I mean, we're already wet so it's not a big deal for us to cross now, I don't think. But what about Rain?"

She watched as Nash looked at the stream they still had to cross, at Rain, then back at the stream. Then he sighed and said, "We're going to have to hope he figures out that he's got to cross if he wants to follow us."

Amanda's heart fell. She'd really hoped Nash would've had some great idea about how to suddenly get the dog to trust them and to let them carry him across when they went. But she'd had a feeling he was going to say exactly what he said.

"He's kept up with us so far. I have faith in him," Nash told her firmly.

Having no choice, Amanda nodded. As they prepared to cross the stream, she spoke to Rain. Telling him what a good boy he was. How he needed to follow them. How it was only water. But Rain simply sat with his head tilted, staring at her.

"You ready?" Nash asked.

She wasn't. But like most things that she'd been through lately, she didn't exactly have a choice. So she nodded. After grabbing the pack, Nash took her hand and they started across the stream. Rain paced the bank as they left, looking as stressed as Amanda felt.

After she and Nash had reached the other side of the stream, they were dripping wet, of course. He suggested they turn their backs on each other once more while they wrung out their clothes, getting as much water out of them as they could. Amanda agreed. It was bad enough they had to walk while dripping wet every time it rained. She'd never take being dry for granted again. Or having a mattress to sleep on. Or food. There were a lot of things she'd change about her thinking when she got home.

Once they'd gotten redressed, Amanda felt much better. It was silly, she was only slightly cleaner than she'd been before they'd found the pool, but emotionally, she felt lighter.

She looked across the rushing water but saw no sign of Rain, which made her better mood take a nosedive.

"He'll find us. I know it," Nash said quietly.

"I hope so."

Doing her best to shrug off her sadness that Rain hadn't immediately followed them, Amanda did her best to think about something else. Namely the man at her side.

Things between them felt different now, but not in a bad way. The sexual tension was even higher than it had been before, but now that they'd acted on those feelings, and were on the same page about seeing each other once they were home safely, the air between them felt more intimate.

Amanda had no idea what the future would bring, but for the first time since she'd been kidnapped, she felt as if things were going to be all right. She didn't feel quite so alone in the world. Nash wanted to see her again, wanted to date. It was something to look forward to. And there was no doubt that Amanda was looking forward to getting to know Nash on a more even playing field. One where she wasn't quite so out of her element.

CHAPTER EIGHT

One more week.

Seven days.

One hundred and sixty-eight hours.

Ten thousand and eighty minutes.

And thousands and thousands of steps.

Honestly, Buck had hoped he was wrong in his estimate of how much longer it would take them to get to the border. Now, he was hoping he hadn't *underestimated*, because both he and Mandy were more than ready to be out of this jungle.

His backpack was light, since all the cans were empty. They were surviving on the meat he managed to catch in his snare each night and the bits of edible fruit they found while walking through the rainforest.

The only one of them who seemed unfazed by the long trek was Rain. The dog seemed to have boundless energy, even though he was super-skinny and had started limping a couple of days ago.

To both of their relief, the dog had found them less than a day after they'd crossed the stream and reluctantly had to leave him behind. He was cleaner than he'd been before, so he had to have gotten in the water at some point. Truthfully, Buck was just as relieved as Amanda was to have him back, flitting around them as they walked.

Buck and Mandy talked about their lives back in Virginia a lot. He knew about her previous teaching job, and why she'd felt as if she needed to quit instead of taking a leave of absence. She told him more about the decision to leave Virginia and come to Guyana to volunteer at the school and orphanage. She spoke fondly about each of the children, and Buck was impressed that she seemed to know each and every single one of them so well. Their quirks, their strengths and weaknesses, and their fears.

She was every child's dream teacher, and the kids who she'd been responsible for were lucky to have her as their teacher and mentor.

He, in turn, told her how he became a Night Stalker pilot, and what it meant to him. He recited their creed, and even told her about some of the missions he'd been on with his teammates. Late at night, as he held her in his arms, they'd covered more controversial topics, like politics, religion, and whether or not euthanasia should be legalized for humans.

Buck had never clicked with a woman the way he had with Mandy, and all he wanted was to get her safely back across the border. They hadn't had any issues with the rebels, and in the six days since bathing in that pool, he'd let down his guard a little, feeling safer with every step closer to Guyana.

The longer he spent with Mandy, the closer he felt to her. They'd crammed a year's worth of getting to know each other into a week and a half. He'd learned more about her in this jungle than he ever would've while casual dating someone back home.

As a result, he was even more sure that he wanted a future with her. Wanted to introduce her to his friends. Integrate her into his life back in Norfolk.

But today he was feeling...off. They were close to the border, he could feel it. But some sixth sense told him that the closer they got to safety, the more dangerous their trip would become. If the rebels truly believed someone was in the jungle, the best bet for finding them—and getting them back in their clutches—would be to ambush them right before they crossed back into Guyana.

Mandy had been silent for hours now, as if she could feel the tension in the air. Or maybe she was simply too exhausted to come up with a new topic for them to discuss.

"Tell me about your parents. You said they died when you were seventeen in a drunk driving accident? If you can talk about it without too much pain, that is," Buck added.

"I don't mind. I still miss them more than I thought I would. I mean, of course, right after they died I was devastated, but as I get older the pain is still there. It's just changed. Now I get sad thinking about how my dad will never get to know my future husband…if I have one. And I can't call up Mom to ask her things like how long to cook a turkey, or ask her to teach me how to sew a button back onto a blouse. Those are silly things, but—"

"No, they aren't," Buck interrupted. "They're completely normal. And you have every right to mourn the loss of them."

"Thanks. My parents were great. I had an awesome childhood. I grew up in Richmond. We were middle class, so not rich, but we had enough for me to play sports and be involved in clubs and things like that. I was in my senior year when they were hit head-on by that guy…so drunk he didn't even know he was going the wrong way on the interstate. They were both killed instantly, which in hindsight is a small relief, because the thought of either of them suffering is too much."

"What happened to the drunk driver?"

Her lip curled. "He had broken bones, a concussion, and didn't remember a thing about the accident…or so he claimed. His license was revoked, and he was sentenced to a few years in jail, but of course he was released early, because no one ever serves all the time they're given. I was obsessed with keeping tabs on him, and about five years ago, on a snowy night, he stole a car from a bar where he was getting blitzed and crashed it. This time killing only himself, thank goodness."

Buck literally didn't know what to say to that.

"Sorry. That sounds heartless, I know."

"No, it doesn't," he said firmly. "It sounds human. For what it's worth, I'm truly sorry."

"Thanks."

"You mentioned something before about a fundraiser..."

"Yes. Along with the lawsuit against the guy's estate—which my pro-bono lawyer won on my behalf—the community was awesome. Raised a ton of money to help me with college expenses and just in general, because they felt sorry for me. I saved a lot of it, and when the opportunity in Guyana came across my social media feed, I had enough to quit my job, pay my rent for six months, and come down here. I needed to figure out if I wanted to continue in the education field. I'm happy to say it worked, I have my passion back again, but for younger kids. I'll have to update my teaching license, but that won't be too hard, I don't think. I'll always be grateful for my experiences here... except for the whole kidnapping thing, of course."

"Of course," Buck said with a small chuckle.

He was so impressed with this woman. She had such a refreshing take on the world. When things didn't go her way, she didn't wallow in self-pity. She changed direction and kept moving forward. He liked that. A hell of a lot.

"What about you? Tell me more about your family," she urged.

Buck had no problem with her request. "My sister's a brat," he said with a grin, making Mandy laugh. "She's older than me and loved bossing me around, tormenting me when we were growing up in Kansas. We had one of those underground tornado shelters in the backyard. You know, the kind that was in *The Wizard of Oz*? Where you lift up a door and go down some steps? Except ours was dark and dank and smelled funky, like mold and dead animals. Once, Natalie told me she had something cool to show me, and when I went down the stairs ahead of her, she shut the door, latching it from the outside. I heard her laughing hysterically as she ran away. I cried and pounded on that door, but she left me down there for what seemed liked hours, though she claims was only about twenty minutes."

"Why'd she let you out?"

"Because Mom said she wanted to take us out for ice cream, but she couldn't find me."

Mandy giggled. Buck loved the sound. It was carefree and open, and he wished, not for the first time, that he was hearing it while they were home safe and sound on his couch, watching TV, or over a table sharing a delicious meal.

"Sounds like a typical older sister. Was she protective too? Or just annoying?"

"Protective," Buck said quickly. "When I was in the fifth grade, there was this girl who delighted in tormenting me. I don't know why. My sister attended the middle school right next to the elementary school, and she'd come over and get me at the end of each day and we'd walk home together. Eventually, she arrived while this other girl, Lena, was picking on me, and Natalie walked right up to her and shoved her. *Hard*. In today's day and age, she would've gotten in big trouble for that, rightly so, but back then there weren't as many teachers keeping an eye on the kids after school.

"She told Lena that if she caught her within ten feet of me ever again, she'd regret it. And of course, Natalie shook her fist as she said it. It was overly dramatic, and I don't think my sister would've ever actually punched anyone, but the threat worked and Lena left me alone after that."

"That's awesome."

"Yeah. My parents were extremely proud when I became a Night Stalker, but Natalie refused to come to my graduation, and she gave me the cold shoulder for over a year. When I'd finally had enough, and flew out to Washington to confront her and find out what her problem was, she admitted that she was scared for me. She'd researched what Night Stalkers did, and she hated that I'd be putting myself in danger. She told me that she didn't want her little brother to die, and that's why she'd put distance between us. Because she was afraid for me and couldn't deal with knowing what might happen to me."

"Awww, that's kind of sweet."

"Maybe. But I told her she was being a bitch."

"Nash! You did not!" Mandy scolded.

"I did. Told her to get over herself. That I could die tomorrow walking across the street. Or *she* could. There's no guarantee in life. You have to live each day as if it's your last. And I was done with her shutting me out of her life. I wanted to talk to my niece and nephew, and wanted to be involved in all their lives, even if I didn't live in the same city or state as her and her family."

"Did it work?"

"Yup. But only after we had a five-hour conversation about how careful I am, how I know what I'm doing, the hours of training I've had, and will continue to have, and the credentials of my copilots and teammates. I answered every question she had—that I was allowed to—and by the end we were both exhausted, but she was satisfied that I was doing what I loved, even if it was dangerous, and she admitted she was proud of her little brother."

"I like that for you both."

"Yeah."

"Your parents are still in Kansas?"

"Yup. No clue why. It's cold, and flat, and windy."

"I could go with some cold right about now," Mandy said with a small laugh.

"Yeah, me too," Buck agreed.

She'd been walking beside him while they talked about family, and he'd taken her hand in his...which felt good. Sweaty, but good. Besides, at this point, sweat was the last thing he was worried about. Neither of them was currently at their best, but their experience had let them cut through the superficial shit couples dealt with at the beginning of a relationship. What was a little sweat between friends?

They hadn't repeated the amazing kiss they'd shared in the pool, but it was never far from Buck's mind. He'd never felt as connected to another woman as he did Mandy. It was the same feeling he had about his teammates, with Obi-Wan...without the physical part, of course. They'd shared an intense experience together, and were working together to get through it, much as he and his fellow pilots did. It hadn't been a life-or-death situation, at least not since they'd evaded detection back at the LZ and when they'd first fled the area around the rebel camp, but no less intense.

"I want you to meet them," Buck blurted. "My family." When Mandy looked at him with longing in her eyes, he knew he'd made the right decision. "My mom will love you immediately. She'll want to know all about your students and how you decided to get into teaching. My dad will just nod his head and say in his gruff voice something along the lines of, 'You're too good for my son.'"

She laughed.

"And my sister will probably try to include you in whatever shenanigans she has planned next for her little brother. She'll be thrilled to have an insider who can work with her to cause havoc in my life. Last Halloween, she showed up on my doorstep dressed as Bigfoot—you know, with the whole hairy getup—and tackled me to the ground. Scared the crap out of me."

Buck decided he was going to make it his mission in life to make this woman sound as happy as she did right that moment as she laughed.

"She sounds fun."

"Natalie *is* fun...when she isn't annoying," Buck agreed.

He was about to launch into another story about his annoying sister when Rain burst out of the trees in front of them, planted his feet, and growled low in his throat.

Any amusement Buck was feeling disappeared in an instant. This wasn't the stray dog they'd gotten to know. In fact, during all the time they'd known him, Rain hadn't made more noise than a few whimpers and whines.

But right now, his teeth were bared and he was making some seriously scary sounds in his throat.

"Easy, boy," Buck said, pushing Mandy behind him. He had no idea what had gotten into the dog, but he wasn't going to risk Mandy getting bitten.

"What's wrong with him?" she whispered.

"I don't know." But they were at a stalemate. The dog wasn't moving, wasn't responding to Buck's gentle tone, and he didn't seem inclined to stop growling anytime soon.

"We're just going to keep walking," Buck said softly to the dog.

As if he could understand him, Rain violently shook his entire body and took a step toward them.

Buck stepped backward, pushing Mandy as he went. That went on for several steps, Rain growling and moving forward slowly, head down, and Buck and Mandy backing away from him.

Then suddenly, Rain darted to the right, scaring the shit out of Buck. For a second, he thought the dog was lunging at them.

He quickly moved forward, hoping to get away from the stray he'd become very attached to—but Rain was having none of that. He swerved back in front of them and growled once more.

Confused and frustrated, Buck stood stock still, not sure what to do. The last thing either of them needed was a dog bite, especially considering Rain almost certainly had never had any inoculations and could be carrying some sort of doggy disease.

Rain walked to the right again...then stopped and looked back at them, letting out a small whine.

"I think...does he want us to go that way? To follow him?" Mandy asked, sounding unsure.

Buck's head tilted, much as Rain's did when it seemed as if the little dog was thinking. "Actually, I think maybe he does."

In an experiment, Buck took a step forward, not surprised this time when Rain growled again and moved to get in front of him, prevent him once more from going any farther in the direction they'd been heading.

When Buck took a step to the right, Rain's ears perked up and he quickly took the lead, looking back as if to say, "Yes, follow me!"

Buck looked from the dog to the path they'd been on, then down to the compass he'd attached to the zipper of his flight suit. They'd been steadily walking east, toward the border, but Rain wanted them to turn south, which would make their trek to Guyana even longer. At this point, he just wanted to get out of this stinkin' jungle. And he had no doubt Mandy shared his thoughts.

But there was even *less* doubt that Rain was trying to tell them something. That he wasn't happy with the path they'd been on for hours.

The dog wasn't always around when they were walking. Sometimes they'd see him trotting alongside them or trailing behind. Every now and then, he'd end up in front. Sometimes they'd go all day without seeing him, but he was always there when they woke the next day, eagerly anticipating whatever Buck managed to snare for them to eat. He and Mandy had actually had a discussion about how silly it was that they continued to share their precious calories with the dog, but neither had stopped.

Twice, Rain had brought his own contributions to the meals, in the form of a small mouse and a squirrel he'd managed to catch. The first time that happened, it was a shock, but Buck had cooked the mouse and fed the entire thing to Rain. Mandy swore the dog had a proud smile on his face as he waited patiently for his meal. The second time, it seemed almost normal to be cooking a rodent that the stray dog had provided for them.

But *that* Rain was nothing like the dog who stood before them at the moment. His muscles were shaking, as if he was a second away from pouncing. His ears were twitching back and forth and his nose was in the air, constantly sniffing.

Looking from Rain to the path, then back to the dog, Buck made a decision. The animal had trusted them not to hurt him, to provide for him...Buck would do the same in return. If Rain didn't want them going east, it would be stupid to continue in that direction. At some point they'd have to head east again, but it wouldn't hurt to go south for a while. Just in case.

"Come on," Buck said in a low voice, reaching for Mandy's hand once more. It was slow-going through the trees, but Rain never got so far ahead that they couldn't see him. In the past, the dog would run ahead, only reappearing every now and then, as if checking on them. But now it was as if he was purposely moving at their pace, carefully leading them where he wanted them to go. Never getting out of their sight...and maybe more importantly, never letting them out of *his* sight.

He could feel how tense Mandy was and hated that he had no words to comfort her. He wasn't sure what had gotten into Rain, but as crazy as it might seem, he trusted the dog's instincts.

They walked for about twenty minutes, and just when Buck thought they should attempt to head back east, toward the border, an out-of-place sound reached his ears.

Rain heard it at the same time, because his ears flattened and he growled low in his throat. Not at him and Mandy this time, thank goodness. The dog was staring to the left...

To the east.

Buck pulled Mandy behind a large group of trees and crouched down with her. To his surprise, Rain joined them, lying right by Buck's side. He was alert, his gaze fixed on something Buck couldn't see.

"Is that...people?" Mandy whispered.

"Sounds like it," Buck said.

"It could be the good guys." But she didn't sound sure.

"I doubt it. Look at Rain."

The dog was shaking so hard as he lay next to him, it was almost alarming. And it wasn't because he was cold. Buck reached out a hand and cautiously placed it on Rain's head. "Easy, boy," he crooned, amazed the dog was allowing him to touch him.

"He's scared. Terrified," Mandy said.

"Yeah."

As they hid behind the trees, they heard men walk by. Two, based on the voices. Not close enough to see them, but their conversation carried easily in the suddenly quiet jungle. They were speaking in Spanish, which Buck was able to understand, thanks to the classes he'd taken in both high school and college.

"This is stupid. We don't have any proof anyone was left behind."

"Right? I don't care what Carlos says, we're wasting our time."

"If one of the brats was enough of an idiot to miss that chopper, there's no way they would've made it this far on their own."

"What if that bitch is with them? Having an adult with them would give a kid a better chance to survive."

"Would it? She had no fuckin' clue what she was doing. Don't you remember the walk to camp? How pathetic she was?"

Both men laughed. Buck hated the way they were talking about Mandy, but he controlled his anger. He wasn't going to do anything stupid at this point in their journey. They were almost home free.

"How much longer do we have to monitor the border? Hell, we don't even know where whoever's out here will try to cross—*if* anyone's out here at all."

"No clue. Carlos said we have to stay, so here we are."

"This sucks!"

"Yes."

The two men's voices faded as they walked farther away from where Buck and Mandy had hidden. The danger they were in seemed sky high right now. They had no idea how many men had been assigned to patrol the jungle near the border, or how long they'd be on the lookout.

The good news was, the rebels themselves had no idea if they were actually looking for someone or not. And they seemed to assume if someone had missed that helicopter, it was a child, or perhaps Mandy and a kid. That would work in their favor, Buck hoped.

Turning, he looked down at Rain. The dog seemed less tense but still on alert.

"You knew, didn't you, boy?" he asked quietly.

Rain looked up at him as if he could understand what Buck was saying perfectly.

"Good boy. You're the best boy. If I had it, I'd be giving you an entire steak just for yourself tonight."

"Nash?"

Hating the fear he heard in Mandy's voice, after one last affectionate stroke of the dog's head, he faced her.

"They're looking for us," she guessed.

"Wrong. They have no idea *who* they're looking for, or if there's anyone to find at all. They're here just in case someone didn't get on that chopper. They don't know for sure. That works in our favor. We just have to be more cautious from here on out. And them patrolling in this area lets us know that we're close to Guyana. Besides, Rain will alert us to anyone who might be out there."

His words seemed to calm some of the anxiousness Mandy was feeling. He saw her shoulders relax a fraction. "If we'd kept going in the direction we were going before...we might've run right into the rebels, wouldn't we?"

"There's no way to know for sure, but I'm guessing so, yes."

Moving slowly, Mandy let go of his hand and moved around him on her knees until Rain was between them. She leaned down and kissed the top of the dog's head. The look Rain gave her, Buck could only describe as adoration. He could relate; he had the same feelings toward this woman.

"Thank you, Rain. You did good. So good. You're so smart and brave. You didn't know how we'd react to your growling. We could've gotten mad or thrown something at you, but you didn't want us to go that way, did you? So you herded us this way. Did I say you were smart? You're the smartest dog in the world!"

The whole time she was speaking, she was stroking Rain's head and back. The dog seemed to arch into her touch, and he'd completely stopped shaking.

Mandy took a deep breath and looked up at Buck. "What now?"

"We keep walking. Following Rain's lead."

"I mean, I know I said he was smart..." To Buck's amusement, Mandy covered the dog's ears with her hands before continuing. "But do we really trust him to lead us to the border? He could actually lead us west, toward some unknown place he came from."

She was so damn cute. Buck touched the compass hanging from his flight suit. "I have a compass, remember?"

"Oh, yeah." She was back to petting Rain's head now.

"Besides, where he came from obviously wasn't a good place. Especially if it was with the rebels who'd joined the camp the morning the kids were rescued. You saw how terrified he was of the two men who were talking. How hard he was shaking."

"Right. Nash?"

"Yeah?"

"I'm taking him with me when we leave. I'm not leaving him here. I can't."

Buck wasn't exactly surprised by her declaration. She wouldn't be the woman he admired and wanted in his life if she could turn her back on Rain.

"Okay."

"Okay?" she asked with an adorable tilt of her head. She had dirt on her cheeks, a scrape on her forehead from a branch she hadn't ducked under fast enough, and her hair was sticking up in spikes all over her head. And he'd never seen a more beautiful woman in his life.

"Yeah, okay. I'll do whatever I can to help. There will be a bunch of red tape. He'll need inoculations, licenses, maybe a letter from a veterinarian. I don't know. But we'll figure it out."

She stared at him for a moment, then went up to her knees and lunged at him over Rain's prone position between them. "Thank you."

"You don't have to thank me. I've become pretty attached to the little guy myself."

She pulled back, much to Buck's disappointment. He loved the feel of her against him. "Oh, did you want to take him home with *you*?"

"He likes me, but he's devoted to you," Buck said with a shake of his head. "He belongs to you. But I wouldn't mind visitation rights."

Her smile lit up her face. "Of course."

It seemed so...normal to be talking about visitation rights for a dog, as if the outcome of their little jaunt through the jungle was a given thing. And as far as Buck was concerned, it was. There was no way they'd get this close to freedom, only to let the rebels find them now. He'd get Mandy, and Rain, safely across the border or die trying.

Not that he wanted to die. No, he had things he wanted to do with his life. Namely, get to know the woman next to him without worrying about things like finding food, being hunted, and not getting bitten by the hundreds of deadly critters crawling and slinking around this rainforest.

"I'm thinking now is our chance to head due east," he said. "Obviously I don't know the perimeter the rebels are walking to search for someone who may or may not be trying to get to Guyana, but since they just went by, I'm guessing we have a window of opportunity to slip past them."

Mandy nodded. "I trust you. Whatever you think is best, that's what we'll do. Lord knows I have no clue about anything out here."

"That's not true. You've held up very well, and you even started our fire last night."

"I did, didn't I?" she said with a small smile.

"Yup. Next thing I know, you'll be Jane of the Jungle."

She huffed out a quiet breath of laughter. "Not quite."

Buck smiled to himself, amazed that he was feeling anything other than a sense of duty and urgency to get the hell out of this jungle. He hadn't expected to spend almost two weeks trekking through the wet, hot hell that was the rainforest, but there were quite a few good memories he had of his time with Mandy.

"What do you think, Rain? Is the coast clear?" he asked the dog lying between them.

In response to his words, Rain sat up, looked at him then at Mandy, before lifting his nose to sniff the air. Then he stood on all fours, did a full-body shake, and stepped out from behind the trees, facing due east.

He turned his head to look back at them as if to say, "You comin'?"

"Seems like the coast is clear," Buck said. He stood and held his hand out to Mandy. "What do you think? Shall we get the hell out of here?"

"You think we'll get across the border today?" she asked, as she took his hand and used his leverage to stand.

"Looks promising, if those rebels are anything to go by."

"What are we waiting for? Let's go then!" Mandy said eagerly.

This time when they started walking, Buck was on alert. At the first sign of anyone anywhere near them, he'd take cover. He had a feeling, though, that Rain would alert them to any rebels who might be near long before Buck heard or saw anything. The dog was incredibly in tune with his surroundings and had probably saved their lives today.

If he hadn't forced them to change direction, it was likely they would've run right into the two men. He owed that dog everything. He vowed to do whatever it took to make sure Rain was able to go home with Mandy. The dog might have to wait in Guyana for the permissions and paperwork, but Buck would make sure he was left with someone responsible, who would treat him like the king he was until he could get to Mandy in Virginia.

For a man who'd taken pride in having a very orderly and uncomplicated life back home, he was certainly collecting his fair share of...complications. He felt bad for thinking about Mandy and Rain as such, but there was no doubt his life was about to change.

He wouldn't be living just for his job anymore. He wanted to make things between him and Mandy work. But their futures were uncertain at best. She still had obligation here in Guyana to fulfill, and he, of course, had his own responsibilities. But she'd be worth whatever he had to do to cultivate the relationship they'd started in the jungle.

CHAPTER NINE

Crossing the border was anticlimactic. Hell, Amanda didn't even know they were safely back in Guyana until they came upon a dirt road with a sign indicating how far it was to Baramita, a town not too far from the Venezuelan border.

"Are we...did we make it?" she stuttered.

"Looks like it," Nash said with a smile. "Although we aren't out of the woods yet. The rebels illegally crossed the border to snatch you and the kids once, they could do it again."

He wasn't saying anything Amanda hadn't already thought about. She couldn't think of anything *but* that. She still had about three months left in her agreement with the school, but the thought of staying was terrifying. She assumed security would be increased, to keep everyone safe, but what if that wasn't good enough? What if the rebels were so determined to get back what they'd lost, the boys and girls—even Amanda herself—that they returned with more men and more firepower? They'd certainly learn from the mistakes of the first kidnapping, probably separate the kids as soon as they were back across the border, with the men who'd been promised the girls taking them immediately.

She shuddered. And of course, Nash noticed.

"What? What's wrong?"

"Nothing," she said without thinking.

"Don't do that. Talk to me, Mandy."

He was right. They'd been through one hell of an experience together, and it felt disrespectful for her to clam up now. "I just... I was thinking about what would happen if they *do* come back."

"I'm sure there've been changes at the school to make sure everyone's safe," Nash told her.

"Yeah."

"Let's just see what we find at the school before you do any worrying. You'll also feel better after you get a shower and some real food in you."

"How are we gonna get to the school? I have no idea where we are or where it is," Amanda said.

"Hitchhike. How else?" Nash answered with a smile.

But that didn't assuage Amanda's worries. "Is that safe?"

"In normal circumstances, no. But we're in Guyana, and I'm armed, and we have Rain...I think we'll be okay."

"Will someone pick us up if we have Rain? And we aren't looking very...trustworthy."

Nash chuckled. "You mean since we've just spent two weeks trekking through the jungle and look like escaped convicts?"

"Yeah, that."

"Have faith, Mandy."

That was the problem. She wasn't the same naïve woman she'd been when she'd arrived here in South America. She'd come to teach children and found herself in a life-or-death situation. It had been, what...a month since she'd been kidnapped? She felt as if she were a completely different person now. Amanda wasn't sure she could look at anyone without suspicion ever again.

They walked along the dirt road, and it was amazing how good it felt to not be in the jungle. Oh, there were still plenty of trees on either side, but walking on an actual road felt liberating.

But...also a little strange. Like they were too exposed. Rain seemed to think so too, as he kept to the side of the road, walking amongst the trees instead of out in the open.

It occurred to Amanda then that the little dog might not even want to come with them back to the school. That thought made her extraordinarily sad. She didn't want to leave him. Didn't want to have to worry about him every day and wonder if he was all right.

He'd stuck by their sides like glue ever since they'd heard the men patrolling the border. But the truth was, she had no idea if the dog would want to leave the only home he'd probably ever known.

The rumble of an engine sounded so out of place, it was hard for Amanda to identify at first. She'd spent weeks getting to know the sounds of the jungle—rain, birds, random animals—that an engine seemed almost foreign now.

But Nash didn't hesitate. He stuck his thumb out in the universal hitchhiking sign and, to her amazement, a battered gray pickup stopped. The man behind the wheel gaped at them.

"Thanks for stopping. We could use a ride," Nash said.

"Are you Amanda Rush?" the man asked in accented English, staring at her with such surprise, it made her uncomfortable.

"Why are you asking?" Nash asked, tone much harder than it was a moment earlier, as he stepped in front of her to block the man's view.

Amanda felt Rain lean against her side at the same time, as if he was prepared to protect her from anyone who dared lay a hand on her. It was comforting to be in an overprotective male sandwich between Nash and the dog, but she was also extremely curious as to how this man knew her name.

"I've been driving up and down this road every day, hoping to run into you!" the man exclaimed. "We got word from Desmond Williams over at the orphanage that you and an American pilot were missing, and to keep an eye out for you. And here you are! You *are* Amanda, right?"

"I am," she said, before Nash could reply. "Thank you so much for looking for us."

"Well, I'll be damned," the man said. "Never really expected to find you. The jungle usually chews people up and refuses to spit them out. Come, hop in the back of the truck, and I'll have you back to the school before you can blink."

"My dog can come too, right?" Amanda blurted.

The man's gaze dropped to the dog at her side. He looked surprised again, but shrugged. "Makes no difference to me."

This was the moment of truth. Did they get in or did they not? But this man wouldn't know her name if he was one of the rebels. She didn't remember anyone back at the camp asking her name. They might've heard the kids mention it, but they all called her Mandy. And there was no *way* they'd know her last name. This man had to be on the up and up.

She looked at Nash to see what he thought.

He looked wary but not overly suspicious, which was a huge relief.

Keeping himself between her and the driver, Nash urged her toward the back of the truck. He helped her climb inside, then hopped up himself.

Rain stood in the road looking confused...and worried. His brown eyes were glued to the both of them, and for a moment, she wasn't sure they'd be able to get him to come after all.

"Come on, Rain," Amanda coaxed, slapping her thigh. "It's okay. You're coming with us. Jump up. You can do it!"

With one last look around, Rain crouched, then leaped.

Amanda couldn't help but laugh as she held out her arms to catch the dog literally throwing himself at her. She fell backward into the bed of the truck with an armful of smelly, dirty dog. Nash was there to make sure neither of them fell right back out of the truck.

"Ready?" the man called from the cab.

Nash gave him a thumbs-up.

Amanda sat up and watched intently as the man backed the truck up and turned around on the road. She was ready to jump right back out if it looked like he was going to drive them in the direction they'd just come from.

It wasn't until they were on their way—in the opposite direction from the border—that she finally relaxed.

"We did it," she said, just loud enough for Nash to hear.

"We did," he agreed.

Amanda hugged Rain against her chest and rested her chin on the top of his head as they headed—hopefully—for the school and orphanage where her whole ordeal had started. She had mixed feelings about what was to come. Not that she wanted to go back into the jungle, but she, Nash, and Rain had gotten into a routine. It was comfortable. Predictable. Whatever lie ahead of her was not.

As if he could sense her unease, Nash wrapped his arm around her shoulders. She leaned into him and closed her eyes. With this man next to her, she felt stronger. Which wasn't smart, as he'd probably be leaving as soon as they got to the school. His copilot was probably waiting anxiously for him, and Amanda had no doubt the rest of his team would be equally worried by now. He'd have his own issues to deal with.

Things would change between them, and she could only hope he'd meant what he said about seeing her once she got back to Virginia. It might've been something he'd said in the heat of the moment, and, once reality hit and he got back to his life, he might regret being so impulsive. That would hurt, but she'd rather know right off the bat than be led on or have him date her briefly out of some sense of obligation.

Nash Chaney was an honorable man, and if he said he'd do something, she had no doubt he'd follow through on his promise to take her out when she returned to the States. But she didn't want to be a chore, a task he had to complete to keep his word.

She liked this man. A lot. She still dreamed about the kiss they'd shared. It was intense, and the best kiss she'd ever received. They hadn't repeated it, but he'd shown affection in other ways...holding her hand, making sure she got the first pieces of cooked meat. And of course, he still slept with his arms wrapped around her every night.

But ultimately, she was worrying for nothing. She couldn't control anyone other than her own actions. And at the moment, all *she* could do was go with the flow. Things would work out or they wouldn't. That was the bottom line.

One day at a time. Right now, she just wanted to see how things went after they arrived back at the school. She was anxious to see the kids. To make sure they were all right. See for herself that they were safe and sound.

The truck didn't drive very long at all before it began to slow. Looking around the cab, Amanda saw the familiar road that led to the orphanage and school where she'd spent three months of her life. She couldn't help but smile.

They'd done it. Against all odds, she'd made it back to where her nightmare had begun.

As the truck bumped down the road, she saw people begin to stream out the doors of the school building, next to the building where the kids slept and ate every day.

Her smile grew, so much that her cheeks hurt. The truck pulled up, and Nash was out and holding out a hand to her as soon as it stopped. She took it and turned to see all "her" kids running toward her.

She vaguely realized Rain had jumped out of the back of the truck as well, but most of her attention was on the children. Michael was leading the group, and the smile on his face was almost as wide as her own. Andrew, James, Natasha, and Sandra were there.

She scanned the faces of the children and realized they were *all* there.

Michael ran straight into her, almost knocking her on her ass. Only Nash's hand at her back kept her upright. But he stepped back when she was swarmed by the kids. She laughed as they all tried to touch her, to prove to themselves that it really was her and she was all right.

Everyone was talking at once. Asking where she'd been, trying to tell her all about the helicopter they'd been in. Their excitement and relief was contagious, and once more, Amanda felt something click inside her. This was what she was meant to do with her life. Teach. Mold and help guide kids to be the best people they could be when they grew up. She hadn't been with this group of children for that long, but they already meant the world to her.

She did her best to touch each child, to comment on how healthy they looked, how smart they'd been during their escape. They soaked up her praise, just as they always did.

They had a million questions, but she wasn't ready to answer them just yet and wasn't sure what to say, anyway. All she kept telling them was that she was fine. Tired, hungry, and dirty, but all right.

As her gaze ran over the children again, she realized one was missing. Little Bibi. Looking around, she saw some of the adults standing back, smiling and observing the reunion between the children and herself. Desmond was there, also with a small smile on his face. As were the other three teachers.

Blair was there too—and she was holding Bibi. A very unhappy little four-year-old. The girl was squirming and trying to get out of the woman's hold, but the matron of the school wasn't letting her go. She might be in her early seventies, but she was obviously still strong enough to subdue the child.

And Blair *wasn't* smiling. She looked...shocked. Amanda could understand that. It wasn't as if they'd been able to call ahead of time to let everyone know she was back. But she was confused as to why she wouldn't let little Bibi come greet her.

Her attention was diverted from the owner of the orphanage by Joseph, wanting to know the name of the dog.

Rain was standing a little ways away, next to Nash, looking very unsure about all the excitement going on.

"That's Rain. He found us in the jungle and was our faithful companion. He helped save our lives by alerting us when the bad men were around. Made us go a different direction."

"And the man?" Natasha wanted to know.

"That's Nash. He's one of the helicopter pilots who came to save us all."

"I'm so sorry I told you James was missing," Michael said miserably.

Amanda hugged him tightly. "It's okay. I love that you were looking out for everyone."

"But I made you miss the helicopter!" he said, tears forming in his eyes.

"Look at me, Michael. Everyone, listen. Are you listening?"

A bunch of little heads bobbed up and down.

"I'm okay. I survived. That's the important thing. I would much rather have gone through what I did because you were concerned about your fellow students, than to not have experienced it and left someone behind. You did the right thing, Michael. And I'm proud of you. I'm so proud of *all* of you."

"All right, everyone, break is over. We're so glad to have Miss Mandy back, but it's time to return to class. Let's give her a little space. You'll see her later, after lessons are over," Blair called out.

Looking over to where she'd been standing, Amanda no longer saw Bibi. She assumed one of the other teachers had already taken her back into the classroom. She was disappointed; Bibi was one of her favorite children. She'd taken an immediate liking to Amanda, and had become one of her constant companions since her arrival at the orphanage.

The kids started making their way back to their classrooms, but Michael walked over to Nash and stuck out his hand. "Thank you for keeping Miss Mandy safe and bringing her back."

Nash shook the boy's hand solemnly. "She kept me safe too. We worked as a team."

Michael looked a little surprised, then nodded. "Yeah, she's pretty cool," he said. Then he turned and ran back toward the school, joining his friends and classmates.

After the children were gone, Blair walked over. "It's good to have you back."

Amanda was surprised at the somewhat chilly reception from the founder. They'd never been super close, but they'd still shared quite a few quiet evenings together, talking about the kids, the mission of the program, and what Blair hoped to achieve in the future.

Blair had opened up in regard to what she missed the most about living in the US, and how eventually her plans were to return. She'd even admitted that she might consider adopting one or two orphans, but never mentioned any specific children.

But the woman who'd indulged in those intimate late-night chats didn't seem like the same one standing in front of Amanda right now, speaking in a flat tone. She seemed almost...annoyed? Which made no sense.

"I'm assuming you'll want to get cleaned up. I won't keep you. The authorities will also want to talk to you about your ordeal. Get your statement. I'll call them and make sure they know you're back." She turned to Nash. "Your friend will also be informed that you've returned. He hasn't left. He's waiting at the nearby base for some word of your whereabouts. I'm sure you'll want to join him as soon as you can. I'll arrange transportation for you."

"I'd appreciate that."

"Your things are in the storage room," Blair told Amanda. "I'm sorry, but we didn't know if you'd be back, and it was...

distressing for everyone to see your things in your room. So we moved them."

Amanda was taken aback. She hadn't been gone *that* long. And she couldn't deny that it hurt...the assumption that she wouldn't make it back.

Well, without Nash, that probably would've been her fate.

"Mandy will be coming with me to the base," Nash told Blair.

Mandy looked over at him in surprise. She was?

"Because this op was sanctioned by the vice president himself, she'll need to explain her side of what happened as soon as possible. It'll be less disruptive for the children if we do that away from here. I'm sure they wouldn't be comfortable seeing all the police and military personnel coming in and out to talk to Mandy."

"You are correct, that's probably best. And that dog won't be allowed to stay anyway. It probably has a hundred different diseases. It's not healthy to have around the children," Blair said, looking at the dog with disdain. "I have work to see to. I'm glad you're back, Amanda. Come find me when you return, and we'll discuss where we stand with your volunteer agreement, and what duties you'll take on until it's time for you to return home."

With that, Blair turned and walked toward the school.

Amanda could only stare at her in surprise.

"Wow. That was...interesting," Nash said.

Amanda nodded. "Something's wrong. She's never acted like that toward me before."

"Maybe she's overwhelmed."

"Do I really need to come with you to talk to people about what happened?"

"Do you want to stay here?"

The thought of being separated from Nash was an uncomfortable one. She'd gotten way too used to being with him. She'd have to eventually, of course, but the longer she could delay that separation the better, as far as she was concerned.

"Not really. But can I get my clothes first? I mean, it sounds as if it's all packed up already, so it shouldn't take long."

"Of course. I'll make sure that happens."

Amanda looked down at Rain, who'd stayed at Nash's side throughout her reunion with the kids, but he'd come to stand next to her once the children left. "You don't have a hundred diseases, do you, boy?" she asked quietly. She was heartsick at the thought of having to be separated from the dog who'd worked his way under her skin, in a good way.

It hurt more than she wanted to admit to hear Blair dismiss out of hand the possibility of Rain staying with her at the school. And she didn't understand the comment about "where we stand with your volunteer agreement." As far as Amanda knew, she still had three months to go. She'd been there three months already, and spent one month in the jungle. Maybe *that* was what Blair wanted to discuss? Whether her time in the jungle counted as part of her six months or not.

And she was equally confused about what "duties" she'd take on until she went home. She was here to teach. Would she not be teaching anymore? And if so, why not? What would she possibly be doing here if she wasn't spending her days with the kids?

Her mind was spinning. Something seemed way off, but she didn't have the brain bandwidth to figure it out right now. Her belly was growling and she was eager for Nash to reunite with his friend. Obi-Wan had to be just as worried about Nash as she'd been about the children.

So, reunite Nash with his teammate. Then she felt as if she could eat an entire cow all by herself, then sleep for three days straight—after spending an hour in a very hot shower, of course. But first, apparently she needed to speak to someone, explain what had happened from the day of the kidnapping and beyond.

The next few hours promised to be very busy, but Amanda blocked it all from her mind. One minute at a time. That's all she had to get through. Whatever happened would happen. Besides, Nash would be there.

It was scary how fast she'd come to rely on him to watch over her. It wasn't a bad feeling, just new. One she knew she'd have to break, because sooner rather than later, he'd go his way and she'd go hers.

As they waited for their ride to the base, Amanda closed her eyes and leaned against the man who'd been her rock. They'd met under pretty shitty circumstances, but she couldn't regret anything that had happened. Because it had brought Nash into her life. For how long, she had no idea, but she would treasure every minute she had with him, since she had first-hand knowledge that the future could change on a dime.

What she'd thought was her path in life had changed so many times in the last few weeks, months, she had no clue which direction she was going now, or even how she was going to get there.

All she could do was hang on for the bumpy ride and hope for the best.

CHAPTER TEN

The second Buck saw Obi-Wan, he grinned. His friend looked like shit. As if he hadn't slept well in weeks. Which was only fair, since Buck's sleep had been crap as well.

The man driving the car that picked them up at the orphanage hadn't said much on the way to the military base, but the second they pulled into the lot of the very building where they'd made their plans to rescue Mandy and the kids, Buck finally relaxed.

The scene at the orphanage was weird. He couldn't put his finger on what had made him so uneasy, but something wasn't right. Which was why he'd said Mandy would be coming with him back to the base. She probably didn't need to, but not only did he feel reluctant to part from her, he couldn't leave her surrounded by the somewhat hostile vibe he'd felt at that place.

And it seemed as if she felt the same way, since she'd agreed so readily. He knew if she hadn't felt something was off, she never would've wanted to be away from the children she adored. Especially the ones she'd bonded with even more deeply during their kidnapping nightmare.

"Buck!" Obi-Wan exclaimed, not hesitating to throw his arms around him and pound on his back a few times.

It felt good. Buck wasn't a man who shied away from physical displays of affection. Maybe that was because his parents hugged each other and their kids all the time while he was growing up. Or because he had a sister who had no problem showing her love by hugging him. Regardless, he returned his friend's enthusiastic greeting, then pulled back.

"You know the colonel is gonna ride your ass for that stunt, right?"

Buck winced. Yeah, he knew that. Night Stalkers weren't supposed to leave their aircrafts, yet not only had Casper done it —with disastrous results—now, so had he. "At least our chopper didn't get blown up as a result," he said with a chuckle.

"True. Laryn will be thankful, since it's bad enough she has to get Casper's new chopper up to snuff. If she had a second one to deal with at the same time, I think she'd quit on the spot. And I'm assuming this is *the* Amanda Rush?"

Turning, Buck smiled at Mandy, who'd been hanging back, giving him space to greet his friend. He held out his hand and, to his great satisfaction, she took it and let him pull her forward.

"Yes. Mandy, this is Obi-Wan, my copilot and one of the best damn chopper pilots in the world."

"Obadiah Engle," his teammate said, holding out his hand.

Mandy shook it, a small grin on her face. "I guess I know why people call you Obi-Wan."

"Yup, because I fly my choppers like they're starfighters," he teased, returning her smile.

"He really does love *Star Wars*, so that's definitely part of it, but apparently when he went to the recruiting station, the recruiter was trying to say his first name. He said, 'Obi-What?' There were other guys in there signing up, and they thought he said, 'Obi-Wan.' Two of those recruits happened to be in his basic training platoon, and they introduced him as Obi-Wan to everyone."

"It stuck," Obi-Wan said, with the same huge smile on his face. Then it faded. "Are you guys all right? I did my best to persuade the colonel here to let me do some flyovers with the FLIR to find you, but apparently that first flight we did ruffled quite a few feathers over in Venezuela. He was told if another helicopter crossed into their airspace without prior approval, it would be considered a declaration of war."

"Fuck," Buck muttered.

"Exactly. But I wasn't about to leave without you. I knew you'd make it out of that jungle, just had to give you some time. I'm sure Colonel Burgess will appreciate you not getting captured and making him have to do a shit-ton of paperwork to get your ass home," Obi-Wan told Buck.

His friend was joking, but Buck could hear the concern and worry in his voice. He clapped a hand on his shoulder. "I'm sorry," he said in a low voice. "I'm sorry I left you to deal with everything back here."

He shook his head. "Not a problem."

"And I'm sorry I forced Nash to leave you and the kids," Mandy said.

"I heard about why you ran off. Have to say, I was pissed at the time, couldn't imagine what the hell you were thinking. But after hearing the entire story, I get it."

"I put Nash in danger. I put *everyone* in danger."

Obi-Wan shrugged. "You're here now. Safe. I'd say it all worked out in the end, and that's all that matters. Sometimes the path to get where you want to be is full of twists and turns, but all that's important is that you keep going until you get there… which you did."

Buck appreciated his friend being diplomatic and not making Mandy feel worse than she already did about her actions.

"Now, I'm guessing you both want to take showers and eat.

Your room is in the same place it was, Buck, and I think they have a bunk for Amanda right down the same hall. I can meet you in the cafeteria in about an hour? Is that enough time to scrub off that jungle rot I can smell on you?" Obi-Wan asked with a grin, letting them both know he was kidding.

"Perfect."

"And there's a firepit around here somewhere, I'm sure, where we can put those clothes. I think they could probably stand up on their own at this point."

To his relief, Mandy chuckled.

"Come on. Apparently Obi-Wan's been practicing his stand-up comedy routine—don't quit your day job, buddy—and we've got a date with a hot shower." Buck still had Mandy's hand in his, and he didn't feel the least bit self-conscious about it. They'd been through an intense ordeal together, and he didn't give a shit what others thought about the obvious display of affection. He wanted Mandy to know that he was serious about seeing her when she got back to Virginia.

Besides, the thought of being separated from her was...unsettling. They'd spent every minute of every day together, except for when he checked his snares, and it felt strange to even think about being away from her now.

"Whoa, is that a *dog*?" Obi-Wan asked incredulously. "It looks like a cross between a wolf and a sloth or something."

Buck couldn't believe he'd forgotten about Rain. He'd been so excited to see and talk to Obi-Wan that he'd gotten out of the transport car and hadn't even thought about the poor dog.

Turning, he saw Rain was sitting in the middle of the parking lot right next to one of Mandy's suitcases, which they'd grabbed from storage at the school, looking a little lost.

Mandy let go of his hand and crouched down. "Come 'ere, Rain."

The dog immediately trotted over, allowing her to pet him.

"That's Rain," Buck told his copilot. "He kind of found us

when we were in the jungle. Decided we were a better choice than the asshole rebels who were obviously abusing him. And the olives we kept feeding him while they lasted didn't hurt."

"We can't leave him out here," Mandy said, sounding stressed. "He won't understand. And he might wander off, feeling rejected."

"Of course we aren't leaving him. He'll come inside with us. That won't be an issue, will it?" Buck asked his friend, communicating with him nonverbally by opening his eyes a little wider and raising a brow.

Obi-Wan immediately shook his head. "You're kind of a sensation around here, Amanda. Especially when everyone heard what you did because you thought a child was missing. If you wanted King Kong himself to move into your bunk room, I'm sure no one would say a damn word."

Buck could see Mandy visibly relax when she heard she wouldn't be separated from the dog who'd played such a huge role in their ordeal.

"He saved our lives, you know. Prevented us from being recaptured," Buck told his friend.

Now *Obi-Wan's* brow lifted.

"It's true. We were headed straight into the path of two rebels who were patrolling the border, in case their suspicions were correct and there was someone who hadn't reached the chopper. Rain pitched a fit and made us go in a different direction. He knew they were out there, and if he hadn't insisted we turn, we would've come face-to-face with those men."

"Huh. All the more reason for him to stay with you guys. I'll make sure everyone hears that story, so there're no complaints. But...and I hate to bring this up...what happens to him when we leave? Will he stay with you at the school, Amanda?"

"That's what I wanted, but I don't think Blair will approve him. I'm not sure what I'm going to do, but eventually I'm hoping to bring him home with me. I'll need to find a vet and get him paperwork, and figure out what else I need to do in order to bring him back to the States when I go."

"Lucky dog," Obi-Wan said with a small smile. "I'll see what I can find out for you. We're kinda remote here, but there has to be a veterinarian somewhere. And someone who can foster him until you leave."

"Oh, thank you so much!" Mandy gushed.

"My best friend is standing in front of me with a smile on his face and looking none the worse for the wear after his time in the rainforest. It's the least I can do for the woman who's made him look more content than I've seen him in a long time." Then Obi-Wan gave them a chin lift. "See you at the chow hall in an hour."

He headed in the direction of the main building on the small military compound, while Buck, Mandy, and Rain walked in the opposite direction, toward a smaller two-story building that served as housing when needed. Buck had grabbed Mandy's suitcase and easily carried it in one hand while holding Mandy's in the other one.

"Will we get in trouble for bringing him inside?" Mandy asked. "Do you think he'll even come in with us?"

"I think he'll go wherever you go," Buck reassured her.

Sure enough, when they got to the building and Buck opened the door, Rain trotted inside as if he hadn't lived outside his entire life. He followed Buck and Mandy up the stairs to the second floor.

"I have no idea where Obi-Wan arranged for you to stay, but I thought you could shower in my room for now. I can stay outside while you take your time."

"Thank you. I have to admit that the thought of you going one way and me going another wasn't sitting well with me. I probably shouldn't admit that, for fear it'll freak you out," she said a little sheepishly.

"Not at all. I'm having the same feelings," Buck reassured

her. It was a relief that she felt the same way he did. He wasn't sure how he was going to be able to leave her here in Guyana when he flew home to Virginia, but he'd cross that bridge when he had to.

He led them to the room he'd stayed in before leaving on the mission to rescue the children, and, after opening the door, saw that everything was exactly how he'd left it. He put her suitcase on the twin bed, then turned toward her.

As he stared at the woman standing uncertainly in the middle of his room, with the unkept and scruffy dog at her side, he felt a sense of rightness move through him. This was where his entire life had been leading him. He was thirty-seven years old and he'd yet to meet a woman he couldn't bear to be parted from. Now his future was standing six feet from him—and he made a mental vow not to screw anything up.

"Will you...will you help me with Rain?"

"Of course." Buck had no idea what she needed help with, but anything she wanted, he'd bend over backward to try to give her.

"I want to get some of the mud and gunk out of his fur, but I'm not sure how he's going to react to the shower," she said, looking down at the dog with concern.

"I'm no groomer, but I'm thinking we might need to cut some of his fur to get those mats out. Let me run and find some scissors. You can go into the bathroom and get things ready. There's one towel on the rack, or there should be at least. And I've got some soap in the shower. I'll see if I can find anyone to get us more towels."

Mandy nodded.

It didn't surprise Buck in the least that Mandy was more concerned about taking care of the dog before she got clean herself. That was simply the kind of person she was. Kind to her core. It was probably why she was such a great teacher, and why the children at the orphanage were so devoted to her.

He left the room, and returned just a few minutes later. He could've used his KA-BAR to cut some of the matted hair off the dog, if necessary, but he'd lucked out and found a Guyanese officer leaving one of the rooms who happened to have some scissors. He had no problem giving Buck a pile of towels, as well.

When Buck entered the room, he heard Mandy talking low and calmly to Rain. Telling him how much better he was going to feel once he was clean. How he'd feel like a brand-new dog. He pushed the bathroom door open...and smiled at the scene in front of him.

Mandy was sitting on the floor with Rain between her legs. She was petting the dog, and they both seemed to be enjoying the one-on-one time together.

"Got what we needed," Buck said, feeling kind of like an interloper.

As if he knew exactly how Buck felt, Rain padded over to him and leaned against his leg. Reaching down, he ruffled the fur on the dog's head. "You're not going to bite us, are you, bud?" he asked. "I mean, when we throw you in that shower and get to work scrubbing the jungle off you?"

"Of course he isn't," Mandy said with a laugh as she stood. "He's too much of a good boy to do something like that."

Buck wasn't so sure. He was pretty positive the dog had never been inside a shower stall before. "How are we going to do this?" he asked.

"Do what? Get him clean? We'll get in the shower with him and turn on the water," she said matter-of-factly.

"I hate to point this out, but that shower stall isn't very big. I'm not sure there'll be room for all three of us in there."

But Mandy simply shrugged. "We'll figure it out. I'll sit on the floor with Rain, and you can stand and direct the water."

Thank goodness the stall had a removeable showerhead. The kind with a long hose attached.

Mandy kicked off her shoes and stepped into the shower

with the rest of her clothes still on, and then turned on the water. She let out a girly screech as the cold water hit her, then giggled.

Buck could only stand there and smile. If someone had told him a month ago this was where he'd be—taking pleasure in a woman standing in his shower in dirty shorts and a T-shirt, with a grubby stray dog, while he was about to join her wearing his filthy flight suit—he would've laughed in their face. Yet, here he was. And enjoying every second.

"Okay, bring him in. The water's warm now," Mandy said.

Buck urged the suddenly unsure dog into the small enclosure, following along behind him and shutting the shower door. He was right, it was a very tight squeeze. Mandy sat on the tile floor and reached for Rain. "It's okay. I know this is scary, but you're doing such a good job. I promise this will feel good. Trust us, buddy."

Bathing Rain took much longer than Buck thought it might, but by the time they were done, he felt closer to Mandy than ever. Taking care of another living being with her was...intimate. They worked together to reassure him, to cut off the mats that were too stubborn to comb out. The amount of dirt that went down the drain was shocking.

When it was over, Rain looked like a completely different dog. His fur was actually a light golden brown, not the dark brown he'd thought it was.

Since they'd had to snip off so much hair, what was left was sticking up in every direction, kind of like Mandy's. In fact, they looked a lot alike at the moment, which made Buck chuckle. Then he had to explain to Mandy what he was laughing at. To his relief, she joined in and wasn't offended he was comparing her to the dog.

When they finally opened the door to the shower, Rain bounded out, clearly relieved his ordeal was over. He shook violently, sending droplets of water across the small bathroom.

Mandy giggled, and once again, Buck felt as if he was in an alternate world. Giggling women, a bathroom that smelled like a wet dog, now with water over every surface, and him standing completely dressed in his shower.

"I'll get him dried off and leave you to the shower," Buck told Mandy, as he stepped out of the small stall.

Without hesitation, he reached for the zipper of his flight suit. He quickly stepped out of it, leaving it in a puddle on the tiled floor. Keeping his back to the shower so he didn't alarm Mandy, considering the more-than-obvious erection tenting his tighty-whities, he took off the grubby tank he wore under the suit, grabbed a few towels from the stack on the counter, and opened the door.

Rain was quick to leave the room, and Buck followed suit.

As soon as the door shut behind him, he let out a long breath. He felt overheated, even in just his underwear. Being around Mandy was making him feel all sorts of things he'd never felt before. None of them bad, just overwhelming at the moment. Because Buck knew without a doubt his life was forever changed, and all because of the woman on the other side of the bathroom door.

"Come 'ere, Rain. Let's get you dried and comfortable. I promise I'll hurry in my shower so we can get you some grub. Something better than squirrel and olives. We'll need to get you some sort of leash and collar too. Someone around here will surely protest if you're wandering around without them. They aren't so bad though. You'll see."

Now he was doing it, talking to Rain as if the dog could understand him. But he had a feeling he just might. He had a way of staring into Buck's eyes with an otherworldly knowing.

The sound of the shower behind the door he'd just closed was enough to make his dick twitch in his underwear. Knowing Mandy was in there was torture...getting naked, letting the water sluice over her skin as she ran a washcloth over her body. But it was also gratifying. The idea he'd been able to provide her with the things she needed to feel clean again.

Buck had never really thought of himself as a protector in the strictest sense of the word. And yet he couldn't deny the sense of satisfaction he felt right now was immense.

After drying Rain as best he could, he stood in the middle of the small bunk room with his eyes closed, taking measured breaths and waiting for his turn in the shower.

They weren't on the run from anyone. Didn't have to worry about being bitten by venomous spiders or bugs in the middle of the night, and soon their bellies would be full. Things had turned out better than he ever could have hoped...

So why Buck still felt a slight sense of unease was confusing as hell.

CHAPTER ELEVEN

Amanda never wanted to leave the shower. It was literally the best shower she'd ever had in her life. She'd soaped up three times and washed her hair twice—quickly. She was now taking a couple extra minutes just to stand in the hot water with her eyes closed, enjoying the feel of not having to be on edge. She was safe. Nash was in the other room, making sure no one barged in on her. Rain was out of harm's way and clean.

Smiling, she opened her eyes and turned off the water. Nash still needed to shower, and she didn't want to make him wait any longer. She dried herself, feeling so much lighter and happier now that she wasn't covered in grime. And even more so when she was able to put on a clean pair of underwear, shorts, and a T-shirt.

She felt like a completely different person than the one she'd been a month ago, when she'd innocently been teaching a class before getting kidnapped.

She opened the door to the bathroom, expecting to see Nash waiting impatiently for his turn. Amanda should've known better. He probably wouldn't have cared *how* long she took in the shower. In fact, he wasn't waiting for her to be done at all. He was lying on the twin bed, Rain next to him, his furry little head on Nash's chest.

Both man and dog were sound asleep.

Amanda didn't want to be a voyeur, but she couldn't help staring at the man she'd spent the last two weeks with. The neatly trimmed facial hair he'd had when they'd first met was longer and scruffier. His hair was mussed, he had streaks of dirt on his face, and was wearing nothing but the tight briefs he apparently wore under his flight suit.

She felt awful for not immediately turning away or waking him up, but Amanda couldn't take her gaze from him. He'd told her that he was only five-eight, not very tall for the average man, but for a pilot, he'd explained, his height was ideal, since he could fit in even the smallest cockpits and still maneuver around. And his body was perfectly proportioned.

Except, as she'd noted in that stream in the rainforest, he'd been given *more* than his fair share when it came to what was between his legs.

Even asleep, he looked impressive. And now that she was safe, Amanda allowed herself to feel some of the things she'd pushed to the back of her mind while trekking through the jungle, hoping they weren't being hunted.

She was extremely attracted to this man. And not just physically. He was gorgeous, that was for sure, but it was more than that. It was how he talked to Rain, how he had no problem giving the stray dog some of their precious food, how he took care of her, how he put himself between her and anything that could possibly hurt her. It was his sense of humor. How much he loved his family and friends. His positive attitude. She had no idea why some woman hadn't already snatched him up.

As if he'd felt her gaze on him, Nash's eyes suddenly popped open and he caught her staring. Amanda's face immediately heated, and she did her best to pretend that she'd just come out of the bathroom. "All yours," she said, gesturing behind her. "I tried not to use all the hot water."

He grinned as if he knew she'd been ogling him. He didn't try to cover himself—why would he? He had to know how hot he was—he simply nodded and swung his legs over the side of the mattress.

"Sorry I fell asleep on you. I was just going to lie down for a moment, then Rain joined me and the next thing I knew, I was dreaming of a pile of French fries and a huge steak."

Amanda smiled. "Oh, that sounds like heaven."

"I was going to make Rain a pallet on the floor, but he had other ideas," he said, the humor easy to hear in his tone.

"He's not stupid. He might have lived his life outside, but who can pass up a comfy mattress, fluffy blankets, and a warm human to snuggle up to?" Amanda asked.

As soon as the words were out of her mouth, she realized she was really talking about herself. And all of a sudden, thoughts about the upcoming night popped into her head. It would be the first night she wasn't sleeping in Nash's arms since they'd met. She was very happy they were safe, had made it out of the jungle alive, but she wasn't as thrilled with the thought of being alone tonight. She'd never had a problem sleeping by herself before, but that was then. This was now. After everything she'd been through, being alone seemed scarier than ever.

"It won't take me long to get ready. Then we can go and grab something to eat. You think Rain will be okay in my room until we get back? We'll bring him something that hopefully he'll like better than canned olives."

"I don't know, he loved those olives," Amanda said. "And I'm sure he'll be fine. He looks perfectly willing to lie on that bed for hours. But is he even allowed to be in here? On the furniture?"

"I guarantee not one person will kick him out once they hear about what he did out there. Give me five minutes and I'll be back," Nash said.

Amanda sat on the bed after Nash disappeared into the bathroom, feeling the warmth of where he'd been lying under her thighs as she waited. Rain woke up, if he was ever really asleep, and scooted closer to her. She petted him absently as she stared into space, wrestling with her feelings toward Nash.

She was opening herself up for heartbreak, but she couldn't stop thinking about a future with him. He seemed to like her well enough, and he *had* asked her out when she got back to Virginia, but they weren't alone in the jungle anymore. She had a feeling once he got back to his routine, back amongst his friends, things would change.

She remembered Sandra Bullock in the movie *Speed*, saying something along the lines of how relationships that start under intense circumstances never last.

But oh, how she wanted to test that theory.

She was obviously sitting there lost in her own head for longer than she'd thought, because before she knew it, Nash was exiting the bathroom. And she wasn't surprised in the least that she was even more attracted to him in that instant. He smelled amazing, clean and fresh, and his beard had been neatly trimmed. The cargo pants he'd put on hugged his muscular thighs and the olive-green Army T-shirt accentuated his wide shoulders.

"Ready? I could eat a horse. Metaphorically, of course," he said with a grin.

Even his smile made Amanda want him more than she'd thought possible. "Ready!" she said as cheerfully as she could. She wasn't going to dwell on anything other than getting through the next minute at a time. Whatever happened would happen, she kept reminding herself. If Nash decided he'd rather be friends, she'd have to be okay with that. For now, she wanted to fill her belly with as much food as it could hold.

She took a moment to tell Rain to be a good boy, and that they'd be back soon with a huge plate of food for him, then she and Nash left the room to head to the small cafeteria. It was mostly empty by the time they arrived, as it was well past lunchtime, but they were each able to get a heaping tray full of food.

They ate quickly, without a lot of conversation, too intent on assuaging their hunger. Obi-Wan appeared when they were almost finished.

"What happened to an hour?" Nash joked. "Pretty sure my watch didn't break while I was in the jungle. You're late."

But Obi-Wan didn't laugh. Didn't even crack a smile.

Amanda tensed. That didn't bode well for whatever was on his mind.

"The colonel got a call from Blair Gaffney, at the school. She wants to talk to Amanda as soon as she can get back there." He glanced at her, his expression sympathetic. "Said she wasn't comfortable having you there anymore, in case the rebels decide to retaliate."

Amanda frowned, the food she'd just eaten sitting like a concrete lump in her belly. "But their objective was the kids, wasn't it?"

Obi-wan nodded. "That's what we assumed."

"There were other teachers there. Women. And they didn't take *them*. Hell, if I had run for the other door, like they did, the rebels probably wouldn't have taken me either," Amanda protested, not sure why she was arguing the point.

"Blair apparently believes they'll be upset if they learn you evaded them in the jungle, what they see as their own backyard. She thinks they might want to make a point or something. She doesn't want you to finish out your remaining months."

Obi-Wan's words weren't exactly a surprise. Not after Blair had said she wanted to talk about Amanda's agreement when they'd arrived back at the school.

She had such mixed feelings. She would miss the children terribly...but honestly, the thought of staying at the school where she'd been kidnapped, that had kicked off a horrible ordeal, wasn't exactly appealing.

"All right. What happens now?"

"You'll need to give your statement to Colonel Khan. Give him as many details as you can about what happened, what was said, descriptions of the men who took you. Then we'll take you back to the orphanage so you can talk to Blair and pick up your belongings," Obi-Wan said.

"I guess I need to get a plane ticket. Arrange to get over to the airport near the capital."

"I've already talked to our colonel back home...it's been approved for you to fly back with us."

Amanda stared at Obi-Wan. "What?"

"Since the rescue operation was officially for you, the reason we're here in the first place, you've been authorized to come back with us," Obi-Wan repeated.

Everything was happening so fast. Amanda's head was spinning. Was it just that morning she'd woken up in the jungle? "Oh, but...I haven't had a chance to make sure Rain is taken care of! To talk to a vet, to get the paperwork I need to bring him back to the States."

Obi-Wan nodded, lifting a reassuring hand. "I hope it's okay, but I've taken the liberty of getting a few balls rolling. As soon as I heard that Blair wanted you out—ungrateful bitch—I had a feeling your first concern would be for the dog...and also the kids. Colonel Khan has agreed to have some of his soldiers guard the school for the foreseeable future, in addition to Blair's increased security. To make sure the rebels don't try to take the kids a second time."

Amanda's eyes teared up. She wasn't sure why she was so emotional about everything. Maybe because it was so much change, so quickly. Or the fact that she thought she'd had another couple of months to figure out her life before heading back to the States.

Up until now, Nash hadn't said much, but his hand rested on her knee under the table, giving her support without saying a word. It felt good to have him next to her, silently giving her strength as her life spun out of control.

"Can you give us a few minutes?" Nash asked his friend.

"Of course. If you're done, I'll take your trays up," Obi-Wan said. "I'll meet you later outside the colonel's office. I want to see what I can do to speed up the process of getting Rain vetted and the necessary paperwork completed."

"Can you even do that?" Amanda couldn't help but ask.

"Watch me," Obi-Wan said with a cocky grin, before heading away from the table with their empty trays in his hands.

"Can you pack up a to-go box for us to take to Rain?" Nash called out.

Without turning, Obi-Wan lifted his chin in the affirmative, making his head tilt back, giving his copilot the answer he needed.

Nash turned in his chair and took Amanda's hands in his. "Talk to me, Rebel. Are you freaking out? What do you need from me?"

"I just...this morning we were in the jungle," she said, repeating the thought she'd had a moment before.

"Right? It feels a little surreal for sure. I'm guessing I'll have a belly ache later from all the food I just shoved down my gullet. How are you feeling about your time here being cut short? Should we fight this? Because you're a volunteer, you don't have a contract, nothing that's legally binding...but I'm sure there's *something* we can do to make Blair reconsider."

Amanda was taken aback by Nash's use of the "we" pronoun, and not "you." She'd always been independent, didn't have a choice, and it felt amazing to not be alone right now.

"Um, honestly? I think I'm ready to go. I'm going to miss the kids horribly though. I had thoughts of maybe adopting one or two. Which probably sounds crazy, considering I'll have no job when I get back to the States and I'm single. But hopefully by the time the paperwork is pushed through I'll have found a job."

"It's not crazy. It's something I have no trouble imagining."

"I really bonded with Bibi. She's only four, and she's had such a hard life already. I wanted to bring her home and show her that the world isn't the horrible place she probably thinks it is after losing her parents and being brought to the orphanage. And maybe Michael. He's older, and the chances of anyone adopting him are slim. But he's extremely smart and sweet."

"Just because you're leaving doesn't mean you can't adopt them, or any other kid," Nash said gently.

He was right. For some reason, Amanda was thinking her ability to adopt any of her students was being taken away, along with her volunteering position. But just because she was leaving, essentially being fired, didn't mean she couldn't still adopt. It might be more difficult from afar, logistically, but surely Blair and Desmond would feel more comfortable with a long-distance adoption when they personally knew the person who wanted to take in the children.

"Yeah. I'll need to think about it, but you're right."

"What about Rain, if Obi-Wan can't get the approvals necessary to bring him back right now? Will you be okay leaving him here? We'll find someone trustworthy to foster him."

"I don't have a choice, do I? I mean, it's not as if we can smuggle him across the border."

Nash raised a brow at that.

"*Can* we?"

He chuckled. "I'm not saying it would be smart, but if you're going to be crushed, go into a mental decline, hole up in your apartment and become a depressed hermit, I'll make it happen."

It was hard to believe she was chuckling after she'd just been ready to sob, but this man had a way of making her see the brighter side of things. "I really, really, really want to take him with us. I think he'd be confused and scared if he was left behind. But I understand that might not happen, so as long as we can leave him with someone who'll take care of him, not abuse him, I'll be okay with that."

"All right. And last...are you okay with coming back with us? It'll be a long trip, and flying in a chopper isn't exactly the most comfortable mode of transportation. We have an expanded fuel tank and, if needed, can refuel in flight. But again...it's not the most pleasant way to fly."

"I'm more than all right with that," Amanda reassured him. She wanted to admit that she felt more comfortable being with him and Obi-Wan than being left on her own, but decided just reassuring him that she didn't mind flying in the helicopter was enough.

"Okay. Let's go feed Rain, then meet with Colonel Khan. You can tell him your story, then we'll go back to the school so you can talk to Blair and say goodbye to the kids."

"I guess there was more to my stuff being packed up than her just not wanting the children to suffer bad memories, huh?" Amanda asked.

"Looks like it."

"I can't believe this. I really thought Blair was becoming a friend. I know she's in her seventies, and I'm not even thirty, but I still thought we clicked. Guess I was wrong. I'm ready. Let's get this done."

"If at any time you need a break, don't be afraid to speak up. The colonel can seem gruff, but he's fair and a good leader," Nash told her.

"I will."

Then Nash leaned forward and rested his forehead against hers. "I'm proud of you, Mandy. None of this has been easy, and you've held up extremely well. Just a little longer and you'll be home safe and sound, and all this will be a memory."

"All of it?" she blurted, then blushed with how desperate she sounded.

Nash eased back and put a finger under her chin, forcing her to meet his gaze. "Not all of it. In case you're wondering, my mind hasn't changed about wanting to date you when we get back to Virginia."

Relief made Amanda almost dizzy. "Mine either," she said shyly.

He smiled at her. "Good. I was afraid you might change your mind, now that we're out of the jungle and you aren't so reliant on me anymore."

He was worried that *she* would change *her* mind? Hardly. But she felt a little smidge of relief that he wasn't as sure of what was happening between them as he sometimes seemed. "Not a chance," she reassured him.

In response, he leaned forward and kissed her briefly. A mere brushing of his lips against hers, but that small touch made most of her doubts disappear. He wasn't regretting telling her he wanted to date her. Wasn't backing off to put space between them. If anything, he seemed to be doing his best to get even closer. Which Amanda was completely on board with.

"Come on, let's do this. Hopefully after your meeting with the colonel, Obi-Wan will have more info on Rain's situation."

"Will you stay with me while I'm talking to him?"

"Do you want me to?"

"Yes."

"Then I'll stay."

"Thank you." Amanda didn't like how needy she felt. How off-kilter. But for some reason, instead of feeling completely safe, as she had when they'd first arrived at the base, it now felt as if a black cloud was hanging over her head.

As she walked out of the cafeteria with Nash at her side, her hand in his, at least she felt as if she wasn't alone. Like if the sky fell in, Nash would be there to help her get out from under it. Maybe that was premature, but he'd shown himself to be someone she could not only rely on, but lean on when things went awry. She could only hope it continued, because she had the sudden idea that life wasn't done kicking her in the teeth.

CHAPTER TWELVE

"And that's why, all things considered, I think it's better if you cut your time here short and head back to the States now."

Amanda was sitting in Blair's small office at the school, listening to her explain why she was essentially firing her. It wasn't because she wasn't a good teacher, or because she didn't get along with the other staff, or because the children didn't like her. It was simply a precaution...or so she said.

But Amanda couldn't shake the feeling there was more to it than that. Blair wouldn't look her in the eyes for more than a few seconds at a time. She fidgeted and shuffled papers around as they spoke. It made no sense, and while a part of Amanda was relieved she was going home, it also felt like a slap in the face that Blair wasn't trying to get her to consider staying on...or apologizing for what she'd been through.

It wasn't as if Blair was paying her, other than room and board. She was there as a volunteer. So being fired was...weird.

Something occurred to her then. "Have you heard something the military hasn't about those men coming back?" she asked.

"Of course not. But it's better to be safe than sorry, isn't it? When they hear the American they took outsmarted them, escaped, and evaded capture as she walked back to the border, they'll probably be even more determined to come back for you."

"How would they hear about it?" Amanda asked.

"What?"

"You said *when*, not *if* they hear. How would they ever know unless someone from the school told them? And why would anyone do that? *How* would they do that?"

"Of course, I meant *if*," Blair backpedaled. "No one around here associates with dangerous people like the ones who took you."

But now that Amanda had the thought, she couldn't shake it. Was someone she worked with a spy? Were they even now informing the kidnappers that she was back? That if they wanted to get their hands on her, they'd better hurry up because she was leaving?

The hair on the back of her neck stood up, and suddenly Amanda wanted nothing more than to get the hell out of there.

This entire situation was infuriating, but she wasn't going to beg to stay where she wasn't wanted. If there was the slightest chance she could bring danger down on the school, and the kids and staff, she'd leave.

But there was one more thing she needed to discuss with Blair before she returned to Nash, who was probably getting anxious as he waited just outside the door. She'd told him she wanted to talk to Blair alone. Even though he'd been there with her when she'd told the colonel everything she could remember about her ordeal, this was something she needed to do on her own. They'd already collected her belongings and stashed them in the car he'd borrowed to drive her to the school. All that was left was for her to talk to Blair and say goodbye to the children. The latter would rip her heart out, Amanda had no doubt.

"I'd like to talk to you about adoption. Obviously the time isn't good right now, given how soon I'll be leaving, but I'm going to put in an application when I get home to Virginia. I wanted to give you a heads-up, so you aren't surprised when my paperwork comes across your desk."

"Adopt? Who?" Blair asked tersely.

Once again, Amanda was surprised at her reaction. She kind of thought she'd be thrilled. They'd talked more than once about how wonderful it would be if some of the children could be adopted. If they could somehow gain the attention of more people from the US looking to take children from other countries who needed homes and families.

"Well, Bibi and I have gotten very close. I'd love to make her my daughter, and continue to be her teacher, friend, and her mom. And I was thinking Michael, as well. I know he's older, which makes him harder to place, and he deserves a shot at a more stable life."

Blair was frowning so hard, Amanda was concerned that she might have a coronary right then and there. Every muscle in her body seemed tense, and it looked as if she might shatter if she so much as made one wrong movement.

"I see."

That was it. Just two words.

Amanda decided to let the silence play out. She refused to break it, wanting to see what Blair would do. Whether she might try to alleviate the uncomfortable atmosphere that was thick in the room.

"I'll watch for your application then."

Amanda was disappointed in the woman she'd once looked up to. She had no idea why Blair was opposed to the idea of her adopting some of the children, but it was *more* than clear by her tone that if Amanda did submit an application, Blair would likely do what she could to discredit her to whomever ultimately made the decision on the children's futures.

It made no sense. None.

But then...Amanda remembered the way Blair had held on to

Bibi when she'd returned earlier that afternoon. How she'd refused to let the girl go so she could come greet Amanda.

Did the woman want Bibi for herself? If so, why didn't she simply say so?

Amanda was more confused than ever, but for now, she was done trying to figure out why Blair was acting so strangely. She wanted to go home. Get away from the uncertainty and weird vibes she was getting from a place where she'd felt more than comfortable just a few weeks ago. Now it felt oppressive. She wondered what she'd missed before. Had it always been this way, and she'd just been too naïve to see it?

Was Blair involved in something dangerous? Was she more than simply the owner and director of the orphanage?

She shut that thought down. There was no way a seventy-two-year-old grandma-looking woman, a widow, would do anything to put the children under her care in danger. No way.

"I'm going to say goodbye to the children now," Amanda said, not asking but *telling* the other woman. "Thank you for the opportunity to volunteer. I wish you all nothing but the best. You'll be seeing my adoption application in a few weeks."

With that, Amanda stood, nodded at Blair and headed for the door with her head held high. She'd done nothing wrong, and she resented Blair for making her feel as if she was leaving under a cloud of suspicion.

She'd put herself in danger trying to help these kids. Why Blair was acting as if she was somehow the sole reason the kids were taken in the first place, and it would be better if she wasn't around, was beyond her.

The second she opened the door, Nash was there. He was frowning and looking at her in concern.

"You okay?" he asked quietly.

"No. But I will be. I want to go see the kids."

He nodded and took her hand in his, escorting her down the hall and toward the door that led outside. The kids would all be in the dorms eating by now, as classes were over for the day. After dinner, they'd have time for themselves, to play, read, whatever they wanted to do. Then they had an hour designated for homework before they were expected to do chores, bathe, and brush their teeth before going to bed.

The next thirty minutes were excruciating for Amanda. She did her best to keep a smile on her face and reassure the children that she was fine, and that they'd be fine too. She explained that she had to go home, but she loved each and every one of them. She promised to write—though she had doubts Blair would ever give her letters to the kids.

Something had changed at the school, and Amanda didn't know what. But what *hadn't* changed was the innocence of these children. It had been dinged a bit with the kidnapping, but thank goodness the outcome was ultimately positive. They'd been rescued, thanks to an empathetic vice president who'd tasked Nash and Obi-Wan with coming down to rescue them.

Amanda didn't want to think about what would've happened to them all if the VP didn't have the connection to Guyana that he did. Colonel Khan might have attempted to help, but his hands had been tied because of tense relations between Guyana and Venezuela.

She'd been lucky. As had these kids. And leaving them felt wrong. Like she was abandoning them. Which has a horrible feeling.

She was exhausted and wrung out by the time she'd finished hugging everyone. Bibi had clung to her, crying and begging her to stay...then asking to go with her. Michael had come to Amanda's rescue by peeling the little girl off her and carrying her away. The look of sadness and disappointment on his face almost had Amanda breaking down right then and there.

She walked out of the dorm holding on to her composure by a thread. By the time the car door closed behind her and Nash had the key in the ignition, the tears had already started. Refusing to look back as they drove away, Amanda sobbed.

* * *

Buck hated this. Mandy had cried uncontrollably all the way back to the base. She'd continued crying as Obi-Wan greeted them and helped him carry her stuff to the hangar where the chopper was being loaded for their departure the next day. She cried while greeting Rain, after Buck took her hand and led her back to his room.

It wasn't even a consideration that he was going to drop her off at the room she'd been assigned and leave her to cry alone. No way in hell.

She was still crying as she came out of the bathroom after getting ready for bed, changing into an oversized T-shirt that she obviously slept in. She wasn't bawling now, but her eyes were continuously leaking.

Rain had whined a few times, clearly concerned, but Buck didn't have the words to reassure him. Hell, he didn't know what to say to Mandy to help her through her sorrow. All he could do was be there for her. Let her know she wasn't alone.

The bed in his room was tiny, but then again, the places they'd slept in the jungle weren't exactly spacious. Buck got her under the sheet, then climbed in behind her, wrapping an arm around her waist and pulling her against his chest. He tucked her in close and simply held her as she continued to cry.

Rain was distressed, and he got up onto the bed with them, curling into a ball and resting his head on Mandy's feet.

"I'm sorry," she whispered.

"Shhhh. You're good," Buck told her.

"I'm just...I didn't think it would hurt so badly to say goodbye to the kids. But after all we've been through together...

I think they thought they did something wrong that made me want to leave."

"I'm sure they don't think that," he reassured her.

"The thing that hurts the most is that I have no idea what Blair will tell them. She was...so *cold*. I'm not even sure that's the right word, but it was as if I was sitting across from a total stranger in her office. And I'm guessing being able to adopt is probably out."

"Why?"

"She didn't sound receptive at all when I told her I'd be sending in an application."

"Really? That's shocking. I mean, isn't it the goal of every orphanage to get the kids adopted?"

"You'd think so. Nash?"

"Yeah, Rebel?"

"I think...I don't even like to say this out loud...but what if she had something to do with it?"

"With what?" Buck asked, not sure what she was talking about.

"The kidnapping."

Buck's first inclination was to disagree. To reassure Mandy that there was no way the seventy-two-year-old director of the school would do something so awful.

But honestly...he didn't know the woman. If Mandy thought it could be possible, he'd listen to her reasoning before forming an opinion.

"Why would she put the lives of the children in danger? And one of her staff was killed in the process. It doesn't make sense."

"I know. But the woman I talked to today was *nothing* like the one I'd gotten to know. She was emotionless. Almost...blank. And when I said I was thinking about adopting Bibi? You know, the youngest little girl? There was a look in her eyes that actually scared me. I think she wants Bibi for herself."

"So she what, arranged for over twenty kids to be kidnapped

because she was...jealous?" Buck felt Mandy stiffen against him. "I'm not disagreeing with you," he said quickly. "Just trying to understand, and playing a bit of devil's advocate. It's how my team and I prepare for missions sometimes. When we try to figure out how things might go."

"Sorry. I just...there's something else. Blair was explaining that it would be safer if I wasn't there because when the rebels hear that I was actually in the jungle, and managed to escape from them, they wouldn't be happy. They'd come back for me in retaliation or something."

"It's not an impossible scenario," Buck said rationally.

"Yeah, but she said when. Not *if* they heard, but *when*. How would they find out unless they had some connection to the school?"

It was Buck's turn to stiffen. She wasn't wrong. That *was* suspicious.

"What if she arranged for the rebels to come? To take some of the kids? It's no secret among the staff that the older kids aren't her favorite. She seems almost annoyed by them most of the time. I didn't think much about it, since she left their care to others and spent all her time with the younger ones. But the day we were taken? The older and younger classes were combined for a special art lesson. On a normal day, there only would've been eight kids in that classroom—the kids who were ten and up. Six boys and two girls."

"To what end would she arrange something like this?" Buck asked. He wasn't feeling warm and fuzzy about anything she was saying. Of course, there was no proof that Blair was involved. But he couldn't dismiss Mandy's suspicions.

"To get rid of the older kids? To make more room for younger children?"

"But kids grow up. The girls and boys she loves today will be older in a few years."

"I realize that, but...God! I don't know."

"What about you? Were you supposed to be there that day?"

"Yes. I worked mostly with the older kids."

"Then what if it wasn't the kids she was hoping to get rid of... but you?" Buck asked into the quiet of the room.

When Mandy didn't respond, he went on.

"You said yourself that she was especially fond of Bibi, but the girl had bonded with you. What if she was pissed about that? What if she arranged for the rebels to come to the school, but they were only supposed to take *you*? Or maybe you and some of the older boys, to make it look legit?"

Mandy shook her head. "They ordered me to leave with the rest of the staff. I refused."

But she sounded unsure about that...

Buck urged Mandy to roll to her back. He was hovering over her now. Her eyes were bloodshot and her cheeks were red. Her hair was once again sticking up all over the place, which he found endearing and adorable.

"Close your eyes. Think back to that day. I know it's difficult, because it was extremely chaotic. Think about what was said, what the rebels did. This time, keeping in mind your suspicions about Blair...look at the scene from a new perspective."

She did as he requested, closing her eyes and furrowing her brow as she thought back to that day.

"They burst into the room, scaring everyone half to death. They had rifles and they pointed them at all of us. They ordered the children to one side of the room and the adults to the other. Then started separating the boys from the girls. They..." She hesitated, then gasped slightly. "One came over to where I was standing with Bibi, kind of in the middle of the adults and kids. Bibi was crying and wouldn't let go of me. The man grabbed my arm and shoved us both toward the door.

"Things got crazy and confusing then, Barry tried to bum-rush one of the men and he was shot, freaking out all the kids even more. They all started screaming. The rebels seemed to panic, and they started pushing *everyone* toward the door, all the kids. The guy still had a hold of my arm. He was pulling me along, but he didn't have to bother. I went willingly. I didn't want to leave the children."

"Did they try to take any of the other volunteers?"

"No. They all ran out a side door as soon as the kids started screaming."

"And was Blair there?"

"No. But that's not unusual. She didn't teach on a daily basis. She was probably in her office in the other building."

Mandy's eyes opened, and she stared up at him. "If she did arrange the kidnapping, what now? We have no proof. Nothing to prove that I was the target, or that she wanted the older children gone for some reason."

Buck hated this. Hated that Blair had hurt Mandy's feelings by dismissing her so abruptly today. And now she'd caught on to the fact that there was potentially something really bad going on at the orphanage. That a woman she knew and trusted might have betrayed her in the worst way. But they didn't have proof, and Buck wasn't sure what, if anything, could be done about it.

"Tomorrow, we head home. I'll talk to my friends, see if we can't get someone to look into what's going on down here."

"I'm scared for the kids."

Of course she was. Buck wasn't surprised in the least that Mandy's concern was for the children she was leaving behind, and not on the possibility she'd been the target of the kidnapping in the first place.

"We'll figure this out. And if Blair did have anything to do with what happened, we'll make sure she pays for what she did," Buck said as diplomatically as he could.

"This sucks," Mandy said with a sigh.

"Yeah."

She looked up at him. "I'm better now. Thank you for getting me back here. I don't remember much about the ride from the school. I was too upset. I can go to my room. I'm sure you'd rather not have me hogging half this tiny little mattress."

"Actually, I like having you here," Buck said honestly. "And with everything you just said, I'd feel more comfortable having you near...just in case."

"You think she'd do something now? Right before we leave?"

"No clue. But I don't want to take any chances. I doubt anyone would be able to get onto the base to get to you, but we don't know what kind of connections the woman's made since she's been here."

"I'm sure I'd be fine down the hall," Mandy said quietly.

"Do you *want* to leave? Am I crowding you?" Buck asked, suddenly feeling stupid for not realizing that she might not want to be in his bed right now.

"No! I just...I don't want to be an obligation," she admitted.

Buck put his hand on her cheek and leaned down until they were almost touching, but not quite. "You aren't an obligation. Maybe at first, before I knew you, you were an *objective*. A mission. But that stopped from almost the moment I looked into your terrified eyes, and you asked about James. Seeing how worried you were for that kid, how unselfish, it changed how I thought about what you did, and what I was doing. Besides, I've gotten used to sleeping with you in my arms. I have a feeling it's going to be hard to get used to sleeping alone again."

"I don't want to leave," she said.

Buck closed the scant distance between them and kissed her. It was a light and easy kiss. Not the one he wanted to give her. But he didn't want to pressure her in any way. She was feeling vulnerable right now, and he'd be a dick to take advantage of that.

"Sleep, Rebel. We have a long day of travel tomorrow. It'll be loud, uncomfortable, and you'll be more than ready to see the backside of me and Obi-Wan by the time we get to Virginia."

"I highly doubt that," she said softly.

"Roll back onto your side, so we can both fit on this mattress," Buck ordered.

She did so immediately, and curling up against her back felt like coming home to Buck.

Rain let out a huff of annoyance and jumped off the bed onto the floor. He walked over to the pile of blankets Buck had left for him and scrunched them with his front paws until he was satisfied they were exactly how he wanted them.

"Nash?" Mandy said after a long moment.

"Yeah?"

"I'm *glad* Blair fired me. I want to go home. I don't feel safe here anymore."

His heart broke for her. "I'll get you home, Mandy. As soon as I can."

"Even though the last month has sucked, and I've been more scared than I've ever been. I've been dirty, hungry, I have more bug bites than I can count…I wouldn't change anything, because that would mean I wouldn't have met you."

It was Buck's turn to feel emotional now.

"Thank you for coming after me," she went on. "For not leaving me alone out there. For being an honorable man. For watching over me, taking care of me, protecting me. I'm not usually so helpless, I promise."

"You weren't helpless, Mandy. You were out of your element. And you could've made that time we spent in the jungle a nightmare. Instead, it felt like kind of an adventure. You make a good partner. We make a good team."

He wasn't blowing smoke up her ass either. Things had been dicey out there, but she'd done whatever he'd asked of her without hesitation. Allowing him to use his skills to keep them both safe and get them back across the border.

"And I wouldn't change anything either, because meeting you has changed my life."

He meant that. One hundred percent. He had no idea what his future held, but he really, *really* hoped it included her.

To Buck's surprise, he heard slight snoring coming from the woman in his arms.

He couldn't stop the quiet chuckle from escaping his lips. She'd literally fallen asleep in the middle of a conversation.

"I'm going to do everything in my power to make sure you never regret meeting me. From here on out, your life is going to be full of nothing but good things. I promise."

He held her, enjoying being on a comfortable bed, in an air-conditioned room, and not having to worry about someone stumbling across them in the middle of the night and holding them at gunpoint.

Tomorrow was a new day with new challenges. But the sooner he and Mandy were in the air, the better. They were starting another chapter, and he was determined to be at her side every step of the way.

CHAPTER THIRTEEN

Nash had been right. Traveling in his helicopter was nothing like flying on a commercial airplane. At first it was exciting. Amanda had never been in a helicopter, and seeing Nash and Obi-Wan do their thing behind the controls was pretty cool. But it fast became boring and uncomfortable. She didn't have her tablet, had no music to listen to. Was just sitting on a hard seat in the back of the chopper, staring into space.

But it did give her lots of time to think. About her time in Guyana. About Blair. About the kids and the kidnapping. About the time she'd spent with Nash in the jungle. All of it. All in all, Amanda decided she was a very lucky woman. Lucky in that she'd had the opportunity to do what she'd done...quit her job and come down to South America to volunteer at the school. Lucky that Nash had found her before the rebels. Lucky that he'd been able to pilfer supplies from the camp without anyone seeing him. Lucky that Rain had found them and decided to stick with them. And Lucky that Nash was the kind of man he was. There were some men out there who would've taken advantage of their situation. Not-so-honorable men who would've demanded sexual gratification in return for protection.

By the time they landed in Virginia, Amanda was more than ready to get the hell out of the helicopter though. And Rain agreed.

Looking down at the dog, Amanda felt a huge wave of relief sweep over her. Somehow, Obi-Wan and his contacts at the base had been able to get the paperwork required to get Rain into the country. A veterinarian had come to the base and given him the necessary shots and signed the papers. She had no idea how much it cost, but Obi-Wan refused to entertain any kind of suggestion that she would pay him back once they reached Virginia.

Rain was now the proud owner of a leash and collar, as well, not that he necessarily liked either. Amanda assumed it was because he'd never had to wear them. But like the even-tempered and devoted dog he'd turned out to be, he didn't attempt to remove the collar. Simply looked up at Amanda with his huge brown eyes and sighed.

When the door to the helicopter opened, they were parked on some kind of runway. Amanda could see buildings not too far away, including one that looked like the hangar the helicopter had been parked in back in Guyana.

But it was the group of people hovering around the chopper that she couldn't take her eyes off.

She assumed these were Nash's friends. His fellow pilots.

"Buck! Good to see your ugly mug!"

"'Bout time you decided to come out of the jungle and get back to work!"

"Good job on rescuing those kids!"

"Thanks for not destroying my baby."

The last was said by a woman with dark hair drawn back into a bun at the nape of her neck, who was wearing a set of coveralls. And if Amanda wasn't mistaken, she had a wrench in one of the cargo pockets along her thigh. This had to be Laryn. The mechanic.

Amanda liked her immediately. Not sure why, but she gave off a friendly vibe.

"Hey everyone! It's good to be back," Nash said with a huge smile on his face. Then he turned to her—and for some reason, Amanda internally panicked. She was usually pretty good with people. Could hold her own in a crowd. But she was much better with kids. And these were Nash's best friends. She didn't want to let him down. Her hair was probably sticking up in every direction again, she was tired from the long flight, and she would've rather met everyone when she felt more secure. She was still feeling a little...off...from everything that had happened.

But when Nash held out his hand, offering to help her down from the helicopter, she settled. He wouldn't do anything to embarrass her. Besides, from everything she knew about these men, and Laryn, they were extremely nonjudgmental. She hoped.

He let go of her hand once she had both feet on the ground, but only to turn around and reach for Rain. The dog allowed Nash to pick him up and lower him to the ground as well. He'd come a long way from the skittish animal they'd first met in the jungle. Rain looked around warily and huddled next to Amanda's leg.

Nash didn't take her hand again, but he also didn't step away from her.

"Everyone, this is Amanda Rush. Mandy. The reason we went down to Guyana in the first place. The reason those kids are all safe and healthy back at the orphanage and school she worked at."

"Hi!"

"Good to meet you."

"Glad you're all right."

"Who's the dog?"

Amanda smiled. "This is Rain. He found us in the jungle and stuck with us for the olives we could give him...and probably because he had no other place to go."

"He's adorable!" Laryn gushed, squatting down so she could be eye-to-eye with Rain. "Hey, boy! Aren't you the bestest dog in the world? You like olives, huh? I don't blame you. They're awesome!"

"Why don't you talk to *me* in that tone of voice?" the man beside her complained with a smile. "That lovey-dovey tone?"

Laryn stood and frowned at him. "Because you'd probably wonder what the hell I was doing and whether I'd lost my mind."

"She's not wrong," another man said. "I mean, it sounds perfectly normal when talking to an animal, but if she did that to you? It'd be weird."

Everyone chuckled.

Laryn stepped closer to Amanda. "Welcome home, Mandy. We're all sorry that you had to go through what you did, but those kids were lucky to have you with them."

"Thanks," Amanda said, feeling shy all over again. Out of her element.

"I've always wanted a dog," Laryn continued, her gaze going back to Rain. "A beagle. I want to name him Waffles. Don't know why, just always thought that would be a cool name for a dog. But I'm gone too much with work. It wouldn't be fair."

"I'd be happy to dog sit anytime you wanted," Amanda offered impulsively. She wasn't sure why she'd said that. She had no idea what the future held, and she'd just met this woman. It was possible they wouldn't even like each other once more time went by.

Laryn's eyes sparkled, and she looked at the man at her side. "Hear that, Tate? She said she'd dog sit."

"I'm standing right here, of course I heard her," the man said, gazing at Laryn warmly. "We'll talk about it more later. I'm Casper," he said, holding his hand out toward Amanda.

The team leader, Amanda remembered. "It's nice to meet you."

"This is Pyro, my copilot. And Chaos and Edge," he said, gesturing to the other men. "I'd tell you their real names, but you probably wouldn't remember them, and they likely wouldn't answer to them anyway since they've gone by their call signs for so long."

"Kylo Mullins, Arrow Porter, and Roman Aldrich," Amanda said without hesitation. "And you're Tate Davis. You have a twin who's a Navy SEAL. And Obi-Wan is Obadiah Engle. Nash told me all about you. Not much else to do in the jungle. And I'm good with names. Have to be as a teacher."

Everyone was gaping at her as if she'd just recited the first eight hundred numbers of pi.

"Anyone care if we stop jabberwalling out here and head inside? I want to get Mandy home."

Everyone spoke at once, apologizing and immediately starting to walk toward the large hangar. As they did, Nash leaned down and asked, "You okay?"

It reminded her of the jungle. How he was constantly checking on her. His concern felt like a warm blanket being wrapped around her after coming inside after a snowstorm.

"I'm good," she reassured him.

"They're a little much all together, but any one of them would give the shirt off his or her back if you needed it."

She nodded. From everything Nash had told her about his friends and coworkers, they were a tight group. She loved that for Nash.

Looking down at Rain, she saw his head was on a swivel, taking in his new environment. He stayed right at her side, the leash lax, not pulling, not trying to bolt at the scary sounds of people and aircraft all around him. Not for the first time, she wondered about his history. How he could be so accepting of seemingly anything. Most strays she knew were jumpy and definitely wouldn't have adjusted as well as he had. He was one-of-a-kind, and she was thankful to Obi-Wan all over again for doing what needed to be done to get him into the country without a lot of hassle.

The next hour went by in a blur for Amanda. Nash had to report to his colonel, and she was left with Laryn and Casper while he did that. She found the couple to be hilarious and kind. They picked on each other in a sweet way and were obviously madly in love. Laryn once again brought up the idea of getting a dog, but insisted it had to be the right dog. Not a designer dog, not one bought from a breeder. She wanted one that needed a home. Which endeared the woman to Amanda all the more.

Then Nash returned, and relief swept over her. Though internally, she frowned. If she was this happy to see him after he'd been gone an hour, what was it going to feel like when he left her at her apartment?

She didn't want to think about that, about how attached she'd gotten to the man…how she was so used to having him around.

She supposed it was only natural, after the experience they'd shared. He'd been her rock. He'd literally saved her life. There was no way she'd have been able to make it back to Guyana without him. And now, after spending almost every minute of every day together for so long, she'd have to watch him go back to his normal life, as if she wasn't being torn apart inside.

But she'd do it. She wouldn't do anything to make him feel guilty or bad for getting back to his usual routine. Besides, she had Rain. She wouldn't be alone. The dog would protect her, maybe not in the same way Nash had, but he'd at least alert her if something was wrong. She hoped. She was probably putting too much responsibility on the dog. But he was smart. *Very* smart. After all, he knew enough to tell them not to take the path that would've led them straight to the rebels.

"What are you thinking about so hard over there?" Nash asked, as he drove them to her apartment.

She had a lot of things to do. Needed to let her landlord

know she was back early. Get her car out of storage. Make sure all the bills had been paid properly while she'd been gone. Go grocery shopping, do laundry, find a vet for Rain so he could get examined here, register him with the city, look for a job.

All her responsibilities suddenly felt overwhelming. But she didn't want Nash to feel as if she couldn't handle herself. She was a grown-ass woman. She'd be fine.

"Just how crazy it seems that it wasn't so long ago when we were tromping through the jungle, sleeping on the ground, and eating random animals you managed to snare."

"Right? Life changes on a dime. I've learned that over my years of flying. It *is* crazy. But I've also learned to go where the wind takes me and go with the flow. Doing anything else would be like punching a brick wall. It gets you nothing but a busted hand and doesn't faze the wall in the least."

Amanda chuckled. It was a good analogy.

It felt so strange to pull into the parking area of her apartment building. It seemed like just yesterday she was leaving, and yet it also felt like a lifetime ago. She was a completely different person now than she was when she'd left. Which added to her feeling of being off balance.

Nash carried the three bags she'd brought with her to Guyana and walked her toward the entrance to her building. It was after dinnertime, and her neighbors had always been quiet, which was probably why she didn't see anyone as she led Nash up the stairs and down the hall to her door.

Putting the key in the lock felt surreal. Even though she'd done it more times than she could count, this felt like the first, because of everything she'd experienced since she'd last been there.

Nash stepped in and put her bags down just inside the door. Amanda unclipped the leash from Rain's collar and turned to look at Nash. She wanted to ask him not to go, but he probably had just as many things he needed to do as she did. And she had no idea what else to say to him, now that the time had come to say goodbye.

"I've got your number, and I'll text to see how you're doing soon."

Amanda's mouth felt dry. She was having a hard time swallowing. She nodded.

"You'll be okay?"

She nodded again.

She wanted him to tell her that he'd call her for their *date* soon. That he'd see her tomorrow, which was stupid, because they'd both probably be very busy in the next few days, weeks.

She wanted to tell him how grateful she was...how much she'd miss him...ask him not to go. But she said none of those things. Simply stared up at him, trying desperately not to cry.

Nash stepped forward and put his hand behind her neck. Her heart sped up. She wanted his kiss. Needed it.

But he didn't kiss her. Not the way she wanted him to. He simply pressed his lips against her forehead then stepped back.

Disappointment swept through her. This was it. He was going to walk out that door and forget all about the weird, impulsive woman he'd had to chase down in a freaking rainforest because she'd been stupid enough to run away from the chopper that was there to rescue her, instead of toward it.

"You're an amazing woman, Amanda Rush. I'm a better man for having met you. I'll text soon," he repeated.

And then he was gone. Leaving her in the quiet apartment feeling adrift. Lost.

And so incredibly alone.

The tears started then, and she couldn't do anything other than sink down to her butt right there in her small foyer and cry. She *hated* crying. Wasn't usually the kind of person who burst into tears at a moment's notice. But she was exhausted, could still smell the jungle on her even though she'd taken that amazing shower in Nash's room at the base in Guyana, and the sounds all around her were so different from what she'd gotten used to, it made her feel completely out of her element once again.

Rain nudged her arm, and Amanda gladly lifted it to hug the dog against her side. He licked her face as if trying to wipe away her tears, but they kept coming.

How long she sat there on the floor, Amanda didn't know, but eventually her butt went numb and she knew she needed to get herself together.

This wasn't like her. She was a strong, independent woman. Taking a deep breath, she slowly stood. Crying wasn't going to change her circumstances, and it certainly wasn't going to get her unpacked and all the other chores that needed to be done accomplished.

Looking down at Rain, who amazingly hadn't wandered off to check out his new environment, but instead had stayed right at her side, she said, "What d'ya think, boy? Want to see your new digs?"

As if he understood every word that came out of her mouth, the dog tilted his head and whined deep in his throat.

Amanda chuckled and wiped her face. "I need to figure out what I'm going to feed you. And make you a bed. And a hundred other things, but first...the grand tour."

An hour later, Amanda was lying in bed, Rain at her side—which felt amazing and reminded her of how Nash would cuddle up against her back at night. Of course, that made his absence feel all the more real, but she refused to cry again.

The vibration of her phone on her nightstand almost made her pee her pants in fright. It had been so long since she'd heard the stupid thing make any noise. It wasn't as if she'd used it much while she'd been in Guyana, and she couldn't imagine who would be texting her.

Reaching over, she picked it up and stared at the screen.

Nash.

He'd texted her. Not in a few days. But in only a few hours. Maybe he forgot to tell her that she needed to come to the Navy base for something. Maybe there was a meeting she had to go to because of the government sending the Night Stalkers down to rescue her and the kids.

Holding her breath, Amanda opened the message.

Nash: My apartment feels empty. I mean, it IS empty because I have to go to the store, but it's weird that you aren't here.

Every muscle in her body sagged. To have confirmation that she wasn't alone in how she was feeling was an incredible gift. Nash didn't have to admit that. Most men wouldn't. They wouldn't want to put themselves out there like he had for a woman he'd just met. But things between her and Nash were nothing like a *normal* relationship, thanks to everything they'd been through together.

Amanda: Same here. I have Rain, but he's currently snoring loud enough to wake the dead.
Nash: lol I can imagine. He's settling in okay though?
Amanda: Yeah. I need to get him some real dog food, although I'm sure he'd prefer he kept getting olives and fresh jungle kill.
Nash: Not exactly practical here in Norfolk...the jungle kill, that is.

This felt nice. Joking. Chatting. Reminiscing in a way.

. . .

Nash: I realized after I left that I didn't say nearly the right things. I didn't ask if you were still willing to go out on a date with me. One that didn't include sleeping in the dirt and walking in the rain. I'd like to feed you good food that I don't have to kill and skin beforehand. I didn't tell you how proud I was of you and how you handled everything. I didn't tell you how hard it was going to be for me to walk away from your apartment. I'm sorry, Rebel. I fucked up. But I couldn't leave it like that. I think I was just scared that, now that we're home, you wouldn't want to see me again. That you'd chalk up everything that happened to extraordinary circumstances and come to your senses.

Amanda was floored by what she was reading. That Nash would open himself up so willingly. He was definitely different from any other man she'd met in the past.

Nash: By the way, this is dictated. I'm not that fast of a typer on the tiny phone keyboard.

She chuckled out loud, and Rain stirred next to her. "Sorry, boy. Didn't mean to wake you up. Go back to sleep." She ran a hand down his back to soothe him, feeling his muscles relax once more. Amazingly, two seconds later, the dog was snoring once again. His ability to sleep was impressive.

Nash: Mandy? Did I freak you out? Are you regretting the decision to go out with me? Because if so, I'd never force you to do anything.

. . .

She rushed to respond.

Amanda: No! I was just feeling overly emotional at how awesome you are. I would love to go out with you sometime.
Nash: How about tomorrow?
Amanda: Yes!
Nash: I have to go into work in the morning, more AARs... after-action reviews. I have to give an in-depth report about everything that happened.
Amanda: Will you get in trouble for anything?
Nash: Doubt it. I'm a Night Stalker. We get away with shit other people don't.

At least he was honest about it. Yes, a little cocky too, but since she'd been on the receiving end of his skills, Amanda wasn't going to call him on it.

Nash: How about I pick you up around five? That should give you time to get some stuff done. I'm sure you need to get groceries and probably a million other little errands. Will that work? I want to take you to Anchor Point. It's a bar, but it has awesome food. I've been craving their fries. They're so damn good.

Amanda: Sounds perfect.

And it did. Suddenly all the fears she'd felt hanging over her were gone. She supposed she should be embarrassed that all it took was a man asking her out to make her self-esteem rise and for her world to feel right again...but Nash was no mere "man." They'd been through a hell of an experience together. Had bonded in a way she never had with anyone else. She wasn't going to beat herself up about wanting to be with him. To see him again so soon.

Nash: I feel I should probably warn you...when my team finds out that we're going to Anchor Point, they'll probably show up. Just because they love the place, and they're curious about you. If that's a deal breaker, we can go somewhere else. Or I can tell everyone to stay away.

Amanda: I'd love to see where you and your friends hang out. And I'd like to get to know them too...if you don't mind.

Nash: I don't. Thanks for being so easygoing about the possibility of them butting in on our date.

Amanda: Maybe they'll give me some dirt on you. lol

Nash: Oh jeez, now I'm rethinking going to Anchor Point. Ha! If you need anything tomorrow, shoot me a text.

Amanda: Okay.

Nash: Good night.

Amanda: Night.

She stared at the message string for a moment with a smile on her face, before putting the phone back on the small table next to her bed. It had been a long, weird day. With too many highs and lows. All of a sudden, she couldn't keep her eyes open a moment longer. Amanda took a moment to appreciate how comfortable it was being in her own bed, with her own pillow, in her own apartment, before succumbing to the exhaustion dragging her into sleep.

CHAPTER FOURTEEN

It had taken all of Buck's control not to text Mandy every hour. The clock was moving extremely slowly, and it was driving him crazy. He had a ton of stuff to do, but she was all he could think about. It felt weird to not have her at his side. They'd been so close for weeks and leaving her at her apartment was utter torture.

He hadn't said *anything* he'd wanted to say, which was why he'd sent her that long text last night. Thankfully, she still seemed to want to go out with him. He was afraid he'd blown it.

Today's meeting with Colonel Burgess had gone as expected. He wasn't happy that Buck had gone against protocol and left his chopper, but once he'd heard the circumstances, he begrudgingly accepted what he'd done. He was much more interested in hearing about the connections they'd made with the Guyanese military, and he informed Buck that the vice president had been personally calling him to find out the result of the mission.

The colonel warned that he'd probably need to report to the VP at some point, which Buck had no problem doing. It was surprising that the man had taken such a personal interest in the children and Mandy, but he was extremely grateful he had.

It was hard to admit that if he hadn't gone down to South America, he might never have met Mandy. She was almost all he could think about now. Buck felt like a teenager again with his first crush. Except his feelings toward Mandy were no mere crush. They went deeper. She felt like his other half. It was a strange thought, especially since it happened to fast...but not unwelcome.

Honestly, if Casper hadn't gotten his head out of his ass after years and realized that he and Laryn were meant to be together, Buck might be a little more reluctant to get involved with Mandy. But his team leader had put a spotlight on what the rest of them were missing out on. Yes, his circumstances were very different. Laryn almost always traveled with them when they were deployed, since, as head mechanic, she was responsible for the upkeep on the helicopters. But she still worried about Casper every time he climbed into a cockpit, whether waiting back on a naval carrier or back home in the States.

It was the respect and love the two of them had for each other that made Buck realize a true relationship was possible.

Made him more determined to see where he and Mandy could take things between them.

He had a lot of things he needed to do, but he'd put everything off to take Mandy on a date. He'd originally planned to take her someplace special. Fancy. She deserved that, after all they'd been through. But for their first date, he decided low-key might be best, and his favorite place in the world to hang out and eat was Anchor Point. It was a hole-in-the-wall joint, but as he'd told her last night, they had great food. Especially French fries. Whatever seasoning they used made them super crispy and delicious.

And, as expected, when his friends got wind that was where he was taking Mandy, they'd invited themselves along. Buck didn't really mind. He wanted Mandy to like the men he worked with as much as he wanted them to like her. It was *very* important to him that the people he loved most in the world got along, because once his fellow pilots decided you were a part of their group, that was it. You were included in their ribbing, their jokes, their dramas. It was just how they were. They worked hard, played hard, and were as loyal as could be.

So...he was going on a date with Mandy and five of his best friends. It would be comical if it wasn't so ridiculous. Buck was glad he'd warned her that they might be there, and even more relieved that she didn't mind.

He pulled up to Mandy's apartment at ten minutes to five and saw her walking outside with Rain. As soon as the dog spotted him, he whined and pulled on his leash, making Mandy glance up. The way her expression morphed from neutral to absolute happiness tugged at Buck's heartstrings. It felt good to be looked at the way she was staring at him right now.

She let go of Rain's leash, and the dog made a beeline for him, almost looking as if he was smiling as he ran. When he got to Buck, he ran a few circles around him, all the while whining in what Buck would like to think was joy. Then he lay on his back and gave Buck his belly to scratch.

Laughing, he did as he was basically ordered, squatting down and petting the exuberant dog.

"I think he's liking his new life," Mandy said dryly.

"He's settling in?" Buck asked.

"As if he's always been a spoiled rotten apartment dog," she said in the affirmative. "You wouldn't know a few weeks ago he was a skittish stray living in the jungle, afraid of men, and hyper aware of everything around him."

Buck stood. "It's because he trusts you. Knows you'd never put him in a situation that would cause him harm. And it all started with a can of olives."

Mandy smiled. "I love him so much. It's weird, because I never really saw myself having a dog, but I can't imagine him not being around. Even though he's a bed hog."

"He is?" Buck asked in surprise. "He always slept in a tiny ball when we were in the jungle."

"I know. I was shocked myself. But last night, I woke up freezing because he'd dragged the covers away from me and was lying under them, fully stretched out."

Buck laughed. "It's probably too late to make him sleep on the floor now, huh?"

"Probably," Mandy agreed. "But it might be time for me to get a bigger bed."

And just like that, Buck's thoughts went into the gutter. All he could think about was Mandy lying on a king-size bed, completely naked, waiting for him to join her. It was ridiculous, as they hadn't done more than kiss, but it was still something he wanted. Badly.

"I need to get him back upstairs and grab my purse," she said, oblivious to the carnal thoughts running through Buck's head.

"You think he'll be okay while you're gone?"

"Yeah. I've been in and out all day today, and every time I came home he was sitting by the front door, waiting patiently. Nothing was chewed up in my apartment and he hadn't peed or pooped on the floor. It's amazing, actually. And I have no idea how he knows when I'm about to walk through the door. I know he wasn't sitting there the entire time I was gone, because there was an indentation on the couch where he'd slept."

Buck shrugged as he walked next to Mandy and they made their way into the building with Rain. "The same way he knew not to take that one path, I'd guess. Instinct."

"Yeah. He's smart," Mandy agreed, reaching down to pet the dog's head.

It didn't take long for her to grab what she needed from her apartment. They said goodbye to Rain, told him to be a good boy, then headed back down to the parking lot.

"You want me to drive?" she asked, gesturing to her older-model Volvo XC60 in the lot.

"You went and got your car today? I could've helped you with that. Or one of the guys."

"I know, but it wasn't a big deal. I called a ride share and went out to the storage place. I'd paid in advance, so they gave me a refund on the time I didn't use. I needed my car and didn't want to inconvenience anyone."

"You would never be an inconvenience," Buck said sternly. "Not to me or any of my friends."

"Thank you. But honestly, it was easier for me to just go out and get it without having to wait for anyone."

Buck stopped in the middle of the parking lot and turned to Mandy. He noticed that she'd taken care with her appearance today, and it was almost like looking at a different woman, considering he'd gotten used to her without makeup, her hair sticking up in all directions, and dirt covering every inch of her body. He'd thought she was beautiful in the middle of the jungle, and she was just as beautiful all cleaned up. She was pretty because of who she was as a person, not because of her outer appearance. But he appreciated the effort all the same, because he'd gone to the same lengths she had. He'd wanted to look good for her.

Remembering what it was he'd wanted to say before getting sidetracked by her looks, Buck said, "You aren't alone anymore. I get that you felt that way before. No parents, no siblings, no close friends. But you have *me* now. And by default, you have my friends. I have no doubt they'll be your friends soon too. It would please me to help you out when you need it, just as I hope it'll make *you* happy if I ask for your assistance with something.

"I'm not taking you out tonight because I want a fling, Mandy. There's something about you that's different from any other woman I've dated. I'm excited to see where this takes us. And people who are serious about each other don't hesitate to ask for help. To reach out when they need something. And it goes both ways. I want someone I can rely on as well."

"I'd like that."

"Good. And no, to answer your question, I can drive us tonight. I promise not to keep you out too long, since we have to get back to see how Rain's doing. Even though he did good today, we probably shouldn't push our luck."

Buck was well aware he was using the "we" pronoun, as he often did with Mandy...but he didn't feel freaked out about it. It simply felt right.

"Yeah. I felt bad leaving him, but I got most of my errands done. The immediate ones, that is. At least I have food in the house now. Including dog food. I got a couple different brands just in case he didn't like one of them."

"Mandy, the dog was probably eating dirt and rotting animals when he couldn't catch a fresh one. I don't think he's gonna be picky about what kind of dog food you bought him."

"Whatever," she mumbled.

Buck chuckled. "But I'm glad you've got food again. I didn't have a chance to do any of that. Been in meetings and trying to answer everyone's questions about what went down."

"Oh, when we come back, I can send some stuff home with you so you at least have something to eat for breakfast," Mandy told him, sounding and looking alarmed that he hadn't had time to go to the store yet. Her tender heart was showing itself again.

"I wouldn't mind that," he told her, as he opened the passenger-side door of his Subaru Outback for her. She smiled at him as she sat, and he waited until she'd buckled her seat belt before closing the door and jogging around to the driver's side.

As he drove toward Anchor Point, he said, "I also wanted to let you know I called a guy I know to have him start looking into Blair."

"You did?"

"Yeah. I know you're interested in adopting Bibi and Michael, and with Blair acting weird, and with our suspicions about the raid on the school, I wanted to have him start looking into things sooner rather than later."

"Who is this guy?"

"His name is Tex. Once upon a time he was a Navy SEAL himself, and he has some crazy computer skills. Anyway, if there's something going on, he'll probably dig it up."

"Okay. But even if he does find something, it's not going to change anything now," she said reasonably.

"You're right. But if she did have anything to do with that kidnapping, you can bet I'm going to do everything in my power to get her kicked out of the country. It's not safe for the kids who are still there, or anyone working for her."

"True."

"I don't know how or what will happen, if anything, but I just wanted you to know. If there's dirt to be found, Tex will find it."

"Thank you."

"You don't have to thank me. I might not know the kids the way you do, but your actions proved your love for each and every one of them. I saw it with my own eyes, when you thought little James was missing and ran to look for him, sacrificing your own rescue in the process. I saw it when you had to say goodbye to them at the school. I heard the agony in your voice when you told me you weren't sure Blair would put in a good word to allow you to adopt."

She gave him a small smile, and Buck reached for her hand, relieved and pleased when she didn't hesitate to intertwine her fingers with his own.

"Besides," he said, wanting to lighten the mood, "if the bitch had anything to do with the hundred or so bug bites on my ass that I got from sleeping on the ground in the jungle, I need revenge."

At that, Mandy giggled.

"What? You probably don't have any on *your* ass because I protected you when we slept. All snuggled up behind you. My ass was the one out there flappin' and apparently attracting all the bloodsucking creatures of the rainforest."

Mandy giggled some more. "Right, but *you* don't have bug bites on your boobs like I do, because I was protecting your front side every night."

Immediately, Buck got hard. Thinking about her tits, and kissing each and every one of the bites she claimed to have. Shit. He needed to get himself under control. Tonight wasn't about sex. It was about sharing her with his friends. About showing her off. About getting to know her without the drama they'd endured for the last couple weeks.

"True. So we're even?" he asked.

"I don't know about that, but I'll go with it for now," she said, still smiling.

Thankfully by the time he pulled into the Anchor Point parking lot, he'd managed to get control over his libido. The lot was full, and he had to park near the back. Which was annoying, because there weren't any lights in the back part of the lot, so it would be very dark by the time they left.

He met her in front of his car, and this time, Mandy reached for *his* hand as they walked toward the door, and Buck felt on top of the world.

They joined the rest of his friends in a back corner of the bar, and they immediately did their best to make Mandy feel at ease. They wanted to know all about her, where she'd worked previously, what she was planning on doing now that she was back in Virginia, about the kids she'd taught down in Guyana, how she got into teaching...it was a little like the third degree, but done in a friendly and open way that Buck didn't think Mandy minded, considering she patiently answered their hundred-and-one questions.

They asked so many questions, in fact, she actually didn't have much time to ask any of her own in return. Something she pointed out hours later.

"I feel as if you guys know me really well now, but I don't know you at all," she complained. That was after enjoying two beers, which seemed to go straight to her head, despite the meal she'd eaten earlier. Her cheeks were flushed, and she'd run a hand through her hair several times as the evening continued, making the smooth hairdo she'd had at the beginning of the night a thing of the past. She looked more like the woman he'd gotten to know in the jungle, which pleased Buck to no end.

"You know us," Edge countered. "I'm the good-looking one, Chaos is the clumsy one, Pyro is the one with the best sense of direction, Obi-Wan is the charmer, Casper has the brains, and Buck is the all-American pretty boy."

Everyone laughed.

"What does that make me?" Laryn asked. She'd been kind of quiet, content to sit next to Casper, drinking water with her meal then nursing the same beer the last couple of hours. But Buck had no doubt she'd been observing carefully. She was protective not just of the helicopters she slaved over, but also the men who flew them.

"You're our *real* leader," Edge said wisely. "Without you, we'd be nothing."

"Damn straight," Laryn said with a grin.

Buck leaned back with satisfaction. He loved these people so much. Because of them, he loved his job, felt safe when he flew in the worst of circumstances, and he knew he could rely on them for whatever he might need. The addition of Laryn to their inner circle was a good one. She softened their sharp edges a little and offered a new perspective on the things they talked about.

"It's getting kinda late and I'm tired," Laryn announced. "I'm going to use the restroom before we head home though. Mandy, want to come with?"

"Sure."

Buck stiffened. It wasn't that he didn't want Mandy to go

with Laryn, it was more that he was unsure what she might say or do. Laryn was a tell-it-like-it-is kinda girl, and if she didn't like Mandy, she might say something that could hurt her feelings. And that was the last thing Buck wanted.

"I'll be back. I probably should get home to Rain anyway."

Buck nodded, then watched Laryn and Mandy weave their way through the crowd toward the restrooms.

"I don't understand why women have to go to the bathroom in pairs," Chaos grumbled. "I mean, they have stalls, it's not as if they can hold hands and sing kumbaya while they're pissing."

"Safety in numbers and all that," Casper said with a shrug.

"Nothing happens at Anchor Point. This is a safe bar," Pyro argued.

"No bar is completely safe," Obi-Wan argued.

"Right? The parking lot is dark as fuck," Edge agreed.

"Is Laryn going to be cool with Mandy?" Buck blurted, looking at Casper.

"Of course. Why wouldn't she?"

"It's just that she has a tendency to speak her mind. Which I love, but Mandy is still trying to acclimate back to life here in the States. Where she was in Guyana was extremely rural. And of course, there was all that time she spent in the rainforest. I just don't want her to feel—"

"Relax, Buck," Casper said. "Laryn likes her. Said she's a badass."

"She did?"

"Yup. Said anyone who can survive what she did is okay in her book. Then she said if she could put up with *your* ass for as long as she did, she has to be all right."

Everyone laughed, but Buck didn't care that they were laughing at *him*. He was simply relieved that Laryn seemed to like Mandy.

He took a deep breath then swallowed the last of his water. He'd switched over an hour ago, not because he was getting tipsy, but because he was driving and he'd never do anything that might put Mandy in danger. Also, he wanted to be fully alert in the bar's dark parking lot when they left.

"Heard you called Tex today," Chaos said, changing the subject. "He have anything to say about this Blair person?"

Buck had given his teammates a basic rundown of the situation in Guyana and what had happened when Mandy returned to the school. They were concerned, and agreed that Tex, if anyone, could probably shed some light on the situation.

"Not yet. He needs some time. He's got a shit-ton on his plate, and after what he and his wife went through recently, he's slowing down some. Says he won't stop helping people altogether, but he's trying to put a little more space between him and the assholes he comes into contact with on a daily basis."

"That was some nasty business," Edge said softly.

Everyone was silent for a moment. They'd all heard what happened to Tex. How *he'd* been kidnapped. They'd even donated money toward his ransom. Thankfully, he had more than enough friends with the necessary skills, who'd been able to immediately get to work tracking him down and figuring out who'd kidnapped him, and where he'd been taken.

"Anyway, he said he'd get back to me with what he found. Would email me anything pertinent," Buck said.

"Good. If you need anything from us, let us know," Casper said sternly. "We're a team. We stick together."

"I will. And I appreciate it."

"Nothing to appreciate. It's just how we operate," Obi-Wan told him.

"I'm headed out," Pyro said. "I'll see you guys tomorrow."

"Same," Chaos said.

"Might as well go too," Edge said as he stood.

Soon it was just Casper and Buck at the table, waiting on the women.

"Relax, Buck. They won't be too much longer. Then you can

go home and have some alone time with Mandy. Sorry we all crashed your date, but we wanted to get to know the woman you seem to be enamored with. And for the record...I like her. We all do."

Buck nodded. He didn't need his team leader's approval to date Mandy, but he was relieved he had it all the same.

He couldn't resist looking over at the hallway that led to the bathrooms. He could admit that he was anxious to do exactly as Casper suggested...spend some alone time with the woman who'd gotten under his skin.

CHAPTER FIFTEEN

Amanda was nervous.

She'd had the best time tonight. Nash's friends were hilarious, and friendly, and she felt included and welcomed by them all. It was as if she'd known them for years rather than just a few hours. She liked how they fought over who would pay for the drinks. She liked how concerned they were about Nash when they'd heard he'd run after her into the jungle. She liked how down-to-earth they all seemed.

She'd done some research about Night Stalkers earlier in the day and was more than a little impressed. After reading about these amazing pilots—who'd done their fair share of rescuing men, women, and children in the past, as well as the military men and women they transported—she was even more grateful for Nash coming to her rescue like he had.

Because who was *she*? No one. A random teacher who'd made a stupid mistake in her panic by not verifying a child was actually missing before running off. And yet he'd never made her feel bad about that. Had done everything in his power to make her feel safe. In her eyes, it wasn't his piloting skills that made him extraordinary, it was his compassion, his personality, his apparent need to serve, and his desire to protect others.

Amanda liked him. A lot. And now that they were back in the States, safe and sound, and he'd said the things he'd said to her via text, it was getting more and more difficult to hide her feelings. To hide her desire.

Hearing him say he didn't want a fling only made her need for him intensify.

Would it be stupid to throw herself at him? Probably. But even knowing that didn't make the desire for him any less. Sitting next to him in the bar, watching him with his friends, seeing him laugh, feeling his hand on her thigh, his thumb brushing back and forth as they sat next to each other...had ramped up her need for him all the more.

Nash Chaney was a good man. And she wanted him. Badly.

Yup, the night had gone extremely well. The only question mark was Laryn. Amanda liked her a lot, just as much as the first time they'd met. But she was quiet all evening, despite a razor-sharp focus. She also had an incredible ability to keep what she was thinking off her face. Amanda couldn't read her at all.

Well, except when she looked at Casper. The love she had for the man was easy to see, and her man returned it tenfold. It was beautiful.

When they got to the bathroom, they did their thing. And when they were washing their hands afterward, Laryn glanced at her and said almost casually, "Night Stalkers aren't supposed to leave their choppers."

Amanda grabbed a paper towel and turned to face her as she dried her hands. "I know. Nash told me."

"Tate did the same thing with me, but there was a Navy SEAL who would've died if he hadn't gone."

Amanda nodded. Nash had told her the story of how Laryn had gotten kidnapped out from under Casper's nose because he'd left her alone in the helicopter in Turkey, while he'd gone to help Pyro with two injured SEALs.

"For Buck to have done that, it was a big deal. A *huge* deal. He could've gotten reprimanded. Lost pay. Lost rank. There must've been something about the situation that spoke to him on a level that was unlike any other he'd been in."

"It was intense. There were kids. The rebels were coming," Amanda said. She wasn't sure what point Laryn was trying to make.

"It was stupid for you to run away."

"It was," Amanda agreed without hesitation. She wasn't offended. It *had* been stupid.

"But Buck leaving his chopper wasn't exactly smart either. So don't you go thinking you were the only one to make a mistake that day."

"Thanks. Nash admitted the same thing to me."

"Always knew he was smart," Laryn said with a small smile. "But I have to say, I'm impressed. You thought a kid was missing, and you didn't hesitate to go find him."

Amanda nodded. "I should've made sure James wasn't there before just running off."

"Maybe. It's easy to second-guess what you should've done after the fact. Tate should've made me go with him, not stay in the chopper by myself. I shouldn't have gone with him on that mission in the first place, although I don't regret it, because his instruments weren't working correctly and I managed to fix them in-flight. There are several things we each could've done differently, but we didn't, and what happened, happened."

Amanda nodded.

"I like Buck. A lot. He's like a brother to me. I don't want to see him hurt. And I know this is ridiculous, me asking you about your intentions when ultimately it's your business, and Buck's. But I've been watching over these men for years now, and I can't just turn off my concern."

"I don't mind. I'm glad he and the others have someone to look after them. I like him too. He's different from any other man I've known."

It was Laryn's turn to nod. "More intense, right?"

"Oh yeah."

"And bossy. Cocky. Protective."

"Yes, to all three. But I don't like him just because he kept me safe in the jungle. It's because of his personality. His kindness toward others. His...I don't know. Everything? All I know is that when I'm around him I feel...seen. Seen in a way I haven't been before."

"I get that. Tate makes me feel the same way. From what little I know of you so far, I like you, Mandy," Laryn said. "And I think you'll be good for Buck. I just wanted to make sure you don't have blinders on. His work is tough. They leave at a moment's notice sometimes. He might not know how long he'll be gone. He can't talk to you about where he was or what he did...top secret and all. What he does is dangerous as hell. Do you know much about Night Stalker pilots?"

"A little. I researched them today."

"Good. But that won't give you the half of it. Trust me when I say, what those men do out there is insane. The way they can maneuver their helicopters is downright scary...and impressive. Are you going to be able to handle that? Being alone a lot? Having him gone and putting himself in danger?"

"Yes," Amanda said with conviction. "I don't need a man to be happy. I've been able to function without one just fine up until now. I want to make Nash's life easier, not harder. I'll miss him like crazy when he's gone, but I trust that his skills, and those of his friends, will keep him as safe as he *can* be. And you'll be there to make sure his helicopter isn't going to fall out of the sky."

"Damn straight."

"Thank you for what you do, Laryn. Nash has spoken very

highly of you. He knows how hard he and his fellow pilots are on their machines—we talked about it a little while we were in the jungle—and he's impressed that you don't even blink when they come back from a mission with, in his words, their choppers a little banged up."

Laryn chuckled. "A little banged up? Yeah, that's one way to describe it." Then she sighed. "I'm being a bitch, aren't I? Jeez, I never wanted to be this person. What right do I have to question you about your feelings toward Buck? You're probably so irritated right now."

"I'm not," Amanda insisted. "I think it's lovely that you care about Nash enough to want to make sure I'm not just after his hot body."

Laryn laughed. "They are built, aren't they? All of them. They're the hot squad, for sure."

"Totally."

The women shared a grin.

"Right, hopefully you don't think I'm a horrible person for interfering. I want to state for the record...I'd love to hang out with you sometime without the guys around. I mean, if you want to."

"I do!" Amanda was quick to say. "I don't have a lot of friends here. I mean, I hung out with some of the teachers at the school where I used to work, but you know how it is once you leave a workplace. The people you thought were friends seem to just fade away, and you realize you weren't actually as close as you thought."

"I get that. That's happened to me as well, although probably not as much since I tend to work with mostly men. I definitely don't have a lot of female friends, and I like you. You seem pretty down-to-earth. Not like a lot of women around these parts, who just want to sleep with a sailor or soldier for the thrill of the chase or something. And don't get me started on the ones who are looking for a baby daddy they can force to pay child support for the next eighteen years."

"Ugh! There are women who do that?" Amanda asked.

"Oh yeah. It's gross."

"No wonder you wanted to make sure my intentions were good."

"Come on. Let's get back out there. I'm sure Buck is probably anxious as hell right about now."

"Why?" Amanda asked.

Laryn grinned. "Because I'm sure he wants you to himself after we all crashed his date. And he's also probably worried about what I'm telling you right now."

"Do you have juicy stories about him?"

"Oh yeah."

"Then we totally need to hang out again."

Laryn was still laughing as they exited the restroom, and Amanda saw Casper and Nash standing at the end of the hallway waiting for them.

Laryn headed straight for her man, and Amanda smiled a little shyly at Nash as she came toward him.

"Everyone else leave?" Laryn asked.

"Yup. You good?" Casper asked her.

"We're good. Great. Peachy. Right, Mandy?"

"Right," Amanda agreed, giving the other woman a sincere smile.

"Awesome. Did you tell her all sorts of embarrassing stories about us?" Casper asked.

"Whatever," Laryn said with a roll of her eyes. "We were just peeing. Come on, stud, take me home."

Whatever Casper saw in Laryn's eyes had him wrapping his arm around her waist, pulling her against his side, and leaning down to whisper in her ear as they walked quickly toward the exit. Neither said goodbye, but Amanda wasn't offended. If she had a man whispering in her ear, probably telling her all the things he wanted to do to her when they got home, she wouldn't remember to say bye to anyone else either.

"Hey," Amanda said. "Sorry if we took too long."

"You didn't. You sure you're good?"

"Of course. I'm fine. Laryn and I were just getting to know each other better."

One of Nash's eyebrows quirked upward, showing his skepticism.

"Seriously. It's good. I like her a lot. She's pretty no-nonsense, which is awesome."

"She didn't scare you away? Having our first date with all my friends didn't make you change your mind about going out with me?"

Taking a chance, Amanda stepped toward Nash, right into his personal space. His arms immediately went around her, holding her against him. "No way. You're stuck with me, Nash. For as long as you want me."

"That's good, because I'm gonna want you for a very long time."

Amanda could feel his erection against her belly, and all the desire she'd been attempting to control swept over her in a rush. Her nipples hardened, goose bumps broke out on her arms, and she leaned into him a little more. They stared at each other for a long moment before his head lowered.

He kissed her. Right there in Anchor Point. It was as if they were the only two people on the planet. Arcs of electricity shot from her lips straight down between her legs. Amanda shifted in his arms, wanting more. Needing—

"Get a room!" someone yelled, then laughed.

Amanda jerked.

"Easy," Nash soothed. Then turned his head and yelled, "Fuck off!"

Amanda couldn't help but giggle. He sounded so put out. She wasn't exactly thrilled to have one of the best kisses of her life interrupted, but she also wasn't ready to entertain the entire bar with their make-out session either.

"Come on, let's get you out of here," Nash said. He turned her so she was against his side and headed for the door. When they got outside it was pitch dark, and Amanda didn't see Casper or Laryn around. How long had they been kissing anyway?

Nash led her to his car and opened the door for her. Once she was inside and settled, he shut it and went around to the other side. They were on their way in moments. Licking her lips, Amanda could still taste Nash on them. Her arousal had dimmed a bit, but it quickly ramped right back up.

"You want to come in and check on Rain with me when we get back to my place?"

"Sure," he said without hesitation.

Amanda decided she was a grown-ass adult and she shouldn't beat around the bush. She just needed to say what she wanted. "And since you didn't get to the store today, and I did, how about instead of me sending something home with you for breakfast, you just stay and eat with me in the morning?"

She held her breath as she waited for his response.

"Be clear about what you're asking, Mandy," Nash said seriously. "I don't want there to be any misunderstandings between us."

"I want you," she blurted, with more confidence than she was feeling. "I missed you last night. The feel of you sleeping against my back. But it's more than that. I want *all* of you, Nash. I want to feel your bare skin against mine. I want to feel you so deep inside that I can't tell where you stop and I start. I want everything."

The look he gave her was so intense, so full of desire, it was all Amanda could do not to jump him right there in the car.

But he didn't say anything. Simply turned his attention back to the road...which was kind of freaking her out.

Until she noticed his white knuckles, the way a muscle in his jaw was ticking, and the erection in his pants.

"Nash?" she said quietly. "Too much too soon?"

"No," he replied, the word deep and grumbly. "I'm just trying really hard not to blow my load in my pants right now."

She smiled, feeling relief course through her veins. "So you'll stay?"

"Oh, I'm staying," he said firmly. "And I'm going to give you *everything*. You won't regret this, I promise."

"Of course I won't," Amanda told him.

The drive back to her place didn't take nearly as long as it did to get to the bar. At least it felt that way. Neither said much, simply enjoyed the anticipation of what was to come. Literally.

Nash parked and said, "I'll come around." Then in seconds, he was opening her door. He took her hand and held it tightly as he practically ran toward her apartment building.

"We have to take Rain outside so he can pee," she said, more to remind herself so she wouldn't immediately jump Nash the second they got inside her apartment.

"I know. I'll do it. It's dark out. Not safe."

Nash's sentences were short and succinct, as if he was hanging on to his control by a thread. It was empowering to shake this man enough that he could barely get full sentences out. It felt amazing.

When she opened her apartment door, Rain was once again sitting in the small foyer waiting for her to return.

"Hey, boy," she said happily.

His tail wagged furiously behind him, but it wasn't until she crouched and said, "Come 'ere," that he moved. Rain bounced forward, almost knocking Amanda over with his exuberance.

"He seems relieved that I came back," Amanda said, as she did her best to not get licked to death. The dog with her now was a completely different animal than the terrified one they'd first encountered in the jungle. It was amazing how a little love could have such a profound impact.

Rain turned from her to greet Nash. Not quite as enthusiastically, but his tail was wagging just as fast. "You need to go potty? Come on, let's go," Nash said, reaching for the leash Amanda had hung on a peg next to the door. It was obvious he was in a hurry to get the dog's needs seen to, but then again, Amanda was just as eager to have him return as well.

"You want a snack or something?" she asked before he left.

"I want a snack all right," he said. "You. I'll be back soon."

Amanda shivered at the promise in his voice. As soon as the door shut behind them, she turned and hurried to her bedroom. This wasn't how she saw the night ending when she'd agreed to go out with Nash, but she wasn't sorry. Not in the least. She just hoped the sex would live up to both their expectations.

CHAPTER SIXTEEN

Buck had never been so hard in his life. It felt as if his dick was going to snap off inside his pants. He couldn't believe Mandy had invited him to stay the night. It was a dream come true, and he couldn't wait to get back inside her apartment and finally do all the things he'd fantasized about.

He had no idea what she and Laryn had talked about in the bathroom, and ultimately he didn't care, as long as it didn't result in Mandy pulling away. But apparently, whatever had been said resulted in the opposite. For which he was more than grateful.

He hadn't lied when he'd texted her last night. His apartment felt extremely empty. And he hadn't slept well at all. It was amazing how fast he'd gotten used to sleeping with her in his arms.

Looking down at Rain, who was taking his dear sweet time finding a place to piss, Buck thought about how fast he'd gotten to this point in his relationship with Mandy. He hadn't dated anyone in a long while. He'd had a couple of one-night stands in the last few years, but of course, they'd lacked any kind of connection, which made them awkward and unsatisfactory.

Being with Mandy was going to blow his mind. He knew that

without a doubt. She'd gotten under his skin in the best way, and he couldn't wait to show her how important she'd become to him in such a short time.

Finally, Rain did his business and immediately turned back to the door of the building. He really was a smart dog, and Buck was more than pleased things had worked out with him being able to come back to the States with Mandy.

He took the stairs at a jog and was back at her apartment in a flash. "You're going to be good tonight, right?" he asked the dog before he opened the door. "Sleep on the floor and not horn in on my woman?"

Of course Rain didn't answer, but the look of adoration on his furry face anytime he looked at Mandy didn't bode well for Nash getting the bed—and Mandy—to himself. He didn't care if he had to share the bed with the dog, as long as it didn't hinder his ability to show Mandy how much he appreciated her making the first move in asking him to stay the night.

"Mandy?" he called out, once he'd locked the door.

"I'm back here in my room. Last door on the left!" she shouted.

Buck's cock throbbed in his jeans. Fuck, he wanted this woman. His skin felt too tight and his clothes extremely irritating. All he wanted was to strip naked and take Mandy fast and hard. But he'd go at whatever speed she needed. The last thing he wanted to do was freak her out. Scare her with his intensity in the bedroom.

To his relief, Rain padded over to a pile of blankets in the corner of the living area and got to work scrunching them into whatever he deemed to be acceptable in order to sleep.

Buck quickly walked down the hall toward Mandy's bedroom, not sure what to expect when he got there.

What he saw endeared her to him all the more.

She was standing next to the bed, looking uncertain and shy. She had on a tank top and a pair of panties, and that was it. Her hair was once more sticking up on one side, and she'd removed the makeup she'd put on for their date. She looked much more like the woman he'd gotten to know in the jungle at that moment.

The only light came from the lamp on the small table next to her queen-size bed, so the room was dim but not dark, which was a relief, because Buck wanted to see her. All of her. Every remarkable inch.

She was slender, a little on the skinny side after their time in the rainforest, but he could fix that with some good nutritious, hearty meals. Her tits were proportionate to her small frame, with the cutest damn nipples he'd ever seen. How could nipples be cute? He had no idea, but hers were. Her white panties allowed him to see that her pubic hair was trimmed but not shaved, which he actually preferred over the bare look.

His hands went to his shirt without thought, ripping it over his head and discarding it carelessly to the floor. He wanted to strip completely naked and tackle Mandy, but that would surely scare the crap out of her.

"How do you need me tonight?" he asked, barely recognizing his own lust-filled voice.

"I don't understand the question," she said, with a small tilt of her head.

"You want slow and romantic. Lots of kissing, caressing, tender words? You want to be in control? Do you want fast and hard? Me getting inside you as quickly as I can—after making sure you can take me without pain, of course—and fucking you until we both see stars? I want to make this good for you, Mandy, and until I know your preferences, what you like, I need you to talk to me. Tell me what you want from me."

She licked her lips, making them shine, and all Buck could think about was how they'd look sucking his cock. He was dripping now, more than ready to be inside her. She was going to blow his mind, of that he had no doubt.

"I don't know *what* I want, or how. All I know is that I want you more than air to breathe. More than food in my belly. More than anything. And I'll take you however I can get you. Slow and romantic, fast and hard. I'm not scared of you, Nash. Of this. I'd like for you to take control this first time. It'll take the pressure off of me. Tell me what to do. What *you* want."

Oh man, she had no idea what she'd just unleashed.

"If at any time you need to slow down, all you have to do is say the word. I'll stop immediately. If you simply want to cuddle like we did in the jungle, that's good too. I'm in this for the long haul, as I already told you. We don't have to do anything tonight other than reconnect, now that we're safe and comfortable."

"I don't want to just cuddle," she said, sounding a little exasperated. "I want you to fuck me, Nash. I need you."

"Take off your tank and underwear," he ground out, feeling as if he was two seconds away from exploding.

She moved without hesitation, pulling the tight material up and over her head, then shoving the scrap of cotton hiding her sex from him down her legs. She stood there, looking a little nervous, but with her chin up. Like the sex goddess she was to him.

Buck moved quickly, toeing off his sneakers, shoving his own pants and boxers off, then reaching down to remove his socks. And then he was as naked as she was. They both took each other in, and Buck swore he was drooling.

Mandy was the most beautiful woman he'd ever seen. And not just her physical beauty. But because she'd asked for what she wanted. Because she was willing to put her trust in him. Because she obviously wanted him just as badly as he wanted her.

"Should I get on the bed?" she asked softly.

"No. Stay right there."

Buck took a few steps forward until he was right in front of her, then he went to his knees. Looking up, he saw the confusion on her face, but as soon as he touched her, put his hands on her hips and eased them around to cup her ass, the confusion immediately morphed into desire.

"Nash," she whispered.

Damn, he loved the way his name sounded on her lips. All breathy and needy.

He licked his lips, needing to taste her. To imprint her scent, her touch, her flavor on his very soul. "I'm going to devour you, Mandy. Turn you inside out, just as you've done to me. I've never met anyone like you and never will again. I'm not going to screw this up. I promise."

"I know you aren't," she said, resting her hand on his head and staring down at him with such tenderness, such…dare he say it…love, that it made a shiver go from his head to his toes.

Then he was done talking.

Buck tightened his grip on her ass cheeks and pulled her forward at the same time he lowered his head. His tongue ran up her slit, parting her, ending at her clit, which he immediately latched onto and sucked. Hard.

She bucked in his grasp, a little squeak leaving her lips as the hand on his head tightened, and her other went to his shoulder to hold on.

He wanted to say, "That's right, Rebel, hold on tight," but his mouth was otherwise occupied.

She tasted divine, and he immediately felt drunk. Immediately needed more. Needed to make her come and drink from the source.

As he feasted on her pussy, Buck experimented. Figuring out what turned her on the most. Every woman was different, and he loved learning what set *his* woman off. He roughly shoved one leg to the side, widening her stance. It put her a little off balance, and she used both hands to hold on to his shoulders now.

Her fingernails dug into his skin, and the slight pain turned him on even more. Buck looked up as he used his tongue as a vibrator on her clit, and the sight of her lost in her own desire made his cock jerk. Her nipples were hard as little rocks, and her upper chest was flushed a bright pink. Her head was thrown back, and she was breathing in short, panting breaths as he brought her closer and closer to the edge.

But he needed her eyes on him. Needed her to see who was making her feel this way.

"Eyes on me," he ordered gruffly.

She immediately complied, lowering her head and staring down at him. Buck deliberately stuck his tongue out and licked her once more, loving how she shivered in reaction. He moved one of his hands around so he could slowly insert his index finger inside her body as he concentrated on her clit. She was tight but dripping wet, soaking his finger down to the knuckle as he fucked her slow and steady.

"Nash!" she moaned, as she began to writhe against his finger.

This was how he wanted her. Out of her mind with desire. Only thinking about one thing. Well...two—him, and her approaching orgasm. He intended to push her over the edge as many times as he could. He wanted, *needed*, to see her lost in mindless pleasure over and over. Reduced to an elemental state of nothing but endorphins and the need for more.

He held her tightly as she jerked and moved against his finger, and as she began to shake, Buck flicked her clit harder and faster, memorizing what kind of pressure she needed to come. It didn't take long, which was a huge turn-on. Then he felt her orgasm on his tongue and all around his finger, buried deep inside her body.

She was still coming when he abruptly stood, picking her and throwing her onto the mattress. She let out an *umph* when she landed, but immediately reached for him, making Buck's lust rise even higher.

Since she was so much smaller than him, Nash had no problem positioning her any way he wanted. He turned her onto her belly, then grabbed her hips, forcing her to her knees. He buried his face into her pussy from behind, loving how she immediately cried out once more and widened her stance, giving him consent and more room to work. Her chest was lying on the mattress and her ass was in the air. It was carnal and hot as fuck, and Buck was out of his mind with need for this woman.

Thoughts of taking her this way were overwhelming, but he didn't want that tonight. He wanted to look into her eyes and see everything she was thinking and feeling when his cock breached her pussy for the first time. It would be everything... and he wanted to be connected to her emotionally when it happened.

His life was changing with every second that passed. With every lick, every suck, every moan, she was imprinting on his very soul. He already knew he couldn't live without her. Couldn't do what he did without knowing she was at home waiting for him. He was moving too fast, but fuck it. He didn't care.

"Nash, I need..." Her voice trailed off.

But her words were just what he needed to get control of his overpowering lust. "What do you need? Tell me, Rebel. I'll do whatever you want."

"You. I need *you*."

"You've got me. Be more specific," he urged. He was being extra controlling, but he couldn't help it.

"Fuck me, Nash! I want you inside me."

He moved her before his brain even processed what she'd said. She was on her back and he was hovering over her. She made him feel ten feet tall. He'd never been the biggest guy growing up, had been made fun of for his height time and again. But tonight, as he covered Mandy's small five-foot frame, he'd never felt more masculine. More like a man.

Just as he was about to ease into her, enter fucking paradise, he remembered.

"Damn it. Hang on," he panted, as he abruptly pulled back and leaped off the bed.

Mandy rose to an elbow and stared at him in confusion. "What are you doing?"

"Condom," he bit out, frantically searching his pants for his wallet. He found it, retrieved the condom, then dropped his wallet without thinking twice about it, ripping open the packet with his teeth. It was almost physically painful to touch his cock when it was so hard, but he rolled the damn rubber down his length and immediately climbed onto the bed.

"I've got the shot," she informed him when he'd returned.

Hearing that made Buck's cock even harder, if that was possible. "That's great, but I'm using a condom until I can prove to you that I don't have any diseases or infections."

"I trust you, Nash."

"And you have no idea what that means to me. Your trust. But I'm still using it."

"Do you not trust *me*? I haven't been with anyone in years," she said, a little uncertainly.

He was fucking this up. They should've had this conversation before things between them had gone this far. He leaned down and took her face in his hands. "I trust you," he told her firmly. "I just want to prove to you that I'm the man you think I am."

"I know who you are," she said softly, reaching up and holding his wrists. "You're the man I'm falling in love with."

"Fuck," he breathed, her words spearing him straight in the heart. She was so damn brave. Putting herself out there like that. He wanted to return the words, but his throat was too tight. He was barely hanging on to his control. He was going to come like a teenager if he didn't get a handle on the situation.

One hand moved to brace himself on the mattress over her, and the other went to his cock. He gripped it tightly at the base, stopping his immediate need to come. "Spread your legs. Wider, Mandy. Open up for me. Let me in."

She did so immediately, ramping up his lust. Running his cock through her soaking-wet folds, he lined them up, then pushed just the mushroomed head of his dick inside her. It felt amazing. So damn tight. It took all his control not to shove the rest of himself in on a single thrust.

Mandy wasn't looking at him, her gaze was locked between their legs, where they were barely joined. He loved seeing the lust in her eyes, but wanted her to be looking at *him*.

He moved his free hand to her face and tilted her head upward until he could meet her gaze. "See who's about to be inside you, Mandy. The person who'd move heaven and earth to make you happy. Who will do whatever it takes to satisfy you."

"I see you, Nash."

And she did. She kept her gaze locked on him as he very slowly pushed inside her tight sheath.

They both moaned when he finally bottomed out inside her.

Fuck, she felt incredible. Her muscles twitched all around him, giving him a crushing hug from the inside. He couldn't move. Didn't *want* to move. Wanted to live right here for the rest of his life...which would make things extremely awkward for sure. But he'd never felt anything so all-consuming. It was overwhelming and almost scary.

Mandy seemed to know he was having a moment, because her arms went around him and she caressed his back, from his ass to his shoulders, as he struggled to overcome his intense emotions.

Eventually, his body's needs won out over his feelings. He moved his hips back, then sank into her body once more. It felt amazing. *She* felt amazing.

Buck propped himself over her with both hands and, keeping his gaze locked on hers, began to move harder and faster. Each thrust feeling more like coming home than the last. She was smiling gently at him, but he wanted her as lost in emotions as he was. Sure, she was obviously enjoying this, but he needed her to feel like she had a little bit ago. Thinking about nothing but getting off and doing anything and everything she could to get there.

He thrust into her harder than before, and was rewarded by a gasp. "You like that?"

"Uh-huh."

"You want more?"

"Uh-huh!"

He gave her what she wanted. Buck began to pound into her, afraid at first that he was hurting her, but quickly realizing she was loving his enthusiastic thrusts. But she wasn't mindless. Not yet.

Concentrating on what she needed to come was helping him hold off his orgasm. She would always come first. In more ways than one.

Shifting, he sat up on his knees, pulling her with him until she was straddling him.

"Nash!" she exclaimed, grabbing at him to stay upright.

But he had her. She wasn't going to fall on his watch. He couldn't thrust as well in this position, but he could reach her clit better. He immediately found it, strumming it roughly. Mandy began to squirm and gasp. Leaning forward, Buck took one of her nipples into his mouth and sucked hard.

That did it. She began to writhe against him, riding him as best she could in his tight hold. He felt her orgasm starting. It was more erotic than what he'd done earlier. Better than feeling it against his finger. He wanted to experience this every day.

"That's it, come for me, Rebel. Come all over my cock. Give it to me."

And she did. Squeezing him so hard it was painful, but in the best way. Her orgasm immediately triggered his own. He exploded into the condom, feeling as if he'd been wrung inside out. He'd never felt such a powerful release before. He was addicted to the woman still trembling in his lap.

He eased her onto her back, pulling his semi-hard cock out of her as he moved. He hated to leave the warmth of her body, but he was going to negate the purpose of the condom.

Mandy looked sated and relaxed, but he wasn't done with her. His hand went between her legs once more, and her gaze immediately flew to his as he began to lightly flick her clit.

"Nash?"

"One more, Mandy. I need one more."

"I don't think I can."

"Yes, you can. I know it."

She didn't look so sure, but she didn't pull away. Didn't tell him to fuck off. So he continued. The sight of her juices coming out of her cunt was erotic as hell. He'd done that. *He'd* turned her on so much that she was dripping. He couldn't wait until he could watch his come mixed with her own leaking out of her body.

It didn't take much to set her off again. She was very sensitive now, and he didn't need such a rough touch to make her thighs start shaking and her heart rate soar once again. Buck loved learning how to satisfy her. What she needed. It was a heady feeling knowing he could control her passion like this. He vowed never to use the knowledge against her though. Only for her pleasure.

When she went over the edge this time, it wasn't as explosive as before, but it was no less satisfying to watch.

"Enough!" she begged, when he was still stroking her slowly after she'd finished shaking.

Buck immediately moved his hand, resting it on one of her tits, loving how his palm covered the entire thing, the way her nipple was still hard and pressing against his skin.

He leaned over her, resting on his side, their bodies touching from hip to chest. He fingered a lock of her bed-head hair tenderly as he stared down at her, waiting for her to recover and open her eyes.

When she did, the love he saw there was humbling. And scary. Because Buck wasn't sure he deserved it. Deserved *her*.

"Hi," she said a little shyly.

Which was cute as fuck.

"Hi," he returned. "You good?"

"I'm perfect."

"It wasn't too much? *I* wasn't too...much?" he asked, feeling uncertain. The sex had been the best he'd ever had, hands down, but he wasn't sure where she stood.

"It was perfect," she breathed.

Buck relaxed. Thank fuck.

"I'm going to go check on Rain, get rid of this condom. Don't move. I'll be right back."

"I don't think I could move if my life depended on it," she mumbled.

Buck was grinning as he reluctantly got off the mattress. Walking butt naked into the bathroom, he did what he needed to do, then quickly looked into the living area. Rain was snoring loudly on the pile of blankets in the corner.

Returning to the bedroom, Buck saw that Mandy had indeed moved. She'd pulled a sheet up and over her body, which was a disappointment, but he understood. They were still new to each other. He didn't comment on it, just crawled under the sheet with her. She turned onto her side, and he immediately cuddled up behind her, as they'd done for so many nights in the jungle. There was something so right about the position. About being here with her like this.

They were silent for several moments before Buck whispered, "I'm falling in love with you too." He hadn't been able to speak when she'd said the same words before, but he needed her to know how he felt.

She squeezed the arm that was around her waist and sighed with contentment.

At least, that's what he hoped she was feeling.

"Thanks for being here. For not freaking out when I asked you to stay over."

"Why would I freak out when it's what I wanted too? I'm glad you were brave enough to say what you wanted, because we're here as a result."

A few minutes later, he heard her breaths deepen, and he was content to simply lie there and hold her as she slept. His life had changed for the better, and he'd never be so glad in his life that he'd been the one to volunteer to go to Guyana for the mission.

Soon, Buck heard the sound of toenails on the laminate floor. Rain came into the bedroom and jumped onto the bed. He did a few circles at their feet before lying down with a huge sigh.

Buck could only smile and be thankful the dog had waited until they were done with their sexy times before coming in. He truly didn't mind Rain being on the bed; after all the dog had done for them and how hard his life had been, he deserved the best they could give him. But Buck drew the line at him being there when they were making love.

He fell asleep feeling more relaxed and satisfied than he'd ever been. Life was good, and would hopefully only get better with Mandy at his side.

CHAPTER SEVENTEEN

Amanda was on top of the world. She didn't have her life figured out, but having Nash in it was a bonus she'd never expected to enjoy when she'd made the decision to go to Guyana. A week had gone by since their return, and she and Nash had settled into a comfortable routine quite easily. He'd been sleeping at her apartment most nights, because of Rain, but she and the dog had gone over to his place one night as well.

It was as if they'd known each other all their lives. He was comfortable to be around and was always looking after her. He made breakfast for them every morning, and even though he had to get up early to go to the base to work out with his team, and for meetings of one kind or another, she'd always been a morning person so it wasn't a big deal to get up when he did.

Sleeping with him—actually sleeping—was amazing as well. He was just as much a cuddler now as he'd been in the jungle. Having him at her back while she slept was a comfort Amanda didn't know she needed or wanted.

And the sex? Yeah, that was a big perk.

She supposed it shouldn't be a surprise that Nash was pretty dominant in bed. He moved her where he wanted her, did what he wanted to her, and seemed to have a thing for making her orgasm over and over. Not that it was a hardship in the least. But he always made sure she was with him all the way, and that he wasn't doing anything to hurt her or that she didn't want.

The most surprising thing was how much Amanda enjoyed letting him take charge. Not having to think about how to position herself, or wonder whether or not Nash might like something, was a freedom she hadn't expected. It allowed her to simply feel, to enjoy the sensations he brought forth, and she could be more in the moment with him.

But he also didn't expect sex every night, which was nice. Some nights all they did was watch TV then curl up together in bed and talk about nothing and everything. It reminded her of the jungle, how they'd talk to pass the time.

And he was great with Rain, volunteering to take him out to do his business, and he'd even taken time off to go to the vet with her to get him checked over. They'd learned the dog was in surprisingly good condition for being a stray from the jungle. The vet guessed him to be around three years old. He was underweight, but not dangerously so, thanks to the nutritious food Amanda had been feeding him.

While Nash went to the naval base every day, Amanda spent her time researching options for upgrading her teaching certificate to include younger grades, and emailing some of the contacts she had for schools in the area about possible job openings. But it was the wrong time of year for hiring, most schools already had all the teachers they needed, which wasn't exactly a surprise but kind of frustrating all the same. She couldn't live off her savings forever.

That morning, Nash had woken her with his head between her legs, eating her out to a monster orgasm before grinning like a loon and casually walking toward the bathroom with a huge hard-on, which he refused to let her do anything about, saying he'd take care of it in the shower because he wanted her to get more sleep. Now, with Nash at work, Amanda was sitting at her small kitchen table, back in front of her laptop.

Once again, she was researching the best way to get her credentials to teach younger grades...when Rain's head suddenly came up off the dog bed that Nash had brought home one day, saying he needed something better than blankets on the floor.

The dog growled low in his throat, a sound Amanda had only heard one other time—when she and Nash were in the jungle, and Rain was trying to prevent them from going down the path that would lead to the rebels.

Surprised, she looked at Rain. He'd left his comfy bed and was now standing between her and the foyer, staring at the door and still growling.

"Rain? Come here," Amanda said.

The dog wouldn't budge.

The hair on the back of Amanda's neck rose. She had no idea what Rain sensed, but it couldn't be good if he was acting like this. She stood and hesitated, not sure what to do.

A second later, there was a loud pounding at the door.

Amanda jumped, the sound scaring the crap out of her.

Rain barked. A deep sound that startled Amanda almost as much as the knocking. She'd never heard Rain bark. Not once. The fact that he was doing it now wasn't exactly a comfort.

"Amanda Rush? Open the door. DEA. We have a warrant."

What the heck?! DEA? A warrant? Amanda was so confused. But the man pounding on her door obviously wasn't going away. And she certainly had nothing to hide. She would've thought they had the wrong apartment altogether, except the man had specifically said her name.

She quickly hurried to the door, grabbing Rain's leash on a hook next to where she hung her keys and purse every time she walked into the apartment. She quickly attached it to his collar and took a deep breath before unbolting and opening the door.

Three men immediately pushed inside the small foyer, forcing Amanda to take several steps back to give them room.

Rain alternated between barking and growling menacingly.

"Keep your dog under control or we'll have to remove the threat," one of the other men said firmly.

Shocked that this was happening, Amanda backed against the wall and kept a tight hold on Rain's leash. Two of the men walked past her into her apartment without a second glance and the third thrust a piece of paper toward her.

"Search warrant. We've received a tip that there's a large quantity of cocaine in this apartment. That it was brought into the country recently. You've been working and living in South America, correct?"

"Um, yeah. Guyana. But I didn't bring any drugs back with me. I don't do drugs," Amanda protested.

"The information was credible, and in light of where you've spent the last few months, that's why the judge approved the warrant. If there's anything here, we'll find it. Please step outside and let us do our job."

Amanda was so confused and scared. Nothing like this had ever happened to her before. She held the warrant in her hand as she was escorted to the door. She had no idea what her rights were in this situation. Could she say no? Could she refuse to let them look through her stuff? She had nothing to hide, but she felt violated all the same.

"Can I have my phone?" she asked, as she stood in the hallway of her apartment building, trying to ignore the way the neighbors—the few around at this time of day—were peering out of their doors, attempting to see what was going on.

"Not right now," the agent said. He didn't close her door, just turned his back on her without a second glance.

Looking down, Amanda was embarrassed that she was still wearing her pajamas. The oversized shirt she usually wore to bed and a pair of ratty old sweats she'd pulled on when she'd gotten up. She was decently covered, but barefoot and braless, and she felt exposed and judged by both her neighbors and the three men who thought she was some kind of drug dealer.

She was left in her hallway for over an hour as the men searched her entire apartment. Eventually, she and Rain sat on the cold concrete while waiting for the agents to finish. Rain had stopped growling and barking, but he immediately climbed into her lap when she sat down, and every muscle in his body was tense. It was more than obvious he was doing what he could to protect her. It was sweet in a sad way.

All Amanda wanted to do was call Nash, but the agents wouldn't let her have her phone. Wouldn't let her go back inside her apartment. She couldn't go anywhere either, because she didn't have her keys. She could see them hanging on the peg by her open door, but she had a feeling if she tried to grab them, she wouldn't like the consequences.

The third man, the one who seemed to be in charge, was keeping an eye on her while also overseeing the other two agents as they worked.

Finally, they seemed to finish the search. The three men came out of her apartment. The two agents who'd been rifling through her things didn't give her another glance as they walked past her and Rain in the hallway. The man in charge didn't say he was sorry, didn't explain that they hadn't found anything, though that was obvious—she'd told him he wouldn't, that she hadn't brought drugs into the country when she returned. The guy simply nodded at her and left.

Feeling dirty, and desperately wanting a shower, Amanda went back into her apartment. She closed and locked the door—and gasped when she looked around.

Everything was in disarray. As they searched, she'd heard the clanking of dishes and pots and pans, and could see the men tossing the pillows off her couch from her spot in the hallway. But seeing how everything she owned had been inspected and combed through made her feel a sense of violation she'd never experienced before.

She understood that if she *did* have drugs in her apartment, they most likely wouldn't be sitting around in plain sight. That they would've been hidden. But this felt like a slap in the face. At least they hadn't slashed open her pillows or Rain's new bed.

Looking down at the dog at her side, Amanda saw he was practically vibrating with nervous energy. He hadn't liked the men being in her apartment any more than she had.

Suddenly needing to be anywhere but here, Amanda hurried to her room to change.

She almost cried at seeing every drawer empty and her clothes piled on the floor. The agents had also removed the mattress from the frame and propped it up against the wall.

Swallowing hard, Amanda grabbed a bra, a pair of jeans, and a T-shirt from the pile and turned her back on the bedroom. She changed in the hallway and, still fighting tears, went back into the main living area. Her phone and laptop were sitting on the table where she'd left them earlier. She grabbed her phone, shoved her feet into a pair of flip-flops, grabbed her purse, and picked up Rain's leash that was still attached to his collar.

The dog had followed her from room to room, staying right by her side. He was a comfort for sure. Amanda wasn't certain what she would've done without him by her side.

Her first inclination was to call Nash. But what was he going to do? He was at work. He couldn't come running home every time she needed something. She wasn't hurt. She wasn't in jail. Nothing had happened to her person. Had she been inconvenienced? Yes. Had she been a little scared? Also, yes. But this experience was nothing like what she'd been through not too long ago.

She'd be fine. She just needed some air. To get away from the apartment for a while.

Rain jumped into the backseat of her Volvo and as soon as

she got in the driver's seat, he rested his chin on her shoulder. Reaching back and giving his head a pat, Amanda pulled out of the parking lot and drove off.

Eventually, she found herself at a park on the other side of the city. It had large trees and a huge open space where people could run around, or lie in the sun if it was a warm day, or even play a game of Frisbee or something.

It was silly to continue driving. She had no idea who'd given the DEA the "tip" that there were drugs in her apartment. It didn't make sense. She didn't interact with a ton of people, and since she wasn't working yet, she didn't have anyone she spoke to on a regular basis who even knew where she lived. The only people she interacted with were Nash and his friends.

And she didn't think for one second that any of his fellow pilots, or Laryn, would've done such a vile thing.

She'd been racking her brain for most of the drive. It could've been one of her neighbors. A few of them knew she was going to South America. Maybe they were upset she was back. Maybe one of them had been hoping she'd stay gone so they could have her apartment. It had the best view...but she honestly couldn't see anyone doing such a thing, especially over something ridiculous like an apartment. This felt like harassment, plain and simple.

The agents knew she'd been in *Guyana,* specifically...so someone had to know her fairly well to be able to communicate that to the authorities, maybe even give them other reasons to check out their "tip."

Taking a deep breath, she got out of her car and opened the back door for Rain. He'd been cooped up for a while now. This park was a great opportunity for him to run, to stretch his legs. She wasn't afraid he'd disappear, Rain had been glued to her side ever since he'd found them in the jungle. He knew he had a good thing going, and she highly doubted he'd run off now.

But when she encouraged him to run around, he sat at her feet and stared up at her.

"It's okay, Rain. I'm all right. You can go play."

Rain didn't budge.

Sighing, Amanda walked over to one of the picnic tables situated at the edge of the huge open space. The park was nice. She'd never been here before, it was a little far from her apartment, but it granted her the peace and quiet that she needed to think.

She climbed up and sat on the tabletop and propped her feet on the bench, staring into space as she did her best to work through what had happened. She desperately wanted to talk to Nash, but she didn't want to be a clingy girlfriend. She wasn't hurt. Wasn't really threatened. Just embarrassed and confused.

She'd tell him tonight for sure. Wouldn't have a choice; the second he walked into her apartment, he'd know something was up, considering its state.

The more she thought about it, about who might've called in the so-called tip the DEA had received, the more Amanda couldn't shake a particular suspicion.

A sick feeling welled up inside her...

Could the tip have come from the very people she'd thought were her friends down in Guyana? Were they upset that she'd left? Did they know she hadn't had a choice? That Blair had basically kicked her out?

But what good would lying about her to the DEA do? She was gone. They could be mad or upset, but nothing that happened to her in the States would ultimately have any effect on them or the school.

Unless...

She didn't want to believe it. But it was literally the *only* thing that made sense.

The only person who might want to discredit her, might want to smear her reputation, was the one person who knew she wanted to adopt two of the children at the orphanage. Proving

Amanda was unstable or unsuitable to be a mother would be the perfect way to kill any adoption application.

Was it a huge leap to think that Blair might've had something to do with this? Not really. She had more connections than the rest of the workers and volunteers. And she certainly hadn't been happy when Amanda told her that she might want to adopt Bibi, the little girl Blair seemed so attached to.

Suddenly, anger replaced the uncertainty and confusion. She had no proof Blair had done anything, but there was no one else who had a reason to get the freaking DEA to knock on her door and search her place.

Pulling her cell out of her pocket, Amanda decided she was going to confront the woman. She probably wouldn't admit anything, that she'd been the one to contact the DEA, but at least she'd know that Amanda was on to her and maybe she'd think twice about doing something like that again.

She had Blair's office number saved in her contacts, and she clicked on it, eager to see if her suspicions were correct.

The phone rang four times, but it wasn't Blair who answered.

"Desmond Williams."

"Desmond? It's Amanda. Why are you answering Blair's phone?"

"Thank you for calling, and for your interest in our school. Yes, we can always use donations."

Confused, Amanda said, "Did you hear me? It's Amanda Rush. I'm calling from the States."

"I can hear you just fine. And yes, blankets would always be welcome. As would food. Anything that is nonperishable is best."

Something was wrong. Way wrong. It was obvious he didn't want someone to know she was on the other end of the line. Blair? Was she in the same room, listening to the call?

"I'm calling because the Drug Enforcement Agency came to my apartment today, saying they got a tip that I'd brought a bunch of cocaine into the country. They also knew I'd recently come from South America. Do you know anything about that?"

"I don't. But I'm not surprised. You can come by anytime with those donations. We'd be happy to have them."

"Was it Blair? What's going on, Desmond?" Amanda was frustrated. And alarmed. Something was happening, and she obviously couldn't get any answers from Desmond because of whoever was listening to his conversation. "Are the kids okay?" she asked, suddenly needing to know *that* more than she needed intel about what had happened with the DEA.

"Yes. The kids are wonderful. Happy and healthy, thanks to donations like yours."

Relief made Amanda feel dizzy.

"I must go now, but we appreciate your interest in donating. We are a small organization and need all the help we can get."

"If you can call me later, please do," Amanda said quickly. "I'm worried."

Desmond hung up without responding.

Amanda had resisted calling Nash earlier, but after that phone call, she didn't hesitate to reach out. She didn't have the resources to figure out what was going on. But Nash did.

Rain whined at her feet. Maybe he felt her seesawing emotions. Amanda moved so she was sitting on the bench and reached down to reassure the dog. "It's okay, Rain. I'm okay. Something's going on back at the orphanage though. I have no idea what. But I think they need help. Maybe the rebels are back, and they've taken over. I don't know. Nash will know what to do."

Clicking on Nash's number, Amanda held her breath, hoping he'd pick up.

He didn't. It went to voicemail.

She left him a vague message, asking him to call her when he could. Letting him know it wasn't anything life-or-death important, just something she needed to talk about.

Not sure what else she should be doing right now, Amanda decided to head back to her apartment. She needed to put everything back to rights. The more she thought about it, the more anxious she was to do just that. Nash wouldn't be happy if he got there and saw the state those agents had left the place. His protective instincts would kick in and he'd probably freak out. She wanted to prevent him from doing anything that might hurt his career.

She got Rain back in the car then headed toward her apartment. She wasn't worried that Nash hadn't called her back yet. He'd warned her that there'd be times when he was in meetings and couldn't use his phone.

Amanda arrived back at her complex and, after Rain did his business, she grabbed the mail from the mailroom then headed up to her apartment, determined to straighten the place up as best she could before Nash got home from work.

She put her keys and Rain's leash on the hooks by the door, threw the mail onto the counter to go through later, and decided to start with the kitchen.

She'd just finished putting all the pots and pans and dishes back in their proper places when her phone rang.

Seeing Nash's name on the screen made something inside of her ease. He'd help her figure out what was going on, of that she had no doubt.

"Hey," she said, answering the phone.

"What's up?" Nash asked, sounding more than a little concerned. "Are you okay? Is Rain okay?"

The fact he was worried about the dog was as sweet as his concern for *her*. "We're both fine."

"Good. What did you need to talk about?"

Suddenly, Amanda wasn't sure it was the best idea to tell him everything over the phone. "How was your day? Are you coming home soon?"

He paused. "Talk to me, Mandy. What's going on?"

Damn. Figured he'd be able to see through her attempt to stall.

"First, I'm fine. Rain is fine. We're in my apartment, door is locked. All is well."

"Okay, now I'm starting to freak out. Do I need to tell Casper that I can't attend this last meeting so I can get to you?"

Wow. That was even sweeter. "No. But in order to tell you what I need help with, I should start at the beginning. And the beginning's *not* the part I need you to do anything about. It's the second part. Okay?"

"Okaaaay," he said, drawing out the last part of the word.

"The DEA came here this morning with a search warrant, saying they got a tip that I had a large amount of cocaine in my apartment."

"Excuse me?"

She needed to hurry and get through this, so he didn't have a coronary. "They entered, searched, found nothing, and left. It's all good."

"It's not all fucking good!" Nash exclaimed. "What the actual fuck?"

"Nash, seriously, I'm okay. I'm still working on cleaning the place, but that's neither here nor there."

"The hell it is! They trashed your apartment?"

Of course that's what he'd get out of that part. She wouldn't call her apartment trashed, but it was definitely...in disarray. "*Nash*. That's not what I need help with. Will you listen for a sec?"

"Talk faster, Mandy. I'm seriously not happy here."

She could tell from his voice that he was probably two seconds from heading to her apartment. And while she wouldn't mind seeing him after her stressful morning, she needed him to hear the rest.

"I went for a drive to clear my head and get away from here, and tried to figure out who might have called in the bogus tip about the drugs. I don't know that many people in Norfolk anymore, no one that I'm close enough to who would do something like that, at least. But then I started thinking about Guyana. And how the agents knew I'd just come from there. I got suspicious, then mad...and I called Blair."

"Blair."

The one word was said with such disdain, but Amanda wasn't exactly surprised. She continued. "Yeah. But she didn't pick up her office line. Desmond did. And it was weird, Nash."

"In what way?"

"He pretended I was someone calling about wanting to donate to the school. He wasn't answering my questions directly, as if someone was in the office with him, listening. Maybe it was Blair he was worried about talking in front of. But I'm *more* afraid that maybe it was the rebels. That they're back or something. I asked if the kids were okay, and he said they were, but I'm still worried. I thought maybe you could find something out? Ask your friend—you know, the one you said was looking into Blair—and see if he can find out anything?"

"I'll do that right now. You're at your apartment?"

"Yeah."

"Stay there. Make sure the doors are locked. And don't open it for anyone except for me or one of my friends. I don't care if the DEA comes back and demands you open it, or if the fucking president is on the other side. You *do not* open that door. Understand?"

He was being bossy and scaring her a little, but Amanda quickly agreed. "I won't."

"Good. I'm going to find out what's going on, I just need you to be safe while I work on things here. I'll talk to Casper, and once I make the calls I need to make, I'm coming home. I'll be there as soon as I can."

"Be safe. I'm fine, Nash. A little shaken up by everything, but good now."

"I'm sorry I wasn't there."

"Nash, you can't be by my side at all times."

"I know, but it doesn't mean I don't want to be. I hate that you had to go through that today by yourself."

"I had Rain."

"Which I'm grateful for, but a dog isn't the same as having a pissed-off Night Stalker by your side or at your back."

He wasn't wrong.

"Drive safe. Don't get a ticket or anything."

He chuckled, and Amanda was glad to hear it. He was still stressed, that was obvious, but the fact that she'd been able to make him laugh, even a little, made her feel good.

"I won't. I'll call if I find out anything before I get home."

"Thanks."

"See you soon."

"Okay."

Nash hung up, and even though Amanda didn't have any answers yet, she felt better now that he was looking into things. It felt weird to rely on someone else like she was on Nash. She'd always been super independent, had to be. But having him on her side, being able to call him for help…or heck, just knowing he was upset on her behalf and willing to leave work immediately to get to her if she needed him…felt awesome. As if she wasn't quite so alone in the world.

Things between her and Nash had moved fast, but they felt right. Their time in the jungle had sped up their relationship tenfold. And she wasn't upset about it in the least.

CHAPTER EIGHTEEN

As soon as Buck disconnected with Mandy, he dialed Tex's number. He'd planned on leaving a message, but to his surprise, the man himself answered the phone.

"Tex here."

"It's Buck. Nash Chaney. I'm calling about Guyana."

"Right. Actually, I was going to get in touch with you soon about that. I'm still looking into the school, but I've found out some unusual things. At least, I *think* they are. First, according to emails I've hacked into that have gone back and forth between volunteers who are still working at the school, it sounds like Blair has moved one of the children into her room at the school. I haven't been able to find any paperwork saying that she intends to adopt the child, but maybe the little girl was having a hard time adjusting to everything after being kidnapped?"

"Bibi?" Buck asked.

Tex sounded surprised when he answered, "Yes. How did you know?"

"She's obsessed with that girl. At least from what I saw. I'm calling about something else though." Buck quickly explained what happened to Mandy this morning. About the search warrant thanks to an alleged "tip" about drugs in her apartment. He also told Tex about her phone call with Desmond. "She's worried the rebels are back and holding people hostage there at the school or something. I'm hoping to find out if that's the case or not. If everyone is all right."

"I'll find out where the tip came from and get back to you on that. It'll be easy enough to hack into the DEA database to find the notes on the call. On the other issue, as of this morning, things seemed to be fine at the school. Staff emails were being sent and received, and phone traffic seemed to be normal, as well. I don't have eyes down there, as they have no video monitoring devices, but electronically, there's been no unusual activity. But I can do a deeper dive, see about getting my military connections to check on the orphanage."

"I'd appreciate that. As would Mandy."

"I did find out some interesting details about the director though."

"Such as?"

"She's been in and out of mental hospitals for years. Since before her husband passed away."

"For what?"

"There haven't really been any firm diagnoses that I can see. Lots of words bandied about…borderline personality disorder, depression, anxiety, schizophrenia, bipolar…you name it, doctors have considered it."

"But there's been nothing concrete?"

"Nope. She's been prescribed lots of different drugs over the years, but after she left the country for Guyana, as far as I can tell, she hasn't been taking anything."

"That could be bad," Buck said, more to himself than to Tex.

"I'll keep working on it and get back to you as soon as I can. I don't blame Amanda for being worried about the kids and her friends who work down there."

"Appreciate it."

Tex hung up without another word. And while Buck felt better that the man was doing what he could to find out what was happening in Guyana, the need to see for himself that Mandy was all right was overwhelming. He couldn't believe the DEA had searched her apartment. After what she'd already been through with the rebels, that had to have been traumatic for her.

He went back into the conference room he and his fellow pilots were using to go over intel for an upcoming mission. They'd taken a break, so he'd been able to check his messages, and he'd stepped out to call Mandy back.

"Everything okay?" Obi-Wan asked when he entered the room.

"No. I need to head out."

"Mandy?" Pyro asked, sounding concerned.

"Yeah." He once again went over what happened to Mandy, from her scare with the DEA to her concerns for the school in Guyana, and he wasn't surprised when his fellow pilots and friends were outraged on her behalf.

"Mandy would no sooner have drugs in her apartment than Mother Theresa."

"Give me a fucking break!"

"I bet they trashed the place while looking."

"You need us to come with you?"

His friends were the best. This was why he'd lay down his life for any one of them, because he knew they had his back without question. "She says she's good. Locked inside her apartment now. So I don't think I need any backup, but if I do, I'll call. Okay if I head out early?" Buck asked Casper.

"Of course. We're almost done here anyway. We can fill you in on what you missed tomorrow."

"Thanks."

"And keep us in the loop," Casper said sternly. "If something's up, we want to know."

"I will. I've got Tex looking into what the hell is going on."

"All right, but seriously, you know we're here for you. And if Tex finds anything hinky going on in Guyana, I'll talk to the colonel about seeing if we can head down there and offer our assistance," Casper said.

"Thanks, guys," Buck said, feeling emotional all of a sudden.

"Is Mandy your girl?" Casper asked.

"Yes." That was an easy question to answer.

"Then she's one of us. Fuck with one of us, fuck with all of us," Casper said firmly. "And if I need to call my brother and get the SEALs involved, I will. I went through hell when Laryn was taken from me, and I wouldn't wish that on anyone. Not that Mandy will be taken again, but if someone's messing with her or threatening her, we won't let what happened to Laryn happen to her. Now get. I'll touch base later."

Buck nodded, then turned to leave. He was anxious to get to Mandy's apartment. To see with his own eyes that she was all right.

It didn't take much time to get to her complex, and the entire time, Buck was thinking hard about what his next steps would be if Tex found out the rebels had returned to the school to exact revenge or to re-kidnap the children.

He took the stairs to her apartment two at a time and knocked on the door, calling out as he did. "Mandy? It's me. Let me in."

The door opened almost immediately, and then Mandy was in his arms. Buck felt like he could breathe normally for the first time since they'd spoken on the phone not too long ago.

He hugged her tightly, then pulled back, running his gaze down her body to see for himself that she was truly all right.

"I'm good," she said softly, obviously knowing what he was doing. "It was kind of scary at the time, as I didn't know what was happening. I had to stay outside, and I was still in my freaking pajamas. But the more time that passes, the less confused and the more angry I get. I mean, I'm a *teacher*! Not a drug dealer. How anyone could think I'd have anything to do with drugs is beyond me. Did you find out anything about the school? Are they okay?"

"Tex is looking into it, and he said he'd get with me as soon as he learns anything." Looking over her shoulder, Buck's lips pressed together. He could see down the hall to her bedroom, and while she might've had time to clean up the kitchen and living area, her room still looked like a disaster. He got angry all over again at the breach of privacy.

"It's okay," she soothed, seeing where his gaze had landed. "It's not that bad."

"I'm going to make sure whoever called in that tip regrets it with every fiber of their being," he said from behind clenched teeth.

To his surprise, Mandy chuckled. He looked away from the messy bedroom to her face. "What's funny?"

"Just that I had the same thought myself. But I'm guessing you have the means and ability to do much more than I'd be able to. Nash, you should've seen Rain. He actually barked! I wasn't sure he could. But he knew those men were here before I did, before they knocked. He growled in his throat, then stood between me and the door and *barked*. I was shocked."

Buck had mixed feelings once again. He was proud of the dog for protecting Mandy, but pissed that he'd had to do it at all. She should have been safe in her apartment. Shouldn't have to worry about people coming into her personal space and invading her privacy.

"Good boy," Buck said, praising Rain, who had gone back to his bed after greeting Buck at the door.

"How did the rest of your morning go?" he asked. "I mean, before the DEA fuckup. You have any luck finding a job or figuring out the certification thing?" Buck was doing his best to control his emotions. His anger. He wanted to *do* something, but all he could do at the moment was wait for more intel to come in from Tex. So in the meantime, he needed to do whatever he could to make Mandy feel comfortable. As if things were under control. And to do that, he needed to stay in control himself.

"Not great. I mean, I've narrowed down the list of schools that have online programs, but I haven't found any open positions."

"What about subbing?" Buck asked, remembering she'd mentioned that at some point in the last week.

"I heard from a teacher who I used to work with about someone she knows who teaches first grade, who's about to go on maternity leave. The admin is looking for a long-term sub, which would be ideal...but I'm not sure it's a great idea."

"Why not?"

"Because it's on the naval base."

"Why is that not a good idea?" Buck asked, genuinely confused.

"Because you work there."

"And?"

"And I don't want to crowd you. Home in on your turf."

Buck shook his head in exasperation. "How is working at the same naval base as me homing in on my turf?"

"I don't know. It just feels...weird, somehow?"

"It's not weird. It's perfect. We could save gas. Only take one car to work. I could come over to the school and see you at lunch. Sounds *ideal* to me." And it did. With any other woman, she might have a good point. He might've felt as if having her so close all the time would be suffocating. But he liked the idea of her being on the naval base. It didn't guarantee she'd be safe from any kind of violence, but he thought it would at least be a little safer than if she was in one of the public schools in the area.

"Really? You aren't just saying that?"

"No."

"Maybe I'll call tomorrow and see if I can put in an application, or at least talk to someone in administration about the position then."

"Good. Have you eaten?"

She wrinkled her nose. "No. Didn't really feel like it."

"How about I grill us some chicken or something. It won't take long. We can have some of that flavored rice you like so much to go with it."

"Sounds good. I can work on putting the bedroom back in order while you cook."

"No. We'll do it together after we eat. For now, sit. Relax. You've had a hard day."

"I can help."

"I know you can. But you can sit and relax too."

Mandy rolled her eyes. "Fine. Whatever. Can I at least go through my mail while you slave over our dinner?"

"By all means." Buck didn't let go of her though, still had his arms around her. He leaned down and rested his forehead on hers. "I'm sorry you had to go through what you did today."

"Me too."

"We'll figure this out. Promise."

"I hope so."

He kissed her then. A loving kiss that hopefully proved how much he cared about her.

Forcing himself to let go before the kiss turned into more—he really did want to feed her, and his stomach was growling as well—Buck headed for the kitchen sink to wash his hands and to get ready to make their dinner.

Mandy went over to the edge of the counter and grabbed the letters lying there, where she'd obviously placed them when she got home. She carried them over to the table and sat, then began to go through them.

Buck was drying his hands when he heard her gasp. Looking over, he saw Mandy staring at an envelope with wide eyes.

"What is it?"

She looked up. "It's postmarked from Venezuela," she said in a whisper.

"What the hell?" Buck said under his breath. "What *now?*" Those words were a bit louder.

Showing how off-kilter she was still feeling, Mandy didn't even try to open the letter, she simply held it out to him as he walked over to her.

The letter didn't have a return address, and her address was typed on the front. But it had definitely been postmarked from Venezuela.

Buck hesitated. He probably shouldn't open it. Should probably call the authorities in case it contained drugs or something that might incriminate Mandy.

But he couldn't *not* open it. He needed to know if there was an immediate threat toward the woman he was beginning to think he couldn't live without, or if it was something else entirely.

Taking a step away from the table, away from Mandy, in case there was powder or something inside, Buck pulled out the knife he always carried from one of the pockets of his cargo pants and carefully slit open the top of the envelope. He pulled the piece of paper from inside and placed it on the counter. He held his breath as he unfolded it.

Thankfully, there was nothing inside except for the paper. The letter was also typed, and was short and to the point.

> *We're watching you.*
> *We have eyes everywhere.*
> *We always finish what we start.*
> *We will be victorious.*

Buck's hands were shaking at the threats. *No one* threatened his woman. No fucking way.

"Come on. We're leaving."

"What? Where are we going? What does the letter say?"

Buck didn't want her to see it. Didn't want the vile words rolling around in her head, as they were in his.

But she was at his side, looking over his shoulder before he could shove the letter back into the envelope. She gasped again.

"Is that from the rebels? The people who kidnapped me and the kids?"

"I don't know. Possibly."

"Holy shit! How the hell would they get my address?"

"I don't know. And that's why we're leaving. Whoever sent this knows where you live. Go pack. Whatever you need for at least a week. I'm not going to risk you staying here and having this not be some sick prank or an empty threat."

"Where are we going?"

"My place. It's doubtful anyone will know *my* name or where I live. But even if they do, my apartment is more secure than yours. Everyone has to be buzzed into the building. You can stay with me until we figure this out. Until Tex gets back to us with intel."

"I don't want to be a bother," Mandy said softly.

Turning, Buck took her face in his hands. "You will *never* be a bother. You don't think I want you in my space? My bed? I do."

"But you haven't complained about staying here."

"Of course not. Because this is your home. Where you're comfortable. But things have changed. Circumstances have changed. I won't risk your well-being, Mandy. We could go to a hotel, but my place will be more comfortable. For you and Rain."

"I don't know what to say."

"Don't say anything. Go pack. I'll get Rain's things together out here. Grab whatever will spoil from the fridge too."

"I don't like this. I mean, I love that I'll be with you, but I don't like being forced out of my home. Being threatened. Not knowing what the hell is going on."

"I don't either, which is why I'm going to figure it out. Fix this."

Mandy leaned against him and wrapped her arms around his waist. "I don't want you to get sick of me. To resent me being in your space."

"I won't. I couldn't. I *want* you in my space. I'd think you'd have figured that out by now, considering how much I hog your bed when we're in it together. I can't get enough of you, Rebel. I love being around you, near you, inside you. That's another reason I have no problem with you working on base. Our relationship is not like anything I've ever experienced in the past. The more I'm around you, the more I *want* to be around you. Dead stop. So this isn't a bad thing. I hate the reason you're moving in with me, but I love the fact that you'll be there. That your things will be mingled with mine. That you'll be in my shower, my bed, my kitchen. Okay?"

"If you're sure..." she said hesitatingly.

The fact that she wasn't protesting, insisting she could stay at her place, that she wasn't scared of the threats in the letter, was telling. She was probably terrified, but protesting because she thought it was what she should do. He'd do whatever he needed to in order to make sure she realized he honestly wanted her at his apartment and it was no hardship for him whatsoever.

"I'm sure," he said firmly.

"Okay. I won't be long."

Buck nodded and let go of her when she pulled away. He had things he needed to do. Phone calls to make. Things to pack. But he took a moment to close his eyes and breathe. They'd make it through this. They had to. The alternative was unthinkable.

CHAPTER NINETEEN

Amanda couldn't help but feel as if she had a huge cloud over her head. Like something was going to happen. Even though, ever since she and Rain had moved into Nash's apartment, things had been good. It was a weird dichotomy. Waiting for the other shoe to fall while absolutely loving the direction her life had taken.

She'd gotten in touch with the principal at the school on the base, and he was thrilled she was interested in the long-term sub position. It wouldn't start for another month, and she had to apply, but Amanda was fairly sure she was going to get it.

She had also applied for an online program to upgrade her certificate. She had to take some classes but the process didn't seem too complicated, which was a relief.

Rain had settled into Nash's apartment as if he'd always been there. The only difference between a week ago and now was that the dog wouldn't let Amanda out of his sight. Instead of sleeping in the living area, he now had a second bed in Nash's bedroom. When she got up to pee, Rain went with her and sat outside the door while she did her thing. They'd also had to put his bed in the living area in a place where he could see her in the kitchen, when she was in there helping Nash. It seemed as if even the dog felt the tension in the air, and even *he* was worried about the letter she'd received in the mail. Either that, or he was still remembering the strangers who'd come to her apartment and was waiting for more.

Things with Nash were better than ever. She'd never lived with a man before, but Nash was surprisingly easy to cohabitate with. He cleaned up after himself, didn't expect her to do all the chores, even though she was at home during the day while he was at work, and he'd eagerly made room in his closet and dresser for her things.

But while her personal and professional life were going well, Amanda still felt a sense of unease. She'd tried to get a hold of anyone down in Guyana every day since receiving the threatening letter, and no one ever picked up the phone. Nash's friend Tex had confirmed that everything at the school and orphanage seemed to be operating as usual. The rebels hadn't kidnapped anyone, and there wasn't any unusual digital activity. He was still researching to see what he could dig up around the time of Amanda and the kids' actual kidnapping, but so far he hadn't found anything pointing to Blair's involvement.

Nash was getting anxious, because his Night Stalker team was preparing to deploy soon. He couldn't say where or for how long, but it was obvious he was reluctant to leave when things with her situation were unresolved. Honestly, Amanda didn't really want him to go either, but what choice did they have? He had a job to do, and she would never make him choose between her and doing what he loved.

The only thing in Amanda's life that *wasn't* great, was that she didn't leave Nash's apartment without him. She felt cooped up. She was grateful to have a safe place to hunker down while his friend looked into what the hell was happening, but she still felt stifled.

KEEPING AMANDA

She'd been reading books, playing games on her laptop, starting early on the lessons she had to complete in order to get her new certification...but she was still bored. And nervous about her future.

After Nash went to work that morning, a week after she'd received the threatening letter, and after a few hours of doing busy work to keep her mind occupied, Amanda decided it was time for her daily call to the school in Guyana. She was desperate to talk to someone, *anyone*, about what was going on down there.

Not really expecting anyone to pick up, just like the last several times she'd called, Amanda was busy getting a treat for Rain out of the cute little jar Nash had come home with a few days ago, when the ringing in her ear stopped and someone actually answered.

"Hello?"

"Oh my God, Desmond? It's Amanda."

"Mandy? Oh! It's so good to hear from you! Are you all right?"

His voice had instantly lowered, but Amanda was relieved to be talking to someone, and that Desmond wasn't pretending she was a vendor or some random person calling to donate to the school. Hopefully that meant no one was listening and they could talk freely.

"I'm all right. Are *you*? I've been trying to get a hold of someone for ages and no one's been picking up. What's going on? Are the kids okay? I'm so worried about everyone!"

"Things are bad," Desmond said, making Amanda's stomach roll. "Blair, she's... I don't know how to tell you this...but she's gone."

"Gone? Gone where?" Amanda asked.

"We don't know. Let me back up," Desmond said. "After you left, she was like a completely different person. We thought it was because she was worried about the rebels coming back or something, but I don't think that was it. She stopped taking care of herself...showering, washing her clothes, even leaving her room or office much. She began to mumble to herself a lot and basically ignored everything about running the school. I stepped in to make sure bills got paid and the children were fed.

"Then she moved Bibi into her room. And she wouldn't let anyone in to see the little girl. She claimed she was teaching her personally and taking care of her, but the few times anyone saw her, the girl looked just as disheveled as Blair. It was if she were a dog with a bone, possessive and aggressive if anyone dared question what she was doing. She's been moody, secretive, and downright mean to everyone, kids included."

"Holy crap, Desmond. And now she's gone? Where's Bibi?"

"She took Bibi with her. Disappeared in the middle of the night. Didn't even take anything. All her suitcases are still here, all her personal things. We're all extremely worried about Bibi. I don't know what switch flipped in Blair's head, but it seemed she couldn't even take care of *herself* before she left. How can she care for a four-year-old?"

"Does she have her passport?"

"We think so. We haven't been able to find it anywhere. We also found a copy of paperwork that Blair had filled out, including forged signatures, saying that Bibi was legally hers. We think she might be trying to leave the country. We've called the police, but they don't seem too interested in helping us figure out where they might have gone."

Amanda's heart was beating a million miles an hour. She felt panicked and absolutely helpless to do anything.

"Something is wrong with Blair. She's not right in the head. Right before she left, it was almost as if she didn't even recognize me, and I've worked with her since she first arrived here. But Mandy...there's something else."

"Oh man, what?" she asked.

"Some of the other volunteers heard her mumbling your name. Pacing back and forth in her room and talking under her breath. They heard her saying things like, 'the plan should've worked. Should've known they would fuck it up. Mandy should be gone for good. Bibi's mine. She'll never get her.'"

Amanda was literally at a loss for words. She had no idea what to say to that. She'd had her suspicions, of course, that someone at the school was behind the kidnapping, but to hear confirmation that it had been Blair, the woman who'd hired her, who she'd shared so many personal talks with, was heartbreaking.

"Desmond, she's...she's not well. A friend of Nash's found out that Blair's been in and out of mental hospitals. It's likely that she's gone off her meds or had a break in reality or something." Amanda told Desmond everything she could remember from the conversation she'd had with Nash about Blair. She'd kind of felt sorry for the woman at the time, but now? Knowing she'd disappeared with little Bibi? It was hard to feel sorry for her at all.

"Well, hell," Desmond cursed. "I don't want to think Blair was behind everything these poor kids suffered, but with everything *else* that has happened recently? I don't know what else to believe."

"How are all the kids doing now?" Amanda asked, feeling heartsick about Bibi and Blair, but worried about everyone else as well.

"They're really good. We've kept most of what's happening from them. But I'm worried about what will happen next. Without a director, we might have to close. I don't know what will become of the children who live here. Blair might have lost her mind, but she was a great fundraiser. Had a lot of connections back in the United States and even here in Guyana. Without that money..." His voice trailed off.

Amanda closed her eyes and sank into one of the chairs at the small kitchen table. She didn't know what to say. How to reassure Desmond that everything would be all right. How could it be? Without funding, the orphanage would surely have to close. Thinking about what would happen to Michael, Sharon, little James, and all the other kids was enough to have tears leaking from her eyes.

"Be careful, Amanda," Desmond said, sounding stern. "If Blair was the one behind the kidnapping, and if she was hoping you would disappear forever, you could be in danger."

"I got a threatening letter," Amanda admitted. "It's written to look like it's from the people who kidnapped me and the kids. It was postmarked from Venezuela."

"It could have been from Blair," Desmond said. "As I said, she's been secretive and holed up in her room or office with Bibi. She knows a lot of people. And if she somehow arranged for the kids and you to be taken, then she has connections to people in Venezuela. It wouldn't have been hard for her to have a letter mailed for her, in that case."

Damn. He was right. But it was so difficult to believe that *Blair* hated her so much she'd go to the extremes that she had to...to what? *Kill* her? That was truly crazy.

"Watch your back," Desmond told her. "Blair could be anywhere, and while things are uncertain here, they're also much calmer. The volunteers and older kids aren't quite so on edge with her gone."

"I'm going to see what I can do to help the school," Amanda said, needing to concentrate on something *other* than a woman she'd seen as the grandmotherly type having gone off the deep end, attempting to kill Amanda just for bonding with the child Blair had chosen as her favorite. "Fundraisers, things like that. Those kids need that school. The orphanage. They need stability, and you and the other volunteers have given them that. I don't know how, but I'll find a way to get some funding so you don't have to close."

"That would be wonderful, but we are also working on

some alternatives," Desmond said. "There are other orphanages. And we're working harder to find homes for the children. It won't be easy, as there are many unwanted children, and too many families who are too poor to take care of the kids they already have, but we won't let them suffer because of this setback."

"You're a good person," Amanda told Desmond. "What if *you* take over as director?"

"Me? Oh, I don't think so."

"Why not?" The more Amanda thought about it, the better the idea seemed to her. "I'm guessing you answered the phone because you're in Blair's office, doing the things she always did. Am I right?"

"It needs to be done."

"Exactly. And you're doing it. I'll be in touch, Desmond. And if you hear anything about Blair or Bibi, will you let me know?"

"Of course. And same applies to you."

"Right. Stay safe down there."

"We will." His voice lowered once more. "She really is out of her mind. Please be careful."

Amanda shivered at the gravity of his tone. At the worry she heard…for *her*. Desmond was six-two and in his late thirties. If he sounded scared of a seventy-two-year-old woman, things were serious. She'd be stupid to discount his warnings.

"I'll call again soon," she said. They both said their goodbyes and Amanda clicked off the connection.

How long she sat at the table thinking about what she'd just heard, Amanda wasn't sure. It was the sound of a key in the lock that had her coming back to the here and now. Looking up, she watched Nash enter. Just seeing him made some of the stress she'd been feeling dissipate. She wasn't alone, and that meant everything to her.

Nash took one look at her sitting at the table and said, "What's wrong?"

How he could read her so well after such a short amount of time, she had no idea, but it was a comforting thought.

"I talked to Desmond."

"And?" Nash asked, putting the bags he was carrying on the kitchen counter and walking over to where she was sitting. He crouched down next to her chair and put his hand on her thigh. All his attention was focused on her. It was a heady feeling. To be so…seen.

She told him what Desmond had said. Didn't leave anything out.

He didn't interrupt, didn't say a word, just kept his gaze on her the whole time.

"I want to help them. I don't know how though. Fundraising, I guess, but I don't know where to start."

"We'll figure it out. How are *you* doing? I know Blair was someone you admired before all of this."

The fact that he was asking how she was feeling made her feel warm and fuzzy all over again. He was obviously upset, she could see that muscle in his jaw ticking as he ground his teeth together. But he wasn't losing his shit, he was making sure she was all right before he did anything else.

"I thought we were becoming friends, but I guess I was wrong."

"Mental illness can change people. I don't think you were wrong. I think something was triggered in her brain and it's making her a different person. It's probably why she called in that tip about you and the drugs. She was desperate to make you look bad just in case you did go through with the adoption request. Having even a hint that you might be involved in drugs would be enough for her to make a case against you adopting."

"I guess."

"I'd like to make some calls. Blair being MIA is worrisome. And the fact that she has Bibi with her, and isn't taking care of herself *or* the child, is not good. Add in that she seems to have a hatred for you that's unnatural…she needs to be found."

"I know. What if she comes here?" Amanda asked. "I mean, she knows my address because it was on the paperwork I submitted to volunteer there. And if she *did* type that letter, that confirms she knows where I live."

"Which is why you're here with me," Nash said. "And if she comes here, we'll find her. Tex is good at what he does. Very good. And he's bitched more than once about the lack of cameras down in Guyana. But here in the States? There are tons of them. If she entered the country with Bibi, he'll find out."

"Nash, there are so many ways she could've gotten in…car, bus, boat, plane. And we don't know *where* she might attempt to cross the border. There has to be thousands of cameras. He can't possibly look at them all to find her."

"No, but he can narrow things down. Desmond said her passport was gone. That'll make it easier because the second it's scanned, it'll leave a paper trail."

"But Bibi doesn't have a passport. What if they crossed over illegally?"

"Breathe, Mandy. I don't know, that's why I want to call Tex. We'll figure this out. I promise. My job is to keep you safe. His job is to find Blair. Your job is to stay aware at all times. Can you do that?"

"Of course."

"Good. I'm going to go change, then call Tex. I'll be right back."

He stood, then leaned over and kissed her. He stayed close and whispered, "I'm not going to let anything happen to you. I just found you, I'm not going to lose you now."

Then he turned and was heading down the hall toward the bedroom.

Amanda closed her eyes and did her best to regain her equilibrium. It had taken quite a beating recently. She felt as if she didn't know which way was up anymore. Who was a friend or who was out to get her.

Rain whined and nudged her with his snout. He'd gotten off his bed after Nash had left and was looking up at her with what she could only describe as a worried doggy expression.

"I'm okay," she said, hoping if she said the words out loud enough, they'd actually be true.

CHAPTER TWENTY

Buck was having a hard time keeping his anger under control. Every word out of Mandy's mouth had made him want ten minutes alone with Blair Gaffney. He wasn't a man who was prone to violence, but just the *thought* that she was responsible for the kidnapping and mental and physical torture of twenty-three innocent children—and could right now be on her way to Virginia to carry out some sort of hateful revenge on Mandy—was enough to make him lose his normally tightly held restraint.

Mandy was taking everything extremely well. And that *also* worried him. He knew how much she adored little Bibi, and the idea that the child was at the mercy of whatever mental illness Blair was suffering was too much to even think about.

He'd left Mandy so quickly because he'd needed a moment to himself. To regain control. So he could think rationally and calmly when he called Tex. Because right now, he felt anything *but* rational and calm.

Buck took a few deep breaths and found they didn't help at all. He was a man of action, and without knowing where Blair was, and what she was planning, he couldn't do a damn thing.

But Tex could hopefully find her, and then they could make

some definitive plans. Call the police, get child services involved. Contact the media to broadcast an Amber alert. Something.

He wasn't sure if he'd been talking out his ass when he reassured Mandy that Tex could find Blair. The man was good, but he didn't know if he was *that* good. Every point Mandy brought up was valid. Finding how, when, and where she'd entered the US —if she'd even done so at all—would be tough. Could take days. Weeks.

Time Buck didn't think they had. His gut was screaming at him that Mandy was in danger. That Blair was coming for her. It made no sense, especially since Blair had essentially "won" whatever competition she thought there was for little Bibi. Mandy was gone and Blair had the child. But according to Desmond, for some reason, there was a deep-seated hatred festering inside the older woman toward Mandy. And that kind of hate didn't go away spontaneously. Since Blair had apparently had a mental break, that hate could be all that was driving her.

Taking another deep breath, Buck changed out of his work clothes and put on a pair of jeans and a black T-shirt. He needed to shower, but he didn't want to delay talking to Tex any longer than he had already. And he wanted to get back to Mandy. Make sure she was really all right. He figured she wasn't, but he'd do whatever it took to make sure she got there.

He strode back into the living area a few minutes after he'd left and found Mandy sitting on the couch with Rain practically in her lap. The dog was scary smart, obviously felt the woman he idolized needed some emotional support.

An idea occurred to him then—what if they secured the paperwork to make Rain an actual support animal? He was completely in tune with Mandy and her emotions, and it would be a comfort to them both if they could stay together everywhere she went, especially when she was back in the classroom again. He wasn't sure how it all worked, but he made a mental note to look into it once things settled down.

Nash went straight to her. Sat on the couch beside her, on the opposite side from Rain, and put his arm around her shoulders.

"I'm sorry I don't have anything ready for dinner."

"Dinner can wait. I'm more worried about you."

"I'm okay. I just...this is so hard to believe."

"I know. You want to listen in on my call with Tex? Or have you had enough today? You need a break from all of this?" Buck asked.

"Listen," she said without hesitation. "I'd feel better if I was in the loop. If I knew what was happening."

"Then that's what we'll do." Buck took out his cell and scrolled to his contacts before clicking on Tex's name.

The phone rang twice before he picked up.

"Hey, Buck. I haven't located concrete evidence of Blair's connection to the rebels, but I will. I know it's there, it's just taking me a little longer than usual to find something."

"We have news," Buck told the other man. "Mandy is here. She talked to Desmond Williams today."

"Give it to me," Tex ordered in a no-nonsense tone.

Buck nodded at Mandy to go ahead. It was just as maddening, infuriating, and baffling the second time he heard the story as it was the first. But Buck stayed calm, determined to be the man she needed right now, instead of the pissed-off soldier he truly was deep inside.

"Shit. Okay. First things first, don't worry about the school. I can take care of that."

Typing on a keyboard was easy to hear in the brief silence that followed.

"What does that mean?" Mandy asked.

"I've got money I can send. And by money, I mean enough to keep the school and orphanage running for years."

"Oh, but that's not why we called—" Mandy began to protest.

"I know. But look, trust me when I say, I've got enough money to be able to fund a *thousand* orphanages from here to eternity. There's no better way to spend it, I think, than on the future of the world. I've already done enough research to know that Desmond Williams is a good man. Compassionate. Smart. Business savvy. He's not going to just blow this donation. And regardless, I'll see to it that doesn't happen. But he'll have enough to get more staff, build more housing, as well as hire security—which is perhaps the most important thing he can do with the money, considering the school and orphanage is so close to the border.

"Moving on to more difficult things…I can find Blair, but it'll take time."

"How much time?" Buck asked.

"I don't know. More than either of us would like though. But the fact that she has a child with her will work in my favor. It'll make her stand out more…hang on…Hmmm, doesn't look like she's used her passport recently."

"Holy crap, you can see that so quickly?"

"Of course. It's an electronic record, and it's easy enough to check the Customs database."

Mandy looked at Buck with huge eyes, as if to say, "What the hell?"

He wanted to laugh, but this really wasn't a laughing matter.

"At least she didn't enter using her real name. I'll keep digging, see what I can find out. And the intel about Blair setting up the kidnapping makes sense, in a warped way, I guess. She probably met with one of the rebels in person, which is why I haven't been able to find an electronic trail. But now I'm more than curious. I want to know who her connection is, and if they're a threat to the kids still living at the orphanage. Because that isn't acceptable. Buck?"

"I'm here."

"I don't like this. Don't leave Mandy alone. Take her with you to the base. She can wait there while you work. With Blair being so unstable, it's not safe for her to be at your apartment alone when you aren't there."

Mandy was frowning now—and looked as if she was ready to cry.

"I don't need a babysitter," she said softly, staring at the phone.

"No, you don't. You need a bodyguard," Tex said firmly. "Look, I know this sucks. But ever since my kidnapping, I'm way more sensitive to this kind of shit. I don't want *anyone* to go through what I did. And if Blair gets her hands on you, or sends someone else to do it—which is more what I'd expect her to try—things won't go well for you. The woman hates you for whatever reason. Doesn't even need to be a good one; she's mentally unstable, so it is what it is. You need to have eyes on you at all times until I can find her. She could be there in Norfolk now. Looking for you. Wanting revenge."

"I didn't do anything to her," Mandy said, her voice wobbling. "All I wanted was to give some children a good home. To love them."

"I know," Tex said gently. "And I have no doubt any kid will be lucky to call you Mom. But that can't happen if you aren't careful. If Blair or someone she's paid off gets their hands on you. This won't be forever. Just until I can find her. Okay?"

Buck hated this. Hated that Mandy was so upset. Hated that someone she trusted was upending her life so much.

"Okay," she said after a long moment.

"I'll see if she can hang out with Laryn in the hangar. When she hears that Mandy might be in danger, she'll go all mother-hen on her," Buck said.

Tex chuckled. "That'll work. And you're right. I can see her now, with her wrench in one hand, ready to knock out someone's kneecaps if they dare look at Mandy the wrong way. Be safe, be vigilant, and I'll be in touch."

The line went dead.

Buck immediately put his finger under Mandy's chin and turned her head so she was looking at him. "*Nothing* is going to happen to you. Tex will figure this out, I will keep you safe. Me and my friends. Life will go back to normal soon. I swear."

She nodded. Then sighed. "Can Rain come to the base with me?"

"Yes." It would probably require the colonel's approval, but Buck would make sure it happened.

"What do you want for dinner?"

Buck shook his head. He wasn't going to let her shy away from her feelings. "Screw dinner. What do you need from me right now?"

"This. You being here. Touching me. That's what I need."

"Then that's what you'll get. Come 'ere." Buck pulled Mandy into his arms and fell backward onto the couch. Rain grumbled, but jumped down onto the floor and went over to his bed. He didn't sleep though. Just kept his eyes on Mandy as Buck got them comfortable on the couch.

He rolled her until her back was against the cushions and he was lying on his side in front of her. They were face-to-face and her hands were between them, resting on his chest.

"This is nice," she said with a small smile. "Usually I don't get to look at you when we're cuddling."

Buck made a mental note to lie like this more often. Anything this woman wanted, he'd move heaven and earth to give her.

They talked for at least an hour. He asked her to tell him more about Bibi, about the other kids she worked with in Guyana. About Desmond. Then he wanted to know more about her parents, about what she was like as a child. Many of the stories she told him, he'd heard before, when they were in the jungle, but they felt different now that deeper feelings were involved. Now that she was far more than a "mission."

He did his fair share of talking too. About his sister, his niece and nephew, his parents. Growing up in Kansas. It felt good to be "normal" for a little while, to not talk about anyone hating this woman enough that they'd arranged to have her kidnapped... a person who, even now, could be on their way to cause more havoc in Mandy's life.

It wasn't until his stomach growled that Mandy insisted they get up and find something to eat. Buck agreed, but only because he felt as if she was truly on a more stable footing. That the time to decompress and simply enjoy being next to another human being who wanted nothing but good things for her had done her some good.

They got up, made a quick meal of ramen with a fried egg, then decided to relax in bed. Buck took Rain outside—there was no question that he would be the one doing that chore for the foreseeable future—then headed to the bedroom.

Mandy was already in bed waiting for him.

Buck paused at the doorway, watching Mandy as she read from her e-reader without noticing him. Seeing her there seemed so natural. So right. It was as if she'd always been with him, which was weird considering how short a time it had actually been. But the circumstances of them meeting and getting to know each other in such a stressful situation hadn't been normal. Had fast-forwarded their relationship in a way that had brought them closer together. Buck couldn't imagine not having her in his life, which was an intense feeling. But right, nonetheless.

He quickly joined her in the bed and snuggled up next to her on his side. She was on her back and started to put her e-reader down, but he stopped her. "No, keep reading. I'm just going to lie here." His head was on her shoulder, his arm around her stomach, one of his legs over hers. Her scent was in his nostrils and the warmth of her body seeped into his own. He felt content and happy. Even lying with her quietly felt intimate in a way he'd never known.

"Are you sure?"

"I'm sure." She needed to lose herself in the fictional world of the stories she loved so much. Where there was always a happily ever after and the bad guy always got what he, or she, deserved.

Buck could only hope they had a similar ending...or beginning, as the case may be. That they'd find Blair, and the older woman would get the mental help she needed, and Bibi would be cared for properly. And, of course, that he and Mandy would live happily ever after.

But deep down, Buck was more than aware that life didn't always turn out the way you wanted. It wasn't a romance novel. All he could do was make sure Mandy was safe while Tex did his thing. He'd do whatever it took to protect the woman in his bed, because he was pretty sure life without her in it would be a dark, cold, and miserable place.

CHAPTER TWENTY-ONE

The next few days were hard. Not spending time with Laryn and her fellow mechanics in the hangar on the naval base, but the not knowing. The waiting. Every day that went by felt like an eternity. Where was Blair? What was she doing? How was Bibi? Amanda had more questions than answers, and it was maddening.

Last night, she'd been so on edge, Nash decided she needed several orgasms to let out some of the tension she carried. By the time he was through with her, she was a limp noodle and didn't have any thoughts in her head except for the man who'd brought her such pleasure.

She was able to rouse enough to return the favor though, going down on him for the first time. Amanda loved the feeling of power it had given her, especially now, when she felt as if she had no control over her life. Watching Nash put his pleasure in her hands—and mouth—had given her back a sense of control she hadn't felt for quite a while. She loved him for that.

No, that wasn't true...she loved Nash because of the man he was. He'd proven to her time and time again that she could count on him. That he wouldn't let her down. That he was there for her. How could she *not* love him?

But she wasn't ready to say the words out loud, afraid she'd jinx things.

After all, they were still in the middle of a crisis. Maybe it wasn't as intense as when they were in the jungle, but there was no clear end to whatever was happening. And until she didn't have to have a *bodyguard*, as Tex had put it, she wasn't going to put any more pressure on Nash than he already had on his wide, capable shoulders.

This morning, however, her stress returned, since they had no more information about Blair's whereabouts than they did a few days ago. It didn't help that there was tension in the hangar. Currently, Amanda was watching Laryn argue with one of her mechanics over something they were doing to the helicopter she was retrofitting for Casper. Apparently it wasn't the first time she'd had to do it in a very short amount of time, and she had no patience for the newer mechanics who thought they knew better than her.

Rain was lying at Amanda's feet as she sat on a surprisingly comfortable easy chair someone had brought into the hangar the second day she was there. She had no idea where it came from, but she assumed Nash had made arrangements for the more comfortable place for her to hang out all day.

The dog had been as good as gold. Not making a peep and not leaving her side. He didn't sleep, but kept his gaze locked on everyone who made their way close to her. For a dog who'd had a horrible life, he'd turned into an amazingly well-behaved animal who adored Amanda, and who was loved just as much in return.

As she was sitting there, bored out of her mind but determined not to let on—because after all, everyone was doing her a favor by letting her hang out in the first place—Amanda was surprised to see Nash enter the hangar and make his way toward her.

But he wasn't smiling. He had a serious look on his face that didn't bode well for whatever reason was behind his visit.

Amanda tensed, hated that she felt that way upon seeing the man she loved. She couldn't wait for the time when she could be happy and excited by a surprise visit, rather than worried about what was wrong *now*.

"What is it? Has Tex found them?" she asked, standing as he got close.

Rain got up to greet Nash, and he gave him a quick but distracted pet before closing the distance between himself and Amanda.

"He found Bibi."

"Really? Where is she? Is she okay? Can we go see her?"

But Nash shook his head slowly, frowning solemnly.

"She's dead, Mandy," he said quietly. "I'm so sorry."

It took a moment for the words to sink in.

"What?"

"A little girl's body was found in a park in North Carolina, not too far from the border of Virginia. She was malnourished, had bruises all over her body, and the coroner believes she died of exposure. That was four days ago. There was no identification on her, so nobody knew who she was. Tex found the report and had his suspicions. He sent in a picture from her file at the orphanage. It's her."

For long seconds, Amanda felt numb. Her mind and body utterly detached from this moment. Then she closed her eyes, the news sinking in slowly.

The little girl she'd wanted to be her daughter—the beautiful, smart, kind, precious child she'd gotten to know—would never grow up. Would never experience the many joys there were in life. Graduations, her first job, first crushes…love.

Amanda's heart shattered.

The first sob took her by surprise, but once the dam was broken, there was no stopping it. The tears came hard and fast, pouring down her cheeks like a faucet had suddenly been turned on full blast.

It wasn't *fair*! Not Bibi. Not that precious little girl...

Nash enveloped her in his embrace, and Amanda collapsed against him, grateful for the comfort he was offering. She buried her head in his shoulder and closed her eyes tightly. That didn't stop the tears though. They came just as fast, soaking Nash's shirt and skin. Bathing him with her despair, her sorrow.

But she kept her eyes squeezed shut. Maybe if she could block everything out, this wouldn't be happening. Nash's words wouldn't be true.

"Why?" she eventually whispered between sobs. "*Why?!* If Blair wanted her so much, why would she do that to her?"

"I don't know," Nash said gently. "But if I had to guess...Blair had no idea what she was doing. If she's in the middle of a mental crisis, she probably can't take care of herself, let alone a child. I'm not making excuses for her, because there *is* no excuse for something like this, but just...trying to make sense of how this could've happened."

Amanda felt as if she were watching their drama from above. As if she were having an out-of-body experience. All she wanted to do was go to sleep. Then she wouldn't have to think about this awful news. About the fact that she'd never see Bibi again. Never hear her laugh. Never hold her little hand...

"Can we get her?" she managed to ask. "I can't stand the idea of her being in a cold morgue by herself."

"Tex is already working on that. If possible, we'll get her transferred here, and we'll have a service for her."

"I want to h-have her cremated," Mandy said with a hitch in her voice. "I brought a kite with me from the States, when I went to Guyana, and she was so fascinated by it. How the wind could carry it so high in the sky...and the way it danced." Her voice softened, and fresh tears spilled over her cheeks. "She skipped around in a field of dirt behind the school, laughing and turning in circles with her arms open, watching the kite. That's how I want to remember her, Nash. Laughing and flying free. Not buried deep in the ground."

"Then that's what we'll do," he said quietly.

Amanda stayed where she was, curled up against his chest, as memories of little Bibi swam through her head. Anger mixed in with her sorrow. This was so damn unfair! She'd had such a tragic short life. She *should've* had the chance to fly herself. Make a difference in the world.

She had no idea how long she cried on Nash's shoulder, but he held her tightly the entire time. Letting her have her mini break-down without interference.

After a while, when she'd gotten control over her tears somewhat, something occurred to her suddenly. She lifted her head and looked at Nash in horror. "This was *my* fault," she whispered. "If I hadn't told Blair that I wanted to adopt—"

"*No*," Nash said forcefully. "Do *not* take this on your shoulders. This is in no way your fault. It's Blair's. No one else's."

"But—"

"Don't," Nash interrupted her again. "I mean it, Mandy. Loving a child is *never* a bad thing. What happened is entirely on Blair. Period. Full stop."

For the first time since hearing the news about Bibi, Amanda studied the man she was clutching as if he was the only thing keeping her from floating away in a ball of misery.

He looked just as shocked as she felt. And sad. And the anger reflected in his eyes mirrored her own, as well. He'd never met little Bibi, had only seen her from afar when they'd returned to the school after getting out of the jungle, but he seemed just as upset as she was. It was a testament to the kind of man he was. A *good* man.

"What now?" she whispered, wanting to comfort him the way he was doing for her, but not knowing how.

"We stay vigilant. Blair is on her own now. And North

Carolina is way too close to Norfolk for my liking. Since the coroner estimates Bibi died four days ago, Blair could be just about anywhere...most likely *here*. If she's had a complete mental breakdown, there's no telling what she could do."

"If she's that bad, how would she be able to think and strategize enough to find me?" Amanda asked.

"I don't know. But I'm not going to take any chances. Not with your safety. I can't lose you, Mandy. I *can't*."

"You aren't going to," she said softly.

"Damn straight. We're going to live a long and happy life. We'll be old and gray and will walk around holding hands, making people roll their eyes at how ridiculously happy we are. Maybe we'll take up cruising as a hobby, see the world from the deck of a boat. Stuff our faces with food, drink good wine, sleep until noon. I don't know. But I want that more than I can express. With you."

"I want that too," Amanda whispered.

"Good. So watch your back. Be aware of your surroundings at all times. Trust no one. That last one sucks, but I wouldn't put it past Blair to hire someone to grab you or hurt you."

A shiver ran down Amanda's spine. Never in a million years would she have thought the woman who'd seemed so kind and smart would end up on the run...*killing* one of the children she'd devoted her life to. And apparently so filled with hate, she was hunting Amanda down. It was unfathomable.

"I'm ready for a more boring life," she blurted, gazing up at Nash. "I thought my life as a teacher wasn't that exciting, but now I'd do anything to get that back."

"You'll have it. I'll do whatever it takes to get that back for you."

He pulled her into his embrace again, and Amanda soaked in the feeling of being cared for, of not being alone during this scary time in her life. If Nash hadn't been here for her, hadn't taken her in, hadn't used his connections to help find out information about what was happening, she'd be completely clueless. He was her world, and without him, she'd feel as if she was adrift on a big scary ocean without any oars.

She felt him take a long, deep breath seconds before he pulled back. "Casper gave me the rest of the day off. I want to take you home. How does a long hot bath sound? You can finish the new book you bought, I'll make us something to eat, and we can cuddle with Rain on the couch and watch a movie or something."

That sounded amazing. But Amanda felt guilty. "I thought you and your team were preparing for a mission?"

Nash shrugged. "We are. But nothing is more important than you and your mental health."

"I'm not sure Uncle Sam would agree," she said lightly.

"You just learned some awful news," Nash replied gently. "Casper knows how that feels. How it feels to have the rug pulled out from under your feet. He'll deal with the colonel and bring me up to speed on anything I missed."

"Will you get in trouble with your boss?"

"No. Colonel Burgess is a good man. Tough but fair. He won't have a problem with me taking the rest of the day off."

"Okay. What you suggested sounds perfect...although to be honest, I feel pretty lazy just sitting around all day. I'm not used to it."

"I think it's *time* you slowed down a tad. Besides, when you start teaching again, you'll make up for the downtime you have now, I'm sure."

He wasn't wrong. Teaching wasn't a seven-to-three kind of job. It was all-consuming, at least for her.

Nash kissed her forehead gently, then took her hand. He leaned down and grabbed Rain's leash and headed for the exit.

Amanda waved at Laryn—who waved back, giving her a concerned look—then focused on nothing but the way Nash's hand felt in hers. She was pretty sure later tonight, she'd break down again while thinking about poor little Bibi, about how things had ended for her. And there'd be many more tears in the days to come.

But right now, she was back to feeling...numb. Disbelieving.

Her life had taken such a strange turn, and it looked like the roller coaster she was on, the one she thought she'd gotten off when she'd exited the jungle, was actually still going full speed. She wanted off, but it didn't seem that was going to happen anytime soon.

Her only hope was that Blair was found. It was hard to believe, in her mental state, that she'd be able to stay under the radar for so long. Someone had to recognize her soon. If not, it was likely this limbo Amanda was in would continue. And that sucked.

She didn't even want to think about what would happen if Blair wasn't found before Nash and his fellow pilots had to leave on the mission they were planning.

A shiver ran through her. She'd never minded being alone before, but now that she'd experienced all that was Nash Chaney...the way he took care of her, how he'd made himself almost indispensable...and with Blair still out there, apparently still holding a nasty grudge against her, being alone felt extremely scary.

One day at a time, she told herself. *That's all you have to do. One day, one step at a time.*

CHAPTER TWENTY-TWO

Buck didn't like this. Not at all. Two more days had gone by since they'd learned about little Bibi's death. Mandy was hanging on, but he could see the stress and sadness in her eyes, her body language, her very essence.

Even though he'd told her not to feel guilty, that nothing Blair had done was her fault, that there was no possible way she could have known of Blair's mental illness when she'd expressed interest in adopting Bibi...the child's death was weighing on her. He wished he could help her more, ease her pain. But unfortunately, all he could do was hold her at night and keep reminding her that he was there. That Tex and the police would find Blair. That everything would be all right.

But that was the thing—he didn't know if it *would* be all right. He had a bad feeling that danger was lurking just out of sight. That something was about to happen. His gut was screaming to lock Mandy away and not let her out until Blair was found.

But Mandy was a sociable person. An extrovert. She needed to be around people to be happy. She was in her element when she was with others. Caring for them. Teaching them.

She'd received word that she'd gotten the long-term subbing job at the school on the naval base. She was thrilled, but knowing she was supposed to start in two weeks just added *more* stress to her shoulders, because of their current situation.

She was worried about the kids. If Blair wasn't found by the time she started teaching, would the children be in danger? Would her fellow teachers? Would Blair be able to get on the Navy base? It was unlikely, but then again, being kidnapped and taken into the rainforest had also seemed unlikely. As had everything else that happened. Mandy knew better than most not to take her safety, or the safety of those around her, for granted.

So Buck took Mandy and Rain to the base with him every morning, left them in the hangar with Laryn, and went to his meetings.

It was awful. This constant worry hanging over his head. It was all-consuming, hoping Mandy was all right, that they wouldn't get any more bad news. He'd spoken with Tex a couple times in the last two days, but the man had nothing to report. He had a few leads but nothing concrete yet.

It was frustrating…yet, Buck wouldn't change anything about his life and the direction it had taken in the last couple of months. Because doing so would mean he wouldn't have Mandy in his life. And there was nothing, no amount of stress or worry, that would make him regret that. He loved her.

But there was no way he could tell her yet. It was too soon, and the last thing he wanted was to add another heavy emotion on top of her stress and grief, or give her second thoughts about their relationship if she wasn't on the same page.

Buck knew what he felt though. Every morning when he woke up with Mandy in his arms, in his bed, he thanked his lucky stars that she was with him. She could have any man she wanted. She was beautiful, smart, compassionate, funny…why the hell she was with *him*, he had no idea. But he wasn't going to fuck things up, no way. He knew what he had, and was determined to make her life better as much as possible.

The time would come for him to say the words in his heart. To introduce her to his family. His mom and dad would absolutely love her. They'd take one look at Mandy and steal her away to monopolize all her time. Natalie would be a touch more cautious, but it wouldn't take his woman long to win her over, as well. And his niece and nephew would be drawn to her like moths to a flame. She was *fantastic* with kids, and his sister's children would be no exception.

She'd fit in with his family as if she'd always been a part of them, of that Buck was certain. But he had to bide his time, be patient. Not overwhelm her. She'd already been accepted by his Night Stalker family. His biological one could wait just a little longer.

She and Laryn had gotten even closer over the last week or so. Whenever Laryn took a break, she'd sit with Mandy and Rain, spoiling the dog without any guilt. Buck had been surprised when Mandy told him they'd had a conversation one afternoon about what Laryn had been through in Turkey. About her kidnapping. To his knowledge, she hadn't talked that much about her experience to anyone, not even Casper. So that she'd opened up to Mandy was a big deal.

He assumed it was because she and Mandy shared the experience of being taken against their will. They'd bonded over a similar emotional trauma. He hated that *either* woman had gone through what they had, but he was beyond relieved that Mandy and Laryn were getting along so well.

Now it was Saturday, and instead of enjoying a day alone with his woman, Buck had attended an unexpected meeting at the base right after lunch. Something that couldn't wait until Monday, as new intel had come in about the mission they'd be sent on soon. He'd brought Mandy and Rain with him, as usual, and left them in one of the empty conference rooms down the hall from where he and his fellow pilots were gathered.

He rejoined her hours later, and they headed straight back to his apartment. Now Mandy was sitting on the couch, quieter than usual, and Buck was desperate to do something, *anything*, to cheer her up. She had to be sick to death of the four walls of his apartment, and sitting around doing nothing while he was at work. She'd been working on lesson plans for her upcoming sub job, but that couldn't occupy all her time.

He'd just made the decision to get her out of the apartment, to take her out for dinner, when his phone rang.

Mandy looked up with a concerned frown on her face, which Buck hated. Didn't like that every time his cell rang, she assumed the worst. That he was either being deployed, or whoever was on the other end would bring more bad news about Blair.

"Hello? Yes, she's here. Okay, hang on."

It was Tex. He'd asked if Mandy was nearby, and if so, requested Buck put the phone on speaker. He would've preferred to know what Tex wanted to tell them first, before he shared it with Mandy. He could only hope the man had good news, and that was why he was so insistent on Mandy hearing it first-hand.

"Can you hear me?" Tex asked.

"Yes, we're both here and can hear you just fine," Buck said, pulling Mandy in front of him and linking his fingers together at her belly, resting his chin on her shoulder. His phone sat on the counter, and he stared at it intently, praying Tex was about to tell them that Blair had been found.

"One of the men involved in your kidnapping was arrested in Guyana last night," Tex said, not beating around the bush. "And he's talking."

That was good news. Buck's hopes rose.

"Basically your instincts were dead on, Mandy. Blair Gaffney was behind the raid at the school. She wanted you gone. Ranted and raved about what a horrible person you were. How you were trying to take over her job. Said you were turning the children and the other employees and volunteers against her."

Mandy inhaled sharply. "That's not true!" she exclaimed.

"Of course it isn't," Tex said calmly. "But in her declining mental state, I'm guessing she truly believed it. The man—who was arrested for being in Guyana illegally—said that Blair wanted you taken, and she agreed they could take the older boys as well, as part of their payment. She was well aware that boys were often taken away from their families and forced to join the rebel army. He said the boys were supposed to be separated from the others, but when they arrived, the children were all together instead. So they just took them all."

"But they didn't even seem particularly interested in me at first," Mandy protested. "Not until one of the men grabbed me. I thought it was because I refused to make little Bibi let go of me, when they were separating the kids from the adults."

"I'm just telling you what the man said. All I know is that Blair was behind it. In addition to the older boys, she paid them funds from the orphanage as well. And apparently she was highly agitated when you showed up again. When the *children* were returned, she was thrilled. She'd gotten them back, which made the orphanage look both sympathetic and triumphant, but you were still gone. It was the perfect outcome for her. But then you came back. I think that's when something in her snapped, and she lost what little common sense she still had."

"Have you found her?" Buck asked, feeling sick inside at the confirmation that the woman had hated Mandy so much, she'd actually arranged for her to be kidnapped by dangerous rebels. She had to know what would happen. That Mandy would've been assaulted and eventually killed. And yet, she'd knowingly paid to make it happen...and used *children* as part of the payment. It was disgusting.

Tex sighed. "No. I *did* figure out how she got into the

country with the little girl. She paid off a mule to smuggle them both in through a checkpoint in Juarez. They crossed at a busy time and were hidden inside a trunk. It was just bad luck that they weren't discovered. Blair then bought a used car —again with funds she'd stolen from the school—and drove east."

"So you know what kind of car she's in," Buck said, desperately trying to find a bright side to this phone call.

"We know what kind of car she *was* in," Tex corrected. "The car was found abandoned at the same park where Bibi's body was found."

"Shit," Buck muttered.

"She's in the wind, I'm afraid. She's not using credit cards, and I'm guessing she's changed her looks. But I'm not giving up. I'm gonna find her, Buck. I give you my word."

"I know you will."

"Thank you, Tex. I appreciate you helping me so much."

"Don't thank me," the man on the other end of the phone said. "I haven't done a damn thing yet. But this bitch isn't going to win. She's pissed me off now. Hang tight, Mandy. Her time's a comin'. I'll be in touch with more info soon."

The phone connection ended, and Buck took a deep breath. It was either that or swear like a sailor, using all the words he'd learned from the Navy SEAL and Delta Force comrades he transported on a regular basis.

"We're going out."

"What?" Mandy asked, sounding confused.

"We're going out," Buck repeated. "We need a break. Both of us. You're going stir crazy, and I can't blame you. We need to stop thinking about that bitch for a few hours."

Mandy turned in his arms. "Is it safe?"

"I'll make sure of it," Buck promised. "Nowhere fancy, just to Anchor Point. We can play some darts, have a beer and some kick-ass food, then come home. How's that sound?"

"Awesome, actually. Nash...do you think I did something to make her hate me so much?"

"Absolutely not." This right here was why she needed a break. He hated that Mandy continued to think for one second she was somehow at fault for anything that happened. "You went to South America with every good intention. I'm sure you worked your ass off at that orphanage to make sure every child felt loved and cared for. Becoming attached to Bibi wasn't some malicious act on your part; sometimes people just click."

"Like we did."

"Like we did," Buck confirmed.

"I can't believe she paid those rebels to get rid of me," Mandy said softly. "And it would've worked if you hadn't been there."

She was breaking his heart. Buck lifted her chin so he could look her in the eyes. "But I *was* there. And you're here. Safe. And I'm gonna keep you that way."

"I know."

"Do you?"

She nodded. "You've done more for me than anyone in my entire life, other than my parents. And it's not out of obligation, because if it was, you would've said goodbye the second we touched down in Virginia."

"Damn straight."

She opened her mouth, and Buck braced himself to hear the words he'd dreamed of her saying. It was the perfect time, and he was more than ready to reciprocate.

But she swallowed hard and smiled up at him instead.

Damn. He'd so hoped she'd admit her feelings. But that time would come. He was sure of it. Because she *did* love him; he already knew that. But it was scary to say the words for the first time. He was living proof. He could man up and say them first, but again, he didn't want to pressure her in any way, or decide they were moving too fast.

He could wait. He was a patient man.

"You want to change before we go?" he asked.

"We're going right now?"

"No time like the present."

"Okay. And do I look all right as I am?" she asked, looking down at herself.

Buck took his time running his gaze down her body. She had on a pair of jeans and a purple v-neck shirt. She looked amazing...but then again, she always looked that way, no matter what she was or wasn't wearing. "You look perfect."

She gave him a small smile. "Thanks, Nash. I know you're a liar, but you're a sweet one."

"I'm not lying," he insisted. "Besides, this is Anchor Point. You could wear your pajamas and no one would look twice."

She chuckled. "I think not. It's a bar, Nash. People are trying to hook up. No one is wearing PJs...unless they're the lingerie kind."

She wasn't exactly wrong.

"What about Rain?" she asked.

Buck looked over at the dog, who was lying on his bed in the corner of the room. For once he was sound asleep. He figured it was because he'd stayed awake when they were at the base, watching over Mandy. He didn't let down his guard until they arrived back home. He was obviously exhausted.

"Rain? You want to come with us, boy?" Buck called out, as if the dog could understand what he was saying. Hell, he probably could.

The dog opened his eyes and stared at them. Buck picked up his keys and held them up. "You want to come with us? Or stay here and sleep?"

In response, Rain sighed and closed his eyes again.

"Right, guess that decision is made," Mandy said with a small giggle. "We won't be long. A couple hours. Be good," she told the dog.

Rain didn't even twitch.

"He's tired," she said, as Buck put his hand on the small of her back to lead her toward the door. "I feel bad."

"He's an amazing dog. I have to admit, I never would've thought after seeing how bedraggled and thin he was in the jungle that he'd turn out to be so handsome when he filled out and was cleaned up."

"Right? Just goes to show that you can't judge a book by its cover. Kind of like Blair."

Shit. He didn't want her to think about that bitch for at least a few hours. The woman had the ability to suck all the joy out of Mandy's life.

"Come on. You need a glass of wine."

"Screw wine. I need a margarita. Or a shot. Or both."

Buck had never seen Mandy drunk. He bet she was hilarious. "Well, I'm driving, so you can have whatever you want."

"Goody," Mandy said, as she smiled up at him. "You don't mind?"

"I haven't had drunk sex with my girlfriend yet. I bet it'll be awesome. So no, I don't mind."

She rolled her eyes. "Of course it'll be awesome, because you'll be there."

"Keep talking like that and you'll definitely get some tonight."

Mandy laughed. Seeing her frown lines disappear and the smile on her face was worth more than all the riches in the world. Buck vowed to do whatever he could to keep this woman happy and content.

* * *

Two and a half hours later, Buck couldn't stop smiling. Mandy was beautiful and kind all the time, but drunk? She was fucking amazing. Laughing, happy, and extremely eager to make sure everyone around her was feeling the exact same way.

She complimented all the waitresses every time they walked by. Telling them she loved their shoes, their hair, the way they effortlessly carried their trays. She thanked men in the bar who were wearing uniforms for their service. She insisted on tipping the bartender very well, every time Buck went to get her another drink.

In short, she was the kind of drunk everyone wanted to be around. Fun and carefree. Seeing her smile and having the time of her life was awesome, especially after the tough few weeks she'd had. Buck wasn't a fan of using alcohol to numb pain or to escape bad experiences, because that shit didn't work for long—those memories always came back tenfold—but seeing Mandy completely relaxed and not thinking about Blair, or the loss of the little girl she'd hoped to adopt, was worth the headache she'd likely have in the morning.

"You know what would've made tonight better?" she asked, leaning against Buck and smiling up at him.

"What, Rebel?"

"Having everyone else here too. Your friends."

"*Our* friends," Buck corrected.

Mandy beamed at that. "Yeah, *our* friends. They're awesome. And not just because they keep you safe when you're flying. Laryn included. Because they're *nice*. And they make you happy."

"*You* make me happy," Buck corrected.

"I'm glad. Because you make me feel like a completely different woman than I used to be. I feel as if I can do anything."

"You can."

"See? That right there. You're so good to me. Why are you so good to me? I'm a mess, Nash. My life is a mess."

"Because you're you," Buck told her. "Because in your eyes, I see my future. A future I had no idea I wanted until you burst into my life."

"You hated me at first. Were irritated that you had to come after me."

She wasn't completely wrong. "I didn't hate you," he corrected.

She grinned. "But you *were* irritated."

Buck shrugged. "Maybe a little."

Mandy giggled again. "Understatement," she muttered, taking a sip of her margarita. It was her third, and while Buck loved tipsy Mandy, he didn't want her incoherent when they got home. He had plans for her. He wanted to see her ride him. Hard and fast. And after she came, he was going to carry her out to the kitchen table and lay her down and feast.

He'd fantasized about that the other morning, while they were eating breakfast. It had popped into his brain out of the blue, and now he couldn't think about anything else. After she'd orgasmed again, he was going to fuck her right there on the table. From behind. It was the perfect height to bend her over and take her. And she'd love every second, take what he had to give her, just like she always did.

"Do I want to know what you're thinking?" she asked with a grin. "You're thinking about sex, aren't you?"

"I'm always thinking about sex when I'm with you," Buck said honestly.

"Not when we were in the jungle. That's gross."

He shrugged.

"You were?" she practically screeched. "Nash! We were disgusting! Dirty and sweaty and tired…"

"You're fucking beautiful, Mandy. How could I *not* think about it?"

"You're so weird," she said with a shake of her head.

It was Buck's turn to laugh. He pulled on her arm and she fell against him, laughing.

"Don't spill my drink!"

He took it out of her hand and placed it on a nearby table. They'd been watching two sailors battle over a billiards table, but all interest in the game had waned.

"I think about you all the time," he admitted. "When I'm flying, when I'm in meetings, when I'm in the car, when I'm in the shower. *Especially* when I'm in the shower. I'm a lucky son-of-a-bitch and I know it, and I can't get you off my mind."

"Nash," she said on a sigh, giving him more of her weight.

"I told you before, this isn't a fling," Buck told her. "I'm in this for the long haul. You are sexy as sin, Mandy, but it's more than sex. Yes, that part of our relationship is awesome, and I think about how compatible we are on a daily basis. But it's more than that. It's how happy I feel when I'm around you. How content. How it feels as if you complete me. And that's cheesy as shit, and I'll deny I said it if you tell anyone," he teased. "But I wanted you to know."

"Okay, that was the sweetest thing anyone has ever said to me. And I'm too drunk to appreciate it fully, or respond with something equally as awesome. So I'll just say...I don't know what I'd do without you. You've gotten under my skin and I like you there. So don't ever leave, okay?"

Buck smiled. "Not planning on it."

"Good. But you *are* planning on giving me an orgasm or two when we get home, right?"

His grin widened. "Oh yeah."

"And carrying me around. And moving me where you want me? I love when you do that." She sighed dreamily. "I never thought I'd like being so short, but with you? It makes me feel feminine, and it's so sexy."

This woman was killing him. The truth was that at five-eight, he'd never been the kind of man who could physically move a woman in bed before. But none of the partners he'd had were Mandy. None were five foot nothing. She was made for him. Together, they were perfection.

"You like me bossing you around in bed?"

She nodded with a shy smile.

"You like me putting you where I want you and doing whatever I want with you?"

"Yes. Because it's not about you doing what you want. Not entirely. It's about you making sure I'm satisfied. That I enjoy what you're doing. If you were cruel about it, or didn't take my pleasure into consideration, it would suck. But you do, so it doesn't."

She was one hundred percent right. Buck would never do anything that would hurt her. He bossed her around because she loved it. Because it turned her on. And in turn, it made their sex life even hotter.

"You ready to go home?" he asked.

She smiled up at him. "Am I ready for you to take me home and give me multiple orgasms and fall asleep, or pass out, whatever, in your arms as you hold me? Yes, sir. I am more than ready."

He was hard and ready for her. He'd take her in the front seat of his car if he could, but that wouldn't be safe. And the last thing he'd ever do was put her in danger, or expose their lovemaking to anyone who might be walking by. He wasn't a voyeur. Wanted to keep his woman to himself. But the ride home would be one of the longest of his life. He couldn't wait to experience drunk sex with Mandy. She was going to blow his mind, of that, he was positive.

It took them twenty minutes to actually get out the door because Mandy insisted on saying bye to all her "new friends." The bartender, the waitresses, the men playing pool…everyone got her unique brand of Mandy-ness.

Buck was smiling huge, arm around his woman, when he was *finally* able to lead her out the door. Other men in the bar were looking at him with envy, not because he was a Night Stalker—*that*, he was used to—but because he was with Mandy. And the feeling that gave him was ten times better than any pride he had in his job.

The parking lot had emptied out a bit since they'd arrived. It was dark as hell, and Buck had once again been forced to park near the back of the lot, in the only space left when they'd arrived during the dinner rush. Anchor Point was popular, for good reason, and while the parking situation *always* annoyed him...now, it had him second-guessing walking to the car, in the dark, with Mandy.

He turned his head, glancing at the door to the bar, wondering if he should escort her back inside to wait for him. When he decided they were halfway to his car already, and it would just be a waste of time, he turned his attention back to where they were walking.

He had a split second of warning, in the form of Mandy's quick inhalation, before all hell broke loose.

Someone ran out from behind a parked car and swung something at Mandy before he could even blink.

The feel of something hitting her head reverberated straight through her and into Buck, since she was plastered against his body when she was struck.

She immediately collapsed, and as Buck struggled to keep her from falling on her face, the attacker struck again. This time the metal pipe, or whatever they were wielding, missed Mandy, hitting Buck in the shoulder.

Pain made him see stars, and his grip on Mandy loosened.

She crumbled to the ground, moaning.

The shock of being attacked and the pain coursing through his body was enough distraction to allow their attacker one more chance to strike.

The weapon swung—and Mandy's groans ceased altogether.

Buck moved before he thought about what he was doing. The karate lessons he'd had as a teen came back to him instinctually. He hadn't used them since he was eighteen, but that didn't matter. Muscle memory helped him kick the metal object out of the hands of the attacker.

KEEPING AMANDA

Ignoring the pain in his shoulder, he swung, catching their assailant in the neck with the side of his hand. Attacks to the throat were off limits in karate competitions, but this was no game. This was life or death.

The karate chop changed to a closed fist, and Buck punched the attacker in the face once they were on the ground. But the person wasn't moving. They were now lying as still as Mandy.

The attack had taken seconds. But to Buck it felt like hours.

Ignoring the blood on his hand, he yelled for help even as he moved toward the woman he loved, sprawled on the asphalt. He could see blood already pooling around her head, and his heart literally stopped beating in his chest. He'd promised to keep her safe—and he'd failed.

She was attacked even while in his arms.

Buck would never forgive himself. Ever.

"Mandy!" he rasped, as he bent over her and put his hand on the wound on the side of her head, where it looked like most of the blood was coming from.

Thankfully someone else exited the bar and heard Buck's cry for help. He came running over and called 9-1-1 while Buck pleaded with Mandy to wake up, to not leave him.

Within minutes, the ambulance and police arrived. Buck hadn't taken his eyes off Mandy since disabling their attacker. The person was still lying motionless not too far away, right where he'd left them.

The paramedics insisted he back up, and letting go of Mandy was one of the hardest things he'd ever done in his life. She still lay motionless on the ground, that damn pool of blood around her head the most terrifying thing he'd ever seen.

His attention was drawn to a second set of EMTs working on their attacker. Buck was shocked to realize it was a woman. What looked like a homeless woman, at that.

But when he looked closer—he saw that it was Blair.

The woman Tex had so desperately been looking for, the

woman Buck had vowed to keep Mandy safe from...They hadn't found her; she'd found *them*.

The crowbar she'd used to attack them was lying a foot from her hand.

Anger hit Buck hard. Mandy had taken a blow to the head from a fucking *crowbar*. He'd let down his guard, and Blair had taken advantage of his inattentiveness, and struck.

As he stood there in shock, watching the paramedics work on getting Mandy ready for transportation to the hospital, Blair regained consciousness. She immediately began to shout about taking what was hers, and injustice, and revenge. Just as they'd suspected, and Desmond had reported, she was completely out of her mind. The woman Mandy had once known was nowhere to be seen.

Buck watched dispassionately as the police put Blair in handcuffs and led her away after she was cleared by the EMTs. He needed to tell the cops that Blair was wanted for suspicion of child abuse and the murder of Bibi—as well as crimes in Guyana—but right now, all he could think about was Mandy.

He followed behind the gurney she'd been put on as the paramedics wheeled her toward the ambulance. They prevented him from getting in behind her.

"I'm sorry, sir, but no one is allowed in the ambulance."

Buck panicked. He had to go with her! He couldn't lose her!

A hand closed on his arm, and Buck fought to get free, to get to Mandy.

"Easy, Buck. I'll take you to the hospital."

Turning, Buck saw Obi-Wan standing there. He blinked, confused. When had he gotten there? How had he even known what happened? How long had the paramedics been working on Mandy in the parking lot? Buck felt as if he was in a fog. He couldn't think straight.

"Come on, I've got you. Did you let them look at you? Are you hurt?"

Buck could only stare at his friend and copilot.

"Right, we'll do that at the hospital then." Obi-Wan steered Buck toward his Jeep Wrangler, which was parked on the street a little ways down from the bar.

Buck stared straight ahead as Obi-Wan drove like a bat out of hell toward the hospital.

"I got a call from one of the bartenders. No clue how he got my number, but I'm damn glad he did. Casper is already contacting the cops about Blair, he'll tell them about Bibi, and get with the detectives in North Carolina. She's not getting away, Buck. She's done for. Mandy is safe."

But she wasn't *safe*. She was beaten in the head with a fucking crowbar! Even if she did survive, she might not be the same person she was before.

Buck couldn't stop thinking about how happy and carefree she was not even an hour earlier. How she'd made everyone around her smile. Her laughter still rang in his ears.

He made a keening sound deep in his throat at the thought of losing the most important person in his life.

Obi-Wan reached over and grabbed Buck's hand, holding on to it with an iron grip.

"She's strong," his friend said firmly. "She's going to pull through. I know it."

Buck didn't feel embarrassed about holding Obi-Wan's hand. He felt as if his friend was the only thing keeping him from splintering into a million pieces right now. His anchor. Just as the man had been at his side through some of the most harrowing missions of their lives, he was there now, in his absolute darkest moment. It felt right.

Obi-Wan gave him the strength to keep breathing.

When they got to the hospital, Obi-Wan didn't park, he pulled right up to the entrance and said, "Go. I'll be in there in a few moments to join you."

As soon as he let go of his copilot's hand, Buck felt adrift again. Lost.

He walked into the emergency room in a daze. Then stopped and blinked at what he saw once the automatic doors to the waiting room opened.

Pyro, Chaos, and Edge were all there. But it was Laryn who was the first to reach him, grabbing him by the hand and pulling him over to the corner the others had apparently claimed as their own in the waiting area. Soon, Buck was surrounded by the people he wanted around him most right now.

"Casper will be here soon. He's on the phone with Tex."

Buck nodded. But it didn't matter anymore. Blair was found. Tex could move on to other cases. Help find other missing people. Track down info for others.

He didn't feel as if Tex had failed him, exactly, because it was more than obvious Blair had been living on the streets. But he couldn't help his feelings of...hurt? Frustration? Anger?...that Tex hadn't come through when he'd needed him most.

Buck had no idea how Blair had gotten to the Norfolk area, or how she'd found him and Mandy, or followed them to the bar...but it really didn't matter anymore.

All that mattered was that she'd done what she'd set out to do—hurt the woman he loved.

"You don't look so good. Have you been seen? Are you hurt?" Pyro asked.

Buck could only stare at him blankly.

"Come on, let's get you taken care of so you can be at your best when you see Mandy."

See Mandy. Yes, that's what he needed to do. He docilely followed Pyro toward the intake desk.

Buck had no concept of time passing. But he was aware that he was brought into a room behind the emergency doors, and a doctor looked him over. Then his arm was put into a sling so his bruised shoulder could heal, and he'd been given some painkillers, which he refused to take. He wanted to be coherent and awake when he was allowed to see Mandy.

But instead of being led to a room to see her, he was brought back out to the waiting area.

"Where's Mandy?" he asked, noticing that Casper had arrived in his absence.

"They took her back to surgery," Chaos said quietly. "She had bleeding on the brain and they need to reduce the pressure in her head."

Buck closed his eyes and swayed hard on his feet.

"He's going down!"

"Get him in a chair!"

"Push his head down!"

Buck felt himself being forced to sit, but everything felt like a blur. Surgery? A brain bleed? This was a nightmare he wanted to wake up from.

Then something else occurred to him.

"Rain!" he said urgently, lifting his head and trying to stand.

But Edge and Pyro, one on either side of him, pushed him back into the seat. "We'll get him. We'll take care of everything. All you have to do is be here for Mandy."

Looking up, Buck stared into Casper's eyes. His team leader was crouched in front of him, meeting his gaze head on. If anyone knew what he was feeling right now, it was Casper. He'd almost lost Laryn. He knew how desperate Buck felt.

"Is she going to be okay?" he whispered.

"Yes," Casper said without hesitation. "Your woman is tough. She wouldn't have gone down to Guyana in the first place if she wasn't. She wouldn't have survived that rebel camp if she wasn't. She wouldn't have made it through the jungle if she wasn't. She's going to pull through. I know it."

Buck was well aware Casper wasn't a doctor. That he had no idea if Mandy would survive or not. But his words were still a balm to Buck's shattered psyche. Exactly what he needed to hear right now.

"Have faith, Buck. In the doctors, in your woman. And when you're able to go in and see her, talk to her, just let her know that you're here. That you aren't going anywhere. How much you care about her. Give her a reason to fight. To come back to you."

Buck nodded, taking his team leader's words to heart. He'd do whatever it took to get Mandy back on her feet. He'd stay by her side no matter what condition she was in when she woke up.

With the vision of her smiling, laughing face in his head, Buck clenched his fists in determination. Mandy would be okay. She simply had to be.

CHAPTER TWENTY-THREE

Buck had no idea what time it was. Hell, he had no idea what *day* it was. All he knew was that Mandy still hadn't woken up. She'd made it through the surgery to lessen the pressure on her brain, but she'd been in a medically induced coma ever since. The doctors wanted to give her brain time to heal. For the swelling to go down.

But every day that went by was one more Buck spent in hell. He wasn't eating very much, definitely wasn't sleeping enough. He wasn't thinking about his job, the upcoming mission, and even poor Rain had been neglected. Thank goodness Laryn had stepped up and brought Rain to her and Casper's place for the time being.

Buck couldn't bring himself to leave the hospital. The nurses and doctors were well used to him by now, and had allowed him to spend much more than his allotted time in the ICU room with Mandy.

The beeping of the machines she was hooked up to were background noise. Buck barely heard them anymore. All his attention was on Mandy. She looked even smaller than usual in the big hospital bed with all the tubes attached to her body.

He sat next to her for hours, holding her hand and talking.

He talked nonstop. Retelling stories she'd already heard from him. Talking about the weather, about Rain, about his family. Anything he could think of.

And he told her how much he loved her. Over and over, he said the words out loud. Words he'd give anything to have said before she was attacked. She had to know how much she meant to him. That she was his world. That he loved her more than he'd ever loved anyone in his entire life.

But the longer Buck sat with her, the more despondent he became. She hadn't moved. Hadn't even flinched. The doctors said that was normal. That since she was in the medically induced coma, she wouldn't be able to do anything other than heal, which was the point.

They also said the swelling had gone down, which was a relief, but the fact that she hadn't moved even one little muscle was freaking Buck out, no matter *what* the doctors told him.

He was sitting with Mandy, as usual, when Obi-Wan came into the room. Buck was surprised to see him, since ICU didn't normally allow more than one visitor at a time.

"The doctor said I had ten minutes," Obi-Wan said, without beating around the bush. "I have news I think you, and Mandy, will want to hear. And since I knew you wouldn't leave her side, I convinced the doctor to let me in."

Buck nodded. His friends had been his rock. He didn't know what he'd have done without them. Casper had talked to Colonel Burgess and gotten Buck's emergency leave approved, Laryn had taken Rain in without question, Obi-Wan and the rest of the guys had taken turns bringing him food and clean clothes, and bullying him into showering when they could get away with it.

"What day is it?" Buck asked Obi-Wan.

"It's been five days since you guys were attacked."

Buck blinked in surprise. "Really?"

"Uh-huh."

"Wow. It feels like it's been a lot longer."

"Not surprising. Anyway, Buck...Blair is dead," Obi-Wan said flatly.

Buck felt not one iota of regret at the news. In fact, he was relieved. *Glad.*

"What happened?"

"She was arrested under suspicion of murder and arrangements were being made to move her to a mental health facility in North Carolina. It was obvious to everyone that she wasn't competent to stand trial, and that she was experiencing a complete mental breakdown."

Buck growled.

"That doesn't absolve her of guilt," Obi-Wan said quickly. "Nor does it make what she did okay, by any stretch. She wasn't going to be freed anytime soon, even if she was deemed incompetent to stand trial. But while she was in a local mental facility, she attacked one of the guards. She'd taken one of the springs from her mattress and tried to use it as a weapon. She had to be Tasered, and she apparently had a heart attack as a result. Even though she was in her seventies, I guess she had the strength of the mentally ill behind her...a Taser was the only way to subdue her."

Buck nodded. He really was glad she was gone, that Mandy wouldn't have to deal with her if she woke up...*when* she woke up. But other than that, he felt nothing.

"Tex is struggling. Wants to talk to you when you feel up to it."

Buck wasn't sure he wanted to talk to the infamous computer geek. All he'd ever heard was how great the man was. He'd done amazing things for Casper and Laryn. Had been an integral part in getting Laryn out of Turkey alive and relatively unharmed. But his Mandy was lying unconscious, and he had no idea if she'd be the same person she was before the attack when she woke up. He didn't fully blame *Tex* for that; the blame was just as much his own. But he definitely wasn't happy the man hadn't been able to locate Blair before the woman found Mandy.

"She was under the radar, Buck. Didn't have a phone, a car, credit cards. She hitchhiked to Virginia and hung out near the base. She never did find out where you lived, but she was able to talk to people around the base, until someone told her a lot of pilots liked to hang out at Anchor Point. She was living in the park right around the corner, keeping watch. Waiting and hoping you'd show up, so she could get to Mandy. Tex literally had no way to track her."

Intellectually, Buck knew that. But rational or not, it still hurt that of all the people Tex had helped out of bad situations, Mandy was one of the few he couldn't.

"How's she doing?" Obi-Wan asked quietly, when Buck didn't say anything.

He shrugged. "The same. No worse, no better."

"What about the swelling?"

"The doctor says it's going down."

"That's good news."

"Yeah."

"Are they going to ease her off the drugs to bring her out of the coma?"

"If she continues to do well, and the swelling goes down a little more, yes."

"You know this wasn't your fault...right, Buck?"

At his friend's words, Buck's eyes filled with tears. He didn't want to cry. Wanted to stay strong for Mandy. But the concern in Obi-Wan's voice did him in.

Once more, Obi-Wan took Buck's hand in his and held on tight. He didn't say anything, just stood by like a pillar of strength as Buck silently cried.

"I love her, man," Buck said after a long moment, when he could speak again. "And I never told her."

"She knows, Buck."

"*How?* How can she know?"

"Because it was in your eyes every time you looked at her. Every time you made her breakfast or dinner. Every time you took Rain out, so she could stay in bed an extra five minutes. It was in every little thing you did for her. It's not the words that matter, Buck...it's the actions. And you show her every single day that you love her. And you know what else? She loves you right back. It's as plain as day to all of us."

Buck looked up at his friend then. "You think?"

"Yes."

Buck took a deep breath, then looked back at the woman lying motionless on the bed in front of him. Obi-Wan was right, of course. He *had* known that Mandy loved him. Every day, she showed him without words how much she cared, the same way he proved that he loved her. With actions. The way she always reached for him in her sleep. How she looked to him anytime they got news about Blair. How she clung to him when they heard about Bibi.

Taking another deep breath, Buck looked at his friend. "I was thinking about making love to her when we got home, and not paying as much attention to our surroundings as I should have. You know how dark Anchor Point's parking lot is. I was just thinking that I should've left Mandy inside, and gone to get the car by myself, when Blair appeared out of nowhere."

"If it didn't happen that night, it would've happened some other time. Blair was patient. She wasn't going to give up. And so what if you were thinking about sex? That doesn't mean you were at fault. I've heard you tell Mandy more than once that what happened to her at the school, getting kidnapped, wasn't her fault. That what happened to little Bibi wasn't her fault. That all the fault lies with Blair. The same applies here. *Blair* was the one responsible for this, not you."

"I've tried to tell myself that, but the bottom line is that I vowed to keep her safe, and she got hurt on my watch."

"Life is a weird thing, Buck. You can make all the promises you want, but life still has a way of kicking you in the teeth when you least expect it. Let it go, man. For your own sanity. For *her* sake. She's gonna need you to be her rock when she wakes up, and you can't be strong for her if you're kicking yourself for what happened. Let me ask you this: you think Mandy's going to blame you when she wakes up?"

Buck didn't even have to think about that. "No."

"Exactly. Let it go. Concentrate on helping her get better. Blair is gone. Dead. She's not a threat anymore. You can't live with that hanging over your head, and Mandy wouldn't want you to. You have your whole lives ahead of you. Do you want to live with regret, or with the joy and expectation of a happy, long life instead?" Obi-Wan glanced at his watch. "With that, my time is up. I'd tell you to let us know when the doc is going to bring Mandy out of the coma, but...you should know, Tex is monitoring the situation and keeping us in the loop."

"How is he monitoring the situation?" Buck asked with a frown.

"How does Tex do anything? I'm sure he's hacked into the hospital files or something. And yes, that's illegal, but shit, is *anything* that man does truly legal? I'll ask Laryn to send a Rain update and more pictures. Mandy will want to see them when she wakes up."

And with that, Obi-Wan squeezed Buck's hand, hard, then let it go and walked out of the room.

Buck immediately turned back to Mandy, taking her hand in both of his. He brought it up to his mouth and kissed the back gently. "You hear all that, Rebel? Blair is dead. She's gone. Out of our lives forever."

"I love you. You love me. Rain is good. Tex is... Shit. I need to call him. This wasn't his fault. I know that...but deep down, I need to blame someone. Blaming myself is easy, but I wanted someone else to blame as well, and I chose him. I know it's wrong—hell, it's not even logical. I'll get my head on straight, I promise. How about you wake up and yell at me to get my shit together?"

For the first time in days, Buck felt a little better. Knowing Blair was dead went a long way toward easing the tension he'd carried on his shoulders. He wasn't sure that made him a decent human, being glad someone else was dead, but he wasn't going to waste time beating himself up for it.

"I love you, Amanda Rush. So much. I'm gonna marry you, we're gonna have kids someday, either biologically or we'll adopt. You're going to be teacher of the century, and we're going to live happily ever after. You just have to wake up so we can get started on that, okay? When the doctor reduces the drugs keeping you asleep, it's safe for you to wake up. I promise. And this time I mean it."

Buck was exhausted. The doctor said he was pleased with how she was progressing. They all just had to wait and see if her brain had suffered any permanent damage from the blows Blair had inflicted. But for the first time since Mandy had fallen to his feet in that parking lot, Buck felt a spark of hope.

There was a chance she might not even remember who she was, or her life. That she wouldn't know who *Buck* was. If that happened, it would be devastating, but he was determined he'd make her love him all over again. He'd won her once, he could do it again. He just needed the chance to do so.

And for that to happen, she had to wake up.

He fell asleep with his forehead on the back of her hand, and for the first time in days, didn't have any nightmares about Blair bursting into the room to finish what she'd started, or the doctor grimly informing him that Mandy had passed away in her sleep.

Instead, he dreamed about his wedding day, with Mandy at his side...about seeing her smile and hearing her laughter.

* * *

This was it. The doctors had reduced the amount of drugs keeping Mandy in the coma enough that she should be able to wake up on her own. For the last day and a half, she'd been restless in the bed. Moaning a little in the back of her throat and frowning as she slept. Buck had sworn she'd even squeezed his hand when he'd ordered her to a few hours ago.

Throughout it all, Buck still talked to her. So much his voice was scratchy and hoarse. If she woke up, and they were able to remove her breathing tube, she'd be moved to a regular room where all their friends could visit her. And someone, probably Tex, had even arranged for Rain to be able to come in as soon as she was moved, as well.

But first, she had to open her eyes and prove that she was still in there. Prove that she was still Mandy.

"How's she doing?" the doctor boomed, as he walked into the room.

Buck winced. His voice seemed too loud after the quiet of the last several hours.

"Better, I think," he admitted.

"Let's try this," the doctor said. There was a flurry of activity as the room filled with nurses. Buck moved to the end of the bed and held on to one of Mandy's feet. He was as nervous as he'd ever been.

The doctor leaned over Mandy—and loudly ordered her to open her eyes.

To Buck's shock, she did as she was told. Her eyes popped open.

"Good job, Mandy! Can you hear me? Squeeze the nurse's hand if you can."

Buck stared at Mandy's right hand, and watched as her fingers slowly tightened around the nurse's.

"Excellent! I'm sure you're confused, and maybe scared, but we're going to remove the tube that's down your throat and keeping you from talking. It'll feel weird, but I promise it'll be over quick."

Buck hated that Mandy was going through this, but was as proud of her as he could be. He squeezed her foot, wanting to let her know he was there but not wanting to distract her from the doctor's instructions.

In seconds, the tube was out of her throat and she was coughing slightly.

"All done," the doctor told her. "You did great. Take a few deep breaths, very slowly. Good. There's someone here who I think you'll want to see." He gestured for Buck to move to the other side of the bed, nearer her head.

Buck was scared shitless. What if she didn't recognize him? What if her brain was too damaged from the blow and the swelling, and she wasn't the Mandy he used to know?

The nurse moved out of his way, and he made his way to Mandy's head. He took her hand in his and leaned over.

"Hi, Rebel. It's so wonderful to see your beautiful blue eyes again," he said softly.

She stared up at him for a long minute with a blank look on her face.

Just when Buck's world almost caved in for a second time in a week, she blinked.

Then mouthed, "Nash."

He'd cried more in the last week than he had in his entire life, but Buck wasn't ashamed when the tears fell again. Not in the least. These were happy tears. Ecstatic ones.

"Yeah, Mandy, it's me. I'm so happy to see you awake."

Her fingers closed tight around his as her eyes closed.

Buck looked up at the doctor in alarm.

But he had a huge smile on his face. "It's okay. She's tired. It's perfectly normal. But it's all good news. She recognized you. She's going to be okay. It might take a while, she'll need some physical therapy, but I have no reason to think she won't be back to normal in no time."

Buck wiped his cheeks with his shoulders, refusing to let go of Mandy's hand. She looked rough. Her hair had been shaved on one side of her head for the surgery, and she still had tubes connected all over. But she was alive. And knew who he was. They could deal with everything else one day at a time.

CHAPTER TWENTY-FOUR

Amanda was so happy to be going home. She was in the hospital for two weeks, and now had spent two more weeks in rehab. The only thing she wanted was to sleep in her own bed. Well, Nash's bed, with the man she loved at her back and her beloved dog at her feet.

Waking up in the hospital with no memory of what happened had been disorientating. And kind of scary. But Nash was at her side almost the entire time. He'd made everything so much better. Not necessarily easier, but with him there, she wasn't as scared as she might have been otherwise.

And it wasn't just him. It was everyone. Casper, Obi-Wan, Pyro, Chaos, Edge, Laryn...they'd all come to see her. They popped in at random times, sometimes staying for an hour or more, other times for just ten minutes, but she was rarely alone. It meant the world to her that they made the effort to come all the way to the hospital, even when they had just minutes to spare. She was sure they had better things to do, but they never made it seem as if they were in a rush, or like they were there out of some sort of obligation.

Her room had also been full of flowers, and every time she

opened her eyes she was reminded of how many people were rooting for her to get better and back on her feet.

It was difficult to comprehend that Blair had done this to her. That she'd stalked her and hit her over the head with a *crowbar*. The fact that she was still alive was a miracle.

Amanda still had headaches from time to time, but the doctor said they should eventually fade and not be so debilitating. She hoped he was right.

And today, she was going home. She was more than ready. The nurses and doctors at the rehab facility were fantastic, but she wouldn't be sad to say goodbye. One of the things she was looking forward to the most was being with Rain. Nash had brought him to see her a few times, and hearing him whine pathetically every time he saw her was heartbreaking. He seemed to understand that she was hurt, and he needed to be gentle with her, because he simply lay next to her with his head on her shoulder, his hot doggy breath on her neck, content to be petted until it was time to go.

A noise at the door had her turning her head. Nash had finally arrived.

It had been extremely difficult not to ask him to stay with her every night, or be there as much as possible during the day. He'd already taken enough leave, and he had stuff to do. She couldn't monopolize his time, no matter how much she wanted to. Besides, she'd been busy working her ass off to regain her mobility and walk without looking like she'd been on a weeklong bender.

Nights were the most difficult. The hospital bed seemed too big, the room too empty. But not having to worry about Blair coming back to finish what she'd started went a long way toward easing any nightmares. And it seemed as if *Nash* had more trauma about the night she'd been attacked than she did, which made sense, as she didn't remember the event itself.

"Hi!" she said, welcoming Nash with a huge smile as he came toward her.

"Hey," he returned, leaning over where she was sitting up in the bed, already dressed and ready to go. He gave her a gentle kiss. "Ready to be sprung today?"

"More than," Amanda said with feeling. "The doc said he'd sign the release papers this morning, so hopefully we'll be seeing a nurse with those before too long."

"Awesome. Rain is excited for you to come home...as am I. We've missed you terribly."

"I can't wait," she said. "I've missed you guys too."

This probably wasn't the time or place, but Amanda had been thinking about things—Guyana, Blair, her time in the hospital, what she wanted in her life—and she couldn't wait another moment to talk to Nash. Before she went back to his place, before she started what she hoped was the beginning of the rest of her life, she needed to clear something up.

"Nash? Can I ask you something?"

"You can ask me anything."

"When I was in the hospital unconscious, after my surgery, you were there, right?"

"Of course. I didn't leave your side," he said. "Why?"

"Did you talk to me?"

Nash had sat down in the chair next to her bed and was holding her hand, something he did every time he came to visit. The first thing he always did was reach for her, as if he couldn't wait one more second to touch her. She loved it.

"Yes. Nonstop. I've heard that sometimes people who are unconscious or in a coma can hear what's going on around them. So I held your hand and talked."

"About what?"

"Everything. Anything. Nothing. I simply wanted you to hear my voice, to know I was there."

"I did," Amanda said. "I heard you. I don't really remember

much of what you said, just your voice in the back of my head. It grounded me. I had a feeling something was wrong, but everything was dark and it felt as if I was looking down at myself from the outside. But knowing you were there, hearing you talk to me, it helped, Nash."

"I'm glad."

"There is *one* thing I distinctly remember though."

"What's that?"

Amanda swallowed hard. This could go really well, or it could backfire on her. But she had to know. Had to know if she'd dreamed up something that she really wanted to be true, or if he'd actually said it.

"You saying that you loved me. I mean, I might have been hallucinating," she rushed to add. "But it seemed so clear. And it's okay if you *didn't* say it...but now I need to know either way. Because *I'm* madly in love with *you*, and I don't think I can go back to your apartment, live with you, get closer to you, if you don't think you could one day come to love me back."

Those last words were said quickly, probably because she knew if she didn't get them out, she wouldn't say them at all. The last thing she wanted was to go back to her cold, empty apartment by herself, but she would. Because loving this man and not having his love in return would slowly kill her.

In response, Nash stood and hovered over her again. His face was an inch from her own as he spoke. "You heard that? You heard me saying that?"

"I think so?" Amanda said, a little uncertainly.

"That's amazing. And yes, I said it. Over and over. I love you, Mandy. More than you'll ever know. What happened to you was the worst day of my life, and the days that followed weren't much better. All I could think of was that I hadn't told you how I felt. That you might die not knowing that you were the most important person in my life. That without you, I'm not sure I can continue on myself."

Relief and joy and love swept through Amanda. She reached up and pulled Nash's head down, kissing him hard. She wanted to deepen the kiss, craved his intimate touch, but he pulled away far too soon.

"I'm not going to get caught making out in the hospital the day you're supposed to leave," he said with a small chuckle.

Amanda pouted.

He laughed some more, then ran a hand over her hair. "I love you, Mandy. You're so damn strong. The doctor said it's a miracle how well you're doing, how fast you're healing."

"I love you too, Nash. Thank you for being here. For looking after me, after Rain, I know it hasn't been easy."

"I'd do anything for you. Don't you know that?"

"I do now."

"I'm shocked that you heard me," he muttered, as if speaking to himself.

She leaned her head into his hand, still cupping her head. "I think it was one of the only things keeping me going. I wanted to give up. To give in to the pain. The oblivion. But you wouldn't let me. I didn't want to let you down. And hearing you say you loved me gave me hope and a purpose, since I loved you back."

"Amazing," Nash said softly.

"*You're* amazing," Amanda told him. "I love you so much."

"It feels great to say the words. I shouldn't have hesitated to say them before," Nash told her.

"Well, we've said them now and we're moving on," she said firmly.

"Yes, we are," he agreed with a smile.

"I don't mean to interrupt," a man said from the doorway.

Nash spun around so fast, it almost made Amanda dizzy. She didn't miss the way he stood squarely in front of her, as if prepared to protect her from any kind of danger. She supposed it would take him a while to let his guard down again. She was determined, in time, to help him relax, to convince him that not *everyone* around them was out to get her.

"Can I help you?" Nash asked the newcomer.

The man didn't move into the room, correctly reading Nash's aggressive body language. "My name is John Keegan. You know me as Tex."

Amanda's eyes widened. She remembered Tex. He was the man Nash had been working with to try to find Blair. The man who'd notified the authorities that the little girl found in the park in North Carolina was most likely Bibi.

"Tex," Nash said with a nod of his head, sounding almost... cold.

Amanda frowned. Why was he being so standoffish? Nash had admired this man. Was grateful for his help.

"I know you probably aren't happy to see me, but I heard Mandy was being discharged today, and I wanted to come down and personally tell her how relieved I am that she's okay."

The men stared at each other without saying anything else.

Amanda let out a quiet breath of exasperation. "Thank you for coming, Tex. It's so good to meet you. I've heard amazing things about you."

His gaze swung to hers, but he still didn't move from the doorway. "Thank you. I understand you're doing well. That the side effects from your injury are minimal."

Nash snorted under his breath.

That was it; Amanda was done with his strange behavior. "Please move over, Nash. I want to shake his hand."

Nash slowly moved to the side, which seemed to be the permission Tex needed to approach the bed. She shook his hand, studying the unassuming man who was apparently capable of hacking just about any kind of electronic out there.

"Thanks again for donating money to the school down in Guyana."

Tex nodded.

"And for finding the connection between Blair and the rebels."

He nodded again.

"And for identifying Bibi."

He nodded a third time.

The air was thick with tension, and Amanda didn't like it. Not one bit. "And for finding the cure to cancer."

Tex began to nod, then stopped himself and gave her a questioning look.

"Just making sure you're paying attention and not just nodding to agree with me. What's going on? Nash, why are you acting so strange? What don't I know?" she asked.

Tex looked at Nash, then back at her. "It's my fault you were attacked."

Amanda couldn't help it. She laughed.

Both men looked a little shocked at her reaction.

"I mean, I don't remember what happened, but I'm pretty sure it wasn't *you* who sprang out of the darkness and bashed me over the head with a crowbar."

Her words were probably a little crude, but she wasn't going to tiptoe around the details of the attack. What was done was done. She was alive and well, and she planned on staying that way.

"It wasn't. But I failed in finding Blair. In making sure she could be detained so she wasn't a threat to you."

Amanda sighed. These men and their God complexes. Their desire to be protectors at all times, even when doing so simply wasn't possible. "It's not your fault," she said sternly. "It's not Nash's fault. It's not the bar's fault. It's not my fault. It's *her* fault. Blair's. You said it yourself, she was mentally unstable. Something clicked in her brain and she snapped. Even if you had found her, and she was taken into custody, she probably *still* would've found a way to hurt me."

"If she was apprehended, she would've been in jail for killing

Bibi," Nash retorted. "She wouldn't have been in that parking lot, and you wouldn't have gotten hurt."

"You want to throw blame around? Fine. It was *my* fault, and my fault alone. *I* was the one who accepted that job in Guyana, where Blair met me in the first place. *I* was the one who didn't fight tooth and nail to get away, when I was grabbed along with the kids when they were kidnapped. *I* was the one who told Blair I wanted to adopt Bibi and Michael. If it wasn't for me, she wouldn't have kidnapped Bibi at all...wouldn't have neglected her to the point she *died*. If it wasn't for *me*, she wouldn't have been in Virginia, waiting in the Anchor Point parking lot."

"That's ridiculous," Nash growled.

At the same time Tex said, "That's going a bit far."

"It's not ridiculous, and it's not going too far. As much as you might like to think so, Tex, you aren't God. You aren't the supreme ruler of everyone's actions. There's this thing called free will. And you might be good at what you do, damn good, but sometimes shit just happens. Blair was under the radar. No electronic trail. No phone, no credit cards, *nothing*. She was a ghost. And you can't track a ghost."

"I can damn well try," he muttered.

"*Try*," Amanda emphasized. "And you *did* try. Extremely hard, if what I was told is correct. Give it up. Stewing about this isn't helping. Maybe use whatever you've learned from this to help someone else. You aren't doing anyone any good wallowing in guilt. And the same goes for you, Nash. Don't think I don't know you're beating yourself up for what happened every single time you look at me. As much as I love your protective instincts, you can't be with me every second of every day."

"I was with you that night. Right next to you, in fact," he said.

"Whatever!" Amanda said with a dramatic flail of her arm. "So you aren't Superman. Big deal! How do you think I would've felt if it was *you* who got hit in the head? You think I wouldn't have felt guilty that you were hurt, when I was the one Blair was after? It would've destroyed me. It's bad enough that Bibi is dead because of me."

"No, she's not."

"That wasn't your fault."

Again, both men spoke at the same time. Both sounded distraught that she believed that.

"Look. Nothing about the last few months has been great. But other parts—like meeting Nash, falling in love, meeting his friends—have been life-changingly awesome for me. We have to take the ups with the downs in life. You can't have one without the other. If you two don't figure your shit out and become friends, or acquaintances, or *whatever* you are again, I'm not going to be happy."

It was a lame ending for her little speech, but Amanda was done. She'd said what she wanted to say, and she just hoped it was enough to get through to both stubborn, uber-protective military men facing off beside her bed.

"I'm sorry," Tex told Nash.

Her man took a deep breath, then nodded. "I appreciate everything you were able to do to help us."

The tension in the room lessened a tad. It wasn't gone, but Amanda didn't figure it would be that easy for either man to let go of their guilt and frustration over what had transpired.

"I did come with other news. It's both good and bad," Tex said.

Amanda braced. Nash sat back down in the chair and took her hand in his once more. Having him there, unconditionally, went a long way toward giving her the courage to say, "Let's have it."

"Michael has been adopted. I know you wanted to bring him here to the States, but there was a childless couple in Guyana that was interested in adoption. They contacted Desmond, he had a background check done, and when they came to visit the children, they bonded with James and Patricia right away. Apparently, Michael was protective of the little ones and always around when they visited with the prospective parents. In the end, they fell for him too. All three children will be staying in their home country with their new parents. Who have plenty of money to care for three kids, by the way."

"Oh," Amanda said. "That's good."

"It is, but I know you bonded with Michael yourself."

"I did. But you know what? Him staying in Guyana, amongst his own culture, is a good thing. And he was always protective. Of me *and* the other kids. I'm glad he found a family of his own."

Tex stared at her for a beat. "You're good people, Amanda. Some people would be upset they weren't able to adopt the child they had their heart set on."

"There are lots of kids in the world who need loving homes," she said quietly. "Yes, I'm a little sad that the life I envisioned giving Michael won't come to fruition, but that doesn't mean he still won't have a great life, do great things. As we were just saying, life has its twists and turns. But every action points us on a different path. Just as my path led me to Nash, Michael's will hopefully lead him to equally wonderful things."

"Smart too," Tex said. He looked at Nash. "I hope you know that I'm always around if you need me. I realize you probably have second thoughts now about coming to me in a crisis, but I'll be there if you, or any of your friends, need help regardless."

"Thanks, Tex. I appreciate it."

Amanda figured that was as close to accepting Tex's unnecessary apology for not finding Blair as the man would get.

"I'll see myself out. Glad you're feeling better. Oh, and that long-term sub job? It's still yours when you're ready. I reached out to the principal and he's aware of your situation. They have another sub working in the classroom, but she's not willing to stay for the amount of time needed. She'll be happy to concede the classroom to you when you're back on your feet. And when that teacher comes back from maternity leave, there's another going on leave to have *her* baby, so he's hoping you can just transition over to that class."

"Oh! Wow, thanks."

Tex nodded, then turned and headed for the door. He was gone a moment later.

Amanda turned to Nash. "Did that just happen?"

He nodded. "Yup."

"Are you really okay with him now? Or were you just lying to get him to leave?"

Nash sighed. "It'll take me a bit, but him coming here...it helped. I don't blame him for what happened anymore. And I'm trying to forgive myself too."

"Good. Because I'm gonna be upset if you continue to beat yourself up about this. It's over. Done. We're moving on. Okay?"

"Sounds good to me. You want kids?"

Amanda was taken aback at the abrupt shift in conversation. "What?"

"Children. I assume you do, since you were ready to adopt Bibi and Michael. Are you dead set on adoption? How would you feel about biological children? Yours and mine, that is."

Happiness bloomed hard and fast. And right on the heels of that emotion was arousal. It had been a long time since she'd felt even remotely sexual, but sitting here, feeling pretty damn healthy, and hearing Nash talk about children—*their* children— had her ready to start making them immediately.

"Uh, *yes*. I'd love my own biological kids."

"Good. Me too."

"Um...now?"

He chuckled. "No. I think we can wait a bit. Get settled. Get married. Buy a house. That kind of thing."

"Wait, was that a proposal?" Amanda asked.

"Not even close. Just me letting you know what my intentions are. I want to spend the rest of my life with you. Make a family. Live happily ever after. My mom is gonna want the big-shindig wedding. She had a blast planning Natalie's, and I know she'll be honored if you let her help plan ours. She loves you already. You won her over with that first phone call I made, updating her on what was going on. And you're going to be an amazing mother. But you need to get your career figured out first. And mine isn't exactly calm and easy at the moment. We'll play things by ear. But one day soon, I'll pull out a big-ass ring and ask you to be my wife. To let me be your husband."

Amanda had a huge grin on her face that she couldn't hold back. "And when that day comes, I'll gladly say yes. I love you so much, it's almost scary."

"I completely agree. But there's something so...beautiful in that terror, isn't there? Knowing you have someone who will be by your side no matter what?"

"Absolutely. Nash?"

"Yeah, Rebel?"

"Is it weird to say I'm glad I was kidnapped?"

"Yes."

"Nash! No, it isn't."

"You asked, I answered. Never be glad for that. But you can be glad we met. You can be glad circumstances led me to you, or you to me, but you can't be glad you were kidnapped. I firmly believe we would've managed to meet some other way. We're both here in Norfolk, it would've happened eventually. And when it did, I also believe we would've clicked just as fast as we did down in Guyana."

"You really think that?"

"Yes. Now, how about I go find a nurse and see where your discharge papers are? I'm sure you're ready to get the hell out of here, and Rain is more than ready for you to come home. He's a damn bed hog, and neither of us have been sleeping well since you've been gone."

"One thing before you go."

"Yeah?"

"I talked to the doctor...and he said that I was cleared for sex whenever I felt up to it."

Nash stared at her with a look so hot, it was all Amanda could do to hold his gaze.

"And I'm thinking we never got that hot night we were planning after the bar."

"You remember that?" Nash asked.

"Bits and pieces. I remember I was drunk, and you were excited about having drunk sex."

"Fuck," Nash said, shifting in his seat and reaching down to adjust his cock in his pants.

"So...no alcohol for me for a while, doctor's orders, but I want the rest. I want to experience Nash in all his controlling, dominating glory, where all I have to do is relax and enjoy. But maybe we can have slow, gentle sex and work up to the other stuff."

"Now I'm *really* going to go and find a nurse," Nash muttered as he stood.

Amanda could see his erection in his pants, and she giggled. "Maybe you shouldn't go walking the halls with *that* going on," she said, gesturing toward his crotch with a nod of her head.

Nash leaned over her and kissed her hard. "Love you, woman. Thank you for being strong. For holding on. For coming back to me."

"Love you too."

Not a day would go by from here on out that Amanda didn't tell this man how much he meant to her. They'd almost lost each other, and she didn't want to have any regrets when it came to him.

She lay back on the pillows and smiled as he strode out of the room. She was more than ready to tackle the rest of her life, as long as Nash was by her side. It wouldn't be easy, life never was, but as partners, they could make it through anything.

* * *

It had been two months since Mandy returned home from the rehab center. Two months since she'd sobbed on his shoulder upon realizing there was a surprise "welcome home" party waiting for her when she got to his apartment.

And Buck didn't take one day of those two months for granted. He and the rest of the Night Stalkers were headed out on a mission the day after next, and he dreaded it like he never had before.

Buck understood it was because he was still feeling overly protective of Mandy. Though he didn't really have a reason to feel that way. She was now working at her sub job every day, and loving it. Rain was content to stay in the apartment during the day and soak up all the attention he could get when Mandy got home. They'd decided not to make him an emotional support dog in any kind of official way. After his difficult start in life, he deserved to be lazy, and to sleep his days away while Mandy worked.

There was no danger lurking around the corner. No worry about the rebels down in South America wanting revenge, since the only reason they'd targeted Mandy in the first place was because they'd been paid to do so.

The colonel had been able to put off any deployment until Mandy had fully recovered. The break had also given Laryn time to finish retrofitting the chopper for Casper. But there was no reason for them to delay any longer. There was a job to do, and the Night Stalkers were needed.

They were knee deep in preparations for deployment, so by the time he got home from work, it was after eight o'clock. He'd communicated with Mandy throughout the day, letting her know he'd be late and not to worry about making him something to eat, since Obi-Wan had ordered takeout for the team.

He was more than ready to turn off work for the moment when he walked in the door.

"Mandy?" he called out, the second he stepped inside.

"In here!" she returned, her voice coming from their bedroom.

Rain was sitting in the foyer waiting for him, as he always was—it was amazing how the dog had the innate ability to know when he or Mandy would be arriving—and after receiving his pat on the head, he trotted over to his bed in the living area and did a few circles before lying down.

Buck walked into the bedroom—and stopped in his tracks.

Mandy was on the bed wearing a tight white tank top and a pair of bikini panties, just like the first night they'd ever spent together. She had a huge grin on her face, her hair was mussed—still a little short, from where it had been shaved off for surgery, and where the rest had been cut to more closely match the shorn side, but growing in fast—and her cheeks were flushed.

She was holding a glass that was half full of a light yellow liquid. It sloshed around precariously as she threw her arms out and said, "Welcome home, honey!"

It was more than obvious she'd been drinking for a while, and was now drunk.

"What're you doing?" he asked, striding forward and taking the glass out of her hand before she spilled it. He sniffed and realized it was a lemon drop, a potent blend of vodka, lemon juice, triple sec, and simple syrup.

She climbed to her knees and shuffled toward the edge of the mattress. When she was close enough, she put her hands on Buck's shoulders and said, "It's time. Drunk sex, baby!"

And just like that, Buck was hard as a fucking rock. His woman was sexy as all get out, and obviously more than ready for the night of fun they'd missed out on all those months ago.

Now that her hands were free, Mandy reached for the hem of

her tank and pulled it over her head. She was still grinning like a loon, now kneeling on the mattress in nothing but her panties.

Buck's gaze took her in greedily. His little rebel was everything he hadn't known he'd wanted or needed in his life, and he literally couldn't imagine her not being in it anymore. It felt as if he'd known her forever. The things they'd been through had been harrowing and horrible, but she'd proven time and time again how fucking strong she was.

"Well?" she taunted. "What you standin' there for?"

Her words were all he needed to shake himself out of his stupor. Buck quickly undressed, leaving his work clothes and boots in a heap on the floor, not giving them a second thought as he reached for the woman he loved.

Mandy giggled, and the sound reverberated deep in his soul. He'd almost lost this. Lost *her*. He'd spend the rest of his life making sure she knew how much he loved her. How important she was to him.

But for now, the only thing on his mind was seeing how many times he could make her orgasm before she begged him to fuck her.

Turns out, the answer to that was just once. She was begging for his cock even before he'd coaxed that first orgasm out of her. She was still a happy drunk, giggling and laughing between her moans. Telling him how much she loved him, loved what he was doing to her, loved how his hands felt.

Her words were as much a turn-on as her body, and Buck found himself smiling as he physically shifted her around on the bed into different positions as he saw fit. In her inebriation, she was pliant and receptive to anything and everything. She was his match. In every way. And Buck was thankful all over again that she was there.

Alive and well. In his apartment. In his bed. His.

They made love for hours, resting between orgasms, cuddling and laughing. Eventually her buzz wore off, and she lost the silliness she'd had while drunk, and their lovemaking got more intense. Slower. More meaningful.

The last time he took her, she was on her back, her legs wrapped around his hips, eyes locked onto his own. It was more intimate than anything they'd done that night.

"I love you," she told him, as he slowly rocked inside her.

"I love you too," he returned, his voice cracking with emotion.

As he held her in his arms afterward, their heart rates slowly going back to normal, Buck sighed in contentment. He'd rolled them until she was lying bonelessly on top of him, her head on his chest, his cock still inside her warm, wet body. Nothing had felt more right than having her in his arms, her soft breaths drifting over his naked chest.

He was going to miss this when he was deployed. Miss *her*. But she'd be okay. His Rebel was strong. Tough. And she'd stay busy with her kids at school and with finishing her certification.

"I'm proud of you," she whispered. "And I'm so lucky you're mine."

He *was* hers. She owned him, body and soul. And he wasn't ashamed to admit that. Not to himself, his friends, the Army, the world. He'd do anything for the woman in his arms. Anything.

Buck opened his mouth to tell her just that, but a soft snore interrupted him.

He grinned. His Mandy. She could fall asleep practically anywhere, and within seconds. It was impressive, actually.

Making a mental note to tell her all the things rolling around in his head in the morning...well, *later* that morning, since it was well after midnight—he'd never hold back his thoughts about her ever again, not after almost missing his first chance to tell her how much he loved her—Buck relaxed.

The last thing he thought before falling asleep was how happy he was. How even when life was hard, with a woman like Mandy at his side, it was easy.

EPILOGUE

Obadiah Engle, known as Obi-Wan to his friends, to practically everyone, had a secret. It was one he'd been keeping from his Night Stalker copilots for a couple of months. It wasn't as if he was ashamed of what he was doing; it was more that he knew his friends would tease him mercilessly when they found out.

And they *would* find out, there was no keeping things a secret around a group as close-knit as the Night Stalkers. But that was fine. Obi-Wan was ready for them to know. He didn't like keeping secrets, even ones that would earn him some good-natured ribbing from his closest friends.

When he'd checked his messages after returning from their latest mission, he had voicemails from the assistant director, the first AD, the set PA, as well as the script supervisor. All with questions or wanting clarification on one thing or another.

Obi-Wan was still pinching himself that *he* was involved in Henry Grubbner's latest war film as a military advisor. Grubbner's films had won several academy awards, and he was known for his uber realism and extremely tough shoots. He was a perfectionist who disliked any kind of criticism, and as a result, went

KEEPING AMANDA

overboard in making sure his movies were as accurate as possible.

His newest movie in the works was about a Night Stalker pilot crashing behind enemy lines in North Korea, and everything he goes through to get to the border and to safety. It was loosely based on the true story of an Air Force fighter pilot...who now lived in Maine and refused to have *anything* to do with the movie. As a result, Grubbner was forced to change it to a helicopter pilot, and he lost the tag of "based on a true story."

During the planning stages of the film, Colonel Burgess was contacted and asked if he had any Night Stalkers who'd be willing to consult. The consultant wouldn't be in the credits or have a role in the actual movie, to preserve their identity because of the top-secret work they did for the Army and Navy.

One thing led to another, and Obi-Wan had been hired as the guy to come on set and make sure everything was as authentic as it could be. The uniforms, the lingo, the choppers. He'd even read through the script and given suggestions on what should be changed to make it more realistic.

Of course, he was still bound by his top-secret clearance, and he wasn't allowed to give any details about missions he'd been on or other government secrets, but so far the entire experience had been...interesting. And now that preproduction had taken place, things were getting more exciting as the entire film crew was in Norfolk to start filming. Eventually, the entire operation would shift to the other side of Virginia, in the Appalachian Mountains, to shoot the scenes with the main character trying to make it undetected to safety. The scenes with the helicopters Obi-Wan knew so much about.

One of the voicemails also informed him of the shooting schedule, letting him know when he'd be needed on set to observe and advise where necessary. Obi-Wan was looking forward to seeing how everything worked and meeting Grubbner in person. Of course, the AD warned him that he wouldn't actually be talking to the director much, as he'd be very busy. But he'd definitely get to meet the man playing the downed pilot in the movie, as well as the supporting cast and crew.

It was a fun change in Obi-Wan's otherwise boring life in Norfolk. He loved being a Night Stalker, loved the missions he went on, but found life as a single military man, in a town full of men just like him, a little unfulfilling.

Now that Casper and Buck had gotten involved with women they were completely devoted to, they spent less time hanging out at Anchor Point and with the rest of the single guys on the team. Which was fine. Obi-Wan didn't feel slighted in the least. But he did see a change in his friends' personalities. They were happier. More content. And he wanted what they had.

He didn't want their *women*, of course. Laryn and Mandy were equally devoted to Casper and Buck, and would never think twice about cheating on them. No, he wanted that closeness his friends had found with another human.

He was close with his fellow pilots, but that was entirely different.

Shrugging off the thoughts, knowing he was feeling particularly melancholy after seeing Mandy exuberantly greet Buck at the base the second they'd arrived on US soil, Obi-Wan headed for the door to the hangar.

"Where's the fire?" Edge called out. "Thought we were going to meet up at Anchor Point?"

Obi-Wan turned and faced his friends. "Can't. I've got a meeting I need to get to."

"A meeting?" Chaos asked. "With who? We just got back."

It was time to let his friends in on the secret he'd been keeping. Taking a deep breath, Obi-Wan said, "I'm a consultant on a project in town. About Night Stalkers."

His friends walked closer, asking questions as they came toward him.

"What project?"

"There's a project about Night Stalkers? Did the Army sanction it?"

"What are you consulting about, exactly?"

Obi-Wan prepared himself for the ribbing he was about to get. "It's a movie. I was asked to be their military advisor. I've been working with the producer, director, and script supervisor on the script, and now it's time for filming to start. I have a meeting tonight that includes the lead actor and actress, and then I'll be spending as much time as I can on set once filming starts."

As expected, his friends were quick to start with the taunts.

"Ooooh, fancy pants!"

"Are you gonna leave us to marry a famous actress?"

"He doesn't need to marry her. He can definitely have a good time while she's here though."

"Who's the director?"

"Screw the director, who's playing the lead? What's the movie about?"

Obi-Wan grinned. He loved these guys. They were his best friends, and he was a lucky-son-of-a-bitch to get to work with them every day.

He told them as much as he could, and when he was done, was surprised when everyone took the information in stride. He figured they'd rib him way more than they had. But Casper and Buck were too ready to head home with their girlfriends, and the others were probably more interested in having some real food and a beer at Anchor Point.

Their long-held traditions were changing. At one time, no one would've missed the post-mission Anchor Point visit, but change wasn't a bad thing.

"Have fun. But be careful," Pyro cautioned. "Rumor has it that Carmen St. James is a bitch."

Obi-Wan rolled his eyes. "She's not going to want anything to do with me. I'm just the military advisor."

"Whatever, Obi-Wan. You're hot," Mandy said with a grin.

"Yeah. If she doesn't take one look at you and decide you're her next conquest, she's stupid," Laryn agreed.

"Thanks for the vote of confidence, ladies," he said with a chuckle. "But that's not gonna happen."

"Uh-huh."

"Sure it's not."

"Stop flirting with my woman," Buck complained, pulling Mandy tighter against his side.

Mandy elbowed him. "He's not flirting, Nash. Geez."

Buck grinned at his copilot and gave him a chin lift. "Have fun. Don't work too hard."

"I won't," Obi-Wan said. "It's not that kind of job. Piece of cake after the mission we just completed."

"Famous last words," Casper muttered.

For some reason, a shiver went through Obi-Wan at his team leader's comment. The team had already been through too much with both Laryn and Mandy's situations. Nobody needed more drama right now. Especially him.

"I'll see you guys tomorrow for the AAR," he told his friends.

"Later."

"Bye."

"Have fun!"

It was a relief to have his secret out in the open. To not be hiding anything from his friends anymore. He fully expected them to continue giving him shit for hanging out with the rich and famous, but the truth was, he was looking forward to this little change in his routine.

Who knew? Maybe he'd meet someone who would shake his life up, much as Laryn and Mandy had done for Casper and Buck. Or maybe he'd have a chance for a hot fling with one of the women who worked on the film.

Either way, change was a good thing. And Obi-Wan was looking forward to it.

KEEPING AMANDA

***

Oh, Obi-Wan will meet someone to shake his life up for SURE. Not only shake it up, but turn it upside down in the best way possible. But of course you know I would never make things too easy for my hero/heroine. Obi-Wan finds himself on the receiving end of so not-so-welcome attention and his snub comes back to not only haunt him, but Zita as well. Find out who, how, and what in *Keeping Zita*!

Scan the QR code below for signed books, swag, T-shirts and more!

Also by Susan Stoker

Rescue Angels Series
Keeping Laryn
Keeping Amanda
Keeping Zita (Feb 10, 2026)
Keeping Penny (May 5)
Keeping Kara (July 7)
Keeping Jennifer (Nov 10)

SEAL of Protection: Alliance Series
Protecting Remi
Protecting Wren
Protecting Josie
Protecting Maggie
Protecting Addison
Protecting Kelli
Protecting Bree (Jan 6, 2026)

Alpha Cove Series
The Soldier
The Sailor (Mar 3, 2026)
The Pilot (Aug 4, 2026)
The Guardsman (Mar 9, 2027)

SEAL Team Hawaii Series
Finding Elodie
Finding Lexie
Finding Kenna
Finding Monica
Finding Carly
Finding Ashlyn
Finding Jodelle

ALSO BY SUSAN STOKER

Eagle Point Search & Rescue
Searching for Lilly
Searching for Elsie
Searching for Bristol
Searching for Caryn
Searching for Finley
Searching for Heather
Searching for Khloe

The Refuge Series
Deserving Alaska
Deserving Henley
Deserving Reese
Deserving Cora
Deserving Lara
Deserving Maisy
Deserving Ryleigh

Game of Chance Series
The Protector
The Royal
The Hero
The Lumberjack

SEAL of Protection: Legacy Series
Securing Caite
Securing Brenae (novella)
Securing Sidney
Securing Piper
Securing Zoey
Securing Avery
Securing Kalee
Securing Jane

ALSO BY SUSAN STOKER

Delta Force Heroes Series
Rescuing Rayne
Rescuing Aimee (novella)
Rescuing Emily
Rescuing Harley
Marrying Emily (novella)
Rescuing Kassie
Rescuing Bryn
Rescuing Casey
Rescuing Sadie (novella)
Rescuing Wendy
Rescuing Mary
Rescuing Macie (novella)
Rescuing Annie

SEAL of Protection Series
Protecting Caroline
Protecting Alabama
Protecting Fiona
Marrying Caroline (novella)
Protecting Summer
Protecting Cheyenne
Protecting Jessyka
Protecting Julie (novella)
Protecting Melody
Protecting the Future
Protecting Kiera (novella)
Protecting Alabama's Kids (novella)
Protecting Dakota
Protecting Tex

Delta Team Two Series
Shielding Gillian
Shielding Kinley

ALSO BY SUSAN STOKER

Shielding Aspen
Shielding Jayme (novella)
Shielding Riley
Shielding Devyn
Shielding Ember
Shielding Sierra

Badge of Honor: Texas Heroes Series

Justice for Mackenzie
Justice for Mickie
Justice for Corrie
Justice for Laine (novella)
Shelter for Elizabeth
Justice for Boone
Shelter for Adeline
Shelter for Sophie
Justice for Erin
Justice for Milena
Shelter for Blythe
Justice for Hope
Shelter for Quinn
Shelter for Koren
Shelter for Penelope

Ace Security Series

Claiming Grace
Claiming Alexis
Claiming Bailey
Claiming Felicity
Claiming Sarah

Mountain Mercenaries Series

Defending Allye
Defending Chloe

ALSO BY SUSAN STOKER

Defending Morgan
Defending Harlow
Defending Everly
Defending Zara
Defending Raven

Silverstone Series
Trusting Skylar
Trusting Taylor
Trusting Molly
Trusting Cassidy

Stand Alone
Falling for the Delta
The Guardian Mist
Nature's Rift
A Princess for Cale
A Moment in Time- A Collection of Short Stories
Another Moment in Time- A Collection of Short Stories
A Third Moment in Time- A Collection of Short Stories
Lambert's Lady

Special Operations Fan Fiction
http://www.AcesPress.com

Beyond Reality Series
Outback Hearts
Flaming Hearts
Frozen Hearts

Writing as Annie George:
Stepbrother Virgin (erotic novella)

ABOUT THE AUTHOR

New York Times, USA Today and *Wall Street Journal* Bestselling Author Susan Stoker has a heart as big as the state of Tennessee where she lives, but this all American girl has also spent the last fourteen years living in Missouri, California, Colorado, Indiana, and Texas. She's married to a retired Army man who now gets to follow *her* around the country.

She debuted her first series in 2014 and quickly followed that up with the SEAL of Protection Series, which solidified her love of writing and creating stories readers can get lost in.

If you enjoyed this book, or any book, please consider leaving a review. It's appreciated by authors more than you'll know.

www.stokeraces.com
www.AcesPress.com
susan@stokeraces.com

facebook.com/authorsusanstoker
x.com/Susan_Stoker
instagram.com/authorsusanstoker
goodreads.com/SusanStoker
bookbub.com/authors/susan-stoker
amazon.com/author/susanstoker

Made in United States
Orlando, FL
02 November 2025